Born in 1942 in North Carolina, Michael Malone is the author of four novels, including *Dingley Falls* and *Handling Sin*. He has also written books on American film and Jungian typology, as well as articles, short stories and screenplays. Both *Handling Sin* and *Uncivil Seasons* are being made into major films with screenplay by the author. Michael Malone lives in Philadelphia and Connecticut, is married and has one daughter.

Also by Michael Malone in Abacus:

HANDLING SIN

UNCIVIL SEASONS

Michael Malone

SPHERE BOOKS LTD

Published by the Penguin Group
27 Wrights Lane, London W8 5TZ, England
Viking Penguin Inc., 40 West 23rd Street, New York, New York 10010, USA
Penguin Books Australia Ltd, Ringwood, Victoria, Australia
Penguin Books Canada Ltd, 2801 John Street, Markham, Ontario, Canada L3R 1B4
Penguin Books (NZ) Ltd, 182–190 Wairau Road, Auckland 10, New Zealand

Penguin Books Ltd, Registered Offices: Harmondsworth, Middlesex, England

First published in Great Britain by Chatto & Windus, 1984
Published in Abacus by Sphere Books Ltd, 1989
1 3 5 7 9 10 8 6 4 2

Printed and bound in Great Britain by
Richard Clay Ltd, Bungay, Suffolk

For Barry Hoffman

"Round up the usual suspects."

The eye of man hath not heard, the ear of man hath not seen, man's hand is not able to taste, his tongue to conceive, nor his heart to report, what my dream was. I will get Peter Quince to write a ballad of this dream. It shall be called Bottom's Dream, because it hath no bottom; and I will sing it in the latter end of a play, before the duke; peradventure, to make it the more gracious, I shall sing it at her death.

Nick Bottom, a Weaver
A Midsummer Night's Dream

1
THE SEA MAID'S
MUSIC

Two things don't happen very often in Hillston, North Carolina. We don't get much snow, and we hardly ever murder one another. Suicide is more our style; we're a polite, college town, and our lives are sheltered by old trees. Maybe once a year a blizzard slips around a corner of the Smoky Mountains and blusters its way east, or a gale swells up from Cape Hatteras and runs across the Piedmont to break up our agreeable liaison with nature; but usually storms lose interest along the way. Whenever one does barge through town, merchants stockpile sleds as recklessly as Carolina blockade-runners once stowed tobacco and cotton. Schools close. Cars spin off the roads. People have accidents.

They commit murders, too, but much more often in thought and word than deed. There is some impertinence in being a homicide detective in a town that wants to go on believing it is still too small and too temperate to require such expertise. That I should be the detective obliged to remind them of their susceptibility seems a further affront to Hillston, for I'm one of them. My mother is a Hillston Dollard. Her family has sheltered the town since its founding; they founded it. They sheltered it with pride; defensive, unchallengeable pride in the town, and the Piedmont that circled it, and the state that circled the Piedmont, and the country that circled the state. That's what Dollards did. It was the family business. For me to be searching for killers among us would have struck Hillston as an improper lack of family feeling, except that, of course, as everyone said, we rarely murdered one another.

The trouble was that now Cloris Dollard was dead, had been found dead last Sunday, her skull crushed. She was my uncle's wife.

"The sky looks like snow," I told Mrs. Lawry Whetstone.

"Never happen, sugar," Susan said.

"Probably not."

I was standing naked beneath my overcoat beside the bedroom window of the Whetstone summer cottage, glumly looking across the January gray lake toward Pine Hills Inn. The Inn was Hillston's oldest restaurant; old enough to boast it had been reduced to the degradation of serving as the stables for invading Federal troops during the War of the Confederacy. My circle ate at the Inn. Snug in a booth there an hour ago, Susan Whetstone had repeated that she just couldn't see the sense in her divorcing Lawry and ruining everything. She'd poked at the shrimp sunk inside her avocado, and brushed her blond hair up from the nape of her tan neck and said, "No, sugar, it's better this way." Susan and I had been having an affair for eighteen months; a year ago, I hadn't thought it was better this way. Now I no longer asked her to leave Lawry, but she hadn't seemed to notice I'd stopped, and she went on refusing to come away with me. It seemed impolite to point out she needn't worry about me, especially after it had become so clear that Susan was not a worrier.

Susan's husband, Lawry, was a vice-president of C & W Textiles, Hillston's biggest industry, a century-old complex of mills and manufacturing that Lawry was determined to haul, against the will of its elderly patriarch, into the hi-tech gloss of what the newspapers were in the habit of calling the New South. Lawry flew around to places like Japan and Houston and neglected to take Susan with him. He'd been away in Atlanta for two weeks now, either buying or selling. "Who knows, who cares," said Susan, no backseat careerist.

I was standing by the window. She was stuffing designer sheets and towels apparently stolen from Hyatt hotels into the hamper, and pulling the beige-checked coverlet over the bed. She found my shorts and tossed them at me. She'd already showered and dressed again; she had a postcoital efficiency I found depressing.

"Justin, it's one thirty. I better run. Laurel Fanshaw told me somebody, she wouldn't say who, was going to bring a motion to *impeach* me off the effing Charity Ball committee if I wasn't at this meeting today. I bet it was Patty. I can't believe you were so gaga over her; she's such a bitch."

"I was sixteen." I lit a cigarette. "You better run."

"Aren't you supposed to be back at work by two?"

"I'm supposed to check Cloris's 'socialite connections.' Aren't you one of them?" I brought Susan her suede boots. "That's what Captain Fulcher told me today." I mimicked my chief's fidgety face. "'Nobody can beat Senator Dollard's wife to death, and rob her blind, in her own house, while I'm at the helm. Check out everybody, Savile, but don't step on any toes. You can be sure nobody in *her* circle carted off a crate of Mrs. Dollard's silverware, right? You know, my wife has the *same* pattern! Grand Baroque.'" I did a set of his mouth clicks.

Susan said, "Funny man. I love it when you do Fulcher. He is so tacky."

"He'd be crushed to know you think so; he wants to be 'in,' like you."

"Not as 'in' as you, sweetie." She shoved her foot into the magenta boot by pushing against my bare leg. "I like that scar on your leg." She opened my overcoat and ran her hand down my calf. "I think it's the fact that it's a bullet wound that turns me on." She walked to the dresser mirror to watch herself slide into her mink coat. "On TV, they said a robber killed Cloris. Meanwhile, it has got to be the creepiest thing I ever heard." Her hand stopped, lipstick poised.

I asked, "Did you ever hear of anybody really disliking Cloris?"

"Come on! You think somebody killed her on purpose? Get real, Justin." The lipstick plummeted into the suede purse. "Bye bye. I loved it today. I'll call you."

Shivering, I walked barefoot into the kitchen; like the rest of the cottage, closed for winter, the room smelled thickly of stale air. Table and counters were piled with summer's leftovers: white sail bags, OFF cans, black flippers, badminton birdies. In their empty refrigerator I kept my bottle of Jack Daniel's. I poured my fourth drink of the day, carried it out on the screened porch, and stared across Pine Hills Lake, a dark flat oval ringed by the coves where, in summer, Hillston resorted in old-fashioned vacation homes. Somewhere on the other side, behind banked evergreens, was the Rowell Dollard cottage. When I was a child, I'd been brought there often, balking, to play with the daughters of the woman whose murder I was now assigned to investigate.

When I was a child, we called the place the Ames cottage, because back then Cloris had been married to a man named Bainton Ames. It was only after his death that she'd married Rowell Dollard, and so become a relative of mine, because Rowell was my mother's younger half brother; and so become, because Rowell was a Dollard and a state senator, just the kind of person no one in Hillston wanted to believe could ever be beaten unconscious and then smothered with her own pillow in her home on Catawba Drive, which was (as Captain Fulcher reminded me) the best street in town.

I'd grown up on Catawba Drive, but had not driven for a long time along its shaded, twisting road until last Monday, when I was called to come look at Cloris Dollard. I was called by authority higher than Captain Fulcher's; because the circle closed ranks.

Because my father had played music on weekends with Cloris's first husband.

Because I'd been a (reluctant) usher at Cloris's second wedding. (Reluctant because I didn't like Rowell Dollard, who persisted in trying to give direction—his own—to my life.)

I was called in because Mother's cousin was the state attorney general. He'd gone over Fulcher's head to relieve me of all other cases so that I could devote my time to discovering who'd killed Cloris, and then telling him about it the day he returned from his golf resort.

Because my mother's oldest brother (Uncle Kip) had died a U.S. congressman.

Because one of my mother's grandfathers had been governor.

There was no need for me to worry about getting back late from lunch. In Hillston, family talked louder than money. Usually, although not always in our case, they spoke the same language. Captain Fulcher did not care for me, but he was afraid to make it obvious. He assumed that sooner or later I would tell Mother's people to find me a job as a judge or a senator, and then it would be better for him if I had never become aware of how covetously he despised me. His pink frantic jowls flinched whenever I referred to Mrs. Dollard as Cloris.

After my childhood I had come to call her Cloris, but I'd rarely seen her. She was only a large, handsome shape passing me on the golf course or on the dance floor of the Hillston Club. Last Monday, I'd stood on the vast yellow carpeting of the vast colonial bedroom, and followed the smear of dried blood and the track of scattered pearls that led to the queen-size bed where Cloris Dollard had lain dead all night on a daisy coverlet, her suit ripped loose at the shoulder, a shoe absurdly dangling from her foot, the pillow now taken away from her face so that Richard Cohen, our medical examiner, could say what was immediately clear: Someone had broken her skull, someone had pushed hard enough on her face to crush her nose. I'd stood, looking down on her body, and remembered her voice when I was a child, a full, warm, smoker-deep voice that made all her words sound like laughs.

And I recalled one moment from the summer I was six. Cloris and my mother, both in their bathing suits, stood on the dock at the Ames lake cottage, watching Uncle Rowell swim out to pull upright the lit-tle sailboat Bainton Ames had just capsized. Cloris was tugging up her suit straps and saying to my mother, "Honey, you're crazy, don't envy me! Thank your stars you're so petite and don't have to lug these damn things around with you everywhere you go!" She put her hands be-neath her breasts and pushed them up. I recall my sudden wonder at all that amplitude of flesh, so different from my slender mother's body. I recall my squirming flush as I realized they were talking about their breasts.

When I called to tell my mother that Cloris was dead, she had sobbed, "Oh, my God, where's Rowell? Is he there? Oh, poor Cloris. I'll come over. Poor Rowell, poor Rowell. And his primary!"

Like her half brother, Mother had been bred a Dollard. She knew that primaries were the family business.

Out on Susan's porch now, hairs rose from the goose bumps on my bare legs. A colder, quicker wind swirled up inside my coat, and my muscles tightened to shrink away from the gusts. Gray swells on Pine Hills Lake slapped up at a gray swollen mass of clouds that had hur-riedly spumed over the sky and blotted the day out. It looked very much like snow. As my head tilted up to finish my whiskey, I noticed a different shade of gray steam skyward from the crest of the piney hill that sloped up from the side of the Whetstone lot. At first I thought of a fire, then saw that it was chimney smoke, then seemed to remember that hidden in that evergreen foliage was the vacation compound belonging to old Briggs Cadmean, president of C & W Textiles.

Hillston was a quiet college town, but it took the clattering noise of Cadmean's mills to pay for so much quietness. For the past fifty years Cadmean had owned the mills; he was the hub of the wheel. Eighty now, he was seldom seen socially. His pleasures had presumably been pecuniary and domestic: he'd made millions, he'd married often. Two wives had left his ugly downtown mansion on the arms of their law-yers; two had left in expensive coffins. Now he lived alone. I'd heard that his children, some of them themselves old, had all fled from him—several by dying. Why should his summer house be open in January? Surely, at his age, he too was not forced out here by a clandestine affair? Did the compound even still belong to Cadmean? I couldn't remember if Susan had said he'd sold it. She'd said something about it today at lunch, but I'd been drinking at lunch, and I forgot things when I drank. What I forgot first was how frightened my Dollard relatives were that I would start drinking again. "Some men can't handle it," Rowell had often informed me. "You seem to be one of them." Rowell had plans for me that meant he had to keep the skeleton gagged in the closet; to him the noise of ice in a glass in my hand sounded like the rattle of bones breaking loose and shaking the doorknob. I threw what was left of my drink toward the lake, and went inside to get dressed.

At two twenty I was walking unsteadily up the wide stone steps of the Municipal Building, when I was stopped by Sister Resurrection, a tiny old black woman who'd been trying to save Hillston for half a century. She always stopped me when I'd been drinking; somehow she sensed that's when I was most likely to agree with her. Now she shook her makeshift cross at me and said, "God's ready to put a stop to all this trash! He got no time to mess with mercy now! Praise Him!"

I said, "Why shouldn't He have time? He had time to start the whole mess."

She had no answer, or didn't care to share it, and marched in her fluttering rags away, insistent that we all rejoice in the imminent Armageddon. I followed her and stuffed five dollars down in her sweater pocket.

Inside on the fifth floor, Cuddy Mangum, Hillston's other homicide detective, stood in the hall, fiddling with his scores on a college basketball pool that was tacked up above the coffee machine. Captain Fulcher couldn't fire me because of my family; he couldn't fire Cuddy Mangum because Mangum was discreetly running the department for him. He wanted to fire us both.

At Cuddy's feet sat the dirty white unclipped little poodle (more or less) that he brought with him nearly everywhere he went, despite Fulcher's demands that he stop. The dog's name was Mrs. Mitchell, or Martha. He'd named her for the wife of Nixon's crony John Mitchell, and with her light frizzy bangs and sharp nose she did somewhat resemble that lady. Cuddy said he'd found Mrs. Mitchell abandoned on Airport Road the day he'd returned to Hillston from Vietnam, when he was feeling that the government had done to him about what it had done to Mrs. Mitchell, when they both had just been trying to help out.

As I came down the hall, Cuddy waggled his eyebrows. "How was your lunchbreak?" And he gave his crotch a few quick pumps.

I said, "Cuddy, that's the kind of gross white-trash social style that gets you assigned to investigate ax fights in the By-Ways Massage Emporium parking lot, while I'm off interrogating Daughters of the Confederacy with our toes dangling in their private pools."

He winked his caustic blue-jay eye down at me. "Is *that* where you were? I told your visitor you were off doing something hushed up and high-class, but *my*, I didn't know it was toe-dangling! Sort of shrivels you up though, in January, doesn't it, all this dangling? Now, was this pool water? You sure it wasn't *lake* water?"

I pointed at my cubicle and felt in my jacket pocket for a cigarette. "Who's in there?"

"I don't know, but I'm in love with her." He blocked me with his tall beanpole body; his white acrylic "ski" sweater smelled like pizza. He sighed loudly. "Now, tell me, Justin Bartholomew Savile the Five, why'd I have to grow up gross and country, and you so classical ivy and antebellum with your mama's folks that used to be the governor and all just running the state so big, why when their wives get whopped on the head, the attorney general has you put right on their case without a kiss-my to our fathead captain, not to mention *me* and my four years' seniority."

"You've got pizza on your sweater. Is that what you got for lunch again? Pizza, a Coke, and a Twinkie?"

"Hey, well, I can't afford to eat in those upper-crust tumbledown spots like where you and Lunchbreak Whetstone just got back from. Ye Olde Pine Hills Inn."

"I guess you want me to ask you how you knew that?"

"Deetection." He stuck his big bony hand in my jacket pocket and pulled out the Inn's inscribed matchbook. "It's never going to work with you and Lunchbreak, you know? What with you thinking *est* is Latin for *is*, and her thinking it's those lessons she took where they teach you how to tell people 'I hear what you're saying,' when you don't plan to pay any attention to what they've said."

"You just don't like Susan."

"Um. There's no putting anything past you today, Mr. Esse Quam Videri." (Once I'd made the mistake of translating for Cuddy the North Carolina state motto.)

I said, "You know, I'm very tolerant of your hillbilly affectations. Mine are just as native as yours. My great-granddaddy studied the classics and went to law school, too."

"Well, you've got me there," he grinned. "In fact, except that I'd have to get so short and pretty and preppie and go act in amateur Shakespeare theatricals, wearing jackass ears and tights, I almost wouldn't mind being Justin the Five, so I could go out gobbling ye olde nouvelle cuisine with a blond adultress in a beat-up barn, and come staggering back to work smelling like bourbon and—"

"Good Christ, don't you ever shut up?"

"Only when I . . ." And he began his graphic pumping again as he wandered back to erase his basketball game scores. Cuddy changed his projections continually on the basis of sudden powerful hunches; he had never even come close to winning the pool. "Ask her if she'll marry me," he called over his shoulder.

I opened my office door and realized what Cuddy had been talking about. She sat in my father's old Yale chair staring with oddly yellow eyes at the papier-mâché ass's head I'd stuck up on the hat rack.

"It was part of a costume," I said.

"Mr. Savile? I was told you'd definitely be back by two o'clock." She turned around the clock on my desk and pointed. It said two twenty-five. "My name is Briggs Cadmean."

I said, "Pardon me" and "I'm sorry," and went around her to hang up my overcoat. I hit into the side of my desk and lurched against her chair. "I was detained. Briggs Cadmean?" She wore a lavender down jacket with jeans and scuffed riding boots. She had a lovely face and an annoyed look. She was clearly not the town's oldest business magnate. I returned stiffly to my seat. "Is the C & W Briggs Cadmean your grandfather?"

With an even more annoyed look she stuffed the book in her lap into a new briefcase. "Father."

"You're kidding."

"No."

"Are you the youngest?"

"Yes. Number nine. Out of wife number four. Now that you have my lineage." She was looking me over strangely. She looked familiar to me, too. But then, Hillston's circle was not large. I was thinking: hunt club (boots), charity tennis, political cocktails, dance. "Excuse me. Haven't we met?"

"Probably." She was not terrifically forthcoming.

"Miss?" I asked. "Mrs.? Ms.?"

"If you prefer to be formal, how about Doctor? Or Professor?"

"Are you an M.D.?"

"No. I teach astronomy at the university."

"My dad taught surgery at the medical school here," I said. "He didn't think Ph.D.'s should call themselves doctors. But I will if you want me to."

"What you call me doesn't matter much, since I'd like to keep this as brief as possible."

We were not hitting it off. In fact, she slid her chair back a significant inch away from me. "I'm here," she said, "because my sister-in-law asked me to drop in. Joanna Cadmean. She'd like to know if you could come talk with her. About Cloris Dollard, I understand."

"Pardon? Joanna Cadmean?" I was looking for a cigarette; I hid them from myself.

"She's the widow of one of my half brothers. And she's staying out at my house for a few weeks. She came here from St. Simons Island for Mrs. Dollard's funeral. She's staying because she was thrown riding; she's on crutches now, with a bad ankle. At any rate, she's worried about something, and she'd like to talk with you."

"What's she worried about?"

"That somebody's trying to kill her, too."

I found a cigarette. "Any particular reason why she thinks so?"

"A premonition."

I leaned my chair back, and dismissed this Joanna Cadmean. We'd already had four other wealthy women call in, frightened that they too would be murdered soon, for their sterling or their diamonds or their too many years of capital and status. I said, "I'm sure it's just that the news of Cloris Dollard's death has upset Mrs. Cadmean." I picked up the silver letter opener Susan had given me, and balanced it on my fingers as I quoted: " 'Such tricks hath strong imagination.' *A Midsummer Night's Dream*."

Her response was to raise an eyebrow. "I saw your performance last week." Obviously, not a theater enthusiast either.

"Mrs. Cadmean," I shrugged, "has spooked herself."

"Yes, she has a strong imagination. In fact, she's a psychic."

"There, you see," I said, and smiled.

"A real psychic."

I smiled some more. "Visions and auras and foresee the future?"

"That's right."

"Tea leaves or Ouija board?"

The yellow eyes were flat as metal. "Please don't be cute."

I let my chair come back down on all fours. My neck flushed. "I'm sorry. Exactly how do you mean, a real psychic?"

She stood up. "If you keep records here, go look up her maiden name. Joanna Griffin. In the fifties she became rather famous for her work with your department."

I stood up. "*That's* who your aunt was? Joanna Griffin? The Hillston psychic?"

"Yes."

"The one who found the two coeds' bodies?" I looked across at Mr. Cadmean's namesake. "Well then! Who's going to kill her?"

Now she looked bemused. "She didn't say. Ask her."

"Why me? Why does she want to see *me*?"

"I have no idea. As I understand it, she doesn't want to talk officially to the police, and I believe she knew your mother. We're out at Pine Hills Lake."

"Ah. You're staying at your father's summer house?"

"The lodge belongs to me." She walked to the door.

"Would you care to have dinner with me tonight, Doctor?"

She zipped up the lavender jacket. "No, thank you."

I wasn't surprised. "Well, then, I'll come out to the lodge after I eat alone. Around eight?"

"Fine. Joanna said to be careful about the road; she said it's going to snow."

I opened the door for her. "Is that a psychic prediction?"

Her hair shook out behind her shoulders. "No, that's probably the weather report. Do you know where the lodge is, Mr. Savile? It's the compound next to Lawry Whetstone's cottage."

I followed her out into the hall, wondering if she and Susan could possibly be friends, and if Susan had told her about us. She so ostentatiously disliked me, I was reluctant to think it had taken only our brief conversation to make her feel that way.

As we passed Cuddy's office, he lunged through his open door and said to Briggs, "Miss, would you like to marry me?"

She surprised me by leaning down to pet the poodle, Mrs. Mitchell, and then laughing. "I might," she said, "but not today."

"Well, how about going out for a pizza and a Twinkie?"

I was pulling on my overcoat. "Cuddy Mangum, this is Professor Briggs Cadmean. This is Detective Lieutenant Mangum, a great believer in marriage."

He cocked his head at her. "Not *the* Briggs Cadmean that owns Hillston! Honey, you don't look at all like your pictures in the paper. Listen, in fact you ought to talk to them. They don't do you justice. They make you look great big and bald and sneaky and about eighty years old!"

Briggs's surprising rumbling laugh suggested to me she didn't care much for her father.

"Excuse me, Cuddy. I'm going to walk Miss Cadmean to her car."

"I don't blame you." He nodded toward the double doors at the end of the hall. "But what about V.D.?" He wheeled around to Briggs. "That's just our captain's name. Van Dorn. We call him V.D. to watch him chew up the insides of his cheeks."

I interrupted their laughter. "I'll be back."

"I'll mention you dropped by. Miss Cadmean, if you change your mind, I could be at the license bureau in the morning." Cuddy ducked back into his office.

I opened the door to what I incorrectly assumed was her father's new Lincoln, then watched as the big black car surged into Hillston's afternoon traffic. Something wet caught on my eyelashes. I looked up, and saw snow floating out of the dark sky.

"Um!" Mangum unlocked the door to the records room. "Joanna Griffin! Amazing. And asking for you like a sphinx out of a story when the only people that call me out of the blue are trying to sell me light bulbs."

"Joanna Cadmean. She married a Cadmean."

"Isn't there anybody in Hillston besides me that's not part Cadmean or a damn Dollard like you?"

"My name's not Dollard. My name's Savile. I'm the only Savile in Hillston. There must be two hundred Mangums."

"At least. And I'm hoping to add more."

"Even if they're part Cadmean?"

"Well, hey, nobody's perfect." Pencil tight in his teeth, Cuddy rummaged through the file cabinets. "Okay, here it is. Griffin, Joanna. Looks like a couple dozen cases here. Also looks like she was what you might want to call a volunteer worker. I don't see where they ever paid her a damn penny."

"How do you charge for visions?" I took the file from him.

"What's her name, Jeane Dixon does all right. Course, she's on a big scale. Like, will Elvis come back from the dead? Lord, I hope so. Well, don't hog it. Read."

The file began in the early fifties, when one day a Hillston girl of good family had walked into the police department and shyly announced to the desk sergeant that she knew where the bodies of two missing local coeds were buried. They'd been missing for over a month. She was taken to the office of the young assistant solicitor, Rowell Dollard.

The girl explained to him and to the incredulous police that whenever she saw photographs of the missing coeds, she saw them being forced down wood basement steps into a black space. She went on to describe in precise detail what turned out to be a half-burnt, long-abandoned country church thirteen miles south of Hillston. Even as the squad cars followed her lead, bouncing over the clay-clotted road into overgrown woods, no one really believed the girl. They didn't believe her until the two corpses were dug from their shallow graves in the church basement, behind the wood steps.

After the department agreed that she couldn't have killed the coeds herself, after a student confessed that he had, they asked Joanna to tell them what her secret was. She said she didn't know. Images like these had been coming into her head since she was little. Naturally, she didn't like it. Not only was she a freak to her schoolmates, the visions themselves brought on violent headaches, and were followed by a terrible depression. She was horrified by the discovery of the bodies. So were her parents. Embarrassed, they had her put under observation at the university, where she was a freshman. There, parapsychologists asked her to look at the backs of cards and read what was on the other side. She did so. The university concluded that if there were such a phenomenon as mental telepathy (and about this they disagreed), then Joanna Griffin was telepathic.

The Hillston police became less skeptical. When a local three-year-old disappeared, his mother begged the police to call in Joanna. Joanna told them where to find the well shaft he'd fallen down, and still lay in, alive. She picked a suspected arsonist out of a lineup, and recounted each moment of his crime to him so vividly that, terrified by her sorcery, he confessed both to that, and to two other unsolved arsons.

Of course, sometimes her sibylline visions were too vague to follow, and sometimes she had nothing at all to tell the department that had sheepishly gotten into the habit of calling her in whenever they had no leads, and the newspaper was publicly wondering why. The papers called Joanna everything from a mystic to a charlatan, and one literary journalist dubbed her "the Carolina Cassandra."

Then suddenly, after two years, Joanna stopped working for the police, and left the university for a term. When she came back to town, strangers continued to pester her with demands that she locate misplaced trinkets and wandering spouses, that she tell them where to find good jobs, that she bring back their dead. She asked them please to stop asking.

"Can you imagine," Cuddy said, "having no choice but to really see what's going on in the rotten world? You know? Not being able to blink your eyes? Seeing all the old smut in the heart and the tumor on the bone and somebody's future that's never going to happen? God damn! Can you imagine being her?"

There was a rumor that she'd attempted suicide in college, but that her family had hushed it up. Then she'd eloped with one of the Cadmean sons, and the visions, as far as anyone knew, had ended. "Marriage'll do that," Cuddy remarked. Perhaps after she had become a member of his family, old Briggs Cadmean forbade her to hallucinate, thinking it unseemly for a daughter-in-law of his to be even mentally trekking through creek bed and alley, feeling her way to the deserted or raped or stabbed. Dreaming her way to death.

Cuddy closed the file of yellowing papers. "I thought I heard she died."

"Christ, I'm almost scared to go meet her."

"Well, if you get a chance, ask her if she can help me win the basketball pool."

"All right. So long, I'm going out."

"You just got here. Why don't you come up to my office and do some police work, just to keep your hand in. Take your pick. Who keeps stealing Mr. Zeb Armel's Pontiac every night and driving it till the tank's empty? And my bet's Zeb, Jr. Who is exposing his private parts to Mrs. Ernestine Staley when she walks down Smith Road to collect her mail? And, my question, why in the world did he pick her? Who held up the Dot 'n' Dash? And, of course, why is there blood and fingertips all over the By-Ways Massage Emporium parking lot?"

"Sorry. I'm on special assignment. I'm going to East Hillston about the Dollard jewelry."

"Across the Divide? Over to where us poorfolk were herded together and told, 'Let them eat Twinkies.' That East Hillston?"

"Right."

"Well, don't ask any tattooed greasers to step outside, General Lee."

I left him at the elevator door and crossed the marble lobby back out into the snow.

Never ask a greaser with tattoos on his knuckles to step outside, especially if he's smiling, and combing his hair with a switchblade. Those were the first words Cuddy Mangum ever said to me. And although we'd been born in the same year, in the same town, they were the only words he said to me until I joined the police department ten years later, and we met again in the hall where I'd seen him today. He'd made the remark our senior year (mine in a New England prep school, his in Hillston High). I was back home to escort a debutante to a dance, and we'd come in our formal clothes at dawn to an all-night diner. As soon as we sat down, three hoods leaned into our booth and began making vulgar cracks. I asked them to step outside. Somebody tall and thin, seated by himself at the counter, all of a sudden spun his stool around and stood up. He said, "Wally, don't talk dirty in front of a lady. I think you left your brains out in your Chevy; why don't you and your pals go look for them, how about?"

And after a volley of muttered obscenities, Wally clanked off and his friends followed.

It was when I came over to the counter to thank Cuddy Mangum that I got the advice never to ask tattooed greasers to step outside. He added, "They never read your rule book, General Lee."

"Mind if I ask, why did Wally listen to you?"

"He's my cousin." And my rescuer spun his stool back away from me, and picked up his textbook and his doughnut.

Ten years after that, when he and I were introduced by Captain Fulcher, I said, "I believe we've already met." Cuddy took a doughnut out of his mouth, and nodded. He said, "Especially now you're in *this* business, don't ask a tattooed greaser to step outside."

2

I inched my old Austin timidly into East Hillston. I hadn't been drinking long enough not to be still afraid of the snow. With me was a list of Cloris Dollard's stolen property that probably wasn't very accurate. She had been a woman of property, but not a careful or frugal one. She'd spent her life as cheerfully as all the money she'd given to Hillston charities, and all the money she'd spent to buy the random wealthy clutter of belongings she'd given away or left behind. What had proved less fragile than their owner (and had not been stolen by her murderer), Cloris's daughters had come from other cities and taken home with them, or stored in the basement. Rowell, who liked to keep things, would not let them touch his wife's room.

I had searched in the house through the clutter, looking for a clue among boxes of clothes, photographs of golf trophies, her first husband's sheet music, and her daughters' camp crafts; among drawers of old theater programs, packets of seeds, keys and buttons whose uses had been years lost. I was looking through a past of good looks, marriages, travel, civic duties, through the loose ends of an easy life, for a clue to tell me that Cloris's death had not happened, as everyone believed, by the unlucky accident of indiscriminate violence, but for a cause particular and personal, and so discoverable. I'd found nothing.

Now I was doing instead what Cuddy had long ago warned me detectives actually do for a living. I was walking, with a list of stolen property, into every pawnshop, secondhand business, and disreputable jewelry store in town. I was waiting for someone to give me a clue. Most of the stores are in East Hillston. None of the owners had seen any of Cloris Dollard's property. Not unless they'd seen on their customers some of the used clothes she was always donating to Goodwill.

The goodwill performed locally by Cloris Dollard and her friends, and by Susan Whetstone and her friends, was for the benefit of this section of town called East Hillston, which meant poor Hillston, which meant the area bordering the side of downtown Hillston that had gone out of business when Cloris and her friends had stopped shopping there twenty years ago and had driven off to the new malls and had never come back, except for charity's sake.

Sister Resurrection walked fast along the streets of East Hillston, dawn to dark, the smell of her rotted sweaters as familiar as her stick with its wood cross taped to the top and her unsparing eyes that kept waiting for God to burn up the world. Men and women who worked the lowest-paid assembly line jobs at C & W Textiles lived here; so did most of Hillston's blacks; so did the few Greek and Italian families, after three generations still known to their neighbors as "the foreigners," who owned corner groceries and submarine sandwich shops. They lived here in all that were left of the massy Victorian frame houses built after the Civil War, when East Hillston had been rich. Boarded up and doled out now as shoddy apartments, the old homes were rotting beneath layers of bad paint and cheap linoleum. Beside them even shabbier little oblong boxes had been thrown up on what had once been big lawns where summer parties played croquet. These little 1940s duplexes, faced with stucco or aluminum siding, now hid behind all the pickup trucks and rusty Chevrolets scattered over the yards. The worst place to be from in Hillston was East Hillston. It was where Cuddy Mangum had grown up.

The Mangums had lived three blocks from the old, shambling two-story Gothic house that somebody named Pope had owned as far back as the town records went. Somebody named Pope had been on the police books as far back as those records went, too. At present, various assortments of Pope brothers and their wives lived in the house and were periodically arrested for stealing cars, hijacking cigarette trucks, and brawling in public. Long ago, their mother Edna had just picked up her raincoat and walked out of the house. She'd left when her youngest boy was twelve. She'd never come back. The boys' father, T. J. Pope, had died while waiting trial for murder: he'd killed a mechanic who overcharged him.

Cuddy said the Pope brothers were hereditarily unreformable, but their marauding was checked by a congenital stupidity (evidenced by their having hidden $3,000 belonging to Cherokee Savings and Loan under a junked bus in an old cardboard suitcase that had "Edna Pope, 1020 Maple Street, Hillston, N.C." tagged to the handle), and so at any given time a few of them were likely to be sidelined by prison.

Cuddy Mangum kept up with the Popes. He called with the latest news shortly after I'd gotten home from East Hillston and was changing into a suit to go meet the psychic Joanna Cadmean out at Pine Hills Lake. His call came when I'd just hung up the phone and poured a drink after listening to Senator Rowell Dollard tell me, again, to go arrest someone for killing Cloris. I thought the ring now was Rowell calling back. My uncle was persistent. He hated to lose. At fifty-eight he played squash twice a week, and he played and played until he won—if I beat him two out of three games, he'd pant, "Let's make it three out of five." Captain Fulcher was scared that if we didn't find Cloris's murderer fast, Rowell would do it himself, and then have all of us fired, as, long ago, he'd gotten V. D. Fulcher's predecessor fired. Rowell liked to do things himself; he'd insisted on acting as a father to me even during the time when I already had one.

The call, however, was from Cuddy. He said, "Lawry Whetstone here, old boy. Understand you've been banging my memsahib. I say, bad show."

"What do you want, Cuddy? A part in our next play?"

"What are you doing right now?"

"Changing my clothes. I told you. To meet the psychic lady."

"You know, I wonder if you're not some kind of pervert. There's something un-American about the way you're always playing the piano and changing your clothes. Want to get in on a real arrest; score with V.D.? Meet me at the Popes' house on Maple fast as you can."

"Christ, what have the Popes done now?"

"Charlene called up the station . . ."

"Graham's wife?"

"Preston's. Charlene is Baby Preston's wife. Can't you keep up? Old Graham's wife gave him the heave while he was in the tank. For trying to collect insurance on a semi he poured kerosene all over and lit a match to about the time everybody was getting out of church and strolling by his house to watch him do it. Whooee, I love those Popes! Graham's wife's the daytime bartender at the Rib House now, but she put on a lot of weight snacking on the job and lost her looks. Charlene called. . . ."

I kept straightening my bow tie. "Jesus Christ, Cuddy, how do you know all this?"

"These are my people, white boy. My grandma's sister married a second cousin of the Popes'. That's why I don't have the heart to go over there alone and arrest Preston for whinging off two of Lùster Hudson's fingers with an ax outside the By-Ways Massage Emporium, which is what hot-to-trot Charlene—who was whinging Luster, as was well known to everybody in East Hillston but Preston—just got through telling Sergeant Davies took place. Now, Officer Davies says we ought to close the By-Ways, says they're showing obscene motion pictures in the back. I says, ummmm, are they ever! but doesn't it make you so mad, Hiram, how they blip off every eighteen seconds and you got to plunk in a few more quarters to get to the good stuff?"

Sergeant Hiram Davies was past retirement age and a rigid Baptist deacon. "Okay, Cuddy, force yourself to hang up, and I'll be right over."

"I knew you couldn't stay away. You love this low-life blood-and-lust detective work, doncha?"

"That and the long lunch hours."

When I skidded scared in the slush around the corner of East Hillston's Maple Street, I could hear gunshots and then I saw Cuddy hiding down beside his patrol car. I braked next to him and yelled, "Get out of here!"

"They're not shooting at me!" he yelled back.

"Jesus Christ! Who are they shooting at?"

He was twisting his arm around inside his neon-blue parka. "How the hell should I know? I just got here! Where the hell is my gun!" He didn't always wear his revolver, and often couldn't even find it.

Up and down the snowy street, lights popped on in the duplexes. People cracked their doors and stuck their heads through. Cuddy hollered at them, "Will you folks please get on back!"

I rolled out of my Austin, slid into the patrol car, and flipped its siren on. Mrs. Mitchell was hiding under the dash. In about five seconds, the shots quit. As soon as they did, a young woman ran out the door of the Pope place and jumped down the cinder blocks that they used for porch steps. She slipped face first in the wet snow, and started to scream as loud as the siren. Cuddy and I scurried to her. It was Charlene. She hissed at him when Cuddy asked her if she'd been shot, and then she went back to screaming. I'd pulled my gun from the shoulder holster I always wore, because once when I hadn't, a drunk at a KKK rally had shot me in the calf and shattered a bone. I crouched, ran toward the porch and yelled into the door. "Police! Come out of there!"

I heard things banging around inside. From next door I heard a man call out, "It's the police for the Popes."

A door at the back slapped shut and Preston Pope came running across the driveway, headed for a van that had white horses in blue moonlight painted on it in iridescent color. Shoving past the metal junk piled on the porch, I leapt down and got to him in time to grab Preston's leg. He kicked like crazy and we whipped back and forth in the snow until Cuddy ran up and shook him off me, saying, "Preston! Cut this shit! I'm gonna hurt you!"

The youngest Pope went limp then, so quickly, Cuddy almost dropped him, and mumbled "Mangum, don't listen to that bitch! I swear . . ." But he gave up the effort and just stood still. We were all three panting, and puffs of smoke from our breath blew all over the place.

Charlene Pope was still out in the middle of the yard hugging herself. Charlene looked like somebody on the cover of one of the magazines you could buy in the By-Ways Massage Emporium. She had bleached white hair and black eyes and breasts hard as apples, and she was somewhere between fifteen and twenty-five. A black acetate bathrobe was slipping down off her shoulder; the only other thing she had on was one pink fuzzy bedroom slipper.

Cuddy scooped her other slipper out of the snow. "Come on, Charlene. Let's all go on back in the house and see what the problem is."

She had a high, twanging voice that got away from her when she raised it. "Y'all got to be crazy out of your minds! I want you to arrest his ass and get him out of here!" She shook both fists at her husband. "Goddamn fuckhead!"

Cuddy said, "Now, don't talk dirty out in the front yard in your nightgown, Charlene." He, Preston, and I went inside, and finally she followed us, already with a cigarette in her glossy purple mouth.

Local news was loud on the color TV, and Kenny Rogers was simultaneously singing a love song loud out of stereo speakers on the mantel above a fireplace that was used as a trash can. The Pope living room looked like a K mart warehouse and like a cheap motel that didn't care who came there or what they did there, and didn't bother cleaning up afterward. Thin green carpeting was oil-slick with grime and puddled with stains and cluttered with bent Coke and beer cans, ashtrays, country-and-western tapes, electric drills, balled-up bags of junk like corn puffs and barbecued potato chips, and God knows what else. Foam stuffing poked out of the black vinyl couch, where a skinny orange dog lay on a beach towel. One shade was ripped in half and there were chunks gouged out of the plaster. On two walls were textured color photograph portraits of various Pope boys and their brides, the boys in rented baby-blue tuxedoes with black piping. On another wall was an auto-parts-shop poster of a hefty blonde naked knee-deep in surf. On the floors along the walls were stacks of car stereos, CB systems, about seventy cartons of cigarettes, and five televisions—one with the screen smashed. I said, "So these are your Popes."

Cuddy said, "My, my, this *is messy*." Two windows were broken and gunsmoke lay thick in the air. He poked open another door and peeked in; he looked down the halls and tilted over to see up the stairs.

Preston picked a revolver up off the floor and handed it to me. "There ain't nothing in it," he said defensively.

Charlene shrieked, "That's right, you'd still be shooting if there was!"

Wiry and sullen, Preston came at her, snow still white in his beard and on his jean jacket. She backed away, making faces. He said, "I wasn't shooting at her, I was just shooting."

"Cleaning your gun?" I asked.

"Blowing off. You know."

I said, "Not exactly."

Charlene said, "He is so *stupid*, I can't stand it another second."

"Well, let me tell you this, this bitch here is a cunt."

"You dumb prickhead!"

They started toward each other again, and Cuddy slid between and elbowed them both. He asked Preston, "Where's everybody else, where's Graham and Dickey?"

"Greensboro. That's where she thought *I* was too."

Charlene hissed back at him. "I came over here to pack up my own personal belongings that don't belong to you."

I said, "In your robe?"

"I was getting ready to take a bath. I can use the tub if I want to, I guess!"

Preston was yelling again. "The hell you can, you can't use nothing in this whole goddamn house, 'cause none of it's yours, 'cause the god-damn water belongs to *me* and the goddamn TV belongs to me too!" He spun around and jerked out the TV cord, which just left the Kenny Rogers tape going at high volume.

"I'm leaving," she said.

"You're not leaving," he said.

"Yes I am too!"

"Go ahead and try!"

"Well," Cuddy said, "why don't you at least go throw on a few clothes, Charlene." He turned her toward the stairs in the hall. "What with all the windows broken, it's kind of drafty." Actually, they had the oil heat up to about ninety degrees; even with the ventilation, the place was so hot I decided to take off my overcoat and brush out some of the slush.

Cuddy put his hand on Preston's shoulder. "Preston, you need to calm down. You don't seem to be paying attention to the fact that you're getting arrested."

Preston said, "What for?" but he was watching Charlene try to go up the stairs while looking back down at us.

I said, "Are you kidding? Assault with a deadly weapon?"

"Charlene's never gonna say that."

"Is he kidding? What do you think your wife's *been* saying?"

"Forget her. Y'all got eyes. She's out of her fucking gourd!"

Charlene yelled from the top of the stairs. "In case you hadn't no-ticed, you stupid asshole, you're *screwed*, Preston! What are you gonna do now, hunh? What are your big brothers gonna do for you now, hunh? Hunh, baby shithead?"

He jumped. "Just let me go kill her, okay?"

Cuddy said, "Whoaa. Let's not do that right this minute. Let's have a talk, you and me, and this gentleman is Lieutenant Savile and that was his camel-hair coat you tore the pocket off of."

Preston said, "I'm sorry."

I said, "It's all right."

Cuddy said, "Now, listen, Preston, you wouldn't like to be moving in with brother Furbus for oh about a year, would you?"

Furbus Pope, the eldest brother, and probably twenty years older than Preston, was in the state penitentiary on a larceny charge.

"Okay, what's the deal?" he mumbled.

"Well, first of all, why did you shoot at your wife?"

"Let me tell you something about Charlene . . ."

"In a minute. Second of all, I'd hate to think for your health's sake, you were going through"—Cuddy glanced over at the floor—"oh, six or seven hundred packs of cigarettes a day while you were sitting around watching all those TV sets."

Preston said, "You want one?"

"And third of all."

Preston now slumped down onto the couch and pulled at his hair. The orange dog finally sat up. I'd decided it was dead.

Cuddy wiggled his fingers. "Third is the matter of a couple of Luster Hudson's fingers, which I hear rumors you took off him with an ax."

"Says who?"

"Guess."

"Luster."

"Guess again."

"That bitch." Preston dug his fingernails into the side of his face and started it bleeding.

"*Now* you can tell me about Charlene." Cuddy sat down. I stood by the door, where I could watch the stairs. The dog came over, sniffed at Cuddy's leg, and then wandered back to the kitchen.

Young Pope had gotten himself so depressed by now, he had to keep taking long breaths while he talked. "Couple of weeks ago I found out Charlene and Luster Hudson had something on."

"Couple of weeks ago you found out," Cuddy said, and looked at the ceiling.

"Well, it was Graham found them out and he told me. So, Charlene she says it's a lie but I don't believe her because she's on nights at C & W along with Luster and she's not showing up home. And then Graham saw her and him dancing at the Tucson Lounge. So I said, 'One of these times Charlene you're gonna open that door and there'll be a gun in your belly.'"

"That's telling her," Cuddy said.

"So she said, 'Don't think I haven't hidden your damn gun where no way you're gonna find it.' So I said, 'I don't need a gun to—'"

I said, "Let's skip to the part where you chop off Hudson's fingers."

"It was Luster came at me with the ax."

I said, "Any particular reason?"

"He had it in his pickup."

Cuddy said, "I think what Lieutenant Savile means is, what did you *do* to Luster before he looked in his truck to see if he had an ax handy?"

Preston mumbled something.

Cuddy took out a package of cheese crackers. "Come again? Seemed like you said, 'Torched his bike.'"

"Yeah."

"Torched his bike."

"I said, *yeah*. I'm looking for Charlene and I seen his Harley outside the Tucson Lounge and so I look in and I see him and her out on the floor and so I take a rag and stuff it in his tank. And so I torch it."

"All right." Cuddy nibbled tiny bites of the cracker.

"So he comes for me at the By-Ways but Graham's with me, so Graham ducks and comes up under Luster's knees and I get hold of the ax and that's when it got his fingers."

I said, "You just left Hudson lying there bleeding?"

"He's the one left, and he knew why, too. I chased his goddamn truck a block but I gave out and threw the ax at it."

"Good Christ," I said. "What about the man's fingers?"

"Aww, shit, it was just the tips. Graham picked them up and looked and it was nothing but the tips."

"I don't suppose you're keeping them in a jar on your bureau?"

Preston was shaking beer cans that sat on the floor; finally he found one with something to drink in it. Mournfully he told us, "Y'all got eyes. Charlene brought this all on herself."

Cuddy said, "I don't see where *Charlene's* the one in trouble."

Preston flared up. "Well, that's where you're wrong because I've about had it with that little girl and she's gonna wind up in a divorce, I swear she is!"

Cuddy said, "That's harsh," and gave me his blue-jay wink.

I hadn't heard noises from upstairs in a while. I said, "Excuse me, I think I'll just go see if Charlene's taking another bath."

"Oh, hell!" Cuddy untangled his long body from the plastic swivel chair. "I forgot! Back stairs!" By the time I got to the top, we all heard the motor rev outside and the tires whir in the snow.

Cuddy yelled, "Too late!" and I yelled, "Is she in *my* car?" and the three of us ran onto the porch, but it was the iridescent van whose engine Charlene was racing out in the street while she shouted through the open window. "*I'm taking it*, it was *my* money paid for it!"

Preston hopped up and down, but couldn't shake Cuddy's grip. "*You get back here!*"

"Get fucked, shithead!" Charlene popped the clutch, tore up a gear, and was gone.

"Sweet lips," Cuddy said.

Preston's mouth was working hard but words had failed him. Then he bolted back inside up to the second floor.

The upstairs of the Pope house convinced me that they'd put all of their housekeeping efforts into the downstairs living room. In a bedroom that could only have been Charlene's, Preston yanked the top drawer right out of a dresser and was shaking his socks and several dozen "Arouse" condom packets onto the floor. Then he slammed to his knees and pawed through everything.

Cuddy said, "What'd she take?"

Preston said, "Nothing," and began tossing undershirts around.

I wandered out to the bathroom. Nobody's been taking a bath, because the tub was full of small gray velvet sacks. I opened one of them.

"Hey, Cuddy, you want to hang on to Preston? We have a problem here."

"What you got?"

I brought the sack back into the bedroom and pulled out an ornate dinner fork. "Cloris Dollard's silverware."

Cuddy said to Preston, "I don't guess you got it with Green Stamps, did you?"

3

Downtown, we booked an even more morose Preston Pope. I left Cuddy with him, and went to visit Joanna Cadmean.

It was snowing so hard by the time I'd driven to the lake, I had trouble finding the turnoff to the Cadmean compound. Although I'd often looked at it from the bedroom of the Whetstone lake cabin, I'd never really seen it, because when you're as wealthy as the Cadmeans, you can afford a lot of trees. Even when my mother's people had had money, they hadn't had that kind of money.

In the black water, a covered sailboat and motorboat and canoe were shadows, moored for winter beside two long docks. A beach (for which somebody had trucked in a great deal of white sand at considerable cost) led up a slope of pines, and at the top, lights looming, sat the huge lodge with its big windows that looked, over the heads of the pines, down on the lake below and the smaller houses that ringed the water.

Inside, the lodge turned out to be the handsome, rustic sort the rich liked to build in the Appalachians and out West in the 1920s, with the cavernous stone fireplace, and bare log beams girdering high ceilings, and a few bluish American Indian rugs thrown here and there. A porch stretched halfway around the first floor, and an open balcony across the second. In the middle of the roof was an odd octagonal turret with outside walkway, like a watchtower. The furnishings were Spartan.

I'd recognized my mother's car among the others clustered along a driveway lit by the porch lights and already glazed with snow. Mother's old sable coat hung on the coatrack in the hall, and my mother, a small, still-pretty woman of a buoyant disposition, sat uncomfortably swallowed by a bent-willow chair near the fire. She was chattering away at someone on the couch when the young woman, Briggs, led me in.

"Justin! Whatever in the world are you doing out here tonight? Oh, Briggs, *you* invited him. I didn't know you knew Briggs, honey. My God, your coat's all torn up. Joanna, this is my son, Justin. He's a policeman. I wanted him to play the piano or use his imagination or something, and Rowell wanted him to be governor, but he's a policeman. I don't know why he ever went into such a morbid profession in the first place, though I suppose you could say his father did cut open people's brains for a living."

"Mr. Savile, hello. It was nice of you to come."

I came around the couch to meet the famous mystic. Expecting . . . I don't know what I expected. Madame Blavatsky? Carmen, in Mexican clothes with gold earrings and big clay beads she'd made herself, ruffling a deck of tarot cards? Saint Theresa?

What I saw was an unexpectedly beautiful middle-aged woman,

dressed in a pastel sweater and tweed skirt very much like those all my mother's friends wore on winter days at home. But despite her ordinary clothes, the chignon in which she wore her waved light hair and the sculpted cast of her features made me think at once of some Archaic Athena, some goddess quietly standing to support a temple. And always afterward, from that first look until the end, I thought of Joanna Cadmean as such a statue, Delphian, cool and impenetrable as stone.

Her right foot, thickly wrapped in Ace bandages, the toes covered by a white sock, was propped up on the redwood coffee table. In her lap was a spiral-bound artist's sketchbook; with a pencil she was drawing faces rapidly, swirling from face to face without lifting the point and, strangely enough, without even looking at what she was drawing. If there was anything else "odd" about her (other than her remarkable beauty), it was her stillness. Her large, wide-set eyes—not at all the sharp Svengalian jabs of light I associated with psychic powers from old movies—were a deep, still gray. Her voice was peaceful, quiet and slow, nothing like the intense, animated cheer habitual with Southern women like my mother, to whom she now said, "Your son came out to see me, Peggy. I invited him out."

As I bent to take Mrs. Cadmean's hand, she quickly turned the page of the sketchbook over to a blank sheet.

"You asked him? Whatever for?" My mother tilted her head for me to kiss as she spoke. "I ought to be grateful, I haven't seen him in ages, except on the stage. He's in the Hillston Players. Weren't you in that a long time ago? They just did *A Midsummer Night's Dream*. He played the one that gets turned into a donkey. I saw him there, and then at Cloris's funeral, and now I run into him all the way out here. You didn't go to Cloris's services, Joanna."

"No. I went to the grave."

"Well, and now you're stuck in Hillston. Joanna fell off a damn horse and broke her leg."

Mrs. Cadmean smiled. "Sprained my ankle. Your mother brought me a CARE package." Beside the couch was one of the wicker baskets my mother called her "Shut-in Surprises." This one included more historical romances than I could imagine a woman like Joanna Cadmean wanting to read.

"It was my fault," Briggs was saying to my mother. "I shouldn't have put her on Manassas."

Mrs. Cadmean pulled a plaid blanket down over her legs. "No, it's not the horse's fault. I started thinking something upsetting, and I frightened him. He wanted to get away from me, that's all. So he threw me."

"Well, that's a weird way to put it," my mother said. "But that's the way Joanna was even when she was little." Mother turned to us. "She used to tell us that we were *colors*. Really! She'd look at us, like this, *hard*, and she'd see these different colors around us like a neon sign. If she didn't like a boy's color, well! She wouldn't have a thing to do with him. Oh, God, Joanna, remember when you told Mrs. Mott at church she had a round lump like a grapefruit in her stmoach and she was dead of cancer a month later?"

I asked Briggs if she had any whiskey.

Mother sang her nervous laugh. "Why, yes, it is so bitterly cold, why don't you just bring me and Justin a teeny, tiny sip of something, Briggs?" She held up thumb and forefinger to measure a quarter inch.

Briggs left the room, and Mother went on. "I was a sort of robin's-egg blue, wasn't I?"

"You still are." Mrs. Cadmean smiled and began to draw again.

"Good! I was afraid maybe you'd say I'd turned all smudgy black inside." Mother touched her finger to the lace wrinkles at the edge of her eyes. She started to remember what colors other childhood friends had looked like to Joanna, while I waited for my drink. My father and I had grown so accustomed to Mother's Ferris wheel of language that on the rare occasions he and I had been alone together, we'd been astonished by the silence and could never think how to get past it. We'd play eighteen holes of golf with fewer words than Mother would use to describe a wait at the bus stop. She'd been by my father's hospital bed talking of orioles who'd come that morning to her bird-feeder, when he'd died, silently, his hand on hers. ". . . And Joanna, what was so spooky was up in Judy Fanshaw's room, you were *eight*, when you said Cloris was stark white with a red rim, like a blood-red moon! and it gave us all the creeps, and *now*, all these years later, here Cloris is, murdered! And the newspaper came over here, Justin, to interview Joanna, but she wouldn't talk to them."

I sat down near the fire. "I don't blame you. Briggs said you live on St. Simons Island now, Mrs. Cadmean. It's beautiful there. How long since you've lived in Hillston?"

"Fifteen years. I left after my husband, Charles, died." Her handsome head was still as marble. "But I come back from time to time. I was here last summer."

Mother scrambled out of her deep chair to help Briggs with the drinks. "I was just thinking last week, Joanna. How Cloris broke down in the middle of your Charles's funeral, because that summer she'd lost poor Bainton in that freak accident on the lake, and now here you'd lost your husband too. Can you believe that was fifteen years ago? Now, here we are at Cloris's. . . ." Mother sipped away a fourth of my already minuscule drink before handing it to me.

The shadows of the flames from the cave-like hearth darkened the pallor of Mrs. Cadmean's face as she turned toward me, wincing as she jostled her ankle. "It was to inquire about Cloris Dollard's death that I asked you here."

Mother said, "The attorney general has assigned him exclusively to Cloris's investigation." The attorney general was mother's cousin.

Mrs. Cadmean said, "Really, Mr. Savile?"

"Oh, Joanna, call him Justin." Mother saw me look inquiringly at my empty glass; she put her arm through mine and led me across the shadowy vaulted room to the huge window at the far end, trilling back, "Ladies, excuse us. Let me just go take a look at this snow. I'm a little worried about driving. But I do have my chains. Do you have yours, Justin?" When we reached the window, she spoke sotto voce. "Will you please be careful?" She nodded at my glass.

"I'm fine."

"Jay, please remember the strings Rowell had to pull to get your license back." Jay was my childhood name, now used in emotional emergencies.

"I'm fine."

Mother pulled away, her nostrils tightened, and she called out, "Look! It really is snowing hard. The ground's completely white."

Briggs came over to watch the swirl of heavy flakes fall into the arc of floodlights. White streaked invisibly into the white sand, and vanished into the lake. Briggs said, "I can't remember the last time Hillston had snow like this."

Mother's eyes widened. "Six years ago," she said. She ran for her coat. "Joanna, I'm going to leave here before it gets too deep. Justin, please don't stay long. Rowell's coming over for a late supper, and I think you should be there." She saw I was tempted to say something, and hurried away to the couch. "Stay off that foot, Joanna. And if that newspaperman pesters you again, why don't I ask Rowell to call up *The Star* and have him stopped? Briggs, would you like one of Mirabell's puppies? She had eleven! Isn't that a very Irish thing for an English setter to do?"

After Mother left, Briggs excused herself to go prepare a lecture.

I said, "I'm amazed. Are you old enough to be an astronomy professor?"

She put another log on the fire. "I'm twenty-nine. How old do I have to be?"

"You don't look it. You're only five years younger than I am."

She said, "You're thirty-four? I'm amazed. You don't act it. Good night."

I poked at the fire with the iron prongs. "I don't think the professor likes me, Mrs. Cadmean."

She smiled at me, the gray eyes steady. "She certainly gave that impression. She's a very serious person. Go ahead and smoke if you like." She said this just as I was telling my hand to move to my pocket for my cigarette case, and wondering if I should.

I sat down in the big bent-willow armchair beside her. "What would you like to know, Mrs. Cadmean?"

"Please call me Joanna. We've met before. Not exactly met. You won't remember. It was a very painful time for you. . . . I was at the cemetery the day of your father's burial. I liked your father. He was perceptive." The eyes smiled. "Not a word I use lightly."

"Thank you." I lit the cigarette. "Yes, it was a painful time." If she had seen me at the cemetery, she had seen me hit Rowell Dollard hard enough to make him stumble back into a wreath of lilies, hit him when he told me that if it weren't for my drinking, my father wouldn't be dead, my mother's life wouldn't be ruined.

Joanna nodded, as if she were following along with my memories. There must be that advantage in having a reputation as a psychic; you simply sit there and nod, and people believe you are seeing straight through to their innermost hearts, either because they want you to, or because they desperately do not. "You look much better now," she said, "than that day."

"Thank you. Let's hope so. I was a raving maniac back then."

"That's not true." She spoke softly and with a compelling self-assurance; all her remarks had this odd quiet authority. On her lap her long white fingers moved over the coarse wool of the blanket, like the fingers of a blind woman touching a face. "Tell me about Cloris's death," she said. And picking back up the sketchbook, she began to draw again.

"Well, I'm not sure what you want to know. Do you mean police details? She was killed between ten and midnight, a week ago Sunday, at her home. In fact, she'd left early from the last performance of *A Midsummer Night's Dream*, the one my mother was telling you we did here in town."

"You played Bottom. I've always liked Bottom for feeling so comfortable in fairyland. . . . I'm sorry to interrupt you. She left early?"

"Sometime after the second intermission. She told someone then that she had an upset stomach."

Mrs. Cadmean looked over at the tap of snow gusts hitting against the window. "Is the theory that she surprised a burglar?"

"Yes. This evening we recovered the silverware and have arrested a suspect."

She didn't seem much interested in this fact. "Some coins were taken? I think I read in the paper."

"A collection that had belonged to her first husband, Bainton Ames."

"Yes. Bainton showed them to me often."

"They were kept in a safe in her bedroom. It was flimsy, easy to jimmy open."

"She was beaten over the head, is that right?"

"With a trophy from her desk. The blow killed her. But the killer also smothered her. With a pillow."

"Another play," Mrs. Cadmean said.

I assumed she meant *Othello*, but the plot of a jealous husband's suffocating an unfaithful wife seemed to have little bearing on the Dollards.

I watched the beautiful profile stare silently into the fire, her eyes darkening, unfathomable as the black lake outside. "Did you find a diary, Justin?"

"Pardon? A diary? No." I stood up. "Why are you asking me all this about Cloris's death? Miss Cadmean said you think someone is trying to kill *you.* Do you think they're the same person?"

The pencil scratched firmly over the page, blotting the drawing. She closed the book, and shut her eyes. Just as I began to worry she was preparing to go into some kind of trance, she said calmly, "You know a little about my . . . past."

"Yes. I know you're the psychic, Joanna Griffin. My partner is a great admirer of yours. The truth is, from the way he's talked to me about you, I thought you'd be a whole lot older. His file on you stops about fifteen years ago. He thought you were dead."

She tugged down the cuffs of her sweater sleeves; it was a curiously nervous gesture in someone so otherwise composed, and one she repeated a number of times during our talk. "Your friend is right. Joanna Griffin did pass away a long while back. I guess you could say I went out of business. So, now I want to be very careful in what I say to you. . . . I asked you about a diary because I think Cloris wants someone to find it."

"Rowell would know if she kept one, wouldn't he? Her husband. Do you know Rowell Dollard?"

Her voice dropped and she looked down at her sketch. "Oh, yes, I know Rowell."

"That's right; he was assistant solicitor when you worked with the department. Were you friendly with him and Cloris?"

"I was friendlier with Cloris earlier, when she was married to Bainton Ames. My husband and I used to play bridge with her and Bainton." Joanna smiled, pulled over the sketchbook, and started a new drawing. "Cloris and I were different in personality."

"Yes." As earth and air.

"But we played bridge very well together. People occasionally accused us of cheating, but it was just . . ."

"Mental telepathy."

"I suppose so."

"Could you use it to help my partner win the basketball pool?"

"Unfortunately, Justin, it doesn't work when *I* want it to. Just when it wants to." Now she began speaking with the slow precision of a translator, her pencil pressing harder into the paper. "Thoughts . . . pictures . . . come to me very vividly. *Very* vividly. At times they are so strong, I have to act. When I went that first time to the Hillston police, about where the two girls were buried? That picture of the graves in that basement felt like the kind of headache where you can't bear the slightest sliver of light in the room."

I said, "I've felt that kind of headache too; without the accompanying epiphany."

She turned and looked so deeply and for so long without blinking straight into my eyes that I grew embarrassed by the intimacy. Finally she whispered, "You have very beautiful eyes. They're quite open."

Neither of us spoke until a whistle of wind blew down the chimney, flurrying sparks in the fire. Then she said, "I have to be careful. I get a strong feeling, inescapable; but who's to know what it means, if it's even true. Sometimes it's nothing."

I said, "Sometimes the bodies are buried there in the cellar." I felt very uncomfortable. "Will you say who you think wants to kill you?"

"One reason I have to be so hesitant is that these pictures are most intense when I'm ill, or upset. Even a fever from a cold. They came strongest when I was younger. They weren't pleasant, most of them. I'll tell you one I never told the police. When Charles was dying, I was at the hospital with him one night when I suddenly saw an image of Bainton Ames out in a boat on Pine Hills Lake." She stopped to erase part of her drawing.

I pulled my chair to the fire. The room was too large, the log beams too high over my head, the corners too shadowy. I began to want another drink. "Was that the same night that Bainton actually drowned?"

She nodded. "Yes. But in my . . . vision, his death was not an accident. There was somebody hidden in the boat behind Bainton, somebody who leapt up and struck him on the head, somebody he knew." She moved her leg slightly with her hands and smoothed the blanket.

A twitch behind my scalp pulled at my hair, even while I was thinking, easy enough to say all this after the fact. "Who was the somebody?"

Again she didn't respond to my questions, but said, "Finally, my uneasy feeling about Bainton's death grew so acute, I told Cloris. She was, naturally, reluctant to believe me. She didn't believe me. In fact, she was angry at me. There was a painful scene. She asked me not to mention my, as she called them, fantasies to her again." The even voice dropped. "Well, that was many years ago."

Snow had stuck in an oval around the corners of the huge window, making an old-fashioned frame. Through it, black lake and black sky were slipping into each other. With my shoe I pushed a log deeper into the fire's cave.

She kept drawing. "You see, Justin, a week ago Sunday, out on St. Simons, I dreamt that Cloris Dollard came to me and told me to find her diary."

"You mean you just *dreamt* she had this diary?"

The gray eyes frowned, disappointed in me. "Dreams are often wiser than the people who have them. They are, in many cases, certainly truer."

I held up my hands. "God knows."

"In my dream, Cloris was dead. Her hair was bloody, and her face blank white. She held out her hand, unclenched her fist, and pearls spilled from it."

"You had this dream the night she died?" I came over to her couch and sat down.

"Yes. She said she'd been killed, because Bainton had been killed."

"Before you'd heard about her murder?"

"Yes."

"You could have read about the head wound, or someone could have told you about it after you got down here, and you fed the details back into the dream without knowing it."

"I could have."

"But you didn't?"

"No." She lifted her long white hand from the opened sketchbook and turned it toward me.

I whispered, "Good Christ." Covering the page was a drawing of Cloris Dollard *exactly* as I had looked down on her that Monday morning. She lay on the flowered quilt, one arm turned back, one foot dangled off the bed's edge. Joanna had drawn the pillow pressed over the head, drawn the pearls on the rug below, drawn even the ripped right sleeve of the suit. Nothing about that sleeve or about the pearls had been in any public report I'd read. She took the sketchbook back from me, and said quietly, "I told you the images I see are very vivid, Justin."

I stood up to walk. "What do you mean, she said she was killed because Bainton was killed? Bainton Ames died years ago. We have a man now in custody, a petty thief from East Hillston. You don't think he killed her?"

"Do you?"

I turned and stared at her. "I don't know. Who do *you* think killed Cloris? If he'd pressed you, what would you have told the reporter?"

She held her hand over her eyes; it was a large hand, milky white, naked without a wedding ring. "Nothing. I don't feel I should say anything, not until there is some other, some *external* evidence."

"Why not? We're not going to arrest someone *just* because of a dream you had."

She shook her head no. I leaned closer and touched her hand and was startled by its heat. "Will you tell me why you believe someone is trying to kill *you*?"

Her eyes went dark for an instant, then she blinked and they were calm again. "Nobody is trying to kill me now."

"But Briggs said . . ."

"I have the premonition that somebody will . . . decide to try to kill me. But hasn't yet. That must sound odd." Her hand came up to her neck, and I thought I saw a white scar very faint on her wrist at the edge of the sweater's cuff.

"Mrs. Cadmean, it all sounds odd to me. I hope my saying so doesn't bother you."

She took my hand and examined it, turning it over, pressing her fingertips into my flesh. "No, it doesn't bother me. I stopped believing some time ago that it was my fault I wasn't as . . ." She let my hand fall and looked up at me. "Wasn't as *numb* as most people. I used to think everyone felt as much as I did; they simply didn't let it show. I was . . ." She looked away. "Deceived. They don't."

"If you thought ordinary people had your gifts, yes, you must have been disappointed." The phone rang, and I jumped. "Shall I get it?"

"I'm sure it's for Briggs. There's an extension up in the tower."

"She's up there on the roof?"

"It's her study. Her telescope's up there."

The phone stopped. The snow had muffled all sound.

"I should go," I said. "If there's ever anything I can do, if you want to talk, will you call?" She nodded, and I found myself leaning down again to take her hand. She raised mine to her cheek and held it there for a moment. Then she said, "Here, take this." She tore a page out of her sketch pad. On it was a drawing of me, done with a skilled and strong line. I asked, "Am I this sad?"

"Yes."

I rolled the paper and put it in my coat pocket. "Do you have a feeling when, if somebody is going to try to kill you, *when?*"

Then Joanna Cadmean made the most bizarre statement of our conversation. She said serenely, "I expect I'll be home long before Easter."

"Back on St. Simons?"

"I mean I will have died. And gone, I assume, somewhere. I don't expect this little world is all, do you? It's certainly never felt like home to me."

"Died! Christ, what makes you think such a thing!"

The beautiful head turned slowly toward me, the eyes still as a statue's. "Cloris told me. I heard her voice. Three days ago, while Briggs and I were in the riding ring. That's why Manassas shied and threw me. It was death. Animals don't like it."

Outside, I wiped snow from my windshield with a pine branch. While the car was warming up, I took out the drawing. It was amazing; it was no more than a few lines, but it was like looking a long time into a mirror. I turned the sheet of paper over. On the back were faint sketches of tiny heads, hideous gargoyles, their eyes tormented, their mouths gaped open with rage.

At the bottom of the drive I looked back up at the lodge. High above me the light from the tower turned the snow to a white mist, as if I were far off, lost at sea, and on top of the Cadmean roof an arctic lighthouse warned me away from frozen reefs.

4

Even though he'd had to leave his wife watching television alone back in Crest Hollows, and shove himself back into all three polyester pieces of his wine-colored suit, and drive his new white Mercury back into town where slush could splash on its chrome, Captain V. D. Fulcher was happy, because he'd heard that Preston Pope had seven place-settings of the Grand Baroque sterling belonging to the Rowell Dollards, and that told him that Preston Pope had murdered

Mrs. Dollard, and that told him the case was closed and that the important people in Hillston would think well of him for letting them forget in a hurry that homicides ever happened in Hillston to important people.

"Except Preston didn't do it," Cuddy said again.

"I don't care which one," Fulcher told him. "Graham. Furbus."

I said, "Not Furbus. Furbus doesn't get out for two more years."

Cuddy tipped a box of Raisinets to his mouth and tapped it. "Furbus is the only Pope that *would* kill somebody. Took after his daddy."

Preston had certainly been saying he didn't do it, and his brothers didn't do it; he'd been saying so for three hours. He was less certain of what he *had* been doing eight nights back. Finally, he decided he'd been out in his van looking for Charlene; that was what he usually did between ten thirty and one in the morning. When I got back to the Municipal Building from the lake, and called my mother to tell her I'd gotten back, Preston was still saying that he'd never seen the silverware until I held up the fork, which was what he'd said to begin with.

I said, "Maybe Charlene brought the silverware over to bathe in."

Cuddy said, "Did Dickey or Graham do it?"

Preston shook his head violently.

"Did you do it?"

"You already asked me that a million times! I swear to God I didn't choke that lady!"

"We know you didn't choke her," I said. "Did you smother her with a pillow?"

"Aww, shit!"

Cuddy bent his head and looked closely into Preston's eyes. "This is real serious, Preston. *Real* serious. This isn't what you're used to, you got to understand that in a hurry."

Preston's pupils blurred with tears that he swiped at with his fists. "I got eyes, I can see shit when I step in it, don't you think I can? Y'all got to help me! Get Graham, he'll tell you I didn't do nothing."

I said, "We have a call in for him right now, believe me. How about this, Preston, did you and maybe Graham and Dickey go over there to North Hillston and rob the place, and you *didn't* kill Mrs. Dollard? Maybe she was already dead?"

"No way!"

"How about, maybe after you *finished* stealing everything, somebody else came in and killed her? Any idea who?"

Preston was sunk down in his chair, rubbing his wrist raw with his chain bracelet. "I don't even know where the lady lives. I just want y'all to believe me, that's all I want."

At nine thirty, Fulcher trotted in smiling, splashed with another pint of his rampant aftershave, and we all went back to the beginning. Preston begged us to believe he would never rob a house with a woman in it, much less kill her. Then he asked Cuddy if he should confess to the burglary (even though he was innocent), so that then he wouldn't have to stand trial for the murder (of which he was also innocent, but for which he might nevertheless go to the gas chamber). Then he said he was so hungry he couldn't think anymore. "Anymore?" Cuddy said, and got him some cheese crackers and a Coke.

Upstairs, just before eleven, Graham and Dickey Pope, dragging two policemen along with them, rammed into the front room like bears after a cub, and yelled at us to give them back Preston. They swore their baby brother had been at home drinking beer and watching the basketball game on television with them every minute of the night of the murder. Told what Preston's alibi was, they swore that, come to think a little harder, they'd been out in the van looking for Charlene with him every minute of the night of the murder. The two of them, dribbling wet snow, crowded in on Cuddy. The younger, Dickey, with his black curly hair and long-lidded blue eyes, was the best-looking of the Popes; as always he wore a shiny cowboy shirt. Graham was ugly and over six and a half feet tall with a beer belly and the short, tangled beard on which Preston had modeled his own. Graham shouted, "God damn it, Cuddy Mangum, you know that boy ain't killed the goddamn woman."

"You watch your mouth," said Captain Fulcher.

"How come all her silverware was in his goddamn bathtub?" Cuddy shouted back at Graham.

The Popes stared at us without a word, and then stared at each other. Finally, Dickey said to Graham, "That little son of a bitch; if he did it, I'm going to kick his ass!"

Graham said to us, "Y'all put the fix in, is that what's going on here? Well, God damn it!" Captain Fulcher had them both locked up as accessories.

We'd already sent Preston to bed; he'd gone back to trying to tell us what Charlene was like.

"He did it," Fulcher said, doing the clicking noise with his mouth that made him sound as well as look like an agitated hamster.

"Nope," said Cuddy.

"Listen to me, Lieutenant."

"All right."

"Somebody killed the Senator's wife. Somebody robbed her first. Preston Pope robbed her and Preston Pope killed her."

"Your logic's real persuasive, but I'm gonna have to disagree."

We were in Fulcher's office, crowded in with his civic awards and bowling trophies. Photos of his children—now teen-agers who wouldn't give him the time of day—grinned gap-toothed in plastic cubes on his metal desk.

Cuddy said, "That house is way out of Preston's league. Besides, if he had been there, he'd have left behind his fingerprints, his car keys, and his dog."

I took out a cigarette, but Fulcher tapped the NO SMOKING Lucite bar on the edge of his desk, and I put it back. He added an apologetic smile. I asked Cuddy, "What makes you so sure?"

"Charlene. Listen, Justin, there wasn't a mark on that girl. Here he was ranting and raving how he was going to kill her for whoring around, and he hadn't even *slapped* her."

Fulcher punched his finger on our report. "Six shots fired!"

"Not at *her*. That's first. Number two is, Preston's got a snapshot of himself and his mama in his wallet. He didn't smother any fifty-year-old woman."

Fulcher looked smug. "His mother deserted him, don't forget that."

With a pencil, Cuddy drew a quick series of overlapping triangles on his pad. "V.D., I'm *real* sorry you took that psychology extension course last summer."

"Don't get smart, mister."

"All right."

"And don't *ever* call me . . . that." Fulcher couldn't bring himself to repeat his initials, and spluttered to a stop.

"So where's the rest, where's all her jewelry and the coins?" I said. "We looked at the Popes'. They're not there."

"They're somewhere," Fulcher announced. "You find them. I want Preston Pope pinned to the wall. I want this case closed fast." He worked into his overcoat. "I'm going home. It's sleeting out there." He called his wife on the phone and told her so.

As soon as the door shut, Cuddy snapped his pencil in two.

"Christ." I lit my cigarette. "Can you believe Fulcher's parents had the gall to name him after General Earl Van Dorn?"

"Yeah." Cuddy threw the pencil pieces at the wastebasket. "Just because they wore silk sashes doesn't mean those damn Confederate generals of yours weren't idiots too."

"What'd you call him V.D. for? You're going to get yourself fired."

"*You* can support me. That suck-butt'll never fire you."

If Fulcher had known Rowell Dollard was going to arrive ten minutes later, no doubt he would have stayed to be congratulated. We saw my uncle as we were on our way down to the lab. Cuddy'd had a patrolman bring over every pair of shoes, boots, and gloves Preston had in the house, to check them out.

Senator Dollard was in the foyer, standing by himself in the middle of the black and white marble parquet floor. He looked like a part of the design, with his perfect white hair and perfect black wool overcoat, and his furled black umbrella with its silver head. His face, ruddier from the cold, was tilted up at the full-length portrait of Briggs Monmouth Cadmean that was hanging lavishly framed above the double doors to the courtroom, with a plaque below it saying he'd given Hillston the entire building. Our hollow footsteps on the marble startled Dollard. He turned, swinging the umbrella like a racquet and reminding me of the last time we'd played squash, when he'd slammed into the wall hard enough to slit open his cheek.

As soon as he saw us, he said, "Has he confessed? Pope?"

I shook my head, and introduced Cuddy, who immediately said that in his opinion Preston Pope wasn't responsible for the crime.

Rowell looked at me the whole time Cuddy was talking; but he turned to Cuddy when he stopped and said, "Then I hope you'll find out who is."

"I'm going to try, sir," Cuddy answered. "I'll be down in the lab, Justin."

Dollard gave a small nod as Cuddy walked away. "Is he in on the case?"

I said, "Now."

From his days as solicitor, Dollard knew this building and our procedures well; he'd followed our investigation the way he played squash, and Fulcher was terrified of his daily phone calls. Mother said Rowell's involvement was his way of coping with what had happened to Cloris, that he would never forgive himself for losing her because he hadn't been there to protect her, because he had never been able to convince her not to leave the house unlocked, not to trust strangers, not to realize that the world was dangerous. He insisted that only a stranger could have killed his wife, because no one who knew her could possibly want to hurt her. "Who in *God's name* would kill Cloris? She had more friends than anyone I ever knew!"

About Cloris, Dollard was right: I had interviewed many of those friends, and by their testimony Cloris Dollard had been the most amicable woman in Hillston. The friends were all certain, like her husband, that she had suffered by hideous chance at the hands of a transient madness. Not only had *they* not killed her, they couldn't think of a single soul who might have, "unless he'd gone crazy." And none of them knew anyone who might have gone even temporarily insane.

Everyone had liked Cloris. She'd liked everyone. I'd talked to a dozen members of First Presbyterian Church who'd spoken with her after services that Sunday morning, when she'd been "maybe a little quiet, but her same sunny self underneath." I'd talked to the daughters whom she'd called that afternoon in Phoenix and Baltimore; they said their conversations had been largely about grandchildren, and unremarkable. I'd talked to Mr. and Mrs. Dyer Fanshaw of the Fanshaw Paper Company, on whom she'd paid an ordinary afternoon call at their estate in North Hillston, two wooded meadows away from the Dollards' own brick colonial. I'd seen her myself in the audience at the Hillston Playhouse during the second intermission of *A Midsummer Night's Dream,* for she'd been chatting in the aisle with Susan Whetstone. Susan had said she couldn't remember what they'd talked about, but it certainly wasn't that Cloris expected to be murdered, although she had mentioned that her stomach was upset. I had in fact interviewed most of Hillston's inner circle, and it had very politely informed me that no one in it was a burglar and a killer.

Although I hadn't let Captain Fulcher know it, I had even checked out that Rowell Dollard had actually gone, as he'd said, to the suite he kept over in Raleigh for nights when he worked late during sessions of the state legislature. If Cloris had died no earlier than twelve, Rowell could conceivably have rushed back in the hour and a half it took to travel the unbanked, unlighted two-lane road between Hillston and the state capital. He could have smothered Cloris, and then sped back to

Raleigh. But so far I could think of no motive. If Rowell Dollard secretly kept a mistress, no one had ever heard of her; if he secretly owed millions, so far I hadn't found out to whom, and at this point he had as much money as Cloris did anyhow. Even if they'd used the estate she'd inherited from Bainton Ames to help build Rowell's career, that career itself was now worth considerably more than his wife's private possessions. If he secretly hated her, Hillston hadn't noticed. Rumor was, among Cloris's many friends, that as a bachelor Dollard had "worshiped" her even when she'd been married to Bainton Ames. They told me now, "He loved her just the same till the day she died." They thought it was the most tragic thing they'd ever heard, for death to part the Dollards after all Cloris had suffered, and when Rowell was destined to even greater office.

Standing there in the foyer under the donated gilt chandeliers, I noticed how Rowell's eyes, which were somewhat protuberant—pressing forward, like his voice and his manner—tonight looked sunk back in his skull, their color dead in the florid face. I said, "Rowell, do you want to see the report on the arrest?"

He hesitated, also unlike him, then answered, "No, just tell me." I gave a summary of Preston Pope's statement while he stared past me down the empty corridor of closed doors, and at the courtroom doors behind us, the doors—he had told me so often—to Washington.

We stood alone in the middle of the big marble floor. When I finished talking, he asked, "But you don't share this Mangum's opinion, do you? About Pope?"

"I'm not sure yet."

"I see. Walk me to my car, Justin, all right? By the way, your mother mentioned something odd at dinner. She said you were out to see Joanna Cadmean earlier. Something about her wanting to talk to you about Cloris." He paused for my response, but I made none, because I wasn't certain what I wanted to say, and he added, "I can't think why. As far as I know, Cloris and Joanna Cadmean hadn't met in years." He waited again. "I did notice she visited . . ." he stumbled, "the grave. It surprised me at the time."

"Isn't that why Mrs. Cadmean came to Hillston, for the services?"

"No! . . . I'm sure she's just here to see her in-laws. She's staying out at the compound with the youngest Cadmean girl, isn't she? The one that teaches at the university?" Dollard walked toward old Cadmean's portrait, then hurried back, as if he couldn't think standing still.

"Briggs," I said.

"Typical of old Briggs to name a daughter after himself. I actually don't think he liked any of his sons."

"I don't think his daughter likes him. Mother told me tonight on the phone Briggs moved out to the lake because she couldn't stand to live in that brick mausoleum with her father."

We crossed to the tall brass-trimmed front doors. Outside, rain had already started washing the slush over the steps and into the sidewalk gutters; by morning there'd be no trace left of the aberrant snowstorm.

Rowell was tapping the umbrella's silver knob against his lips. "Did Joanna Cadmean say what she wanted to know?"

"She wanted to know if Cloris kept a diary. Did she?"

"A diary?" He was surprised. "Why? No, Cloris didn't keep a diary."

"Are you sure?"

"Of course, I'm sure! Cloris was a totally . . . open person. She always left everything out where anybody could see it. I would have known. She would have *read* it to me." He kept shaking his head. "What did she mean, a diary?"

I decided to tell him. "Mrs. Cadmean says your wife told her in a dream to look at a diary."

Thoughts were shifting through his eyes as he stared at me. The eyes looked angry; but then, they often did.

"She said she dreamt Cloris came to her and said she'd been murdered, and told her to read the diary."

Rowell began pacing again, tapping the umbrella tip on the loud marble.

I added, "She described details I just don't see how she could have known."

The ruddiness of his complexion deepened in his neck and ears, and his voice dropped. "Did she say who?"

"Who what?"

He snapped, "Who killed Cloris."

His tone startled me. "She gave the impression that she had somebody in mind, but she won't say who. It's just a dream. I don't know why she chose to tell me about it. Even odder—she talked more about Bainton Ames than anything else. Another dream she'd had years ago, at the time of *his* accident; she dreamt that it was no accident. That it was murder. And she really almost had me convinced."

Rowell kept rubbing his lips back and forth over the umbrella's silver handle. He said, "Do you know who she was?"

I nodded. "A psychic. A mystic. She worked with you back in the fifties."

"She did not 'work' with me. She was somebody who came to the police and volunteered certain premonitions. . . ."

"She knew where the bodies were buried."

The umbrella twitched in his hand and the knob scraped against his teeth. "You understand," he said softly, "this woman is preternatural. You have no idea." He turned around to me. "She's also insane, Justin."

"Insane? She acted perfectly normal. You know, I would have thought you'd be the last person to place any credence in . . ."

His face flushed. "She is *not* normal, how can you say she's normal?"

"I mean, coherent, pleasant; you know what I mean. Obviously she's not *normal*. Listen, Rowell, if somebody tells you they're Jesus Christ, they're crazy. But if somebody tells you on Monday that X is going to be killed on Tuesday and X *is* killed on Tuesday, it doesn't make them crazy. It makes them pretty damn clairvoyant."

Rowell nodded. "Or a murderer."

"Good Christ. You're not suggesting *she* killed Cloris? She wasn't even in Hillston. For what possible reason?"

"For God's sake, of course I don't think that! Don't be absurd! I'm suggesting you stay away from that woman."

His command irritated me. "How much do you know about Mrs. Cadmean personally?"

His voice was curt. "I doubt I've seen her more than five times in the last fifteen years."

"She never remarried. Was her marriage to, what's his name, to Charles Cadmean, happy?"

"I have no idea. I assume so."

"Is there any possibility she might have been involved with Bainton Ames? I'm sorry if this is awkward for you."

He was glaring at me. "Why awkward?"

"I suppose because Bainton was Cloris's husband. And, quite honestly, people have said you were already involved with Cloris back when they were married."

His mouth twisted to a sneer. "People?"

"They don't say it critically."

"They shouldn't say it at all." He put his hand on the door's brass bar. "How I felt about her isn't any of their business. And it isn't any of yours." His voice got loud enough to echo off the marble walls of the large empty space. "And I suggest you spend a little less time listening to Joanna Cadmean's hocus-pocus, and a little more convicting the *thug* who killed Cloris!" The Senator banged open the door, and his umbrella caught in it as it swung shut. When I tried to help, he jerked it free and started down the steps. At the curb, rain was streaming past the tires of the silver Mercedes he'd left parked there.

I was turning away, when, from behind the small antique cannon fixed to the side of the stone steps, someone darted suddenly at Dollard with a long stick. I yelled "Rowell" and sprang down after him, but I saw before I reached her that it was Sister Resurrection, even this late, haunting the streets, assaulting people with the promise of apocalypse. She was dressed as she always was. Rain beads hung from her knots of hair and ran down her shapeless sweaters, soaking into her split and laceless tennis shoes. Rain, like the world and the flesh, had meant nothing to her for many years.

She had her cross pointed at Rowell and was chanting as he shoved past her to pull his car door open, "It won't be long! The dragon coming! I heard the voice say, 'It won't be long.' That old serpent, he got the chain in his teeth, and he snap it! He *snap* it, and crawling out of the lake of fire and brimstone. He shall be *loosed* out of his prison!"

"Get back!" Rowell, his face white, was in his car now, tugging on the door. "Will you get her away!" Sister Resurrection touched her hand, shriveled as a claw, to his. She had a hissing whisper. "God getting ready. We shall arise anew! Say yes! Say yes!" He shook the skinny arm off his sleeve, slammed the door, and left her fallen to the curb.

I tented my coat over my head, and leaned down. "Sister, you all right? You shouldn't be out in this cold rain. Come on. It's late." I pulled her to her feet. She was weightless, and tense as wire, and her smell in the rain even fouler than usual. "You go on home. It's late." I pointed down the sidewalk toward the Methodist church two blocks east, where the minister had made her a place in the basement near the furnace. "You'll catch cold."

I doubt she had heard me, but, still chanting her garbled Revelations, she turned and with her quick stiff stride, hurried away, her makeshift cross in one hand, and Rowell Dollard's black umbrella in the other, jutted out before her like a sword.

5

The Hillston police are stationed in an annex connected through the basement to our new Municipal Building, although some offices (like the detective division) have been moved into the main building itself. The lab people never come upstairs if they can help it, and Etham Foster, who runs the lab, would just as soon nobody ever came down to the basement, either. He's a wary, saturnine black man of about forty, who looks like a basketball player, and had gotten himself through college playing that game, and said he had never picked up a basketball again after the day they handed him his diploma. When I walked into his lab, his long fingers were picking with tweezers at the bottom of Preston's boot. And Cuddy, chewing on a glazed doughnut, was standing like a stork against the wall, watching him.

Cuddy looked up. "Look who's here, come down to pay a call. You and the Senator wrap it all up?"

I said, "Sister Resurrection just scared him to death."

Foster glanced at us, then went back to placing bits of fuzz in a plastic bag as if he were alone in the place.

"Good," Cuddy said.

"She was out front under that overhang, just about frozen."

"You know why she stays around this spot so much? She's got a grudge against the powers that be, and this is where they be."

Foster turned his back on us and switched on the light under his microscope. Cuddy went on. "You know Sister Resurrection used to have a kid, long long time ago? Yeah, ain't that downright amazing to think of? But he went bad, raised hell, and got himself shot."

"I hadn't heard that."

"Well, this is a little bit of local East Hillston lore wouldn't necessarily have come to your attention over on Catawba Drive."

"Who shot him?"

He licked glaze off his fingers. "Cop."

"You're kidding."

"Sure. I'm a great kidder." He walked around to Foster. "Okay, Doctor Dunk-it, what you got?"

Foster slid in another slide without looking up. "No yellow threads anywhere on your man's shoes."

"Good. And no prints of his on the silver, either."

Foster said, "Doesn't mean a thing."

His drawer was filled with fragments of Cloris Dollard's life: fuzz from her yellow carpet, gravel from her driveway, hairs from her cat, blood from the top of a trophy that said she was the best woman golfer in Hillston. Etham Foster knew Mrs. Dollard as precisely as my father had known where against the skull to place the drill. I said, "Tell me about who did it, Etham."

"I told you. Man was careful."

We had little more than that to go on. Since Cloris Dollard had never bothered locking her house, we didn't even know whether her murderer had entered before or after she had come home. Her house was so protected by its grounds that no neighbor had seen or heard a thing, even if she'd struggled. And we'd lost nine hours before the Dollard maid's arrival the next morning. We knew the upstairs phone had been yanked from its cord, and that Cloris's purse had been thrown in the grass by the stone gate, and we had a list of all Senator Dollard thought but wasn't sure had been taken by whoever had pulled open all the drawers and cabinets in the handsome house, and had left in its bedroom a dead woman.

I said, "Pros don't kill people."

Foster finished looking at a piece of glass taken out of Preston's boot tread. "Didn't say pro. Said careful."

"Come on, can't you give us *something*?"

"Give you a Marlboro butt off the driveway that wasn't there more than a day, and nobody in the house smoked."

"It's too bad the neighbors and two ambulances and a half-dozen of V.D.'s new patrol cars drove all over the place before they called you in."

Foster said, "Right," and would I mind not smoking in his lab, and Cuddy said, "He can't be a detective without smoke coming out of his nose." His eyes looked dull blue and angry. "Was Mrs. Dollard taking this guy on a guided tour or what? 'Well, now you've loaded up the silver, and don't forget that little TV, come on up in the bedroom 'cause I've got some jewelry and rare coins I think you'll like, locked up in a little safe you probably wouldn't even have noticed all on your own.'"

"Maybe she thought if she offered him things, he wouldn't hurt her," I said. "Maybe he only hit her because she went for the phone or maybe it started ringing and panicked him into hitting her." I rubbed my hand against the back of my own skull. "Or, let's try this possibility. He already knew the house, and knew her, and he meant to kill her." *But who in the world would want to kill Cloris? She had more friends . . .*

Cuddy said, "How tall was she?"

"Five nine and a quarter, plus heels."

"Preston's too short."

Etham Foster looked back up. "You don't know she was standing."

"And Preston's not strong enough, either. To pull her up on that bed —and what the crap for?—and shove down a pillow so hard he breaks her nose? I don't believe Preston could do it, much less he's just not that goddamn mean!"

I was thinking of how Rowell had flicked Sister Resurrection from his sleeve as if she were a gnat, knocking her down on the curb. I said, "Maybe anybody can be that mean."

Cuddy slapped his hand loud on the counter. "Oh, don't start that dorkshit 'everybody's rotten under the thin ice' moralizing again! The only thin ice you ever knew anything about, somebody served you in a *whiskey* glass!"

Unhurriedly, Foster walked away from us to open the refrigerator and take out a tube of somebody's blood. My blush had brought sweat out over my lip. "Get off my back, Mangum, you've been picking at me since I got down here. Why are you so pissy?" We stared at each other, until he reached up and pulled on both his ears with his knuckly hands. "I'm scared," he said, "the powers that be're gonna railroad Preston because it's easy. Nothing personal."

"Except you think those powers're all my kinsfolk. You're a snob."

He blew out a sigh, and then he laughed. "Whooee, Doctor D, listen to the white folk spat!" Foster ignored him and smeared the blood on his slide, and Cuddy tossed my overcoat at me and said, "Okay, Preppie, let's get out of the man's lab. Don't you ever go home, Foster?"

Foster didn't look up, but said, "Your man had big hands," and he held up his own, fingers spread the way they would have stretched over a basketball. He added, "Shut the door."

Upstairs, while Cuddy fed Mrs. Mitchell a cold hamburger, I told him more about my visit with Joanna Cadmean.

"She couldn't be *that* good-looking."

"That's not the point, Cuddy. The point is, she knows who killed Cloris. The same person who killed Cloris's first husband."

"How about her second husband?"

"Maybe."

He said, "I'm kidding."

"I'm not."

I am an insomniac, like my father, who wandered around his house at night like a ghost and now, from time to time, visits mine. I have always had to drug myself unconscious with cheap detective fiction: reading on about pure nastiness and simple guilt until I can fall backward into nothing, like in snow. When I awaken in the night, I need to get the light on quickly, and find my page, before the real mysteries slip in, before I hear voices, before I see ghosts. When I was little, my father would come at my request with what he claimed was a magic stethoscope, and would check for signs of monsters lurking. I did not doubt his power to keep them away.

This morning I had a nightmare that woke me up. It was pitch-black night in this dream and I was in our old canoe out on the lake. Pine Hills Lake is fairly large—seven miles by almost two—but in my dream the lake was boundless, an unshored, black flat expanse. Out of the silent dark, Bainton Ames's powerboat suddenly came flying at me, his white bowlight shooting up and down across the water. Then the dream went up to that octagonal turret on top of Cadmean compound. Joanna Cadmean was standing there at its window, wearing the gray suit Cloris Dollard was found dead in. And now Mrs. Cadmean's eyes did look like a mystic's, unblinking, crazed. She had her arms out as if she were waiting to embrace someone. I knew it was her eyes making Ames's boat head toward me. Someone was kicking away from the boat, churning foam. And I jumped too, just as the boat ripped through my canoe, and exploded, and flames spumed along the water, rimming me in.

So, I was awake at five, and rather than fight for sleep until Cuddy came to pick me up, I put on a monogrammed robe Susan Whetstone had given me that I didn't much like, and, my bare feet tiptoeing on the frigid wood steps, I felt my way down the three flights from my bedroom to my kitchen.

Most of my salary goes into the mortgage and upkeep and furnishing of a narrow Queen Anne brick house in the south part of Hillston that overlooks the lawn of a women's junior college, named Frances Bush after its nineteenth-century founder: my house had once boarded her students. Five years ago, after I'd finished law school in Charlottesville, and confused everybody and annoyed Rowell by going to work for the Hillston police, I'd bought the house with the money my father left me. No one wanted to live downtown then, and old houses there were cheaper than trailers. Obviously, as had been pointed out, it was too much house for a single man. It was also too much house to heat: the rooms were large and had high ceilings, and on each floor a big Victorian bow window sucked in the cold air robustly with a laissez-faire disdain for my modern fuel costs.

At five, then, in the kitchen, I wrapped myself in a blanket and ate leftover spaghetti while I finished reading the department's copy of the old coroner's report on Bainton Ames's drowning accident that I had started studying before I went to bed, having taken it out of the files last night. There was little in it to suggest that Cloris's first husband hadn't died exactly as the coroner had concluded: accidental drowning while under the influence of alcohol. His dinner companions that night had confessed that the five of them had drunk five bottles of wine, and everyone knew that Bainton did not normally drink.

An unlucky accident, people had said, and added, "but not surprising." Bainton Ames, a preoccupied, farsighted man, for decades chief industrial engineer of Cadmean Textiles, had his eyes focused on future machines or ancient coins or seventeenth-century music; the present had been a blur. When Ames drowned, people said preoccupation had killed him.

One midnight in mid-August fifteen years ago, he had left the Pine Hills Inn, where he'd dined with four men big in the Atlanta textiles business. Against their advice he'd set out across the lake in the twenty-two-foot inboard powerboat Cloris had given him as a lure into the world. Headed back to the Ames cottage on the opposite shore from the Inn, he had presumably slipped, knocked himself out, and fallen overboard. The boat had sped on pilotless into a marina, where it had blown up a gas tank. The explosion had terrified all the residents, and that summer, boating after dark was banned.

A few weeks later they discovered that Ames had not been in the boat when it exploded, because a teen-age boy, swimming around under old Briggs Cadmean's long pier, had bumped into a swollen body bent around a piling, and had unhooked Ames's jacket from the bolt it was caught on.

After her husband drowned, Cloris had their lake house closed. Two years later she married the still-bachelor Rowell Dollard, and he and her daughters persuaded her to reopen it. Rowell bought a new boat.

My father, who every weekend for years had played violin in Ames's amateur string quartet, was furious with his dead friend for ever having tried to pilot the Chris-Craft, even in the daytime. When Cloris later married Rowell, my father said, "Well, good Christ, Peggy, Cloris certainly runs the gamut. First Euclid. Now Mark Antony. Don't you think your brother Rowell is a little too *relentlessly* athletic?"

But the Ames girls liked their sporty stepfather, who taught them how to water-ski and dance. And by all accounts, Cloris loved him. In old photographs of them together, I could see that she shared with Rowell something florid and heated, something that made you think she enjoyed her marriage bed, in the same way she enjoyed her golf and the club dances at which she and Dollard won prizes as the most polished couple on the floor. They traveled. They were well-to-do; especially after Cloris sold Ames's sizable shares of Cadmean stock to a Mr. Paul Whetstone—which turned Cadmean Textiles into C & W Textiles, and turned Lawry Whetstone into a vice-president.

And Cloris had the easy, warm sociability necessary in the wife of a politically ambitious man. So Rowell swam, with the same seriously energetic strokes with which he did his laps on the lake each summer morning, into the state senate. Cloris was proud of him. So were Mother's people. He was proud of himself, as he said when he advised me to do something I could be proud of.

Time had worn away her past with Bainton Ames. She was Cloris Dollard. And Ames was to most current lake residents, "Oh, that accident that blew up the marina. Man fell out of his boat."

All I had to suggest that the man had been pushed rather than fallen, was the distant dream of a woman my uncle thought mad. After fifteen years it was going to be close to impossible to prove Joanna right; the boat was gone, the marina was gone, the body was rags over bones. I didn't even know why I wanted to prove her right; it wasn't Bainton Ames's death I was being paid to investigate.

When I woke up in my kitchen, my head flopped over on the Ames file, my hand still around a fork wrapped in spaghetti, Mother was rapping on the back pane. "Jay! Jay! Wake up!" She had her hand to her mouth. "Lying there like that! You scared the life out of me!" We both knew she'd found my father like that, the day of his first stroke, his arm flung out across his desk; on it, accounts of other people's medical problems.

"Justin, please don't tell me you've been drinking again." She took my face in her hands. "You haven't suffered a relapse?"

"What time is it? No, I haven't been drinking." All my bones felt bruised.

"Quarter to ten." She let out her breath in a little laugh, relieved by her decision to believe me. "It's freezing in this house. My God, son, just throw open the windows; it's warmer outside!"

"To ten?"

She rubbed at the arms of her old sable coat, the gesture, like her face, girlish. "Aren't you supposed to go to work? I let your phone ring its head off."

"I unplugged it. Stop staring at me, I said I haven't been drinking."

"I didn't know you could unplug phones. I'm sorry, but your feet are *blue*, Justin! I'm going to turn up your thermostat. I can't understand why you want to live in a house that you can't live in."

"I like the woodwork on the doors. I don't like flat doors."

I made coffee while mother hurried through the house to see what my life was like. Its reality always seemed to surprise her. I said I wanted to ask her something.

"Rowell said you've arrested poor Cloris's murderer. I'm glad it's over. Ask me what?"

"It's not over." I handed her a cup. "That last Saturday, when you and Cloris went shopping, the day before she died, tell me again, what sort of mood was she in?"

"Fine, she was fine. We had lunch and I bought a scarf and she got some papers copied. That's all. What do you mean, not over?"

"What papers? You didn't tell me about any papers."

"Well, it's nothing to do with her dying."

"I said, tell me anything, it didn't matter what."

"I probably did mention it. You never listen to half the words I say, anyhow." Mother sighed. "Your father always said, 'Half's plenty.'

Well, if it matters, we went to CopiQuik. She said, 'As long as we're right here.' She had a big folder of papers she said had been Bainton's. It surprised me because why after all this time be copying anything of Bainton's, and I remember I said, 'Cloris, whatever for?' Well, she'd found them in a box in the basement, she was a terrible pack rat, like you, because there were these textiles people wanting them now. They wanted to know if Bainton had ever figured out how to make this—now, it was a funny word, inert, inertial?—some kind of loom. Seems like Cloris said something about making copies of the papers to show to old Briggs Cadmean. That's all I remember, so don't ask me anything else. I was trying to get to the off-ramp of that idiotic new beltway before a mile-long truck going ninety hit me."

Further questions led her only, by looping cloverleaf turns of language, to news of her departure. She had, in fact, come to see if I had suffered a relapse; she *claimed* she had come to tell me she was driving to Alexandria, Virginia, to baby-sit her only grandchildren—the two belonging to my younger brother, Vaughan, a gynecologist, and his wife, Jennifer, who were off to Antigua on the Club Med plan. Vaughan was the mirror in whose clean image Mother had always asked me to scrub off my flaws. As a child, he had never given her a moment's trouble. As an adult, all he asked of her was baby-sitting. Vaughan was still annoyed with God for postponing him. He resented the position of second son; in his view I had long ago abrogated the privileges and responsibilities of primogeniture. ("I hate to have to say it, Jay, but it's really pretty crummy the way you've let the folks down; you've really loused up pretty bad.") He never hated to have to say it at all; he couldn't even keep from smiling.

I said, "Tell Vaughan bon voyage."

Mother poked her forefinger into each of my geranium plants on the window ledge, and watered one of them. She asked with sly nonchalance, "How do you like Briggs?"

"Which Briggs?"

"The girl, of course, Justin."

I said, "I don't. Too cold."

"Baloney. Susan Whetstone's the one that's cold. Of course, she must love it over here." Mother patted my hand. "That was pretty catty."

"I'll say." I poured another cup of coffee.

"Look." From her purse Mother took a small newsclipping. "It was in this morning's paper." Beneath an old photograph of Joanna Cadmean that made her look like Grace Kelly was a headline: FAMOUS PSYCHIC COMES HOME AFTER GIRLHOOD FRIEND MURDERED.

I scanned the two paragraphs. "That damn Bubba Percy! He even blabbed that she's staying out at the compound."

"He says maybe the police ought to ask Joanna who killed Cloris."

"Mother, I am the police, and I did ask Joanna."

"You did? Who did she say?"

"She didn't say anything."

I took a pack of cigarettes out of the back of the cabinet where I hid them from myself.

"Oh, Justin, I wish you'd stop smoking. If I could quit after . . . I started when I had you, I was eighteen, and I stopped when your father died, in March that'll be six years, so that's . . . If I could quit after twenty-eight years . . ."

"Then I will too. . . . I'm sorry. I didn't get much sleep."

"Well, you'll quit when you start feeling bad enough about it. You never have been as feckless as you like to imagine. You probably feel bad about sleeping with Lawry Whetstone's wife."

The match burned my thumb. "Who told you that?"

"Nobody. Whatever else would you be doing with her?" Mother sat down with her coffee. "Justin, I had no idea you were so naive as to let me convince you I was. I'm not opposed to adultery; but I am old-fashioned enough to think it ought to be serious."

"Mother, please don't tell me you and Dad were having affairs. I couldn't take it this morning."

She looked fondly at the gold ring that was to me as much part of her hand as the bent little finger she said she'd deformed by playing Chopin's "Revolutionary" étude before her bones were mature. "Your father and I were . . . oddly in love, though he was occasionally a little less aware of it than I was. But of course, I realize not all marriages are lucky. Why, my God, I liked Bainton Ames perfectly well, but it didn't stop me from being really happy for Rowell and Cloris."

"Wait a minute. You *knew* for a fact Rowell and Cloris were having an affair, at the time of her first marriage?"

"Well, nobody *said* it. Rowell was already in politics. But of course I knew. He'd been in love with her for years. And people in our circle more or less knew. I thought you knew."

"It doesn't surprise me. I remember I *was* surprised when she married him. She always seemed very nice. I liked her."

Mother frowned. "I don't understand why you dislike Rowell so. He went out of his way to advise you all through. And after your father died . . ."

I went around the table and pulled my little space heater closer to her. "Dad didn't like Rowell either, you know that. You know what he said to me once? He said Rowell was the kind of man who would have made it to California over Donner Pass."

"Well, I don't know what in the world your father meant by that—which is nothing new."

"He meant Rowell would shoot the Indian. Cut loose the dying ox and pull the wagon himself. Drink the horse urine. Eat the dead. He meant Rowell would *get there*."

My father had added that he himself would have probably been the one who always in a western movie didn't fire his gun in time and was therefore tomahawked by the Apache, who didn't lash his horse hard enough to leap the chasm and couldn't hold fast enough by his fingers to the scrabbling rock of the edge, and so never made it to the final reel.

"Dad said that once Rowell and he were out on the dock looking at some ducks on the lake that Cloris was feeding bread to, and Rowell said, 'Damn, if I had a rifle right now, I could blast them all right out of the water!' "

Mother said, "I thought you enjoyed those hunting trips with Rowell."

Looking down at the Ames folder on the table, I said, "I did. . . . Let me ask you something. What if Cloris found out Bainton had actually been pushed, not fallen, but been pushed out of that boat when he drowned? What if someone had told her that?"

"Who! That's a horrible thing to say! Cloris never thought such a thing."

"What if she'd just recently found it out, just before she died. Would she have told anyone?"

"She would have been *devastated*. When Bainton drowned, Cloris felt horrible! I've always thought that's why she and Rowell waited those two years. That, and his career." She washed out her cup. "Jay, are you going off on one of your tangents?"

"Mother, just a minute, what was Bainton Ames doing while Rowell and Cloris were having an affair? Was he having one? Is it possible he and Joanna were lovers?"

"God, that is the funniest thought imaginable. I don't say this meanly, but Bainton and Joanna both always struck me as a little on the cold side. Bainton never looked up from his designs long enough to even notice Cloris, and I think Joanna married poor Charles Cadmean because he kept asking her and she didn't have anything else to do. Joanna never seemed to care much what happened to her *life*. Why, it never seemed to cross her mind that she was beautiful." Mother stood up and pulled on her gloves. "Of course, she was four or five years younger than I was—I was already up in Virginia when she was in high school and college—and we weren't close when I got back, so I probably shouldn't even talk about her."

"If she didn't love Charles, more reason to turn to someone else."

"Well, it wasn't Bainton. I really have to run, honey. Don't bother to kiss me. I'm sure your lips are frozen. And calm down." And out she fluttered.

I opened the coroner's report again. I knew Ames's death was tied by knots, years tightened, to the death of Cloris Dollard. Except I didn't know it; I had only heard dreams. I needed what Joanna Cadmean had called the "external evidence." I started making phone calls.

To let Cuddy in, I had to get out of the shower and back into my robe. He blinked his eyes at my wet hair and bare feet. "Excuse me! I've been ringing your bell for ten minutes. Guess I caught you on your Lunchbreak."

I ignored this, and started back up the steps to my bedroom.

"Your photos are out in the car. My, it is freezing in here!" He followed me up the three flights, with a loud charade of gasping. "Why don't you move into someplace nice, and level, and warm?"

"This *is* nice. Anybody who has a photo wall mural of Cape Hatteras beach in his living room shouldn't talk about what's nice."

"Everybody in River Rise has got one, they're built in."

"I don't doubt it."

"What's the matter with it? The only time your place is nice is springtime, when you can spy out the top story on the Busher girls all catching the rays on the grass and reaching behind their pretty backs and unfastening their suit tops."

"You're in a better mood. Where were you?"

"At the office. Doing V.D.'s paperwork."

"Where was *I* supposed to be?" I threw the coverlet over my bed, a four-poster I'd bought at a used furniture store that had subsequently changed its name to Antiques Ltd.

"Following a lead on those coins, is what I told V.D. He's not happy. He had to let Graham and Dickey go. Looks like they *were* drinking beer the night of the murder, and looks like they were doing it at the Rib House, and in comes Joe Lieberman and says he's got about twenty folks to swear to it."

Joe Lieberman was the Popes' lawyer; they gave him a lot of business. I'm sure he had three stereos in his car, if he wanted them, and four TVs in his house, and all the cigarettes people would leave him alone to smoke.

Cuddy took off a ski cap that said GO, TARHEELS!, stuffed it in his parka pocket, and sprawled out on the bed. "But V.D.'s got it jimmied so he can hold Preston, the mad-dog killer, and they moved him across town. Preston asked me would I go get Charlene for him. Aww, lordy, humankind, don't it break your heart? So I went over and tried, but she wasn't much up for it."

"Back at the Maple Street place?"

"Nope. Luster Hudson's. He rents a little house off the Twenty-eight bypass, raises hunting dogs. They tried to chew their way out of their pen when I drove up. Ole Charlene finally came to the door in her black number and told me I was lucky Luster was out of town. I said, 'I wantcha, but this is business,' and I told her what had happened to her husband since she saw him last."

"What'd she say?"

"I only knew one lady with a messier mouth, and she had three or four big scars down her face and rolled drunks in Saigon."

"Charlene wasn't sympathetic."

"That about says it all. She told me she had a real man now, a big man she could lean on instead of carry, and she went on with that awhile like a Loretta Lynn song. So the idea is baby peckerhead can insert his privates up his own privy for all she cares. I said, 'Where is Prince Luster so bright and early in the morning when he works the night shift?' She said he quit C & W, and was on to a better life in the dog market. I said, 'Well, even if it does seem the thrill is gone between you and peckerhead Preston, seems like a good proletariat union volunteer like yourself wouldn't want to see a working man railroaded by police and capitalists.' She said Preston'd never worked a day in his life. She had me there. . . . Her new love's off somewhere unknown in the Great Smokies with his dawgs."

"Did she know those silver sacks were in there?"

"I asked her that very thing. Says I, 'Charlene, sweetheart, one more question and I'll let you go on back and feed those dogs before they eat each other and put Luster out of his new business. When you were taking that bath yesterday, did you notice anything in the tub besides yourself—clanky stuff belonging to a rich murdered lady?' That's when the doorknob slammed into my dick and I lost interest."

"Why didn't you bring her in, Christ!"

"Let's hold off a little bit, see what Graham can find out. What's that scratchy singing?"

"It's Ma Rainey."

"Come again?"

"An old blues singer. One of my blues records."

"Where do you get all these folks from?"

"I bet Willie Nelson likes her."

"Sounds like she's singing up from the bottom of the reservoir through a tin can."

"It's a very old recording."

"Hey, well, I *knew* that. You wouldn't have it unlest it was old." His jay eyes peered ostentatiously around my bedroom. "It's all old. My mama had a chest in her kitchen looked like that one." He meant the pine hutch with a white metal countertop where I kept my sweaters and shoes. "Yessir, she was ashamed to death of it, it was so country. I'd been wondering where it got to. All right, let me just lie here and take a nap while you plow through your wardrobe awhile looking for something to put on. Will this old thing hold me?"

On our way out, Cuddy snooped into my front room, and took the cloth off an oil painting. I'd started a self-portrait. In the family attic I'd found the easel that had belonged to my father, who did landscape watercolors and who had, to his deep pleasure, a picture—a clump of spruces at the golf course—hanging in the university museum.

Cuddy said, "The bow tie's good. You got the polka dots just right."

"You don't think it looks like me."

"Looks like a cross between Bobby Kennedy and Susan Whetstone."

"Maybe that's what I look like."

"Well, that's true. But you mostly look like Senator Rowell Dollard. Sorry. And maybe Jimmy Carter before he wore out. When he was leaning back in the porch rocker with his fluffy hair. What was the name of that old girl friend of yours, the one that was so crazy about Jimmy Carter? Why can't I come across somebody like her?"

"You're too ugly."

"I know I'm ugly but it's the kind of ugly that's getting real popular."

He was still talking when we walked outside, to the patrol car. "Savile, the thing you need to do, you want to be a detective like in your books, you got to do more than mope and fuck and puff your lungs to soot. *Dentists* can oil paint. You want a hobby more on the lines of bloating up big and fat and raising orchids. You want to take up something even kinkier than Shakespeare playacting."

"Well, I play the piano in the middle of the night. Not too different from playing the violin on cocaine."

"Shit, you can't count that. All you know how to play is 'Malagueña' and 'The Sting.'"

"That's not true, and I don't think any of your hobbies, like your wall display of a bunch of different kinds of beer cans, puts you up there with Hercule Poirot, frankly."

"Who?"

"Christ, open the door to the car! It's freezing out here!"

"I don't know how you could tell. Hop in the backseat, Martha."

The frizzy little dog scrambled over the headrest. Cuddy, driving with a doughnut clamped in his teeth, now informed me, "Here's the truth. Your trouble is, you're too domestic. You got too many towels. Sideboards. Relatives. You ever hear of Philip Marlowe's mother coming to visit him at the office? Listen, the thing you have to do is to get out in the rain and let your trench coat get all soggy. You got to get lonesome, Lieutenant Savile. You're not lonesome enough, that's your real trouble. That, and a nutty imagination. And don't remind me how you solved who poisoned Mrs. Ormond last year, 'cause that was pure *luck*. Doughnut?"

"No. How can I get lonesome with everybody traipsing in on me all the time?" I shook four vitamin C capsules from the bottle I kept in my briefcase. "I didn't get any sleep and I don't want to get run down and don't say a word." I also had a hangover I didn't mention.

Cuddy pawed through the bag and found the doughnut he was looking for—a vile jelly one. He said, "Anybody else ever tell you you were a hypochondriac?"

"Yeah. She's probably a judge in Atlanta by now."

"Where to, General Lee?"

"Pine Hills Lake. I want you to meet your mystic. Then I'm going to Cape Hatteras, you know, like on your wall."

"Kind of cold for the beach, and I don't know if V.D.'s gonna love your taking another vacation so soon after the last one, when you and Susan Whetstone slipped off to—"

"I'm going to see Walter Stanhope, you know who he is? Well, he used to have V.D.'s job, fifteen years back, before Rowell had him fired, and I found out on the phone this morning from Hiram Davies that Stanhope retired to Cape Hatteras. So I want to ask him something. You want to come? It's four hours."

"No, thanks, I'll just look at my wall. But you got to listen to me, Stanhope's not how to find out who killed Mrs. Dollard."

"Trust me."

"That's what my ex-wife said."

7

Cloris Dollard kept the past, whether she'd kept a diary or not. She didn't sort it, or label it, and from all reports of her habitual sanguinity, she didn't dwell on it. She just kept it in cardboard boxes. Tossed into a fur company's box were hundreds of photographs—her unedited biography from scalloped black and white rectangles of herself as a habitually sanguine child, to color Polaroids of her and Rowell posing last summer at 10 Downing Street in London. Over the past week I had studied these pictures. I felt close to this big, tan, blond woman with the loud, warm voice I could remember yelling at me, "Pull that canoe on in, hey you, Jay Savile! Get your body over here and eat some lunch with my girls!" To Captain Fulcher, the fact that the Senator's wife had been murdered was the tragic but ancillary after-math of the fact that she had been robbed. I didn't believe that any-more. I believed she had been robbed because she'd been murdered. I believed she was dead because Bainton Ames was dead. I believed Joanna Cadmean. And I wanted to hear more of her dream.

At the Cadmean lake house, young professorial Briggs came down from her tower with a green ribbon through her hair, like a vine in strawberries, and engaged in a quick spate of stichomythic wisecracking with Cuddy Mangum about professional women and the merit of the solar system. All she said to me was, "Is Mr. Mangum always so . . ."

"Juvenile?"

"Jocular."

I said, "He doesn't know what jocular means," and Cuddy said, "I do too: well-endowed," and she excused herself to go find her sister-in-law.

Cuddy sighed. "I believe I drove her off with my lewdness. And just when she was about getting ready to want to marry me."

"You've already been married. Why do you want to do it again?"

"Improve," he said. "Besides, Briggs was married before too. Married a hippie when she was a child. It didn't last long. He turned capitalist on her after all he'd said. She woke up one morning and he'd shaved off his beard. Imagine! After that, it all went in a downward spiral."

Another surprise. "Are you making this up, Cuddy?"

"Nope. She told me on the phone last night."

"Why'd you call her up?"

"My my, don't be tetchy. You can't keep 'em *all* on the bench."

Joanna Cadmean came in and sat down on the couch where she'd sat before, the same pillow cushioning her foot on the coffee table. In win-ter light, the great vaulted space of the lodge living room was sharp, even harder than it had felt last night shadowed by snow. She wore the same skirt and the same long-sleeved sweater. On the floor beside her was the morning paper open to Bubba Percy's article on her. Her sketchbook lay next to her on the couch; she picked it up and began to draw in that odd unlooking resolute way, while Cuddy and she talked about her past work with the police. Drawing, she sat in the bright cold light and told of old nightmare visions, of seeing the lost she'd been asked to find, already dead in secret graves, hair growing wild.

I asked her, "Did you ever, do you mind if I say this? Did you ever think you were crazy?"

Mrs. Cadmean smiled at me. "Oh, I expect I *am* crazy."

"I mean, well, want to get away from being you? Want to change? Did you suffer from what people said about you?"

With quick sideways strokes, she crossed out the face she was sketching and turned the page. "When there was that external evidence, Justin, to prove me right, people said I had a great gift. When there wasn't, they said I was a charlatan or a lunatic. Neither the praise nor the censure of other people came to mean much to me."

Cuddy said, "I don't expect there's anybody doubts you've got an amazing gift." I could tell he was as impressed with her as I had been—with her beauty and her strange incandescent self-possession.

The calm gray eyes turned to Cuddy, crooked toward her in the bent-willow chair. She said, "The trouble with the kind of gifts the gods give, Mr. Mangum, is they cannot be declined, or exchanged, or even . . ." She looked down at her drawing. ". . . Set aside for a while. You cannot say 'No, thank you' to the gods." One hand closed over the wrist of the other, covering what I felt must be scars. Then she looked up at me. "Now. Justin. You wanted me to look at some photographs of some men? Men who may be connected to Cloris's death? Are they in that folder? Mr. Mangum, we seem to have made a convert of your friend overnight."

Cuddy said, "Hey, he's got ESP! I mean, not like you, but he's always saying things that you're thinking, or singing songs that are in your head, you know. A couple of years ago one night he called me up and said, 'Are you okay?' and I had in fact just had the puerile notion of sticking a dirty revolver in my mouth—tasted terrible—over some real sad news about my ex-wife getting married that morning. If I'd had ESP, I wouldn't have ever introduced her to her new love, much less hauled that same man across a rice paddy on my back."

"I'm sorry." Her eyes went black in the sudden way I'd noticed before, a bruised look coming into them and then vanishing.

In the manila folder were blowups of a dozen random mug-shots I'd asked Cuddy to bring me—mixed among them pictures of the three Pope brothers. One by one as I handed them to her, she touched her hand over the surface, shook her head and placed them facedown beside her on the couch. She paused no more over Preston Pope's face than any other, although when she came to Graham Pope's, she did go back and hold the two pictures up and comment on the resemblance. The only time she even hesitated was at a photo of a bull-necked blond ex-Marine with dulled eyes and a long arrest record, a local hood, Cuddy said, who had died ten years ago in Vietnam.

"No, I'm sorry," she said. "Nothing. Of course, that means nothing too, you understand."

Then I gave her the photograph I had brought in my briefcase. She dropped it, and as I leaned down to pick it up, I noticed the long fingers of her oddly translucent hand trembling in the folds of her skirt. "Why are you showing me this?" she whispered. Cuddy twisted over to see the picture I'd taken from among the jumbled stack in Cloris Dollard's cardboard box. On the back in her broad script was scribbled *Pine Hills Lake house, 1966,* and on the front Bainton Ames slumped in a beach chair, papers on his lap; near him his daughter lay on a towel, my mother in her bathing suit stood in the sand, holding a cigarette, and in the shallow water, Cloris Ames and Rowell Dollard—both tan and well muscled—stood laughing together, their handsome faces close enough to touch.

I said, "They look like lovers, don't they?"

Mrs. Cadmean turned her eyes to the huge window, where light sparked like static over the pine tops and down across the flat gray lake. I spoke quietly. "Is there anyone in *this* picture you associate with Bainton Ames's death?"

Her response was to struggle up awkwardly onto her crutches and limp across the long room to the window. Cuddy had to jerk in his legs as she went past.

"Did the two of them arrange Bainton's accident?" I asked her.

Her back was to me, her hands tight on the crutches. She shook her head no.

"Did the same person kill Bainton who killed Cloris? Mrs. Cadmean? You said, she died *because* of Bainton. Did the same . . ."

"I know no *fact* to suggest so." Her voice was soft but distinct in the hard angles of the room. "Do you?"

"Not yet. Do you *believe* so?"

She kept staring out to the empty lake as if she were waiting for someone.

Cuddy looked up, his face uncharacteristically hushed, as I walked around him to go stand beside her. It was then that I realized that from the Cadmean window you could see across the northern tip of Pine Hills Lake to the dock and the small half-mooned beach of Cloris Dollard's summer cottage, now boarded up; with some effort I could distinguish part of the back deck, where whoever had taken my old photograph might have stood to snap it—perhaps the other daughter, not seeing what the camera saw. From the tower with the telescope, Briggs could probably see right into the house itself.

Standing by Joanna Cadmean's side, and without turning to look at her, I asked her, "Is it Rowell?"

Her eyes closed, then opened, peaceful gray. They looked a long while at the lake.

I followed Mrs. Cadmean as she moved along the window. "That's what Cloris told you in the dream, and when you heard her voice at the riding stables, she was warning you against him?"

Cuddy looked at me, startled. "Why not?" I told him. "Maybe Rowell just grabbed up the coins and things at random to make it look like a robbery, and dumped them, and Pope somehow stumbled on the silverware."

She said in so low a voice I barely heard her, "Bainton's coins were very rare; some collected by his grandfather were especially rare. I know Rowell liked them. He liked to keep what was rare."

I said, "Like Cloris?"

"Was she rare?"

I said, "But why kill Bainton? What's wrong with divorce! The estate? He built his career on Bainton Ames's money?"

Joanna Cadmean swung her crutches toward me. Her voice was like the light coming off the ice outside. She said, "He built his career on what I told him."

Cuddy asked, "What do you mean, Mrs. Cadmean? The publicity from your discoveries when he was assistant solicitor?"

"At first." Her voice melted into its soft stillness. "My . . . insights remained helpful even after it seemed best not to make them public. . . ."

Cuddy said, "You mean, you were working with Dollard on his courtroom presentations?" She nodded, and he turned to me. "Well, according to Fulcher, your uncle never lost a case."

Yes. Dollard had campaigned on that record, and gone to the state senate on it, and with it won the worshipful envy of men like Fulcher.

Mrs. Cadmean reached her hand out to me. "In the past I've found my perceptions grow stronger the closer I get to the place where the death occurred." She took my hand in hers, its heat and tension startling. "They are stronger here in Hillston than they were on St. Simons."

We were all quiet for a moment. Then I said, "I'll take you over to the Dollards' house."

Cuddy unwound himself and stood. "I suppose we could. Couldn't hurt."

"Let's go now," I said. I wanted to go back there too.

She excused herself to change her clothes, and I was surprised again by her attractiveness when she returned in a stylish red wool dress and wool cape. Outside, she walked awkwardly on the unfamiliar crutches, dodging the puddled ice that was alarming all Hillston, a city unaccustomed to the cold.

Mrs. Cadmean said nothing as we drove in past the Dollard gate and along the crackling driveway up to the imperturbable expanse of red brick and white wood. An orange Pinto was parked in front of high rhododendron bushes whose stiff brown winter leaves seemed to have given up all hope of spring. Inside, a Mrs. Teknik was vacuuming; she had replaced the former black cleaning woman who'd quit. She said that the woman had refused to come back inside the unlucky house. "Colored people," she said, "believe in ghosts."

I said, "So do I."

The house had been restored to order, Etham Foster's men having long since abandoned the search for proof of an intruder's identity anywhere on the premises. Upstairs, Senator Dollard had had the blood-stained yellow carpeting torn off the bedroom floor, and the blond oak queen-size bed was stripped to its mattress. But his wife's clothes still hung in their closets, her toiletries still lined the white wicker shelves in her bathroom. Dust lingered in the light over the vanity table where Cloris Dollard's perfumes, combs, and jewelry boxes sat in geometric patterns utterly unlike the untroubling disarray in which we'd found them that first Monday morning we'd been summoned there. In fact, it was not that the house had been returned to order, it had been put in order: premises that had once looked like an unresolved quarrel between two incompatible decorators now had swung in favor of Rowell Dollard's opulent fastidiousness. Downstairs the stiff silk pearl-hued chairs and settee made a precise square with the gray mantel, and no longer gawked askance at the painted wood secretary I'd seen so piled with magazines and gloves and so stuffed with scraps of paper, pointless pencils, and unmailed letters that it would not close. Everywhere in this house now, the disorder of life was missing.

By holding to the rail and to my shoulder, Mrs. Cadmean was able to climb the curved stairs to the bedroom. Her body heat against my side shocked me; her arm burned across the back of my jacket. Her other arm clutched a shoulder bag. In our slow ascent I said, "I don't like the idea of your being out at the lake by yourself."

"Briggs is usually with me, and before she leaves to teach, she fixes everything so I'm quite comfortable."

"Still, couldn't you go to your father-in-law's in town?" She shook her head. "Way out there," I said. "What do you do?"

She smiled the strange cold smile that had scared me at the end of our first conversation. She said, "Oh, I prophesy."

"If you get . . . worried, you'll let me know?"

"I'll let you know," she said. "Is that the bedroom through there?"

"Yes."

"And, Justin, should something . . . happen to me, ask Briggs for a letter. I don't mean to be coy, I want you to understand. So, tonight, I'm going to write everything down for you."

"All right." My shoulder felt abruptly cold when her hand moved away to take the crutches. I left her, as she had asked, alone in Cloris Dollard's bedroom. The sound of the crutches moved slowly across the bare wood above me.

Downstairs I searched through the wood secretary, the study desk, and bookshelves for anything Cloris might have used as a diary. Then I went down to the basement, where I found no boxes of anything resembling technical papers that might have belonged to Bainton Ames.

"Savile, you are tangling with the big boys now. Why'd you let me go on believing *you* were rich?" Cuddy was in the study, looking at Rowell's framed diplomas.

"I tried to disabuse you, but obviously the idea meant too much to you to give it up."

"Now I see Uncle Rowell's place, and Cadmean's playhouse—not even his real house!—I wonder why I bothered being jealous of you all these years."

"Me too."

"Yassir, things have clearly slumped for you since all the slaves done run off your place and jest left the corn rotting in the fields, like some old tall dead yellow-sashed soldiers." He started on the other wall of bookshelves, reading the spines.

"Christ, you love to talk," I said.

"I can't rely on my features, Lieutenant."

From the other wing the vacuuming buzz stopped loudly. I heard Mrs. Teknik mumble, then I heard a sharp "Where are they?" As we hurried back out into the entryway, Rowell Dollard, his scarf very white between his black velvet collar and his flushed ear, was starting up the stairs.

"Rowell," I called. "Sorry to intrude again. I assumed you'd be in Raleigh."

His face was swollen with suppressed irritation. "I understood from Fulcher that you people were finished here, Justin. I don't mean to be uncooperative, but . . ." Then his eyes were pulled away from us and turned up toward the landing at the top of the stairs where, soundless, Joanna Cadmean stood braced by the angle of her crutches. When he finally spoke, his voice was hoarse. "What are you doing here?"

She answered mildly, "Hello, Rowell."

Florid, he backed down the steps toward me. "Why is she here? Why have you brought her in this house? What in hell kind of hocus-pocus are you pulling, Justin?"

Cuddy loped up the stairs to help Mrs. Cadmean down. I said, "I'm trying to find out who killed Cloris."

"How so?" Dollard snapped.

"Any way I can."

His black overcoat still buttoned, the Senator strode across the entry-way to the study door, his head quivering from the effort to control his voice. "I'm sorry, but this is not tolerable. I'll have to ask you all to leave." The door shut sharply behind him. I suspected he was telephoning Captain Fulcher.

My apologies to Joanna Cadmean for having subjected her to so painful an encounter were acknowledged, if heard, by a nod from some far-distant and chilling place. In the car, Cuddy's little dog whimpered on the floor of the backseat where Mrs. Cadmean sat silently until we were back out on the bypass. Then she asked, "Is there no phone in Cloris's bedroom?"

"There was," I told her. "After the jack was torn out, I suppose they must have had it removed."

"Because standing in there, I kept hearing her phone ring. Very loud. There was no image really of what might have . . . taken place. I simply kept hearing the phone ringing over and over. Except I did see coins. Coins falling in the air. Bainton's, I suppose. I recall from the papers back at the time, one of the men Bainton had been with that night was talking about the coins. Odd. Falling like a storm." In the rearview mirror I watched Mrs. Cadmean's steady, peaceful eyes gazing out as the unleafed trees went blurring past. I noticed that the eyes never blinked.

All the way back to town Cuddy said, "I don't know. I don't know. It's nutty."

I reminded him that he was the one who had first told me just how accustomed the Hillston police were to exactly Joanna Cadmean's kind of detection.

"That's true, but mind if I say something personal?"

"Yes." Mrs. Mitchell nosed herself under my elbow.

"Hate is blind and so are the hots."

"Meaning?"

"You ought to take yourself off this case and go back to your regular assignments."

"Sure!" I leaned over and punched in his cigarette lighter. "And leave you to run the only case the town council and the newspapers care anything about! Get your name on this one, Mangum, and maybe you can squeeze out Fulcher."

"Get fucked, Justin."

"You sound like Charlene. Okay, okay. I apologize. You're just trying to help. Like always. How are hate and the 'hots,' as you so eloquently put it, blinding me?"

We were both angry. I was smoking; he rolled down the window and let in the freezing wind. He said, "You know what I'm talking about. You *want* to believe Senator Dollard killed his wife, because you hate him. You hate the way your momma thought you ought to let her little brother be your great white father. You hate the way she loves him so much and admires him so much and and and. You're jealous."

"Oh, Jesus Christ! Now you sound like Fulcher's psychology course.

And who am I jealous *for*? Cloris Dollard, or my mother? Is it for them I have 'the hots'?"

"You said it, not me. I had in mind Joanna Cadmean."

"I'm not even going to respond to that, it's so absurd."

"I watched you, General Lee. You gloop around her like some soulful teen-ager with sore nuts, mooning over the high school art teacher." The anger loosened and left Cuddy's face; he grinned. "In fact, now I remember, you *were* in love with your seventh-grade Latin teacher, weren't you! What was her name?"

". . . Mrs. Berry."

"That's right. It was because of her you majored in classics. You know what's amazing that I bet you never thought of? We're older now than Mrs. Berry was *then*! What could she have been—twenty-seven at the most? Here she was, an Older Woman—up in a tower of knowledge and power there was no way you could climb—and the damn truth is, she was a *baby*!"

"I'm not going to drop the Dollard case."

"I didn't think you would," he said, and rolled the window back up. "You can lead a horse to water but a jackass likes to mix his own drinks."

8

Graham Pope's former wife, Paula, tended bar at the Rib House, out on the bypass, on the other side of Hillston from Pine Hills Lake. Almost as big as its parking lot, the Rib House stretched between a Toyota dealership and a pitch-and-putt course that was closed for the winter. Its long-tentacled machine, there to feel through the weeds for balls, had been left waiting like a giant mantis in the grass. The Rib House, in a regrettable effort to resemble a Victorian train depot, had stuffed itself with semi-antiques, beginning with a mechanical gypsy fortune-teller in a glass case by the door. In trolley cars, plywood gazebos, and papier-mâché caves, large families ate at long tables without talking—except to yell at their children to stop running back to the salad bar. Even if the parents hadn't apparently worn out conversation years back, they couldn't have heard each other. The Rib House was a clangorous blare of herded suburban flight from life at home together. Hand to my ear, I made phone calls while Cuddy walked Mrs. Mitchell outside.

By half-past five, on every level surface, vast dripping ribs of pig and cow were being devoured. A lengthy ·line of more hungry families craned out necks to meter their progress while they stood discussing whether they should order "The Hombre" or "Big Mama" or "Little Dude," as poster-size menus labeled these platters.

Paula Pope was a creamy, fat woman somewhere near forty-five, with hair so black and skin and eyes so lovely she looked as though some cartoonist had drawn Snow White's face inside a moon. She was working fast, puffing at a loose curl, and frowning fretfully, as she plopped cherries and pineapple chunks into huge frozen pink and lime drinks that she topped with paper Confederate flags. "I'm divorced," she said to Cuddy for openers. "We're friendly, I guess, but we're divorced; so don't come asking me about Graham Pope, because I don't know."

Cuddy said, "How you doing, Paula? This is Lieutenant Savile. Paula Pope."

"Paula Burgwin." She wiped her small hands on a towel when I . offered mine, and we shook. "I got back my own name. Do you know what it cost me? Fifty-five dollars."

I asked her if she'd heard about what happened to Preston, and she nodded the way you nod when the highway patrol asks you if you know what the speed limit is. "What can you tell us about it, Paula?"

"Not a thing, except it's probably not true. You two want a drink?" Cuddy had a beer and I had a whiskey and for a few minutes we both tried to pick up the check.

"You keep up with Charlene, don't you?" Cuddy asked, licking at his beer head. "Preston wants to see her, real bad. Is it all over between them? Because she gave me that feeling."

Paula was mixing two more fishbowls of icy pink foam. "You wouldn't get her to believe it in a million years, but Charlene's acting real dumb." She added, "That don't mean, compared to Preston, Charlene oughtn't to be teaching over at the university." She giggled like a child. "Charlene says there's this brainy girl at C & W that's big in the union that told her she was naturally smart and oughta do something with herself."

Cuddy said, "I'll have to go along with that. Preston, now, *is* slow, no getting around it. So what makes Charlene so unnaturally dumb these days and can I have two bags of those beer nuts over there? And bring Justin something to eat too."

"I'm not hungry," I told her. "I'd like another whiskey. Weak."

"Because she's young, is all," Paula said. "Everybody young's dumb. Weren't y'all dumb? One weak Jack Daniel's." She had a pretty hand, set apart from the creamy arm by a crowded charm bracelet. Her arm looked as if its skin were so tight it would pop if something pricked it.

"Oh, lord," Cuddy said with a sigh. "I've been waiting and waiting for a chance to *get* young. I was always old, working to get myself to where I could have a ball being young, and now Paula, you come telling me, 'Remember when.' I'm so sad, I got to have a pizza, can I order a pizza here at the bar? Justin, I want you to try some of this pizza."

Promptly at five thirty a rail-thin black man complaining about the cold weather came to replace Paula at the bar, and the three of us found a little cable-spool table free in a corner, and I bought her a strawberry daiquiri and had a third drink, and Cuddy ate an entire pizza the menu named "The Kitchen Sink." Paula said, "Charlene traded a moron for a goon, is all."

"I bet you mean Luster Hudson," Cuddy mumbled, cheese stuck to his fingers.

"Thinking there's men like Luster makes me worry I gave up on Graham." Her high, small voice struggled against the dinner clatter around us. "Well, I'll tell you one thing, last night Charlene asked me over there for supper, where she's moved out with Luster, called me up and said we had a lot in common now, and invited me."

"Ex-Popes Club, hunh?" said Cuddy. "Y'all could get a lodge and play bingo."

"That'd be funny if it wasn't sad. So anyhow I went, and you know what that man is doing with a bunch of dogs?"

"Not feeding them," Cuddy said. "And speaking of Luster's dogs, business must be better'n it looked, for him to quit C & W, did you have that feeling? Didn't he make pretty good money on the forklift at C & W? He say anything about that?"

"He didn't say anything about anything. So, do you want to know what he does with those dogs? Well, I happened to go to the bathroom, and I heard this little kitten crying its eyes out in a box with holes punched in it, so I brought it out, and I said to him—Charlene was outside getting the bottle of wine she'd stuck in the snow to cool off." Paula paused to offer me Nachos and eat half a dozen herself. "I said, 'Whose cute little kitten is this?' Just trying to be polite, even though I don't much like Luster and vice versa in a big way—you could tell he was mad at her for even inviting me over and he was about as nice as a snake. You know what he told me? Says, 'I get them from ads. I use them to hunt my dogs with, if it's any of your business.' He sat right there with the TV on, and told me that, like he thought I'd say, 'Oh, that's nice!' He was obtaining those kittens under false pretenses and then siccing his dogs on them, I couldn't even believe it! Then he says, 'Put that damn cat back where you got it,' but I set it down on the floor and it ran right over and climbed up the leg of Luster's jeans, like I'd told it to go scratch out his eyes. And so he yanked it off and threw it against the wall, hard. And so Charlene opened the door and the kitten tears out and runs up a tree and can't get down. So you know what he did?"

"Shot it," I said.

Cuddy said, "I see you're getting a feel for Luster's personality. I had to bring Luster in one time, me and five guys that used to play pro football, and we ran the patrol car back and forth on top of him for a while so we could get in close enough to put the cuffs on."

Paula sucked away half her daiquiri through a straw. "He wouldn't even let me use his ladder to get that kitten. And he wouldn't let Charlene do it either. And so he says, 'I don't have to put up with somebody coming in my house and telling me what to do.'"

I said I could imagine Charlene's response to that.

"She didn't say a word. And you want to know something else, Charlene's scared of Luster. I really think that's why she wanted me to come over, so she wouldn't have to be by herself with him. She was glad he was going off to the mountains. She thinks she's all excited about Luster, but what she is, is scared, if you know what I mean."

I said, "I think that's an interesting observation," and she smiled with a shy hesitation that was taking a while to decide she'd been complimented.

Cuddy licked his fingers. "She told me she had a *real* man now."

"That's right, that's what she thinks she thinks." In one long sip

Paula finished whatever liquid there was in her drink. "I don't know any real men."

"Well, hey, what about us?" said Cuddy.

She looked at me, her spoon poised to scoop up the pink slush. She said, "What about you?"

I said, "I wish I could, ma'am," which she knew wasn't really true, but a way of saying I liked her, and she gave me a nod and closed her mouth over the Snow White pretty teeth and scooped up more daiquiri. I asked her what had happened to the kitten.

"Luster said he didn't want me in his house, is what he said, and I said, 'Thanks for supper, Charlene,' and went and got my car and parked it under the tree and climbed up on the cartop and just about killed myself and got the dumb kitten." She held out her right hand so we could see the red scratch streaks. "It's at home. You two want a kitten? I don't even like cats all that much. You think your little dog would like a kitten, Cuddy?"

I said, "If you ask me, you sound like a real woman."

She dropped the spoon in the empty glass. "Too much of one." She giggled, then sighed. "Well, how bad trouble's Graham in? Did he steal that new Mustang of his?"

"Not that anybody's mentioned," Cuddy said.

I asked her, "Have you ever seen him or his brothers in the company of Senator Rowell Dollard, the man whose wife's been killed?"

She laughed. "I doubt it."

"Ever heard them talk about him?"

"They didn't talk much politics—except 'Shoot them all.'"

Cuddy said, "How about, hear them talk about some old coins, jewelry, a sapphire and diamond bracelet?" Paula turned the charms on her own bracelet; she shook her head. Cuddy went on, "I got two notions: One is, Preston stole that stuff from whoever stole it. The other one is, Preston never saw so much silverware in his life till Mr. Savile here showed it to him. And number two means Graham and/or Dickey dropped those little bags off at the house on their way to Greensboro. Or, number three, old Albert Einstein Charlene needs a real lawyer a lot more'n a real man." Cuddy wrapped his pizza crusts in a napkin to take out to Mrs. Mitchell.

Paula said, "Well, if Charlene put that stuff there, and I'm not saying she did, because I never knew her to steal a thing, she sure didn't know it belonged to that dead lady, because Luster was watching about the investigation on the news, and told Charlene to shut up so he could hear, because she wasn't listening. And I tell you the truth, Cuddy, I wouldn't put a lot past my in-laws, but they're not *killers*. Graham tore in here this morning and said you folks had planted that silverware on Preston because y'all had to get somebody fast, this lady being a Hillston big shot and all. How can you eat all that pizza and stay so skinny? If I *look* at a pizza, all my buttons pop off."

Cuddy held the last cheesy triangle about an inch from her nose. "Honey, don't blink," he said.

She giggled again. "Well, this was real nice, but I've got to go feed a cat. I shouldn't even say this, and this is all I'm going to say, but if I was the two of you, I'd talk to a man called Ratcher Phelps, you know him? He's the one Graham and Dickey would go to if they had something special."

"Who?" asked Cuddy. "I never heard of him."

"Oh, he's tight. Old guy. Only reason I know is I've heard Graham on the phone telling people if they used Ratcher Phelps they had to be careful, because Phelps wouldn't put up with sloppiness." Paula then explained that the only way to open negotiations with this Mr. Phelps was by asking at his East Hillston business, the Melody Store, if he had banjo sheet music for "Moonlight Bay." "You had to say it was your mother's favorite and you wanted to play it for her birthday."

I said, "Mr. Phelps is a sentimental receiver of stolen goods, I take it?"

"Don't Savile here talk old-fashioned?" Cuddy asked Paula. "He likes everything old. He even rides around on horses, pretending to be a Confederate general."

"He's talking about a pageant at the Hunt Club, that's all, Paula. I like your bracelet," I said. "Could I ask you where you got that particular charm there, do you mind?"

She raised her dimpled wrist. "This one? Oh, it's some kind of an old stone bead I dug up myself in the backyard when I was little, I think it belonged to an Indian." The charms jingled as she shook her hand. "This is my whole life, right here."

"Pardon?"

"Well, like here's a Bible-camp medal, third prize for backstroke, if you can believe water could ever hold me up once upon a time, and this is for high school choir."

Her voice came out in slight pushes of air, as if it were trying to escape the weight of her body, as if it were something delicate caught inside, still singing, like the cat in *Peter and the Wolf*. She said, "And this one is one of those Purple Hearts, have you seen one? It was my first boyfriend's that he got in Korea. I was real young. We were going to get married but it didn't work out that way. And here's my wedding ring." She spun it on its chain. "Do you know what I found out? Graham stole it out of a jewelry store in High Point, if you can believe that."

"It has the sad smack of truth," Cuddy said.

"And this little pin here, my mama got this for twenty-five years' service on the loom at C & W. Mr. Cadmean presented it to her himself. They had a whole ceremony. Now they just lay people off and don't even wave good-bye to them. And well, so on and so on. My whole life, right here on my arm." She let it fall onto the table.

Cuddy sighed. "Paula, I sure wish you'd stop talking like the end is near."

A curl shiny as a blackbird spilled over onto her forehead; pushing it back, she touched her broad face, puzzled, as if she'd never felt the flesh before. She said, "Oh, I don't mean my life's over. I just mean I can see what it is now. It'll just be that some more." Her giggle was like a small bell, unreverberant, swallowed by the racket of food. "I mean, I used to wonder, is all, and now I know."

9

"The Popes are out," I said an hour later, flipping my cigarette into one of the big cuspidor ashtrays sitting under Mr. Cadmean's portrait in the Municipal Building's lobby. "From the way Paula talked, I'd say Graham really thinks we're trying to frame his baby brother. You don't suppose V.D. could have actually dumped that silverware in their bathtub, do you? He'd do anything for Rowell."

The instant the elevator door opened on the fifth floor, Captain V. D.

Fulcher was standing there. He yapped at Cuddy. "Where have you been? Is that that dog!" Mrs. Mitchell jumped behind me, and I hid her in my coat.

"Going up, sir," Cuddy said, and pushed the CLOSE button, but Fulcher shoved his fake-madras shoulder against the door. I asked, "You been waiting in the hall for us long, Captain?"

Fulcher had his mouth click going at a quick tempo. "Do you two ever bother listening to the radio dispatch in your car?"

Cuddy said, "I like Loretta Lynn better. He likes Mama Rainey."

"Ma," I said.

"Where've you been all day?" Fulcher wasn't spluttering; that meant Rowell hadn't called him, which surprised me. I said, "We got a lead a couple of hours ago about a possible fence for the jewelry and coins, and we followed it up."

"I don't suppose you found out much of anything?" Fulcher's face was so smug, I started to wonder if, despite our advice, Preston had decided to confess. "Come to my office." Our leader marched ahead.

In fact, we hadn't found out much of anything from our lead at the Melody Store. Ratcher Phelps's response to my wanting to play "Moonlight Bay" on the banjo for my mother was to regret that he was unable to help me, especially considering that he was always happy to assist the police.

"It must have been your overcoat, Savile," Cuddy said. "I should have asked. You just don't look like a banjo player."

Ratcher Phelps smiled. He was a small black man of sixty-some, wearing a black pinstripe suit with an American-flag tiepin, and square yellow-topaz cuff links. He had the rhetorical lugubrious look of a well-to-do funeral director, and smiled with aggrieved disappointment at our suspicions that he might be trafficking with petty thieves. On the way from the Rib House to East Hillston, we'd called in a check on him, and the last charge against Phelps was twenty-five years old, when someone who hadn't liked him much had phoned the station to say there were four-dozen Lady Bulova watches in his car trunk. Since then, not so much as a parking ticket had brought him to the department's attention—although he had a nephew either less virtuous or less careful.

Mr. Phelps's ostensible business was musical instruments. It was in his Melody Store, while mentally adding up the spinets and electric organs all around him, that he told us sadly it was always the same old story. "And the years don't change it and the government won't change it and nothing I see's going to turn it around, and, gentlemen, I guess that if I let it bother my tranquillity of mind, I doubt I'd sleep peaceful, which I do." He counted the burnished trombones and glossy clarinets that hung glittering out of reach on the walls and were purchased through high-interest installment payments by the parents of East Hillston's state-famous high school band.

"That's good. You get your rest," Cuddy said. "Poor Lieutenant Savile here's an insomniac, and my upstairs neighbors are too much in love. Now about these emerald earbobs I was mentioning."

"It is dispiriting and grievous to me," Phelps said, rolling his tongue around the words as if he were readying his lips to play what he had to say on one of his saxophones, "the same old way when white people rob and steal what belongs to some more white people, the first thing to transpire is the black people get paid the call by you people."

"That about takes care of all the people," said Cuddy. "Let's drop all of them for now except the ones called Pope, and talk about a diamond and sapphire bracelet."

"If you young men want a clarinet, a harmonica, if you are inclined to a piano in your home, we can talk till you buy or I close. But, gentlemen, I don't sell jewelry."

I said, "Do you buy it?" and he showed me his cuff links and smiled his sad insincere smile. I tried again. "Do you buy rare American coins, and might you be interested in a reciprocal exchange? For instance, an upcoming appearance of your nephew William Phelps currently involving petty larceny, but susceptible to abatement."

His lips repeated *reciprocal,* either because he liked the idea or liked the word and intended to add it to his already palaverous style.

I said it again for him: "Reciprocal." My lips were a little numb after three drinks, and I thought maybe I'd mispronounced it.

His morose filmy eye lamented the Fall awhile before he said, "Such as, to what?"

"Shoplifting," I said.

"And suspended," Cuddy added.

"I know a Mister Dickey Pope," he said. "Who used to buy strings and picks from me for his guitar. But I haven't seen him since summertime. Maybe he gave up on his playing." Phelps's gloom suggested this would have been a wise decision. "No, not since summertime."

I said, "Anybody besides Popes come to mind?"

"No, sir, they don't. What would these jewels and these American coins happen to look like if I was to happen to glance down at one on the sidewalk in the midst of my constitutional?"

I described them. Only the rarest of Bainton Ames's coins had been kept in the bedroom safe and only they had been stolen; the rest, the less valuable type sets still sat in their small vinyl boxes in the Dollard study. Among the missing, according to the detailed records Ames had kept in his neat, spidery hand, were a 1907 Saint-Gaudens double eagle, an 1841 "Little Princess," a Bechtler's five-dollar gold piece, and an 1880 Stella Liberty head with coiled hair; the last alone was worth at least $65,000.

Phelps shook his head sorrowfully. "Isn't that something? A couple of old dirty coins are worth more than all my pianos put together."

Cuddy said, "I know what you mean," and rapped a beat on a snare drum so wretched-sounding that Phelps's eyes moistened even more. I bought a collection of simplified Gershwin songs, and he came close to selling me a new piano.

"Nice to meet you," I told him.

He moistened his lip. "The feeling is reciprocal."

In his office now, V. D. Fulcher was turning the plastic cube that contained photos of his offspring from child to child. Cuddy and I were listening to him ask us again, "Who is this unidentified black source you say doesn't know anything? There's getting to be too many nigrahs in this case."

I said, "You mean like Etham Foster?"

He bounded across to the file cabinet and jerked open the drawer, flashing the plastic digital watch he wore with the face on the inside of his wrist.

"I mean," he gloated, "I have one of Mrs. Dollard's earrings." There was an unavoidable twitch of surprise from us both that Fulcher must have treasured. "You know who had them? Reverend Hayward."

Cuddy said, "I didn't realize Reverend Hayward was a nigrah! My, my, he looks as white as you do."

Fulcher said, "You're treading, Mangum. That crazy old colored woman Hayward takes care of came into the vestry today and dropped this in the collection plate by his elbow." He unclenched his fist, and green flashed out. "He couldn't get her to tell him where she got it. You know who I mean. The Bible nut. Sister Whatsherface. She had a pretty expensive umbrella, too. Might be connected."

"It's Senator Dollard's," I said.

Cuddy said, "Damn, you *are* psychic."

In the interrogation room, Sister Resurrection, indifferent to a destiny less than universal, paced out a square along the walls, so that Fulcher and I had to keep rotating on our chairs to see her. Harriet Dale, the only woman on the force with whom Fulcher felt comfortable, stood by, boxy and tight-curled. Cuddy had gone back in disgust to the lab.

"We ought to have her sedated," Fulcher said, exasperated.

"Good Christ," I told him. "We ought to let her go home. What the hell good is holding her supposed to do?"

"What's with you, Savile? Ogilvey'll be down in a second. Then we'll make some progress." Ogilvey was our consulting psychiatrist.

"I doubt it."

In the gray cotton dress that Harriet Dale had somehow gotten on her, Sister Resurrection looked a third her usual size, but her sermon was the same, and in no evident way responded to Fulcher's demands that she tell him where she'd found or stolen Mrs. Dollard's earring. By the time Dr. Ogilvey arrived, she was in stride with the measure of the room she walked: "God is sick and tired of all this trash! The day coming He got to lay down His head. God fixing to move the mountains, pull over the sky, and lay down His weary head. No more shall He walk in the garden in the morning. No more shall He fret on the sinner's hard heart. Matthew and Mark can't hold Him back, amen. Mary weeping can't hold Him back, amen. His little baby Jesus can't hold Him back. Hear the voice, hallelujah, say yes. God fixing to loose the Devil's chains."

"This woman is schizophrenic" was Dr. Ogilvey's prompt diagnosis. He threw in "hebephrenic" and "a hundred percent delusional system," and advised us our duty was to take her to the state institution. As for extracting from her the original whereabouts of the jewelry, his offhand estimate was that it would take him five years of daily work to bring her to acknowledge her own name, and in fact he doubted he'd ever succeed. Some years back I'd been forced to talk to several psychiatrists; this was the first time I'd believed one.

"What about if we sedate her?" pleaded Fulcher, but Ogilvey just pulled back on his car coat and left. The captain followed the doctor out, arguing the point. "I'm going home," V.D. let me know over his shoulder. "We're having company and I'm already late."

"Well, Sister," I said. "Would you like a cigarette? No? Mind if I smoke?" Mrs. Dale began giving me a worried look. "Sister, you know that silver-haired man knocked you down last night? That earring belonged to his wife. My mother was a friend of hers. And now somebody's killed her. What's your opinion, ma'am?" Mrs. Dale's head jerked up; she thought I was talking to her. "Share your thoughts. You think that silver-haired man might have killed his own wife? Did that earring fall out of his car?"

Sister Resurrection was edging along the wall and shaking her head. She began again. "Shadrach, Meshach, and Abed-nego they were walking in the middle of the fire. But the flame of the fiery furnace never teched a hair of their head. The dragon he spits up fire in the night. High up. Down it rain."

"Umbrella won't help?"

She shook her head, back and forth. "Down it rain."

I stood up, and scared Mrs. Dale. Clearly she was torn between her assumption that I had interrogation techniques beyond her training, and her instinctive feeling that I was deranged. I said, "I'm going to call Reverend Hayward now and he'll come to take you on home."

This alarmed Mrs. Dale enough to make her step forward. "She hasn't been released, Lieutenant Savile."

"Has she been charged?"

"No, sir. But I don't have the authority . . ."

"I have the authority."

With relief, she gave up her struggle. "Yes, sir." Such is the comfort of rank.

Back upstairs, where I hadn't been all day, Officer Hiram Davies peered at me over his bifocals with eyes earnestly innocent at sixty-four. Behind the front desk he still sat at attention in the uncomfortable wood chair where he sat all day, fearful of sloth and forced retirement.

"Here," he called. He handed me a neat stack of his memo sheets and added a reproach. "I hope I got them all right."

"Hiram, let me ask you a favor? Don't mention my having called you about where Walter Stanhope lived."

"How come? Is something wrong?"

"No, but . . ."

"Nobody told me he wanted his whereabouts kept secret. Lots of people know he moved to Cape Hatteras."

"I know, that's not . . . Never mind, just please don't volunteer the information that I was asking."

His nostrils pinched tight. "Are you saying I'm some kind of blabber-mouth, because—"

One of his lines rang, and he transferred a call downstairs with elaborate precision.

I said, "One more thing, and I'll stop pestering you."

"You're not pestering me."

"Burch Iredell, that guy that was coroner here back ten, fifteen years ago?"

Davies pushed in on his bifocals as if that would help him see what I wanted.

"Is he still alive?"

"What do you want to know about all these old people for?"

"Maybe I'm planning a reunion."

"That's not true. Is it?"

I apologized. "It's just a joke. . . . Is Iredell dead?"

"He's in the V.A. hospital over in Raleigh." Davies sat up straighter, his shirt stiff with starch to hold off the future. "But his wife's passed away. She attended my church for many years."

"Hiram, tell me, do you remember when Mrs. Dollard's first hus-band died? Bainton Ames?"

"Well, yes. Bainton Ames. He drowned."

"Back then, do you remember, did anybody ever suggest he might have been murdered?"

He pushed on his glasses some more, uncertain whether I was check-ing to see if his memory was failing, or actually coming to him for help. "It was 1968. Wasn't it? They thought he'd been blown up with the boat, then along comes his body miles away. Then they thought he'd fallen out."

"That's right. You have a good memory. Anybody think he'd been pushed out?"

Davies's eyes went away to the past and came back puzzled.

He said, "Now, isn't that funny, because Captain Stanhope did ask that same question, now I think back. Is that why you want to see him? There wasn't anything to it. He was fired, you know." He said this as if getting fired were a profound moral failure. Then with careful fairness he added, "He got another job, some kind of security work. But he was pretty bitter. Then I heard he just retired. I heard all he does now is fish, off in the middle of nowhere."

"That sounds pretty good to me, Hiram."

Davies shook his head in a nervous tic, scraping his collar on his thin neck. "No, it's not," he said. "It's not."

Alone in my office I felt myself dropping back into the weighted depression that had always tugged me down when I didn't keep drinking once I had started. The rush of impulse just to walk out and find a bar scared me. Instead, I started smoking. The memos in Davies's small, precise hand all looked accusatory. One said, "Call Candace," which was Susan Whetstone's code name, and the name she wished she'd been given at birth. Another said, "Call Mr. Briggs Cadmean." He was doubtless returning the call I'd made earlier about the papers my mother had said Cloris Dollard was planning to show him. The man who answered the Cadmean phone now didn't say whether he was a secretary or a butler or a son, but he came back on the line finally and told me Mr. Cadmean would be happy to see me; right away would be fine.

Then I called Susan, though I felt guilty phoning her home, and she told me she was coming over to my place tonight, after going to a bridal shower, because we couldn't meet tomorrow because tomorrow, two days early, Lawry was coming home. I said again I really thought she and I should take some time to think things over, and she said she was coming anyhow. I said I was tired, and she said, "Good. You can be passive," and laughed.

I tried the former police captain, Walter Stanhope, long distance again. I'd been trying during the day first to find out his phone number on Ocracoke Island, then to reach him. This time, just as I was hanging up, he answered. He answered like a man who didn't expect to get phone calls unless somebody had died. His voice had an unused, rusted sound, and he said very little except to repeat an inflectionless, indifferent "okay." On the spur of the moment I decided not to explain until we met why I wanted to talk to him. Instead, I said I was coming out to the Outer Banks to fish, and just wanted to pass along Hiram Davies's regards, and maybe pick up some tips about what fish were running.

Stanhope said, "It's January."

"I like surf casting in winter. Truth is, I'm trying to get away from things in Hillston."

"Okay. Up to you."

I told him I'd call tomorrow after the ferry ride.

"Up to you," he said again, and hung up.

My stomach had knotted and was rumbling from hunger. I ate three Tums tablets and tried to call Susan back to say I had to leave town, but now no one answered. I picked up the silver letter opener she'd given me and absentmindedly pricked blood from the palm of my hand.

Across the room, the insignia on the back of my father's old chair said LUX ET VERITAS. He had believed in both. Cuddy Mangum believed in luck. Sister Resurrection and Joanna Cadmean believed in voices. Perhaps because for a short time I'd heard voices too, they made as much sense to me as truth, light, and luck. I had an impulse to call Joanna Cadmean.

Professor Briggs Cadmean answered the phone at the lake house.

"How's Mrs. Cadmean feeling?"

"Fine. She's up here with me now; would you like to talk with her?"

"In that tower? How'd she get up there?"

"I helped her. She thought it'd be interesting to look through the telescope."

"I have to go out of town tomorrow," I explained. "If anybody asks to see her that you don't know, or even if you do know them, stick around, all right? And would you let me know who it was?"

"Is something wrong?"

"Probably not. If Senator Dollard gets in touch with her . . ."

"He called this evening."

"What did he want?"

"I don't know. He talked to Joanna."

"Put her on."

"What's the matter?"

"Probably nothing. I'm sorry. Let me speak to your aunt, please."

"Joanna isn't my aunt. You forget my father's patriarchal persistence. She's my sister-in-law. I have brothers in their fifties."

Joanna Cadmean came on the phone, her voice as peaceful as a hypnotist's. Rowell Dollard, she said, had called and spoken to her abusively, had charged her with insanity ("Not the first time I've heard that, of course"), and had told her never to come to me again with her delusions.

"Did he threaten you?"

"He said, 'I won't let you do this to me.'"

When she again refused to move into town, I suggested she invite some friend over during the hours Briggs had to be away, and she promised she would. For one thing, two strangers, who'd read Bubba Percy's newspaper article, had already come out to the lodge to ask her to tell them where their runaway teen-age son was living, and why he had left them. "I'm going out to Hatteras to see Walter Stanhope, Mrs. Cadmean. Do you remember him?"

There was a long pause.

Finally she said, "I don't think that will serve much purpose, do you? After all these years, surely there's not going to be anything he can tell you."

"Well, the old story is that Dollard pushed him into resigning over a series of bungled investigations. I'm wondering if it was really because Stanhope had gotten on to something about Ames's death. Obviously he's got no stake in protecting the Senator."

Another pause, then she spoke slowly. "Perhaps. But digging up the past? I don't think it's necessary."

"I don't understand. I thought that's what we were trying to do?"

"I confess, I used to be rather frightened of Captain Stanhope when I was young. I don't think he liked having me around much. Even then he seemed to me a very dissatisfied man."

I said, "So am I." I meant about the case, but she said, "Yes, I think so. You have your mother's eyes, but in yours there's a dark rim around the iris."

"Pardon?"

"Midnight blue. Very dark. May I say something, Justin? Let go. You aren't to blame."

"Pardon? Blame for what? What did my mother say to you?"

"She didn't say anything." There was a mild small laugh. "Don't forget. I'm the crazy psychic, I always say weird things. Thank you for worrying about me." She said good-bye.

Down in the garage, Lieutenant Etham Foster was stooped over unlocking his car parked in the space next to mine. I said, "It's only eight thirty. What's your family going to say seeing you so early?" Then I realized I didn't know whether Etham had a family or not. He had never spoken of anything but the problem under the lens.

His sheepskin coat hung on his nearly seven-foot frame, like beach moss on a tall winter tree. He said, "What they always tell me, 'It's in the oven, heat it up.'" This was more of a response than I'd expected, and led me to say, "Give me a second, Etham. Let me ask you something. Wouldn't you figure if you got hit on the head in a powerboat with side rails, you'd fall down *in* the boat, not over the side?"

"No idea. Never been in a powerboat."

I pulled myself up on the hood of my Austin so I wouldn't break my neck trying to talk to him. "So, what's your guess, did a robber kill Mrs. Rowell Dollard?"

"Not paid to guess, that's your department."

"He knows he can't hock those coins. They're too rare."

"Like you said before, he could already have the buyer set. Could be something *else* he wanted; something you don't even know about. Nobody knew she had it but her."

I tossed up my car keys and caught them. "That's good. Nobody but her, and *him*. Like a diary."

"She jots the killer's name down?"

"Maybe it was already in there."

This time when I tossed the keys, his big hand flicked out and they disappeared inside it. He said, "Your mind's racing," and threw them back. Bending himself into his car seat, he added, "I heard you just sprang Jessie Webster on your own hook. You got something on Captain Fulcher you can lean against when he finds out?"

"Yeah. A big family. Is that Sister Resurrection's name, Jessie Webster?"

"Oh, yeah, most of us have real names too. Did you think it was my momma named me Doctor Dunk-it?"

"She might have. My momma named me Justin Bartholomew Savile the Fifth and called me Little Jay until my father died."

"You're still pretty short," he said, and I'm fairly certain he came close to almost smiling.

While I was watching Foster drive off, Cuddy came out carrying Martha Mitchell and digging in the pockets of his bright blue parka for the keys to the new white Oldsmobile he kept parked as far from everybody else's cars as he could manage. He told me that Davies had found out for us that of the four textiles executives who'd eaten dinner with Bainton Ames the night he died, two were themselves now dead, one was on vacation, and the last (a Mr. Bogue, now president of the synthetics division of Bette Gray Corporation in Atlanta), could be reached at his office tomorrow.

"I need my own theory," Cuddy said. "You got yours, and now it looks like V.D.'s getting the idea you and Sister Resurrection pulled the murder off together."

Finally he tugged out of his jeans the big key chain that had long been a department joke, for on it were a rabbit's foot, a miniature horseshoe, and a Saint Christopher's medal ("Don't laugh. Chairman Ho had nothing to match it," he'd say); the dirty snow of the rabbit fur had a Junior Mint stuck to it. "Well, time for Cudberth R. Mangum, M.A.—as my momma once had my name listed in the Hillston phone book—to go slosh around on that water bed you think's so trashy, and flip on the tube. Martha and I got twenty-two channels of big tits and loud guns waiting. I just love it." He cocked his head at me. "You ought to get home too. You don't look so good. You're starting to look like that painting of yours."

"I didn't get any sleep. Or food."

"You coulda had a pizza instead of those bourbons. Go set a couple of your sideboards on fire, warm up your house and crawl in bed. Go home, hear me?"

"I'm going to see Briggs Cadmean."

"Which?"

"The fat, bald one."

"Good."

"Then I'm going to Hatteras."

"You're going off the deep end is where you're going."

I opened my car door. "That's all right, I know the way back."

"Good." Cuddy shook his head as he walked away.

10

I couldn't see the Cadmean mansion until I was waiting, freezing, at its door, and what I saw then was about a block's worth of bricks the color of old blood. Between the house and the street spread a high fence of iron spears; the long front lawn was an arboretum crowded with immense trees, each labeled with a metal plate and all indigenous to North Carolina—balsam fir, longleaf pine, palmetto, spruce; the largest were two magnolias and a red maple with the frayed ropes of an old swing hanging from it. The side of the house was sheltered by a tall latticework walkway, twisted with thick leafless grapevines. It made sense that a little girl growing up here would have started looking out at the stars; she certainly couldn't have seen much sun down below. The big rooms inside were as crowded and dark with wood as the yard. Wood inlaid floors and wood paneling were crammed with wood chests, paintings, Spanish chairs, and marquetry tables. Clearly the strangely empty spaces of the lake lodge had been the girl Briggs's reaction to this press of pudding-thick furniture.

To come upon old Mr. Cadmean's own beaming manner in the midst of this gloom was disconcerting. The elderly black housekeeper who'd finally come to the door led me up a dark, boxed stairway into a pink children's room wallpapered with Victorian Mother Goose characters. There, like a mammoth stuffed walrus in a toy shop, Cadmean lay on the floor in a disheveled gray suit, his huge arthritic hand working delicately to place a mirror into the bedroom of an extravagant dollhouse. Crouched beside him, a beautifully dressed little girl, five or six years old, watched with her lips pursed critically.

"There!" he rumbled. "Now Miss Mandy can look and see how pretty she is." He stood a miniature doll in front of the little mirror.

"Grandpa. I told you already. Her name's Two Eight."

"Honey, Two Eight's no kind of name for a sweet pretty lady. Let's call her Mandy, isn't that a nice name?"

"I don't like it," she said. "Now put this rug down right by the bed." With a peremptory point, the child handed him a doily.

"Mr. Cadmean. Sorry to intrude."

His enormous head swung around as he lumbered up onto all fours. "Oh, Justin, there you are. Good. Come on in here and meet one of my grandchildren. This is Rebecca Kay Cadmean. Isn't she just as pretty as a little doll?" He beamed.

"Grandpa. Be quiet." The child smacked her palm over his mouth.

I'd seen Cadmean rarely since going away to school, but as a boy I'd sat in the pew behind him in church and watched the back of his big, already bald head bounce in time to the hymns, his big hand swipe at a fly or float an envelope into the collection plate. Now, at eighty, he looked almost exactly the same—the fat still solid, the shrewd yellow eyes lidded as a bear's, the small lips curling (like his daughter Briggs's, like the granddaughter's, too), the same habit of patting his stiff bent fingers up against the shave of his cheek, making a rhythmic sound of the scrape.

Rebecca was there for a visit; her mother, who'd brought her, was off somewhere tonight, probably at the same bridal shower as Susan Whetstone. The inner circle wasn't large. We left Rebecca rearranging the doll's furniture as the old housekeeper complained querulously that she couldn't get the child to mind her.

Rebecca agreed. "I'm not going to bed, no way, José."

"Regina Tyrannosaura," Cadmean chuckled at me, and brought me back down the stairs, one hand clenched on the rail, one arm tucked through mine, like a barge hooking itself to a tugboat. "Let's us go down to the office. Can you believe this weather! Had to get two fellows from C & W to come over, unfreeze my kitchen pipes. In Hillston!"

A fire blazed under a walnut-paneled mantel, gleamed on brown-leather armchairs and on a spaniel sleeping by the hearth. The office, as he called it, looked more like a small museum honoring the history of C & W Textile Industries. On its walls were engravings of the earlier factories and framed citations and advertisements for hosiery and under-wear and work clothes ("The Men Who Built America Were Wearing

Cadmean Jeans"), and photographs, and maps of Hillston. On tables sat scale models of textile machines.

Mr. Cadmean banged at the fire with another log from his wood-stack, then opened a liquor cabinet in the wall next to the mantel. Over the mantel was an oil painting of an unhappily beautiful woman in a formal summer gown with a little copper-haired girl leaning against her side, their hands clasped on the woman's billowing lap.

"You don't drink, do you, son?" he asked, holding up a bottle.

"Yes, sir, I'll have a whiskey, if you don't mind."

His mouth, fleshy and pretty as Henry the Eighth's, made a kissing noise. "Allrighty. I had the notion I heard you weren't a drinker."

"I don't drink as much."

His laugh rumbled. "I don't do anything as much." The glass he handed me was cut with a Gothic C. "And I hate it." He clicked his glass to mine. "I certainly do hate it. You know who that is?" I was looking up at the portrait.

"Your daughter, Briggs, isn't it?"

His breath rumbled slowly through his huge body. "That's right. Her and her mother. A sweet, sweet lady." He shuffled closer to the painting, the fire reddening his scalp. "Just that pretty, too. She was my favorite of all I married. Last and favorite. I hated like hell to lose that woman. I'll tell you this, I just about killed your daddy when he told me she was dead. Yep." He shook his ice hard. "I took him by the coat, I didn't even know I was doing it, and just about killed him."

"He was her surgeon?"

"That's right." Cadmean squatted, his stiff joints popping like the fire, and dropped in another log. "Well, hell, poor fellow, his eyes got big as milk saucers. I apologized later on. But I couldn't believe she'd left me, like *that*." He snapped his fingers one sharp crack, then turned around and chuckled. "Your poor old daddy said, 'I'm having you thrown right out of this hospital!' Said, 'You can't hold on to her by *shouting* at her all night long!' I said, 'Try it, Savile, go ahead. I paid for this goddamn hospital!' Yep, I was in a state. Have a seat, son."

"How old was Briggs?"

"Baby was ten years old." An ice cube cracked in his teeth. "Hard-headed as a mule." He sank himself down in the big leather armchair across from mine. "I hear Baby and Joanna drug you out there to the lake on some foolishness."

"Rowell told you?"

"That's right." Ice bulged one cheek, then the other. "What do you think of my daughter? Mighty pretty, isn't she? And sharper than a serpent's tooth and always was."

"She doesn't appear to like me."

Ice glistened between his small, even teeth when he grinned. "Me either, son. You find me a man she does like that's not some Communist hothead or a damn pansy covered with ivy, and I'll kiss his fanny. Baby's done everything she could to spite me. Everything in the world she could think of. Because I didn't have the heart to come down hard. She was like a little doll left me of her mother."

His fire was so hot I had to shove my chair back; beads of sweat were running down the line of my chin. I said, "She seems to be doing all right. A college teacher."

"Oh, shit, college teacher. That's right. Had to go up North to school, just had to go. Like a fool I let her, and the next thing I get's a telegram, a *telegram*, telling me she's married some scrawny little New York draft-dodger Jew she met in all that mess going on back then. Eighteen years old, and she sends me a goddamn telegram. I couldn't believe it!" He pawed at his vest pocket and pulled out a cigar, the tip of which he poked into the fire.

"I heard they divorced."

A long low growl bubbled past his lips.

"She's lived out at the lake since she came home?"

After Cadmean puffed his cigar tip bright red, he stared at it in disgust. "It's hers," he grumbled. "Like a fool I gave it to her mother and like a fool her mother left it to her. Baby hasn't set foot in her own home for five years and seven months. My own flesh!" His fat palm thudded on his chest like a priest's mea culpa, except Mr. Cadmean had given no indication that he believed the cause of their estrangement lay in him. Then, with an abrupt jerk, his body shook off the subject as he pushed out of his chair and refilled our drinks. "Hell. Women! I truly love women. Truly love them all, big, little, white and black. I love textiles"—his twisted forefinger waved around at the room's evidence—"and I love women, certainly do. Any kind of woman except a loose one. That sort I've got no use for. None. I had two divorces with women that turned out to have the morals of a cat, and both times

I was as shocked as a baby with his finger in a lamp socket. How come you aren't married? I had half-a-dozen kids when I was your age."

"I lived with a woman in law school I thought about marrying; she decided she'd rather be a judge."

"You don't *think* about marrying. You *do* it. Judge, hunh? Shit. Isn't that good whiskey? Here, hold this." He handed me his drink while he prodded the fire into a roar. "Justin, let me tell you this. Women are going wrong. Men, shit, men are nothing but rooting pigs and hogs grabbing in slime, always will be. But women, now. Women are the dream, son. The grail. They're what the war's about, what you're beating your brains to get your snoot out of the swill and look up at something better for. Come to America and what do you see? That's right, you see the Statue of Liberty. Hunh? A woman. A dream. A whore's worse than the worst man ever lived on this earth, because a whore's fallen down from the *sky*, son." He raised his huge arm and let it plummet to his side; then he reached over and took back his glass. "From the sky. Am I right?"

"I like women too."

His yellow eyes squinted at me. "You just have to remember one thing. One thing. They're all crazy."

"Is your daughter-in-law, Joanna?"

"As a loon!" His head nestled back and forth in the tufted leather. "Now, tell me, is that what you wanted to see me about? If Joanna was nuts? You could have saved yourself some gas." He leaned across and patted the air as he would have patted my knee if he could have reached it. "But I'm appreciative you came out in all this ice because I am truly enjoying our talk. Folks think I'm some kind of misanthrope or senile fool or whatever they think, because I've got so I can't abide standing around someplace with no chairs listening to a bunch of phony society goats suck up to me and nose their hands in my pockets. I'll do what I do. And one thing I'll do is take care of my own. Because I love my own." He grinned. "And I enjoy talking to my own of a winter's evening. What did Joanna want?"

"She has a feeling about who killed Cloris Dollard. She thinks it's connected to Bainton Ames's death."

"*That so?* Crazy as a loon!" He threw his cigar into the fire. "Who does she think did it?"

"I'd rather not say."

He nodded. "Never any sense repeating geese gabble. I thought you already caught your man. Some East Hillston jailbird."

"No, sir. Actually, Mr. Cadmean, what I wanted to ask you about was some technical papers of Bainton Ames's that Mrs. Dollard brought over here to you shortly before her death. Do you have them?"

The old man pushed his forefinger in at the bubble of his lips. "What papers?"

"As I understand it, designs for something called an inertial loom."

Cadmean looked at his drink, then put it down. "No, I haven't had a talk with that woman in years, except in a goddamn reception line. What are you getting at, son?"

I told him what my mother had said about Cloris making the copies, and he went to straighten a picture frame on the wall. "Well, hell, I don't know what Peggy thought she heard about these papers, but either she didn't hear right or Cloris changed her fool mind. Cloris wouldn't know a technical paper if you blew her nose on it, besides. And Bainton Ames worked for me till he died, you know. Whatever he designed, I'd already have anyhow." He crooked his fingers now. "You know what this is? Come over here."

Behind glass on a mat was a collection of faded checks with an etching of the original Cadmean brick mill printed at the top. He tapped the glass. "This is real currency. See what they say? Three dollars. Twenty dollars. The Cadmean Company. Back before the War between the States, we paid with our own money! Printed it and paid with it. Just as good as a bank's. Better! Who the hell knows you at a bank? What do you want some old papers of Bainton's for?"

"I just wonder if there's some connection between them and Cloris's death."

His palm played its scraping rhythm on his wide cheek. "Oh, shit, son. That doesn't make a lick of sense. Bainton's been dead for almost twenty years."

"Well, almost fifteen. Are you sure you can't recall any such conversation with Cloris Dollard? Do you know what textiles people might be interested in papers like that? Mother said some men asked Cloris about them."

"I can recall plenty of conversations with Cloris. That woman ran her mouth like an automatic bobbin loader. But none worth listening to and none anytime lately." He tapped an old photograph. "Now, look at that factory there. Isn't that the prettiest thing you ever saw? It broke my heart to have to pull that building down. And you know what? We found some old gold-shafts under the foundations! Isn't that something? Going back to colonial times. You heard how people say they were sitting on a gold mine!" His chortle stopped as suddenly as it began. "Now my board's trying to stick up something so ugly it wears down my soul to have to look at it every day."

His arm crooked in mine, he led me around the room as if it were an art gallery. I stopped at a photograph of Cadmean shaking hands with Franklin Roosevelt. "Parachutes," he told me. "Yep. Overnight, we switched from ladies' hose to parachutes, working our fannies off, and here's Mister Frank thanking me personally. All his boys were jumping out into thin air hanging on to my parachute. Wearing my B.V.D.'s." His laugh rumbled down along the arm pressed against mine.

"You go in everyday, then?"

"Damn right I do. Day I don't, send the hearse and start digging a big hole. I love work. Work *is* love, son. Am I right? I love every shuttle, every bolt, every man and woman that works on that place. Hell, some of them have been with me longer than you've breathed the air. Loyalty. That's what work is. I'll tell you one thing. I've got a bunch of young snots pushing at me now, who, you unscrew their heads and you're looking at a goddamn computer inside. Shit, telling me we got to cut back and lay off and get out of cotton. Conglomerating this and importing that and union diddling and tax diddling. That's not C & W. *This* is C & W." He tapped first at an old magazine advertisement claiming that a boy who'd walked barefoot to school had built a factory that now put socks on America's feet, and then at a photograph of a dozen women, half of them black, on an assembly line, each face turned obediently to the camera. "Whites and Negroes, sitting side by side! So listen here, don't say I'm against progress because that's a lie." He steered me to a complicated model on a table by the wall. "You're wondering about Bainton Ames? Bainton Ames was progress. And I grabbed him like *that*." His fingers snapped. "I didn't like the icy son of a bitch, but I grabbed him. I bet you don't anymore know what this is here than those young computer-heads like Lawry Whetstone and all who wouldn't know a shuttle if they got their balls caught in one."

"It's a loom."

"That's right. What kind?"

I shrugged. "Did Bainton Ames design it?"

"He did. Yep. He did indeed, right before he got himself drowned. This pretty thing was our first high-speed shuttleless loom. A rapier loom." He shoved the miniature steel rods in and out on the model. "You know what a shuttle loom does? Shakes. Breaks down. Uses a lot of power. Makes a lot of noise. People go deaf. I went stone-deaf myself once for six goddamn months. Shuttleless loom purrs like a little kitty, compared. No, I don't hate progress, long as it's real. But I'll tell you this. Most of it's a pile of acetate." With a grinning nod, he rubbed my wool jacket cuff between his fingers. "I'm back on my goddamn coal now the Arabs are squatting on our faces, and if I'd had my way, I'd never gone off it. Nice jacket. I bet you understand me, Justin."

"Well, I don't like acetate." I sat back down with the drink I'd left on the table by my chair.

"You don't look like you do. See this?" He tapped a piece of the model. "Bobbin loader. Used to be, back in the sixteenth, seventeenth century, when they wound the yarn around a skein, they called it a bottom. I saw you in that Shakespeare play. Just had to go, with so many of my acquaintants in the cast. Bottom the weaver. I noticed that, an old weaver like myself. You did a good job; I laughed out loud. That Bottom, he got himself into quite a fix, didn't he? Hunh?"

"Yes, sir, he had a most rare vision. I thought I saw you in the audience. Maybe Cloris mentioned something to you there?"

"Never saw her. That place was jam-packed, wasn't it! Hillston sticks by its own."

"Why'd you hate Bainton Ames, Mr. Cadmean?"

"I didn't hate him."

"I'm sorry. I understood you to say you did just now."

"I didn't like him. There was nothing in his head but ideas." Bent over behind the display table, Cadmean kept working the moving parts of the loom model. "Ideas are fine, truly fine, on paper, but they don't warm the bed. A man who lives by ideas will betray his brother. 'But a faithful man who can find?' Proverbs."

The tiny machine clicked and rattled. Squinting over it, he looked at me awhile. "Leave all this old mess alone, son. Bainton's dead and gone. And Cloris left her fool house open to trash and trash got in and killed her. It's happening more now. Even down here. I hate it. But she's buried now. You let Rowell get through his troubles in peace. He's got a primary coming up before long. You're his people."

The fire was hot on the side of my face; I loosened my tie. "I work for the same state as he does, sir. I realize he has a primary. But I have a murder."

Cadmean stopped the loom suddenly with his palm and came slowly back toward the fire, his small lips puffing in and out. "Let me say something. Everybody's got a little shit on their shoes, son. Everybody. People like us don't track it into the parlor and wipe it on the rugs. That's all. You know what I mean?" His stiffened fingers reached across me, picked up my glass, and held it in front of me.

I knew what he meant.

"Now, you excuse me. I've got to go see about that little princess I'm baby-sitting. What do you want to bet she's no more sleeping than a hoot owl? Selma'll bring you your coat. Truly nice seeing you again. You look like your daddy. Take care driving on that ice, now."

Shuffling past, his fingers squeezed an instant into my shoulder, then ruffled the back of my hair. I couldn't imagine how his hand could be so cold in that room. The fire spat back when I flung my ice at it.

11

Oh, I knew what he meant. He meant all the things that our kind of people were too polite to say in Hillston—just as they had been too polite to say Cloris was not faithful to Bainton Ames.

He meant me to translate his parting remark out of the code. "You look like your daddy. Take care driving on that ice, now." He meant me to think about my car accident on Catawba Drive in the snow six years ago, the accident that had brought on my father's second stroke.

"I thought I heard you didn't drink" was code too.

He meant me to remember I was a Hillston Dollard, blood kin to men of high degree, and I was bound in a circle of courtesy, and I was closely guarded there.

Just as my mother's family, when they arranged to have rescinded my expulsion from a New England prep school, never let it be said in

Hillston that I'd been expelled for getting a girl intoxicated and keeping her out all night.

And when I dreamt and drank away my college years, Dollards arranged to degrade an arrest for drunken driving to a speeding ticket, and they never told Hillston I had a drinking problem; they said the late sixties were demented.

And when drinking got to be the only dream I cared about—being a dream of magnificent swaggering prerogative, coarse and bountiful, unshackling me from my future and pillaging my days like a corsair—my people never told Hillston my problem had gotten worse.

And when I dreamt to hear voices uncivil as the times, when ghosts dashed against my windows and whispered to me in bathetic plagiarisms, *God, am I like the rest after all?*, when ghosts could fly faster than I could floor the car, my people told Hillston I was too ill to accept my ROTC commission. They did not say that the pleasant Blue Ridge Mountains hospital to which they'd taken me boarded only those addicted like myself to the heedless fever of drink.

A year later when they came to take me home, we all kept on keeping silence. Only my younger brother, Vaughan, said grief over my commitment had caused my father's first stroke, and Vaughan, everyone knew, cared nothing for Hillston, or even the state. Whenever I'd complained to Rowell, "Pick on Vaughan. Let *him* go into politics," Rowell had impatiently frowned. "He's not a Piedmont man. It's got to be you, Jay. All your uncle Kip has is daughters. And I don't have anyone. There's just you." Whenever I said to my preoccupied father, "Please get Rowell off my back," he told me, "Shrug your shoulders. He'll fall off."

I went to the law school where Rowell arranged to have me admitted.

And two years after that, certainly no one let it be said that drink had made me crash the car while driving my father home from a Christmas party. They blamed it on the snow. And when, in the spring, my father died, Rowell brought me down from the Blue Ridge Mountains hospital to which I'd escaped, so I could stand with my people at my father's grave.

And Rowell stood with me. Even when I struck him for whispering there by the grave what I knew was true. Even when I insisted on living in Hillston as something no Dollard had ever been. For they had been college men, and lawyers, and even some of them drinkers, and some more or less mad, and most had held public office. But none had ever been public officers, in so individual a sense.

Like my psychiatrists, my people had among themselves their theories about why I wanted to spend my time with criminals. My mother's cousin the attorney general wondered if alcohol had given me a taste for gaudy violence. My mother's older brother Congressman Kip thought I'd read too many books. Her younger brother Rowell Dollard said I needed time till ambition took root.

But no one said anything to Hillston. People not in the circle had no idea I'd had a "really serious problem," much less that all my pastimes—playing the piano, painting pictures, refinishing furniture, putting on plays—were hobbies I'd developed in a sanitorium, were habits to replace habits.

Because I said nothing either, not even to Cuddy Mangum, who probably thought my mother's people had pulled the requisite strings to keep me from going off to Vietnam, whereas I'd simply on my own gone off a different deep end. Which is what I meant when I told Cuddy there in the parking lot that I knew the way back.

To Mangum, in the beginning, my joining the police was only another of my social pastimes. My arrival at my first homicide in white tie and tails (I'd come to the victim's house directly from the town's Charity Ball) led him to conclude I'd cast myself as the inspector in a drawing-room romance, a mystery novel.

But I had chosen detection carefully. In college I had studied classics, electing to learn about the distant past because I had known so long so much of a closer past, had been told since childhood so much of what my future would be: It would be the family business, public office. When Rowell decided his ambitions for me would have to be postponed ("After the mountains, you're too vulnerable for courtroom law, and you can forget running for office anytime soon. We're going to have to wait a good ten years to fade this mess"), when Rowell decided to wait, he told me that in the interim I had two choices—I could go into business law, or I could accept a position on his staff.

I chose public office. I chose the police.

Ironically, it was a remark of Rowell's at my father's grave that confirmed my desire. He said, "What you've done grieves me, but I can't say it surprises me. I was a solicitor too long for anything to surprise me. In that building, there're no mysteries in the end."

After my training, I was rushed through promotions because that's what Captain Fulcher thought Dollards wanted him to do. And I knew they wouldn't tell Fulcher anything different. They had to hold me up out of the mud because I was wrapped in the flag of their name.

I had never wanted to be a lawyer. I didn't want to prosecute crime, or to defend it. I simply wanted to solve the mystery. I wanted to pull down my visor and on a common field ride to where mystery contracted to an instant, like the *crack!* of splintering wood, where no one knows from what castles the jousters have come, and Justice is a blind queen on a dais who cannot see the coats of arms on their shields.

Detection was to me a knight, and Law was only a squire to my people. A loyal, discreet British butler. And I had read enough mysteries to know how often the butler turns out in the end to be the villain.

But what Mr. Briggs Cadmean meant me to remember was that I was indebted to that butler's discretion, nevertheless. I had been sheltered by his family service. When Cadmean reached over my chair and held up before my face my empty whiskey glass, and didn't say a thing, he meant that when I had come home from what my family referred to only as "the mountains," the circle had stood by me, in a ring. And they expected that courtesy returned.

Rowell liked to make speeches to me. "You have a duty to this family. You have inherited a sacred trust, and that is the honor of serving your state. Don't you feel that, Jay?"

Well, now I did.

12

"Listen here, Lieutenant. Whatever your name is, y'all got no right to come in here and harass me! They could fire my ass, called off the line by the police like that in front of everybody and his goddamn brother. Y'all think just because I'm nobody and a woman, it's open season on Charlene Pope. First Mangum, now you. And you really want to do something for me, you get that baby Preston's big brothers off my back. I don't belong to the goddamn Popes!"

"Savile."

"What?"

"My name is Lieutenant Savile."

"Listen, right this minute, far as I care your name's Lieutenant Shithead and I don't care if you think I think so either."

Charlene and I were having our talk inside a Plexiglas cubicle from which her elderly shift manager observed the floor; he'd politely offered to go away to buy himself a Coca-Cola.

It was almost ten o'clock at night by the time I'd left my empty glass beside Mr. Cadmean's models and driven across Hillston to stand here looking at the originals. Beyond the window the great hall of machines kept whirring and clattering, even at this hour blending, carding, combing. Fed by their workers, the huge looms tirelessly kept weaving Cadmean's cloth.

Charlene (her bleached white-yellow hair pulled back in a ponytail, and wearing a smock over jeans and an orange mohair sweater) was in the same mood I'd seen her in on Maple Street. Now she also had purplish pouches under her eyes and a large scab in the corner of her lip.

Suggesting she sit down, which she wouldn't, and offering her a cigarette, I said, "I'm not trying to harass you."

"Sure, what do you call this? I smoke my own." She proved it by pulling a pack of Marlboros from her pocket and flicking her plastic lighter on in front of the match I was holding out.

"I'm trying to find out why you'd called us yesterday and said your husband was responsible for the fight at By-Ways Massage."

"You tell me," she mumbled.

"Does that mean you wish you hadn't?"

She shot a fast stream of smoke out of the side of her mouth; she was watching the men and women moving about in the plant beyond the glass, as if she thought one of them might suddenly turn on us with a machine gun.

I said, "One thing I can assume is, you wanted us to come over there and see that silverware. There're easier ways to leave your husband, aren't there, than getting him arrested for murder?"

"Don't you start saying I did things when I didn't do them."

"What things didn't you do?" I noticed a man with prematurely white hair and a black moustache staring in at us as he went by. Turning her back, Charlene hurried to stand on the other side of a tall file cabinet where she wouldn't be as easily seen.

I said, "Well, we don't much think Preston committed the Dollard murder."

"Fine." She was smoking faster than anyone I'd ever seen, holding in her other hand the little tin ashtray she'd snatched off the desk quick as a shoplifter. "I could care less, but fine."

"Or the robbery. We don't think his big brothers did it either."

"How come? Don't put it past them, mister. I could tell you stuff about the Pope boys . . ." She went back to her cigarette.

"No doubt. Incidentally, what was it you took out of your husband's bureau drawer when you left on the spur of the moment in the van yesterday?"

Veins bulged in her neck. "Did that prick tell you I *stole* that money! Goddamn him! That was $675 I *won* in Atlantic City on our vacation and we were saving to go to the beach this summer and it belonged to me and I took it. And just let me see Preston tell me to my face I stole that money!"

"Preston didn't say you stole it."

Confused, she stopped her cigarette midway to her mouth, and I pointed at it. "Did you know, somebody who didn't live at the Dollards' left a Marlboro butt in their driveway the night of the murder?"

She blustered, "So?"

"Mrs. Pope, was that silverware there in the bathroom when you got to the house, or did you put it there? And, if you put it there—for whatever marital cause—where did you find it?"

She stabbed out her cigarette hard enough to shred it. "I'm not talking to you. I never killed a fucking fly. Y'all are off the wall."

Outside, the throbbing noise was endlessly the same. I came around to lean on the metal desk across from her. "Nobody said you killed anyone. Your, I guess, former sister-in-law Paula told us—"

"Paula!" With a jerk she knocked two cigarettes out of her pack; they fell to the floor and I picked them up.

"Paula told us she doesn't think you knew that silver belonged to the victim."

Charlene let me light her cigarette this time; her eyes, black as pea coal, had gotten glittery with fear.

I said, "I wonder if you came across the silver and figured it was stolen and thought you'd get back at Preston for causes I can certainly imagine. If you don't want to come talk to him, all right. All *I* want from you, Charlene, is where you got the sacks."

She was whispering now. "I never saw it."

"That's not true, is it? I should and will pull you in, Charlene, but I don't want to have to."

"Please. Listen to me, Mr. Savile. Y'all *got* to leave me alone! Please! I never saw it."

"Do you know where you were the night Mrs. Dollard was killed? A week ago Sunday?"

Her teeth scraping across her lower lip pulled the scab off so a line of blood the color of her lipstick started down her chin. "I was with a guy called Luster Hudson the whole night, out at his place. Preston and I are separated. Luster can tell you I was there. He's in the mountains now, delivering some dogs."

"You remember that far back? I don't think I would."

"Listen, you sure would if the fucking cops—" She stopped and wiped at the blood with her fingers. I handed her the handkerchief in my jacket pocket; she just stared at it. I said, "Here," and took it and pressed it against her mouth.

Behind us the door swung open, and a small young woman with short red curls and hostile blue eyes charged in yelling, "What's going on here?" Above her jeans she wore a too-large sweat shirt with a badge identifying her as a union representative named Alice "Red" MacLeod. She couldn't have been more than five one or two in her work boots, but she seemed to be under the impression that she was a great deal larger as she elbowed me away from Charlene and repeated, "Okay, what are you doing to her?"

I said, "Pardon me, I'm Detective Lieutenant Savile. I'm speaking here with Mrs. Pope."

"What about?" In her huge sweat shirt she looked like a high school student on a stage crew, but there was none of that swollen adolescent blankness in her face.

"It doesn't concern"—I looked down at her badge—"the union."

She spun around. "What happened to your mouth, Charlene?"

Dabbing with the handkerchief, Charlene shook her head, her eyes miserable. "Nothing. I bit my lip. He's just asking me about Preston, the guy I'm married to, but, like I told you, I moved out. It's nothing, honest. Okay?" She looked at me. "Can I go now? Give me a break, how 'bout. Okay?"

Alice MacLeod said, "You don't have to talk to him, do you understand?" Then she wheeled on me, leading with her tilted chin. "What do you want with her?"

"I don't see how it's your business, Miss . . . MacLeod."

"Anything on my floor on my shift is my business." Her voice was North Carolina, but farther west, mountain sharp.

I said, "Mrs. Pope, the best thing you can do for yourself, listen to me, is cooperate with us voluntarily."

Miss MacLeod pulled Charlene away by the arm. "Do you want a lawyer?" Charlene shook her head no.

Going to the door, I told Charlene, "We're finished for now. If you don't think I'm trying to help, wait till you meet my chief."

She nodded, without meaning it, and I left.

I'd gotten all the way outside and was tugging the collar of my overcoat up over my ears to start the walk past all the railcars and trucks bringing Cadmean raw fibers to weave, taking what he wove away to sell, and past all the hundreds of cars his workers had bought with the money he paid them for making him so much more; I was still standing there staring up at the disinterested stars his daughter studied, when I was jabbed in the back by the fingers of Alice "Red" MacLeod, who still wanted to know what was going on.

Her breath clouded around her face, one of those British schoolchild faces, freckled milk, one of those faces brought over from Scotland's Highlands by vanquished followers of Bonnie Prince Charlie, a stubborn fighter's face. "Is Charlene in trouble?"

"Yes. She has information involving a murder."

"What murder?"

"Mrs. Rowell Dollard's."

She sucked in the cold air.

"Yes. The best advice you can give her is to tell us what she knows."

"She's scared out of her wits."

"Of what?"

"What do you think! Of you. What's your name?" It was not a friendly question.

"Savile. Justin Savile." I took off my glove, found my wallet, and showed her my identification, which she examined studiously. I said,

"You're going to freeze out here. Would you like to step back inside and I'll explain, if you're really interested in helping Mrs. Pope."

"Tell me here."

I told her that Preston was being held for possession of stolen property thought to be connected with the homicide. She listened frowning up at me, her fists balled under her crossed arms. "Okay," she nodded when I finished, "I'm going to talk to her." She spun away, then back around. "Sorry I jumped down your throat. I don't like cops."

"Why not? We're workers too."

"Depends on what you're working for."

"Mind if I ask, is Red a political nickname, or does it refer to your hair?"

She studied my face.

I smiled. "Or your temper?"

A puff of air blew from her mouth. "All three," she said. "Bye." And was gone.

Behind me the lights of C & W spread across the night, like a small town. Old buildings saw-toothed at their roofs with skylights hooked on to the new flat buildings Cadmean didn't like. Other buildings were under construction, their scaffolding bare. Huge spider-tanks were painted pretty colors and inscribed with their owners' initials. High smokestacks spit out the waste of power.

Spits up fire, I thought. Sister Resurrection's fiery furnace. The dragon spits up fire, and down it rain.

13

It was only when I opened the door to my house and realized that all the lights were on and the heat had been turned up to at least eighty and the shower was running hard up on the top floor, that I remembered that Susan Whetstone had told me she was coming over. My rapping on the tub's glass stall, as she had apparently not been able to hear me until then, in no way appeared to startle her. The impenetrability of Susan's composure continued to impress me. Both hands still lathering her hair, she said, "Where have you been?"

I said, "You sound like we're married, which only you are."

She said, "I can't hear you," and slid the door closed.

I walked back down to the first floor, ate two jars of yogurt and a muffin while reading the day's junk mail and bills, I swallowed four aspirin with some tomato juice, I turned down the thermostat, I picked up Susan's mink coat, which was spread open on my couch, and her suede boots, which were toppled over in the middle of the rug; I shut off the lights, climbed the stairs, took off my clothes, and went back into the bathroom. The shower didn't stop until I was brushing my teeth, staring at the red streaks in my eyes.

"Where have you been?" Susan said again.

"Working on the Dollard case. Tell me again, Susan. You can't think of *anything* else Cloris said to you that night at the play except she had a stomachache?"

"Oh, for God's sake, her stomach hurt, and wasn't the play good, and when was Lawry coming back."

"Why'd she ask that?"

"Well, she didn't know about *us*, if that's what you mean. She said something like, 'I think he's annoyed with me.'"

"Annoyed with you?"

"No, with her."

"Why?"

"Who knows, sugar."

"Was she upset, was she joking, was—"

"Not back to this again! I told you, she just yapped at me a few seconds at intermission." Susan dropped the balled-up washcloth to the floor of the tub. "Who cares."

"Seems to me the conversation would stick in your mind a little better considering the woman was murdered an hour later."

"Considering I'm not a psychic, how was I supposed to know that at the time!" Susan stood in the tub, appraising with thumb and forefinger the girth of her waist, the hang of her upper arm, the firmness of her inner thigh. Her thighs were brown and slender. All of a sudden, they reminded me of my mother's. Distressingly reminded me of one hot August afternoon—it must have been the summer of my seventh birthday—when my father was driving us up to Virginia to visit his parents. I had yielded the front seat to my younger brother, Vaughan, and had fallen asleep in the back, my head on my mother's lap, at the cuff of her red-and-white-dotted shorts. I woke up, my cheek sticky hot and stuck to the skin at her thighs. My eyes opened on a magnified world of gold-haired skin, whose tanning over the summer months had been an assiduous undertaking, discussed at length. ("Oh, Rowell, here you are already black as a berry and I still look like an absolute fish!") I pulled away from her thigh and saw the red imprint I'd left, and the stain of saliva that darkened her shorts. Then I lay my head down again in a new place, shivering with the pleasure of the cool, sinking soft flesh. I kept still there, pretending sleep, until finally she carefully slid away from me, and picked up her book.

In the bathroom mirror, now, my adult face flushed with blood. I couldn't stand here naked, looking at a naked woman, and thinking about my mother's thighs. I turned away to wrap a towel around me. Susan was saying, "All right? I talked to Lawry right after I got home from the play. There was a message on the service to call him back and I did. All right? I said, 'Why does Cloris Dollard think you're mad at her?' and he said he had no idea why. All right?"

"I'm trying to find out what her *mood* was, Susan."

"Her mood! What's her mood got to do with a robber hitting her over the head? Justin, come on. Anyhow, why are *we* talking about it? I know, it's your *job*. You better watch out, sugar. You're beginning to remind me of my husband."

I rinsed out my mouth and spat. "I thought you loved Lawry."

"I do. . . . So, I thought you had this case all solved. People were saying at Patty's tonight that they heard on the news you all had arrested some creep. Meanwhile, that has got to be the most boring party I've gone to in a month." She tilted her head, twisting water from her hair.

Susan had tan blond hair and sharp beautiful bones and a perfected body kept the same tan blond color throughout the year by regular exposure to various beaches. Naked, she looked as if she were wearing a white bikini. I handed her one towel that she wrapped around her hair, and one that she tucked in over her breasts.

She said, "Laurel Fanshaw got blotto and puked all over the kitchen."

"Charming."

"She said she'd felt like throwing up ever since she got pregnant. She gave Patty a gorgeous Marimekko wall hanging. I don't see why they wanted to give Patty another bridal shower anyhow; she's already been divorced twice."

"If Patty has a tag sale, let me know, would you? I could use some more pillows and sheets."

"Funny man. And how's your funny partner, Mr. Mangum, the good ole boy? Were you two out together, I bet?"

"Cuddy's fine. Why are you so hostile, you think maybe we've gone gay?"

"Funny, funny. That man is so fake."

"Are you kidding?"

"Oh, forget it." She stepped out of the tub.

I said, "I'm sorry I'm so late. Pardon, pardon, pardon. How come you're washing your hair?"

"I always wash my hair when I'm bored. If you're going to stay out all night playing cops and robbers, why don't you get a TV?"

"I don't like the way they look."

She shoved me away from the sink, leaned into the mirror, and said with the mildest pretense of sincerity, "I'll tell you what I don't like, sugar. I don't like the way *I* look."

"Oh, yes, you do."

"Joel gave Patty a face-lift for an engagement present."

I stepped behind her. "We aren't engaged."

She pressed her fingers against both cheekbones and pulled the tan blond skin tightly outward. Next to the thin platinum wedding band, the big square diamond flashed in the mirror. We both watched my hands come around and loosen the tuck in the towel until it fell away, and move over her breasts, and then downward until they dropped below the mirror's view. In a while she rubbed back against me, her hands still on her face.

She said, "I thought you were going to be passive."

"I am."

"Oh? Something didn't get the message." She looked at me looking at her.

I took her hands and pulled them down around my back and held them with mine. We watched her nipples harden.

"I can't stay too long," she said. "I've got to go out to the airport early. Lawry's in a vile mood about some stupid business deal of his falling through, or something."

"I'm going to have to call him about this Cloris thing."

"Is it midnight?"

"No."

"Do you know if it is or not?"

"No."

"I want to leave by midnight."

"All right."

"You should have come back sooner."

"Do you want me to hurry?" I pulled the towel from her hair.

When I woke up it was nearly four and she was gone and all the downstairs lights were on. I woke up because of another nightmare. I was playing Bottom again, that final Sunday performance of *A Midsummer Night's Dream* at the Hillston Playhouse, a small downtown movie theater we'd bought when it went out of business like most of the stores around it. We were doing the scene in the woods in which my cronies run off terrified after Puck transforms me, changes my head into that of a donkey, and Titania, the fairy queen, takes me off to her bower to make love. Titania, to my disturbed surprise, was Joanna Cadmean. Old Mr. Cadmean sat in the front row, his bent fingers patting the knee of his daughter Briggs, whose hair had been cut to short curls —like those of the C & W union representative, Alice MacLeod. Then it was intermission, and I saw Susan in her mink, standing in the aisle, as I'd actually noticed her that Sunday, talking to Cloris Dollard. Now Cloris was braced on Mrs. Cadmean's crutches, and her nose was crushed in. Everyone pretended not to notice. Then I was in a car with Rowell Dollard, driving through the snowstorm back to the theater—I don't know why I'd left—and trying frantically to get back there before intermission ended and I had to be onstage. I had on Bottom's homespun costume, and the huge papier-mâché ass's head lay on the car seat between us.

In the dream, I knew I had to keep out of my mind my certainty that Rowell had killed both Bainton Ames and, fifteen years later, his own wife. I knew that if I couldn't void my brain of my suspicion, Rowell would be able to read it there and he would try to kill me, too. But the more I fought to erase the images, the more vividly detailed they grew, like an iris opening in a film. Beside me in his black overcoat, his face from the snowlight as silver as his hair, Rowell kept staring, harder and harder, into the side of my head, until I could feel he was seeing through my skull to what was in there. I sped up, pushing the accelerator to the floor, but nothing changed. The tires floated on in snow so deep all boundaries of the road had disappeared, and the front beams shone out at a white, endless lake, billowing around us. Then we were sliding down the long hill and into the curve at the bottom of Catawba Drive, near my parents' home, the hill that had been in my dreams before. And down there, in the middle of the intersection, black rags in the snow, stood Sister Resurrection. Rowell snatched up the papier-mâché mask and jammed it over my head, and, blinded, I still saw the tree like the ghost of a giant looming. Then I heard the siren coming, as years ago I had heard it, waiting in the crashed car, holding my father.

I woke up uncovered and shivering. In the bathroom two white towels lay strewn on the floor. I showered to warm myself enough to stop shaking; then I put on some jeans and a heavy sweater and an old down jacket. My tackle box, and rod and reel, were out on the back porch, icy to the touch.

When I pulled into a truck stop for breakfast an hour later, the world was still dark, and the woodpeckers and mockingbirds were just beginning to complain about the weather.

A poor pink started to wash through that blue-black opulence the sky has just before dawn, and I had come out of the little hills of the Piedmont, and passed in the night with the trucks the scruffy little egg and hog farms ramshackle in leached fields, the red clay and corn-stubble and piny gum woods, lifelong familiar and so invisible. East on 64, I was sloping down into coastal lowlands, into flat earth fallow for the bright-leaf tobacco, and for cotton, the old king—throneless since Appomattox—like Bonnie Prince Charlie after Culloden Moor.

Wind was cold off the bright water of Albemarle Sound. Far away the wakes of menhaden and shrimp boats already ruffled, luring the white gulls down. As I met the ocean, the sun blew up over the horizon line and I turned south off the causeway into the wilderness preserve of the Outer Banks. I was alone on the road for an hour. Shafts of sea oats bowed shaking to a sandy highway that warned of the dangers of leaving it.

Waiting for the ferry to Ocracoke, I fell asleep, and fell back asleep, crossing. And missed again the wild horses, descended from the mounts of buccaneers, that summer after summer I had never seen, though straining beside my father against the boat rail, binoculars at my eyes, gulls screeching in and out of view.

Ocracoke Island, to which former Hillston police captain Walter Stanhope had retreated, hides across rough water at the farthermost tip of Cape Hatteras. These are the barrier isles, spars of sand dunes, some heaped high as a hundred feet, all forever shifting, the longest stretch of wild shore on the eastern coast. Between the Banks and North Carolina are tangled inlets, too shallow, too dangerous for successful commerce, haunts of pirates and blockade-runners. Between the Banks and England swells the gray sea. They call Cape Hatteras the Graveyard of the Atlantic, and boast of over two thousand ships buried there, lost beneath the foaming spume. When I was a boy vacationing on the Banks, my father walked me out along the bleached plank fence on Diamond Shoals to see the black-and-white-striped lighthouse—tallest in the country, the placard bragged. And yet still defeated by the flat sea below, where rusted smokestacks and iron masts speared out of the waves like the arms of monsters drowning. From the Indies with Verrazano, conquistadors came here, and fled, conquered by swamp and the secret spars. It was in through the Outer Banks, past Kitty Hawk, that Sir Walter Raleigh—who wore clothes of silver and in one ear a pearl and who dared more gorgeous madness than other men could dream—sent his colonies, saying, "Bring me gold to win back the favor of my queen." At Manteo the earthworks of their fort are tended grass now.

The Outer Banks are a place to risk a dare, like courting queens, like flying; or a place for men, like Blackbeard, who need to be lost. Walter Stanhope, namesake of Elizabeth's captain, had come back here to retire, among people still holding in their faint Devonshire accents a distant memory of Raleigh's extravagant dream. Stanhope had come to lose himself here at the edge of the sea.

After some inquiries and some wandering among the narrow sanddusted streets, I finally found him, around eleven, out on the island's oceanside, surf casting on the empty beach, a tin bucket wedged in the sand beside him.

"Mr. Stanhope?"

"Right."

"Sorry to startle you. You're not an easy man to find."

"Savile?" He was a thin, reedy man in his late sixties, with a gaunt wrinkled face brown as my gloves. He wore a beat-up winter police jacket and frayed green rubber waders, a crumpled hat and sunglasses, and he clamped in his teeth an empty cob pipe.

"Yes, sir. Justin Savile. Thanks for seeing me. Regards from Hiram Davies. He's well."

"Okay." Pulling down his sunglasses, he looked at me as if people were something foreign and their purposes dubious.

According to Davies, Walter Stanhope had lived alone since his wife had died; he had no other family. He was a native Banker, who actually had worked in Hillston only a decade. It was said that old Briggs Cadmean had been instrumental in maneuvering the city council into first appointing Stanhope Hillston's police chief. What had impressed Cadmean was the man's management of a flare of civil rights disorders in the small coastal town where he was then chief. Stanhope's Hillston predecessor had a brutish reputation that, in Cadmean's view, might give our city a bad name. It had been under that earlier man's regime that Sister Resurrection's son had been killed.

"Drive okay?" Stanhope finally asked, and pushed back up his sunglasses over his eyes.

"Fine. Catch anything?"

"Some." In the bucket two croakers floated.

"Kind of windy out here, isn't it?" I wiped at the tears already chapping my cheeks.

"I guess. Not so bad. Where're you staying?"

"I don't know yet."

The glasses came down again. His eyes were the color of the sea, an impenetrable grayish green. "Lotta places are closed up."

"I noticed. Looks like you lost some houses, too. I haven't been out on the Banks in a while."

Stanhope reeled in, unhooked some kelp from his lure, and cast. The whir of his bright brass spinning reel sent the line on and on over the ruffled waves. "Lost some in seventy-three. Whole place'll be gone before long. The Army Corps of Engineers finally quit messing with those dune walls. Guess they figured they'd poured enough millions into the water. Hurricane tides sucked the groins right out." He stopped with a brusque rasp of his throat, as if surprised to hear his voice go on so long.

I said, "Amazing the sanguinity of the human race, rebuilding on sand that already slid out from under you."

"Amazing the stupidity."

By now I was close to a jog trying to stamp the sting from my numb toes. "Can I buy you a cup of coffee, Mr. Stanhope? Maybe some lunch?"

"I've got coffee home. . . . You really come here to fish?"

"Well, sir, to tell you the truth, I hoped you wouldn't mind if I asked you a few questions about the old days in Hillston, and maybe get some advice. Had you heard that Rowell Dollard's wife was murdered January the ninth?"

His teeth, tannic colored, shifted back and forth on the pipe's cracked stem. "During a robbery, I heard on the news."

"I'm not so sure I think so."

"I'm retired, fifteen years." He reeled in a few turns on his line. "I don't much like looking back. What did Hiram say to you about me?"

"He said your dismissal was totally unjustified." It was totally untrue that Davies had said so, but nevertheless accurate. I added, "A lot of people in Hillston say you were a good chief, Mr. Stanhope. I think maybe too good."

"I don't much like Hillston," he said, and added a few minutes later, "You work under Van Fulcher?"

"Out from under him, as much as I can. We're not friendly."

The sunglasses were pulled back down the hawked nose. "I used to work under some of your Dollard kin. We weren't friendly."

"Fulcher's better at going along with them than you and I are."

I interpreted his tug on his line as a nod. He reeled in, hooked the lure to the guide, said, "I live over there," and picked up the bucket and started toward the weedy dunes behind us, his feet sliding easily as he climbed through the soft sand. Silently we went past a collapsing plank walkway now jutting out into the air, the shore beneath it shifted away; its house's windows were boarded, and old beer cans, left doubtless by partying trespassers, cluttered the porch. "That your car?"

I nodded. "Can I leave it there?"

"Up to you. Austin 100-4?"

"Yes, sir. Used to be a nice green."

"Parts must cost a penny."

"About what I earn."

Far down the beach, scouted by furtive sandpipers, a solitary man moved with a metal detector, as though he had been condemned by Herculean gods to sweep clean the coast. "Stupid," said Stanhope when I pointed at the treasure hunter.

I said, "Well, they used to claim Blackbeard's gold's still buried out here somewhere in the dunes near where he was killed."

"There's no gold." It seemed to be a flat statement about life. Stanhope motioned me across the deserted highway and down a narrow cul-de-sac dark with moss-hung oaks and yaupon.

"There might be," I called ahead. "Things get buried."

His head jerked back at the sea. "Lot of gold out *there*." He said "out" as my father—a Tidewater Virginian, had—"oot." Clearing his throat through a voice that sounded, as it had on the phone, rusty from lack of use, he added, "At Nags Head, men used to tie lanterns to their horses' necks, drive them along the coast dunes. To trick the ships into smashing on the reefs. They'd loot the wrecks after the drowned washed off." He stopped at the door of a tiny bleached-wood cottage and added, "I don't much like people," and took his tackle and bucket inside.

Like its owner, Stanhope's living room was brown and worn and sparse: no pictures, few books. There were, however, long shelves of records, and as soon as he came in, he put on a stack of LP's. The first was string music, perhaps Mozart, very quiet. He also had an old television, with rabbit ears covered by foil, that sat beneath a cabinet neatly lined with conch shells whose shiny peach inner curls were the brightest color in the room.

He asked hoarsely, "Are you hungry?"

I admitted that I was, and at a small Formica table in the small kitchen, we ate the fish chowder he had left to warm on the stove top.

Telling Stanhope about the Cloris Dollard case was not easy, as he did not so much as nod, but I faltered on through his silence until I'd explained everything I'd come to suspect. Then we sat there without a word. Finally he said, "You want that coffee?"

"Thank you, yes. You see, if Cloris found out Rowell had *killed* to get her—and maybe he also had done something under the table about selling Bainton Ames's textile shares to Whetstone, I don't know—but if she was going to *leave* him, or *expose* him . . . Rowell wants to go to Washington, Mr. Stanhope. One more term in the state senate's all, and then he wants to run for Uncle Kip's congressional seat. If he had to choose between Cloris and his ambition . . ."

Stanhope combed the pipestem through thin brown hair paler than his scalp. "Killed the woman he killed for?" he asked in the inflectionless tone his voice kept.

"Well, this is fifteen years later. Maybe they were fighting and he did it accidentally. Panicked and tried to make it look like robbery."

"Why'd he come home from the capital in the middle of the night to accidentally kill her?"

"Maybe she called him in Raleigh; she said she was leaving the play because of a stomachache, but maybe she was actually upset about Rowell. The last time he can confirm his whereabouts in Raleigh is nine fifty. That's plenty of time for him to drive to Hillston. We've got till midnight for time of death."

Stanhope brushed his eyebrows. "Joanna Cadmean put this notion in your head?"

"No, not really."

"Okay."

"Look, you know yourself Mrs. Cadmean's not just some kind of nut. I've been back to the newspaper files on her. The bodies in the basement like that! She's listed as instrumental in the solving of at least thirty crimes."

He poured coffee from a tin pot. "I don't deny it," he said. "Dollard got a lot of use out of that girl."

"She thinks you didn't like her."

"Didn't."

"Why?"

Staring into his empty pipe bowl, he shook his head. "No reason. Superstition. Gut."

"Did Rowell dislike her? I mean, then? He hates her now."

Stanhope looked at me for a while. Finally, he cleared his throat with a cough. "I'll say it this way. How that girl Joanna felt about her —what she called them—visions was how she felt about Rowell Dollard. She'd do anything he'd have wanted her to."

I stopped looking for a match and took the cigarette out of my mouth. "She was infatuated with him?" I didn't want to believe this.

As he handed me his box of kitchen matches, Stanhope nodded. "He was taking her to bed. Not that it's anybody's business."

"Are you sure? It's hard to believe. What happened?"

"Hard to believe of him?"

"Of *her*. Well, she was, what, only eighteen?" I saw Mrs. Cadmean at the top of his stairs. *Hello, Rowell.* "What happened?"

"Guess it ended. Dollard got promoted, moved to Raleigh."

"How do you know they were lovers?"

"People talk. People are sloppy. People are spiteful. And I'm a good cop. Was." He slid his pipe along his teeth.

Leaning over toward him, I said, "Tell me. You *did* think Dollard might have killed Bainton Ames. Didn't you?"

Instead of answering, he dumped the two fish from his pail into the sink and started scraping their scales off.

I went on. "You think what I think, don't you? Rowell was in that boat, he pushed Ames out, and then swam to shore. He's an impatient, violent man. He wanted Cloris, and Ames wouldn't divorce her."

His palm on the fish, Stanhope carefully slit open its belly. "I considered it," he said.

"But couldn't prove it?"

His head shook no.

"Why consider it?"

"It's a long time ago, Mr. Savile."

"It's not since Cloris was murdered."

Stanhope wrapped his fish in foil and put them in the small refrigerator before he said, "Okay. Hiram told you I thought it. I did think it. That he *might* have. That he had motive and means. That's all. Okay, it puzzled me that Ames hadn't been in the boat when it hit. The skull contusion"—he ran his long fingers through the back of his hair—"surprised me. Too deep and sharp to have happened in the water. Far back here on his head. He hit falling, should have hit landing on the boat floor."

"Yes! So how'd he get over the rail?"

"Lots of ways besides Dollard's pushing him. Accept that first off. But I knew about Dollard and Cloris Ames. And I knew Dollard was at the same restaurant as Ames the same night eating dinner."

"He was?"

Stanhope took his pipe off the window counter and sat back down. "He left his car in the lot overnight. I asked him why. He said there was a short in the ignition. There was."

"How'd he get home? He didn't live anywhere near the lake."

"I asked him. He said, a friend."

"Who?"

"I asked him. He said it didn't concern me."

"You couldn't find out?"

"I tried. But then"—he stood up and took the cups—"I lost my job."

I lit a cigarette. "The coroner's report said one of the textiles men Ames had been talking to, the men from Georgia, thought he saw Ames walking with somebody toward the docks; I think the somebody was Rowell. But the man said he couldn't give any description."

"I had a talk later on with one of those Georgia guys. Hogue? Bogue?"

"Bogue. Impressive. How can you remember that?"

His eyes crinkled the deep crow's-feet around them. "It's a case sticks in my mind. Bogue was, all four were, closemouthed about whatever business had been going on at this dinner. It was around the time there was a lot of tangle with pro-union activity in some of the textile mills. I figured they might have been up to Hillston about that, planning strategy. We had our hands full for a while. Back then old Cadmean was dead set against the union. Bainton Ames was dead set for it. On principle. Don't think he had much of a grasp of the politics one way or another. So I figured they were up talking strategy to Cadmean, and then Ames was just supposed to take them out and smooth them over with a polite meal. Pine Hills Inn had rooms back then, they were staying the night." His throat rasped into a cough, and he stopped for a few minutes to rest his voice.

"Anyhow," he went on. "What I remember is this Bogue was itchy to know if we had some coin, some kind of rare gold piece, he said Ames had brought over to the Inn for him to look at. They both collected. This was a new acquisition Ames was excited about. Bogue said he'd looked at it again right before they split up outside, and Ames had put it back in a little envelope in his pants pocket. Bogue wanted to know, if we had it, could he buy it? His friend's just dead a day now. He wants to go see the widow about a coin."

I said, "So, you don't much like people?"

"Not many. . . . Now, the coin wasn't on the body. I didn't see how it could have fallen out, unless Bainton dropped it outside on the dock or in the boat while he was fishing for his keys, and didn't notice. Not like him, though."

From the back of the house the phone rang. It surprised Stanhope, and frowning, he left the kitchen. What surprised me was that he had called Bainton Ames by his first name, and I was going to ask him how well they'd known each other, when he walked back into the room, his thin mouth working hard on the gnawed pipestem. He stared at me so seriously I thought perhaps he had been given news of someone's death. He said, "That was Mr. Briggs Cadmean on the phone. Wanting to know if you were here."

"What?"

"I figured, some kind of family emergency, so I said yes. But that wasn't it."

"How the hell did he know I was here? Hiram Davies! What did he want? Is he on the phone?"

"No." Stanhope went back into his living room and turned off his record player. I followed him. "He hung up. He wanted me to know—"

"I don't believe this!"

"He said you were set on stirring up some nonsense from the past that had nothing to do with the investigation."

Stanhope watched me pacing the little room.

"Said, fact that you'd come down here showed you'd gone haywire, he put it. Said, he hated to say it, but you had a history of mental trouble."

"God damn it."

"Said, I should calm you down. And just as well not mention he'd taken the trouble to call, for your family's sake. Just concerned about you."

We were facing each other across the kerosene heating stove that stood out from his wall. Finally I asked him, "Why'd you tell me, then? And why the hell did he think he could ask you to calm me down?"

"I owed him favors, he put it." Having said this in his flat tone, Stanhope returned to the bedroom. He came back clearing his throat repeatedly, and carrying a scuffed black violin case. For a bizarre moment I thought he was bringing me the one that had belonged to my father, which I knew my mother still kept at home. Then he said, "You called up, I thought about it. I said, okay, come on. So. You came. I don't much like looking back." He set the case down on the worn-smooth corduroy covers of his couch, and snapped open the clasps. "Long time ago, some of us used to play. Not much. Just a little on weekends. Bainton Ames and me."

I understood what he meant. "And my dad."

"Some. It was no big thing."

"I don't know if you knew. My dad died, some years back."

"Yes, I know." He closed the lid on the bright ruddy wood of the violin.

I sat down beside his coffee table; under its glass top, shells were carefully arranged on sand. I said, "I hope you aren't just agreeing that I'm on to something because you knew my father. And otherwise you'd think I was unbalanced too."

"No. But I wouldn't have let you come out. I think it's possible you're on to something. I don't think Mr. Cadmean would bother making a call if you weren't on to something. I just don't know what the something is. When somebody tells me, they hate to mention it, but they're disinterestedly eager to keep somebody else quiet—I wonder why. Where's the string tied? Motiveless benevolence? . . ." He shook his head. "But, you probably notice, I'm not much on the species. Forty years, arresting them for hating each other and trying to grab whatever the other one's got—it's enough."

We sat listening to the kerosene bubble in the stove, and to the wind, and the tireless surf.

I said, "They can surprise you."

"Not enough. I stick to fish now."

I pointed at his shelf of records.

He nodded. "Yes. And to music. Music's just itself. No motives."

"People wrote it. People play it."

"It doesn't care who. Not a bit." As he stood up, he scratched his brown long hands through his hair. "You even bother to bring along any tackle?"

"It's out in the car." I smiled.

"If you want to, go get it," he said, and coughed. "There's a cove on Silver Lake I'll show you, down some; you might get a bass. Crankbait'll sometimes stir one up in winter. Up to you. They call you Justin now?"

"Pardon?"

"Used to call you Jay, didn't they? Seems like they called you Jay last time I saw you." He held the tan thin hand out at the height of his waist. "You ought to quit smoking," he added, and held out my coat.

15

Before I left, my two-pound bass wrapped in foil, Walter Stanhope let me use his telephone to make some calls, which I charged to the department. Mr. Bogue of Bette Gray Corporation in Atlanta told me busily he couldn't possibly remember a conversation with Bainton

Ames fifteen years ago, and thought it could hardly be relevant now, but he'd have his secretary send me a memorandum should anything come to mind. He said briskly that he still very much regretted the loss of Bainton Ames, and now, of Mrs. Dollard. And, yes, he had spoken to a police chief about the coin. He was sorry to hear others were missing now. If we recovered them, he would be interested in purchasing a few from the owner. The coin Ames had shown him fifteen years ago was, he recalled, an 1839 classic-head Liberty quarter eagle minted in Charlotte, North Carolina—it was a poor sister of the star of the Ames collection, an 1841 quarter eagle known as the "Little Princess" among numismatists—but still quite something to possess. He added briskly that he'd lost another chance at just such a piece only two years ago at an auction in Washington, D.C., and concluded in a hurry, "Was that all?" I took down the name of the auction gallery.

Then I called Hillston to tell Cuddy I was going to stay overnight on the Banks. He told me to come back now. He said, "You know that wall in that Shakespeare play you were just in? That wall you peeked through and the lion ate your girl friend? That wall's about to fall on your head, old Mister Bottom. And it was the only thing between you and V.D.'s snapping teeth. I am in reference to that wall being your fancy kin and friends. They are falling off. Old Cadmean called up here."

"And Hiram told him where I was! God damn it."

"I jumped on Deacon Davies, but he didn't mean no harm. He got real peevish: Yes, you told him not to mention it, but how was he to know that meant including not to *Mr. Briggs Cadmean* that had donated the very floor he was standing on! He thought maybe you meant don't mention it to *me*."

"God damn it."

"You already said that. What's with that fat old bald man? What'd you say to him last night? He must have hopped up and down on V.D. bad about your trying to string up Senator Dollard."

"I didn't say a word to Cadmean about Rowell."

"Well, something rubbed him wrong. You better come home. Old V.D.'s saying you may need some quick R and R—by which I mean Restraint and Roughing Up. Says you're bonkers, and he's gonna have Dr. Ogilvey come see you."

"Oh, great."

"Um hum. There's more. Says Harriet Dale, our lady flatfoot flathead, told him she was 'scared' of you, the way you and Sister Resurrection were shooting the breeze on the same frequency downstairs yesterday. Listen here, General, when it gets so the only friends you got at headquarters are white trash and nigrahs, it's time to pucker and pick up the bugle, and I don't mean 'Charge!' As my daddy said after forty-two years on the line at C & W, 'Enough's enough.' And the truly bad news is Preston's told Fulcher he *did* pick up that silverware. Off the side of the road on Wade Boulevard around two in the morning the night of the murder. While out cruising for Charlene. He claims it caught his eye when he stopped for a red light and emptied out his brains into the ashtray. 'Those sacks must have fallen out of the killer's car,' he tells us. I'm real disappointed in Joe Lieberman. He's already talking plea bargaining for Preston. Fulcher's got-Ken Moize and the other justice boys hot to trot. Murder one. They're going for it."

"Where's Charlene?"

"Can't find her. We're looking."

"She might have gone after Hudson."

"The Great Smokies are great big."

"Well, who knows Hudson? Did he have any friends?"

"Let's not take time out for humor. Speaking of which, I'm going out now to eat supper at Ye Olde Pine Hills Inn. I'm trying to go suave, see, and I said to myself now where would old suave Savile take a girl? So what's good there? How's their pizza? I'm taking Briggs. I wanted you to be the first to know, in case you found out."

"Briggs?"

"Junior. The professor. I took six Valiums and called her up and I think I heard her say yes."

"So why are you telling me?"

"On accounta your tone right now."

"She was supposed to stay with Joanna Cadmean."

"I'll talk to Mrs. Cadmean. Not to worry. I'll make her promise to lock up. Listen to this, I'm going to take over my basketball pool, and let her take a whing at it. She never saw a game in her life. But well, hell, why not? So get on back. Not that there's all that much we can do anyhow. If you see some fellows in white coats with a net on the front steps here, don't stop to chat."

"Could you start a check on the late-night gas stations on Raleigh

Road? If Rowell drove back and forth twice that Sunday, maybe he got some gas, God willing."

"Savile, you are *stubborn*. Anybody else ever tell you that?"

"Rowell Dollard, for one. Constantly."

"Well, I hate to spit on your birthday candle, but you got about as much chance of pinning either one of those killings on him—I don't care if he's Jack the Ripper—as you got of getting Lunchbreak Whetstone to cook you three squares behind a picket fence. *Adiós* and happy holiday."

"What holiday?"

"Lawdy, Ashley, you don't know it's a state holiday? Today's General Lee's birthday! Yaahoooo! Shall we rise? We shall rise!"

I said, "Your jocularity is getting me down," and hung up. I felt too tired to drive for four hours. As it turned out, it took me closer to five. And it was eight thirty when I reached Hillston and changed clothes, and headed across town to C & W Textiles.

I was stubborn.

That I was stubborn had moved into familial myth long ago when, at age six, I'd trekked one night in cold rain to the home of a fellow first-grader three miles away, whom I rightly believed had stolen my harmonica. That was, as it proved, my first case of detection, and one involving the police as well, for a patrol car had found me on North Hillston's winding roads, trudging, sodden, home to Catawba Drive—with my harmonica.

That I was stubborn had kept me bloodied facedown in mud through the autumns of junior high school, attempting to play the game of football, for which I had little talent and less bulk.

"No, you have your father's talents, and my character," my mother would say. "That's a Dollard will. We're all stubborn."

"Everybody in the state of North Carolina is stubborn!" was always my father's reply.

On vacations, to the beach or the mountains, the only times I remember his being so garrulous, my father would say (as furious drivers passed him on the shoulder, or waitresses refused to let him order what he wanted), "North Carolina is such an ornery state. Virginia may be stuck-up. But North Carolina is stiff-necked. You won't give in, you won't give up, and you won't move out. Did you know, Jay, even now, ninety-nine and a half percent of the people living in this state were *born* here, and the precious few of us that weren't, are looked on with considerable suspicion?"

In proof, he would always point out that we claimed to be the first colony, even though we were a lost one. That our state was named after the only British monarch misguided enough to get his head chopped off (Charles I), and was half-settled by the crazed Highlanders who thought they could win that kingdom back for Charles III. That our president, Andrew Johnson, had been the only chief executive to get himself impeached. That, in the seventeenth century, we had even been mad enough to declare war on Virginia!

My father would say, "The hornet's nest, that's what General Cornwallis called Carolina. Now, Virginia yields to no one in *considered* revolution, but, good Christ, you Tarheels rebel against polio vaccinations!"

"And proud of it," I would call from the car's backseat.

And Mother would add, "Our Edenton ladies had their tea party long before the bragging Bostonians, and what about our Culpepper rebels, and your great god Thomas Jefferson, sweetheart, did nothing but plagiarize our Mecklenburg Declaration of Independence!"

And beside me Vaughan would turn the pages of his horror comic book as Carolina cars swept in a rage around us, FIRST IN FREEDOM on their plates.

And in school I was taught that we were indeed a stubborn state: the first colony to vote to leave old England, the last to ratify the new constitution. In the Civil War, first we wouldn't secede, and then—though we lost more men than any other Southern state (and my mother, a Daughter of the Confederacy, could tell me the names of all those dead from whom I descended); lost more men than this country lost in Vietnam—we wouldn't surrender, not until seventeen days after Appomattox. And for ten years after that, while Federal troops guarded farmland matted with weeds, we rankled, stiff-necked. And now on the front-bumper plate of Preston Pope's van rides a cartoon Johnny Reb, sword high, screaming, "Hell no! I won't surrender!"

And when at fourteen I broke my heart refusing to stop trying to date Patty Raiford, who was ostentatiously in love with a senior (first of her three husbands), Mother would say to my father, "Little Jay comes by his stubbornness honestly. Honey, he's a Tarheel. My God, if I hadn't been a Tarheel, I would have let you just slip away back to that awful girl from Alexandria. Remember her? She had the biggest bosom you would ever want to see. I never did believe those breasts were real, were they?"

And my father would say with his soft smile, "Good Christ, Peggy, I haven't the faintest idea."

And Mother would lean around from the car's front seat and say to me, "Now, that's a Virginia gentleman, I want you to know. That's a Savile."

At my father's grave, Rowell Dollard had hugged his arm across my back. "You're a Dollard, Justin. I won't forget it. Don't you."

16

Under the lights, coming around the curve onto the Hillston beltway, I noticed the tan Camaro behind me, and the image stirred that when I'd come home, a tan Camaro had been parked across the street near the entrance to Frances Bush College. The car was still behind me after I took the C & W Textiles exit, and when I pulled into the Dot 'n' Dash, it went by at a crawl. I waited; in a few minutes the tan nose edged, bouncing, out from the side street behind the store.

My escort kept behind me as I passed through the chain link gates that hem in the town of Cadmean's mills. For five minutes I leisurely cruised up and down the long parking-aisles, until finally the Camaro simply stopped in an open space behind me, and shut off its lights.

I reversed fast, slowed as I passed by, took down his plate numbers, and then continued on backward until I found a parking space.

Inside at the big board by the time clock, the driver of the Camaro walked by me without a look. Waiting for the elevator, he pulled off his orange John Deere cap and stuffed it in his mackintosh pocket. I remembered that combed-back white hair and the black moustache; last night out on the plant floor, he'd stared in at Charlene Pope and me long enough to make me remember.

The elderly division manager could tell me nothing about Charlene Pope's present whereabouts; her future at C & W—if we were indeed thinking of arresting her—appeared to be in doubt. On the other hand, he was pleased to tell me about the floor's instructional supervisor and elected union representative, Alice "Red" MacLeod, once I had assured him that far from being under suspicion, Miss MacLeod had proved a model citizen of cooperation with the authorities. Flat in the face of his own disapproval, the man obviously liked her, and, fears allayed that her politics had brought her to grief—that she might have incited a workers' riot or kidnapped the governor—he let me know that "in spite of how it looks," Red was "a crackerjack," "a little steamroller," "smart as a whip," "sound as a dollar," and, in general, as industrious, reliable, and judicious as a socialist union troublemaker, only twenty-nine and female, could conceivably be.

This time, instead of talking in an icy parking lot, she and I drank horrible coffee in an institutional lounge walled with vending machines. This time, instead of a sweat shirt, she wore an apple-green turtleneck, and instead of opening with "What's going on?" Red MacLeod whisked in and said, "Have you found Charlene? Hi."

"Hello. No. We have a car cruising the house where she's supposed to be staying. She didn't call in sick?"

"Nobody's seen her since last night. And look, last night after you left, she shut me out *fast*. She wouldn't talk, and she sure wouldn't listen. All she would say was how people had to leave her alone."

Unspiraling a glutinous pastry, Red shook her head; the curls bounced like the ribbons my mother liked to coil with the edge of her scissors into bows on packages. "Look, I'm sorry I couldn't help out. If I get a chance, I'll try again. Okay? How long have you smoked so much?"

I threw onto the tray the empty matchbook inscribed PINE HILLS INN. I said, "Not long enough."

"It is hard to quit." Her eyes were earnest blue.

"But you managed, no doubt. Please don't brag about it."

"No brag. I can't smoke in class, so I had to quit. I miss it."

"Class?"

"Frances Bush. I go in the mornings. This is my last term. That's why I work the two-to-ten. A little old, but better late . . ." Having unwound her sugary concoction, she broke it into six even strands, pushed three toward me, and began eating the others.

"Somehow you don't look like your typical Busher," I said. "There's no name sewn over the rear of your jeans."

She took a count of four, staring at me, and then she smiled. Her left front tooth had a very tiny chip at the corner. "I get tuition," she explained. "The woman that founded the school, Miss Bush, worked this scholarship deal out with Cadmean Company—sometime back in the nineteenth century—for a woman working in the mills. They give one a year. Next fall I'm hoping to go to the university. To law school."

I cracked the edges of my styrofoam cup, bending them down like petals. "And then what? Do you know?"

"Sure!" Freckles of confectioners' sugar stuck on her Highlander chin. "I've always known. I want to be governor of North Carolina."

"Oh, my God."

"What's so funny!" Her freckled fists crossed under her arms.

"Nothing. That's what *I* was supposed to be. But you go on ahead."

"I will."

"Brush off your chin first."

Her hand flew up to her face and then back under her arm. I saw she bit her fingernails. I said, "Mind if I ask you where you live? Not on campus, do you?"

"Why?"

I ate one of the sticky strands. "Because I live across the street from Frances Bush. In the narrow brick house with the blue shutters?"

She didn't appear to know it. After thinking it over, she decided to say, "I just moved to Tuscarora, an apartment."

I smiled. "That's only two blocks away from me. You know, your old academic ancestors used to live in my house; it was sort of a Frances Bush dormitory annex. Sometimes I think I can hear them in the house giggling, and climbing the stairs in their high-button shoes." And sometimes I thought I could hear their ghosts in tears alone in iron narrow beds. I said, "Two blocks away. I'm glad to think I'm bound to have met you anyhow, even without Charlene."

She didn't speak, and we studied each other's eyes. Hers were serious and azure and very tired. Then I told her, "You're twenty-nine, you come from near Boone up in the mountains, you never call in sick, you work too hard, and you've never been married."

She snapped, "Not a crime, is it? Who told you?"

"An old gentleman admirer of yours. Your division manager. I'm thirty-four, I come from Hillston, I've got a law degree and I'll trade it to you right now for the name of that man with the black moustache over there to your left—don't turn your head—by the wall phone, and I've never been married either."

"Do you call in sick a lot?" She bent down and retied her bootlace. "It's Ron Willis, why? Just a loader here at the plant. And a company stool. He's a creep. He's also a junkie."

"Any connection to Charlene? Relative? Friend of any of the Popes? Old boyfriend?"

"I don't know. Do you want me to find out?"

"Would you do that, Governor? And would you tell me too if you could join me for dinner tomorrow night?"

Her leather laces twice-tied, she straightened slowly back up in her chair. "I work nights, you notice?"

"Lunch?"

"I eat between classes. It's ten minutes."

"Are you planning on wending your way to the governor's mansion all alone? Mind if I ask? Or are you living with someone, or engaged or anything discouraging like that?"

"I'm just busy. Why do I have to be engaged?"

"Why do you always answer a question with a question?"

"Why do you ask so many?"

"I'm a detective."

"Why aren't you a lawyer if you've got a law degree?"

"How about breakfast and I'll answer your first five questions, maybe more. I'll even throw in a few pointers about how to get to be governor."

"I'd appreciate it if you'd stop kidding me. Obviously, the idea is to work up in local politics."

"Who's kidding? I can be of assistance. I know an old family recipe for working up in local politics. My great-great-grandfather was a governor of this state. Eustace Dollard."

She sat back. "For real?"

"As far as anyone could tell."

"Dollard. Like Congressman Kip Dollard?"

With a paper napkin I rubbed the pastry crumbs from my fingers. "Don't forget the attorney general."

Her fist went to her mouth. "Oh! And Rowell Dollard. His wife; you must have known her. Look, I'm sorry."

"Thank you." I stacked our cups on the tray, and she pulled it from my hands and dumped the contents in the wastebin. She said, "Thanks for the coffee. I ought to get back on the floor. Let me know about Charlene, will you?" With the sudden celerity that was gradually startling me less, she turned back toward me. "Are you still holding her husband?"

I explained that in all probability Preston Pope would be indicted by the grand jury tomorrow.

"But Charlene says she doesn't care about that. What's *she* so scared of? Being charged as an accessory? Is she afraid of her husband, or his family, or what? Because she sure is scared."

And so it was then that I saw I already knew what Charlene was afraid of. I knew because at the Rib House, Paula Burgwin had told me. Charlene was afraid of Luster Hudson.

Red's fingers were waving in front of my face. "Hey!"

"Pardon?"

"I said, I eat breakfast at the Bush Street Diner. At seven thirty. That's probably too early for you. Bye." She waved the small freckled hand and spun away.

I caught up and walked her back down the twisting turns of concrete steps, each landing painted a different pastel color, and hurried with her along the hall toward the rattling whir of the indefatigable looms. Then, quite suddenly, she turned, startled, her lips parted. She asked, "Why are you whistling that?"

"Pardon?" In fact, I hadn't noticed that I was whistling anything—though apparently I often did. "I don't know. Just popped into my head. I don't even know the name of it." It had been some slow, lamenting tune of which I could do only the first phrases, reiterative and dolorous.

"It's an old mountain ballad; it's 'Lass from the Low Country.' I can't tell you how weird this is. That was my grandfather's favorite song. He used to always whistle it like that." She looked at me solemnly. "I mean, I was thinking so much about him today. Today's the day he died, January nineteenth." Her Scottish face, pink and white and stubborn-chinned, went on staring up at me luminous in the neon light. "Do you do that a lot?" she asked.

"Apparently."

Slowly, she nodded at me, and vanished behind the steel doors.

I didn't move. I felt as if I were being nudged off a cliff, falling into a new self, impatiently telling the old, "Why do you keep saying you love Susan, when you don't?" I said aloud, "I don't love Susan." A man coming out the double doors beside me said, "If you say so, buddy."

I grinned at him. "She doesn't love me, either."

He called over his shoulder. "Join the club."

17

It was ten twenty when Fulcher's call came. I'd gone home and decided against trying to warm the house, and had washed out the lipstick-smeared glass Susan had left on the kitchen table, and then had filled it with bourbon, and then had poured half back into the bottle.

Today I'd driven nine hours on little sleep; my skin was dry, flushed hot, and my bad leg with its chipped bone was hurting. I'd already called old Cadmean's house twice—even though Walter Stanhope's last words, delivered with his bluff hoarseness, had been a warning: "I were you, I'd be leery of the man with the strings. But up to you." Now I was told that Mr. Cadmean was in bed. I had a feeling it wasn't true. I also had a strong urge to call Joanna Cadmean, but decided that she probably was in bed. And in fact Cuddy and Briggs were probably back there at the lodge now. My earlier jealousy of them seemed now a kind of gluttonous evasion; evidence that having invested so much time in wanting Susan, I had to feed any dissatisfaction with amorphous claims to other women. What a loss of my past to admit I didn't want to marry her at all, didn't even like her.

Back in the living room, and without turning on the lights, I sat at the piano and tried by touch in the dark to pick out the melody of "Lass from the Low Country," pick out the sad sweet Celtic grief that had come across the ocean with defeated dreamers.

Above the piano was framed my favorite of my father's landscapes—a pencil-and-watercolors sketch of the Rappahannock River, banked with the tight-leaved lime-green trees of early Virginia spring. I looked up at the picture and saw, reflected in its moon-silvered glass, Joanna Cadmean's face. Slowly she smiled. Then the face contracted, as if she were stepping backward, away from me. My heart loud, I spun around on the piano stool, but there was, of course, no one standing in the dark, soundless room.

Outside, a car motor started. So vivid had been Joanna's image on the glass, that I leapt up—jarring my throbbing leg—and ran to the front door to see if she had somehow gotten in the house and were now leaving. The car had reached the corner, and was just turning into the intersection. It was the tan Camaro from C & W, Ron Willis's car; obviously he had been watching my house again. Spying for whom? Himself, the Popes, Cadmean, Rowell? And why? To find out what I was finding out? Blackmail? It was even possible Fulcher had someone undercover trailing me, gathering violations of the rules manual to back him up when he told my family I was fired.

Dizzy, I closed the front door and leaned against it in the unlit foyer. Something white fluttered at the top of the stairs. Probably what I saw was a sliver of a neighbor's light, shining in through the white window curtain. What I thought I saw was Joanna Cadmean. This time she was standing at the edge of the second-story landing, one hand on the banister. Her hurt foot, unwrapped and bare, was held out in front of her as if she were about to step off into air. A veil of white gauze fell, like netting around a bed, from her head to her feet, enclosing her.

With her free hand she raised the gauze. And beneath it she was utterly naked. Pulling the cloth over her head, she flung it away, and it floated timelessly down the stairs toward me.

I shut my eyes quickly, but when I reopened them she was still there, still naked, moon-pale and gleaming. Then suddenly she raised both arms to me, as she had in my dream the night before, drawing me up to her embrace. But when her hand let go of the rail, she lost her balance and pitched forward and fell, soundlessly. I cried out loud, "Christ!" and plunged for the light switch. Illuminated, the hall shrank, the steps shortened to a finite number, and there was no one on them. I walked back to the piano and my drink.

And then at ten twenty, I felt my way to the insistent phone by moonlight.

"This is Van Fulcher."

Too worn down to be much interested in the tirade I expected, I said only, "Yes."

"I just this second got the call from the station. I want you to get out to Pine Hills Lake right away. Mrs. Charles Cadmean just committed suicide."

The glass fell from my hand. "Joanna Cadmean?"

"I guess so. . . . Yes, right. Mr. Cadmean's daughter-in-law. We've got to handle this right, Savile. I'm going to call Cadmean up right now. I'm at home. It's going to take me a while to get over there. Ambulance and squad car are on the way. I want you to—"

"She's dead?"

"Yes. I—"

"How?"

"Jumped from some kind of tower at the Cadmean lodge out there. You know where this place is?" Fulcher's voice was quick and high with excitement. He always found death exhilarating.

I asked, "Jumped? Who said jumped? Who called it in?"

"Well, it's tragic. Rowell Dollard. He's out there. After what he's already been through! Sergeant Davies took the call. The Senator's badly shaken, I guess. This is ticklish, Savile, its being the Senator who found her. You follow me? So, considering, we'll postpone getting into these stunts I know you've been pulling. And you get out there. Do you know where it is? Savile? Savile, are you listening to me?"

"Yes, I'm going. Good-bye." I picked up the pieces of broken glass as I waited for Etham Foster to answer the phone at the lab.

The moon kept ahead of me, a hard ball of light rising through the black smoke of the clouds, climbing over the black trees, heading for the black glassy lake. I could see up the hill, through all Cadmean's thicket of pines, the harsh blue and red patrol lights spinning. Their colors flickered on the silver Mercedes that was parked in the driveway, right in front of the porch steps. On the gravel beside the car, covered in white cloth, lay the shape that had brought all the lights, and brought the men who now knelt around it, like Magi at a moonlit crèche.

"She's dead?" I asked.

"Oh, yeah." Dr. Richard Cohen, our medical examiner, looked up, bald, unshaven, exhausted. He was my age, with the pouched, weary eyes of a man much older. "Oh, yeah. Dead on impact. Her neck's broken." He pushed himself to his feet, and tapped the edge of the Mercedes' hood. There was a dent in it. And blood on it. Cohen's hand, pale and black-haired, vaulted in an arc from the car roof to the ground. "Like this. She hit here, see. Bounced off."

I pulled my collar up around my ears and closed the lapels over my neck. He nodded, blowing on his hands. "Cheesh, it's colder than a witch's pudendum. I might as well have stayed up in Brooklyn. And they told me this was the Sun Belt."

"Where's Dollard?"

"Lying down inside. I tried to give him a sedative, but he wouldn't take it."

"How did it happen?"

"According to him, she insisted he go up there to that tower with her." Cohen pointed over his head at the octagonal study on the roof of the high lodge. A shaft of light came out of the open door, silhouetting the rails of the balcony. "She doesn't say a word, *bam*, she opens that door. And over she goes. He couldn't get to her in time." Cohen's words floated on the cold air, like mist.

"She was on crutches."

"Right, they're up there, by the rail." He rubbed his eyes. "You knew her? So what was her problem?"

"What was he doing here?"

"Ask him. He told us she called him up, said she was upset and had to talk to him. I wish I'd brought a hat."

I gave him my tweed cap; it fell low on his narrow head. "How long's she been dead, Richard?"

"Less than an hour. You want to take a look? Then I'm headed home, okay? I've got a baby to walk."

Together we knelt down, and he tugged away the sheet and shook his head. "Good-looking for—what?, forty-two, three?"

"Forty-eight, I think."

"Looks younger. Well, okay, she hit here." He turned the head. "This tibula's broken." The arm was unnaturally twisted back. It was the hardest part of her to look at.

"Five ribs broken. Cheek's crushed. But what killed her was the neck. Instantaneous. It's a long drop."

I touched her hand; it still felt warmer than mine. "What's this?" Her wrist was smeared with a small streak of fresh blood.

Cohen shrugged. "Scrape; it's nothing. This is interesting: See these faint vertical white streaks? Old scars. Too old really to tell much, but I wouldn't be surprised if she hadn't made a serious attempt way back when."

"What would you say, could anyone have survived that fall?"

He looked back up at the tower. "Improbable. But people have jumped out of planes and survived it. People do amazing things."

The moon loomed between the vaporing clouds and shone on the motionless face, cool and still, white except where blood gritted the skin. The gray steady eyes were open, unblinking, focused far beyond this moment. The handsome head was twisted to the side, and the line of its profile, Delphian, serene, was as untroubled and disinterested as stone. She wore a dress of thin white wool, too thin for such weather, and around her neck were milk-white pearls, and tight in the hand of her broken arm, a white silk scarf.

"Say, come on; can I go now, Savile?"

"Just a second, do you mind?"

Officer Pendergraph had gone back to the squad car; he was young, raw-faced, and energetically working against letting me see he was bothered by mortality. I said, "You all right, Wes?"

"Yes, sir, I'm fine."

"Was there a note?"

"No, sir. We didn't find one anyhow. We looked."

"Get a statement from Senator Dollard?"

"Dr. Cohen said leave him alone till you people came."

I told Pendergraph to call the station and try to hurry Foster's crew and the photographer. The task relieved him. "They're on the way," he came back to tell me.

The murky vaulted space of the lodge's huge living room was reddened by the embers of a fire gleaming beneath the smooth embedded stones of the mammoth chimney. Beside the antlers coatrack, the telephone was off its hook. I replaced it and called the Pine Hills Inn, too late to page Cuddy Mangum there. I reached him at his apartment in the River Rise complex, and told him not to bring Briggs home, and told him why. Then I walked slowly through all the spare, chilly rooms, checking their windows. Nothing was out of order. Finally I sat down on the couch across from Richard Cohen, who'd pulled one of the bent-willow chairs over to the fire embers and was resting his head in his hands, elbows to his knees. "Your hat's on the table in the front," he said.

"Richard, I want you to tell me two things. What's there to indicate a struggle? What's there to indicate she was pushed?"

His hands opened and his head came up, pale and thin above the wiry black border of hair. "Pushed? Who by? By Senator Dollard?"

"Yes."

"Cheesh!" He nodded slowly. "Well, okay, sure. Somebody could have shoved her; that or jumped, fall would be about the same. Struggle? I didn't see any claw marks on his face, if that's the kind you mean. But who knows." He thought, yawned, and thought some more. "I'd say, pushed her from the back, *bam*, no warning, if he did it. Seems like I saw a snag kind of thing, down the dress front. Rail splinters probably. Headfirst, see." He pantomimed the motion and the fall. "Yeah, headfirst. Gutsy woman, if it was her idea. I'm going, all right with you? Fading fast here."

"You writing probable suicide, or what?"

"I'm writing broken neck for now. You can decide how it got started." He yawned through his words. "Goo'night."

The door to the first-floor bedroom was closed. I opened it. It had been her room. By moonlight I saw the basket of gifts from my mother, still untouched on the dressing table. Over a rocking chair back were folded the sweater and plaid skirt I'd first seen Joanna Cadmean wearing.

"Justin?"

His voice came from a chair in the dark corner. Then Dollard stood, and his silver hair moved into the light. "Justin? Did they take her away yet?" His face was ashy; his pupils black, distended to the rims of his eyes.

"No."

"Justin, *God*, this is dreadful! Dreadful!"

"Yes."

"I should have suspected . . ."

"Yes? Suspected what?"

"She was just standing there by the door, up there. Then she opened it. And went out on the balcony. And just *leaned* . . . and . . . then she was gone. Just gone! I *heard* it, Justin. My God! She was mad . . . mad. Completely insane!" His mouth opened, gulping air like a swimmer.

"Yes. I remember you told me she was insane." I stooped to the lamp and twisted the knob. At the click, Dollard stepped backward and covered his eyes. He wore all gray, gray sweater and gray slacks. He looked old. I said, "I'd like you to take me up to the study now, and show me how it happened." I turned toward the door, and let him pass through first. One of his hands kept rubbing up and down against his arm.

The door to the balcony was open, the tower was cold as outdoors. Its huge gray telescope shadowed a wall. The instrument pointed straight out across the black lake, pointed at the summer house that had once belonged to Bainton Ames. Silent in the room, we listened to a siren coming nearer.

As Dollard told me where she had stood, and how she had moved, I stepped out onto the pine-plank balcony. Yellow crutches lay on its floor. Caught in the rough log rail were tiny threads of white wool. I leaned over. Far down, directly beneath me, gleamed the silver car, beside it the white motionless shape. Beyond the pines, from the foot of the hill, came headlights bouncing. Foster's men and the photographer. It was still too soon for Captain Fulcher. I walked back inside, pulling the door closed with the edge of my sweater.

"Have a seat, Rowell."

"We'll talk downstairs. It's too cold up here."

"In a minute, please. It *is* cold. Why were you and she up here?"

"She asked me. She insisted I look at something. Something to do with Cloris."

"What?"

"She never said." Rowell sank down in a chrome and black leather chair beside a desk heaped with papers and maps of the stars. He said, "I don't think there was anything to show me. She began talking wildly. And then, she jumped! For God's sake, can't we do this in the morning? I'm upset, Justin, God!"

Watching him, I lit a cigarette. I found a paper cup with some water in it to use as an ashtray. "Why were you over here at all?"

"She called me. I've already explained all this. She begged me to come."

"Why?"

He didn't answer.

"Why did you come?" I was speaking as softly as he was. "An insane woman you clearly dislike, calls you up at night, and you drive all the way over here from North Hillston? Why?"

He still didn't answer, and I turned and leaned down to the telescope sight, and looked through it, into blackness. Pushing it upward, I saw very clearly cold and unblinking stars. "Why, Rowell?"

When I turned back to him, Dollard thrust his head forward, the shadows behind him moving. "It's a private matter."

"Not anymore."

His hand pressed hard against his arm. "Justin. She was hysterical. She was raving."

"So you tell me. I'm asking you, about what? What was she raving about before she just turned around on those crutches and pulled herself up and over the rail? In her raving, did she happen to say why she suddenly decided to commit suicide? While you stood and watched? Why did you happen to be here when the impulse just struck?"

He stood. "What's the matter with you, Justin? For God's sake!"

"Tell me why you came here."

"You're the one who let her into my house! Into Cloris's bedroom! You listened to her insane mutterings!"

"So did you, some years back. They weren't so insane then, if I recall your comments to the press."

For a long time, Rowell stared at me, his eyes protuberant, his face tight. Then he stepped quickly forward and touched his hand to my shoulder. "Justin, what I'm going to say is in absolute confidence. I want that understood."

I didn't speak, or move. Finally he stepped back and turned his eyes to the wall of books. His voice was broken by struggles with silence. "When I first knew Joanna Griffin, she was quite young. I was young. We were thrown together by her . . . involvement with, well, apparently, you have read all about that. She . . . fell in love with me, I guess you'd have to say. And, well, we had a brief, a *brief* relationship. I broke it off. She was not a stable person, even then. As she proved. Now, that was thirty years ago! And now!" He stopped suddenly, walked back and sat in the chair. "Now she comes back to Hillston and begins making incredible accusations. By involving you, she involves the police. And then she does this!" He stabbed his finger toward the balcony. "I don't know why!"

I said, "I don't believe you, Rowell."

When he raised his eyes, they were as glazy as marbles. "What?"

"I don't believe she committed suicide." I dropped the cigarette into the paper cup and listened while it hissed in the water. "I think you killed her."

"What did you say?"

"I said, you killed her."

He whispered at me, "You're as mad as she was. In God's name, why should you think such a thing?"

"Why?" I leaned against the books and watched him. "Because I know what her accusations were. Because she made them to me. And to Lieutenant Mangum. Because I know she believed, absolutely believed, that you are guilty of murder. Believed you killed Bainton Ames in order to marry Cloris."

A dusty red mottled his cheeks, spreading up his face to where the vein in his temple jumped.

"I think she believed you killed Cloris too."

"Oh, my God!" All the color disappeared from his face.

"Because Mrs. Cadmean would never have 'asked' you to come over here, would never have 'asked' you to come up in this tower with her, because she was deathly afraid of you. Afraid you were going to kill *her*, too! That's right. So strong was her conviction, that her sister-in-law came to my office Monday to tell me about it." As I went on, Dollard's face froze, like the face of a man put under a spell. "*Because*, Rowell, Lieutenant Mangum just told me he was over here this evening, and he spoke to Joanna Cadmean, and she was not at all in a suicidal state. She was getting ready to go to bed. She had no intentions of inviting you over. And I think a check of the toll calls out of this house tonight is going to prove it."

Outside, light jumped up from the flash of the photographer's camera. I could feel Dollard's eyes frozen on me as I moved out of the room onto the balcony. Down on the driveway, I saw Foster crawl around the front of the Mercedes. I called, "Etham," and the willowy black man leapt to his feet and rammed his hands into the pockets of the sheepskin coat. "Yeah, what?"

I called down, "Thanks, okay? As soon as you're through, they can take her."

"Can I get up there?"

"Come on when you're ready."

Rowell sat rigid in the black chair, breathing with his mouth open.

He said, "Justin, dear God, why are you doing this? I don't understand."

"Why not? You had already called here yesterday and threatened the woman. You came here tonight, and forced, or cajoled, your way in. You ordered her to keep quiet about her premonitions—just as you just now ordered me to keep quiet about your having seduced her. And when she told you she *knew* you were guilty, you shoved her over the balcony. That's all. She probably climbed up here to try to escape you. I expect if she hadn't struck your car, you might have simply driven off and left her, assuming we'd call it an accident. Just as people thought Bainton Ames's drowning was an accident."

A noise came from Dollard's throat, and his hands squeezed on the chrome armrests.

I said, "I'll try hard, but maybe I won't be able to prove you killed Ames. Just as Walter Stanhope wasn't able to prove it."

Startled, his head jerked up.

"But, Rowell, I *can* convict you of killing Joanna Cadmean. And I will."

"I really believe you mean this," he whispered. "You're serious! I'm your *family*." He came fast out of the chair, his voice louder. "After all, *all*, you've already done to hurt your mother, you can't mean to do this! This will kill her!"

"It will hurt her to hear what you are."

Suddenly he made a sound like a laugh, derisive and sharp. "This is insane! Justin, think! Even the accusation could do irreparable harm. And not only to me!" His indignant expression darkened abruptly and his face was purple. "I'm not listening to any more of this. This is intolerable! Nobody in his right mind would put up with it."

I stayed by the door as he strode toward me. I said, "If you'd wanted us to think it was an accident, you shouldn't have broken this chain."

His head swiveled to the brass door chain I held up, its catch twisted where it had been snapped from the bent lock. "And you shouldn't have wrenched her wrist," I said, "so hard you tore off her watch." I stepped over to the corner, bent down, and gathered the two pieces of the watch I'd seen on Joanna Cadmean's wrist both times I'd been with her. The band of gold links was broken. Near the watch lay a brass letter opener. I pointed down to it. "Did she try to protect herself with this? Is that how her arm got broken? Did you take the phone downstairs off the hook so if Briggs called, she'd think Joanna was talking with someone? And your scarf, Rowell? Did Joanna grab at your scarf as you shoved her toward the rail? Is that why it's down there in her hand now?"

Slowly, horror closed Dollard's eyes. I listened to footsteps start to climb the stairs far below us. When they reached the first landing, he shook himself, then walked to the door without seeing me as he went by. I spoke to his back, to the lush gray sweater that looked no less rich and assured now than it had before. I said, "Just don't leave the house. Thank you."

Without turning back, he mumbled thickly, "You're going to regret this."

I picked up the extension phone on the desk and called the River Rise apartment and asked Cuddy how Briggs was doing.

"Cruddy. Same as me," he said. "She's okay, don't worry. It's feeling responsible, you know, that's the worst. I mean, my sense is she and Mrs. Cadmean hadn't met more than a couple of times before now. Listen, she wants to come over, and I'm gonna bring her. We both feel awful, tell you the damn truth. But that lady acted *fine*, Justin. She didn't seem down, she seemed almost, hell, jolly. I swear I can't understand it!"

"It's not suicide, Cuddy."

I heard his long whistle, like a wind. "Dollard?"

"I think so. It looks that way."

"Shit a brick. Well, you were right. And I was wrong. Damn. How'd he get in there? She told me she was going to lock up. I *told* her to."

"I don't know yet. I guess she let him in. Okay, would you go ask Briggs if Joanna told her about any kind of letter or note or something she'd written to me and put somewhere."

While Cuddy was gone, I listened to the ambulance doors snap open and shut, and its motor spit in the cold, and the keen of its siren leaving. Foster opened the study door. I waved him in.

Cuddy came back on and told me Briggs hadn't been left any message about a letter for me. He said, "Be there soon as we can. Justin, I'm sorry."

Foster and the photographer crowded me out of the study. Downstairs, I went to the door and watched Rowell, motionless in his black overcoat, standing outside by his car—boxed in by my car and Foster's and the squad car whose noiseless light kept spinning, throwing fire over the lake.

In Joanna Cadmean's room I began my search for the letter I felt certain she had written me, but had not yet made known to Briggs because she hadn't thought she needed to yet. There were very few belongings through which to search: one suitcase on the floor of the closet. One drawer indifferently arranged in the bureau. She had required little. I emptied Mother's wicker basket, and ruffled the pages of the pile of thick cheap romances, heroines in white by ruined towers, pierced by moonlight.

I found what I was looking for in a book under the bed; one of those small-print, yellowing collections of Shakespeare's *Complete Works*, pages separated from the cracked spine, the kind of book that summer houses have on musty shelves. Mrs. Cadmean had written the letter on the notepaper given her by my mother. She had placed the dozen sheets, whether by design or accident, midway through the play *Hamlet*. Her handwriting was scrolled and ornate, but perfectly clear, perfectly linear on the page. At the top of each sheet the red cardinals sat on a dogwood branch, symbols of the state.

January 18

Dear Justin,

I think it best for me to go back to the island within the next few days. My presence here is unsettling. You said just now on the phone you planned to go speak with Mr. Stanhope. If you did, he may have told you something about an incident in my life, when I was a young girl, and involving Rowell Dollard. It is true. I was hurt by it. Perhaps I should have told you myself, but it has no bearing on this matter.

It is also true that when I first told Cloris of my terrible instinct that Rowell was responsible for Bainton's drowning, she said I had fabricated the story because of my dislike of Rowell. Our friendship came to an end because she didn't believe me.

It is not true that I fabricated the story. But I have to confess. When I said to you that Cloris spoke to me in my dream about a diary, in fact, she had telephoned me, last month, in the ordinary way. You see, not all my conclusions are so, what some have called, unnatural. Let me explain. I have had an interest, since my childhood, in old coins. I suppose I liked feeling on their faces the many hands that had touched them through so much history. Bainton had often shown me his coin collection. I knew it well. And so I noticed in the testimony surrounding his death the mention of a coin he'd brought to the Inn to show someone that night he died. It was a coin he'd recently acquired.

Justin. I saw that coin *this summer*, back in the collection. I know I am not mistaken. I could only conclude that Rowell had taken it from Bainton that night, and all these years later put it back with the others.

This summer I visited Hillston (at my father-in-law's request—he wants even relatives I suspect he doesn't much like, to keep in touch). And this time, I paid a call on Cloris (Rowell was, I believe she said, in Washington that weekend), and asked if we might not reconcile our long silence after our quarrel. She agreed. We had a good talk. Afterward, I asked if I might see Bainton's coins again. I was stunned to see the presumably missing gold piece there. But I didn't mention it. Bainton had died so long ago, and I suppose I felt the cruelty of asking her to accept a truth about Rowell that would shadow the life they had, by all accounts, so happily lived for so many years.

But I did take the coin out of its case, and studied it, and I remember I commented on the fact that it was the only one with no label on its paper envelope.

Shortly before her death, Cloris phoned me. To thank me for making the overture to renew our friendship, and to ask about summer rentals on St. Simons. And she said, laughing, that she had wanted me to have that coin as a gift, since I'd taken such an interest in it, and after I'd left, she'd set it aside to mail to me, along, she said, with a pretty leather diary she was sending to her daughter. But she'd packed them up somewhere, and couldn't put her hands on them—as she said—but they were somewhere in "this madhouse" and one of these days she'd send it along. It was very typical of her.

But I never received the coin. And then, a few weeks later, I had my dream, and the next morning was told that she'd been murdered. Justin, I don't *know* if Rowell killed Bainton. I have hoped you would be able to prove so. I, perhaps foolishly, decided only to intimate my feelings to you, by talking about dreams, without directly producing evidence that would involve me in testimony about the past. My encounter with Rowell at his house, and his truly cruel attack on me over the phone, make even clearer, if I need further proof, just how vicious I can expect him to be.

The coin is a two-and-a-half-dollar Liberty-head gold piece, Charlotte-minted in 1839. Bainton kept very careful records. He had only one. I feel strongly that the coin is still in that house. I think Rowell could not bring himself to discard it—as easily as he has discarded the living.

That was the end of her original letter. In a different pen, another sheet followed, dated tonight.

Dear Justin,

Briggs and your friend, Lt. Mangum, have just left for their restaurant, and I'm going to take my poor ankle to an early bed—with another friend of yours, Shakespeare. (I regret I missed the chance to see you in *A Midsummer Night's Dream*, a favorite of mine—as you might expect.)

I have the strong feeling you're thinking of me now. I thought of calling, but hate to intrude any more than I already have on your sympathetic ear. I will mail all this tomorrow. You can decide what's best to do with it, if anything. I'm going home.

You have been very much in my thoughts. Upsetting thoughts, of your falling a long way. But perhaps only into something new. Everything around you is white. I can't tell if it's something good or bad. (Always the Sibyl's way out, isn't it?) But please take care. You know, I trusted your eyes from the first moment I saw them. They see the possibility that there are more things in heaven and earth than are ever dreamt of in all the Horatios' philosophy. For believing so, dear Justin, I thank you. We are only mad north-by-northwest.

Joanna Cadmean

I folded the small scented sheets back in order. This was no deathbed letter, and not even the Polonian fool Captain Fulcher would believe it was.

On the table by the bed was the sketchbook, some of its drawings torn out. I turned over the pages. A gray shadow of Rowell's enraged face looked out at me, uncannily like the look he had just now given me as he strode out of the study. Across the sheet, Joanna had drawn a series of vertical lines, like the rails of a balcony, like the bars of a cell.

I walked back out into the bitter cold night, and charged Rowell Dollard with suspicion of murder.

II

BOTTOM'S
DREAM

The snow began to fall again early in the morning after Joanna Cadmean died; thick, sticky flakes this time, large as new buds of white azaleas. By dawn they covered Hillston, snowslip heavy on the trees, the downtown stores wheyfaced, staring out at one another across the white, silent roads. I walked onto the steps of the Municipal Building, and saw the whole slumberous city lulled and hushed by snow.

Rowell Dollard was not in custody; he was not even booked. He was in a private room at University Hospital under the care of a personal physician who said his patient was the victim of hypertension and acute prostration brought on by the shock of the violent deaths of his wife and Mrs. Cadmean. The pull of medical rank pleased almost everyone who had been sitting all night in Van Dorn Fulcher's office. Dollard's near nervous collapse was, said the state attorney general, "just the sort of holding pattern we need right now." The A.G.'s name was Julian D. Lewis, and the *D* was for Dollard. He had driven very quickly over from Raleigh for this informal hearing, which was also attended by Judge Henry Tiggs, a man I'd known since childhood. Everyone listened sleepily to Rowell Dollard record his statement for the stenographer, until Rowell simply mumbled to a stop and said someone should call his doctor right away. His statement was the one he had given me: Mrs. Cadmean had jumped for no cause she made known.

By dawn, V. D. Fulcher looked as if he were ready to check into a ward near the Senator's. The captain's pink, whiskery jowls were twitching. His splutter had stammered into incoherence as he tortured himself with calculations: Where should he truckle, and how? Word that Rowell Dollard could legitimately seek sanctuary in a hospital bed was the happiest news the captain had had since he heard the Jaycees were giving him a plaque and Mr. Briggs Cadmean was going to attend. Fulcher's problem was not that I thought there was sufficient evidence to charge Dollard. And certainly not that Cuddy Mangum and Etham Foster agreed with me. It was not even that Fulcher himself— after clicking his mouth hard up in the tower study for fifteen minutes, and twice rereading Joanna Cadmean's long letter to me—not even that he himself did not believe with much comfort that she had committed suicide.

Fulcher's problem was that Hillston's current solicitor had said flatly that there were unignorable grounds for reasonable suspicion against Rowell Dollard, even if he was a state senator. This solicitor, Ken Moize, not only was not a Dollard, he was not a Hillstonian, not even a Carolinian—having only lived in the state since the age of fourteen. Moreover, this outlander Moize didn't even like the A.G., Julian D. Lewis, whose job (Fulcher whispered) he probably coveted. Fulcher's problem was that he needed to decide whether Julian D. Lewis would override Moize to protect his kinsman; or, whether Lewis would feed Moize a little tidbit of Dollard (an indictment), to avoid the public howl Solicitor Moize might let loose if he could prove Lewis party to a cover-up, oust him, and snatch up and wolf down the attorney general-ship for himself.

So buzzed poor Fulcher's mind. He couldn't even be sure but what *Lewis* disliked his cousin Rowell Dollard, jealous of the backing the state moneymen (like Cadmean) had always shown the Senator, their man in Raleigh for many years, and one they'd expect to see go on being their man for years to come. Fulcher's quandary was that if the ship was sinking and he ought to desert, where was the shore? And what if, as he paddled off, whiskers frantic above the waves, he should look back and see the big vessel majestically right itself and sail, with all its power churning, away from him? What then?

So, for most of the night, he sat fretful and let us fill his office with smoke—he couldn't tap his Lucite-bar warning at me because the attorney general, copper as old money from his recent vacation at a golf resort, was pilfering my pack—and let us litter his floor with the yellow crumbs of Cuddy's crackers and the foil of the solicitor's gum. Until finally it was decided that nothing had been decided, except that Joanna Cadmean was a corpse now, in a waiting room at Pauley and Keene Funeral Parlor, dead either by her own hand or by misadventure at the hands of person or persons unknown. And both the city prosecutors and the state prosecutors would study the evidence, and one another, until they could decide, in due time, where the ship should dock.

Only one decision was made: Fulcher decided after everyone but Cuddy and I had left that I had overstepped my authority, and was therefore to take two weeks' leave of absence. Inspired by the convenient collapse of Senator Dollard, he phrased my suspension in a medical way: The leave I was on was sick leave; my sickness was overwork. Clearly, wherever Fulcher thought the big boat of power was headed, he didn't much believe anymore that I was one of its officers, and although still a first-class passenger, I was now one who could with impunity be kept for two weeks from eating at the captain's table.

I left Cuddy in there arguing with him about me. Passing under the wry, yellow, lidded eyes of Briggs Monmouth Cadmean varnished in oil, and clattering across the black and white floor of the rotunda, I walked out. I stood at six in the morning at the top of the steps looking over the still, blanched facade of downtown Hillston, where I had lived all my life, and, shaking, I pulled on my gloves and wrapped my scarf tighter. Across the street, my car was as white as a cairn of heaped stones.

Up the sidewalk through the slant of thick, blossomy snow came a black umbrella. Beneath it a man's ratty overcoat fluttered out as if there were no one in it; the bottom dragged stiff and wet in the drifts. Sister Resurrection was marching from her home in the church to her post by the hall of government. I walked down to meet her, my legs unsteady enough to keep me close to the balustrade.

"Good morning, Mrs. Webster," I told her, and touched my cap. My voice startled me by coming out a hoarse whisper. "Like a fairyland out here, isn't it? Mighty cold for a walk, though."

Although she didn't speak, she did stop, and I bent down to look at her under the umbrella. She wore a child's red toboggan cap and red mittens with white stars over the knuckles. The wizened folds of her neck were open to the gusty snowfall.

I said, "Well, things are bad. That silver-haired man we were talking about; I believe he's killed somebody else now. She was actually, now I come to think of it, a little in your forecasting line of work."

Sister Resurrection walked around me, and began a march as precise as a sentinel's, up and down, at the base of the steps. A hum rose out of her throat, and then a chant. "The King of Babylon," she said, "he wox angry. He got the iron walls. He got the fire burning. He throwing God's childrens into the fiery furnace. But God Almighty don't mess with Babylon. He makes His people for to walk through the valley of the shadow. God Almighty He taken that fire and He wet it with the tears from His eyes. He snatch that fire and He squeeze it." Umbrella high, she balled tight the red mitten of her free hand. "And *squeeze* it. And making a chain to hold the Devil just a little while longer. Just a little while longer. Just a little, my Lord, just a little. And then we laying down our heads and sleep."

I said quietly, "Amen."

And "Amen," she replied, and looked into my eyes and through them and beyond.

I said, "Here, if you're going to stay out, here, Mrs. Webster, do you mind?" and undid my long wool scarf and wound it high around her thin neck and tucked it in. Unmoving, she stared beyond me, then turned back to the march of her weariless warning.

But as I was brushing snow from my car, I felt all of a sudden her scratchy hand pluck at my arm, and when I looked around, she began to tug at my sleeve, her grasp oddly strong. Pointing the black umbrella ahead, she pulled me with her into the street. She let go, hurried a few steps ahead, whirled back, motioning with her fluttery arm for me to come; rushed on, turned back, called me with her arm again. Down the empty streets I followed the small dark figure, no one but the two of us in the white ghost town. The unplowed road billowed around us soft as sheets. On we floated, like sleepers silent, until abruptly she darted off to the left.

Lurching after her into the side street, I saw her stop and rattle her umbrella at the painted glass front of the downtown dance-bar that was calling itself these days THE TUCSON LOUNGE. Gaudy at night with noise and rows of red electric bulbs topped by a red neon cactus, it was in daylight just a dull, raw wall. In its gutter, snow was falling on black plastic bags and soggy boxes of drinkers' debris, bottles and cans and stench. Sister Resurrection wheeled around and pressed against me, her eyes rheumy clouds that suddenly sharpened to jet. Her hand flew up and grabbed at my coat arm and, the fingers wriggling inside the mitten, she pulled me down with her to a crouch at the curb. The hand flew out again and pinched hard at my earlobe. "Trash," she said, and pointed down, twisted her head and pointed back at the window of the bar behind us.

I nodded. "Yes, you're right."

"The harlot sitting on the dragon's back, she wearing the crimson and purple robes, she wearing gold and wearing jewels." Her red-mittened fist jerked away from my face, yanked up her hat and squeezed the ear beneath. She breathed out slowly, "Wearing *jewels*." And for a wink of a moment only, I saw a self come into her eyes, saw her be there seeing me. Then she was gone again; murk clouded the pupils and they lifted skyward.

I touched my ear, burning still where she had grabbed it. "Ear jewels?" I whispered. "Is this where you found that earring? Here in the trash?"

But unhearing she sprang to her feet and scurried through the snow back the way we'd come.

Back in front of the Municipal Building, I heard her as I climbed into my car. "She hold the cup of fornication and drinking the blood of my Jesus outta that cup. She Babylon. God throw her down from the iron wall and dogs shall lick her blood."

At the Bush Street Diner near Tuscarora Road, I was asleep with my face pressed into the side of the booth, when Alice "Red" MacLeod tapped my shoulder, and scared me. "I told you seven thirty was too early for you."

I bolted upright, shaking my head, and she added, "Are you all right?" Tugging on her book bag, she slid into the booth.

I said, "I'm fine, it just doesn't show."

She unbuttoned a plaid parka; beneath it she wore a pink fuzzy sweater the color of her cheeks. "Sorry I'm late; I had some union phone business. More rumors about shutting down my division. This creep named Whetsone had us 'analyzed' and says we're not 'competitive.'"

"We've met," I said.

While we ate eggs and coffee, I explained what it was that had kept me awake all night, that Joanna Cadmean was dead, that the suspected murderer was my uncle. She said, "Justin, I'm really sorry." She thrust forward the stubborn chin. "And it's just disgusting what they're doing about it. They fired you!"

"They suspended me, while they decide if they can afford to fire me."

"What are you going to do now?"

I made an effort at a laugh. "Well, first I'm going to take it lying down for about eight hours."

"How in hell do people like them always end up running the world?"

"God, I hope that's not a serious question."

"Oh, yes, it is. It sure is. It's *the* serious question, Justin."

I looked across the plastic tabletop at the solemn blue eyes. "You called me Justin two times," I said. "Would you mind doing it again?"

Her blush moved up from the neck of her sweater into the freckles, and she frowned. "Isn't that your name?" And she went back to piling scrambled eggs on her toast like pâté, eating quickly and pleasurably. "Aren't you hungry?" she asked, cup to mouth.

"Not really." The food at the diner did not look as if it had improved since my last visit, the night Cuddy rescued me from his cousin Wally's switchblade; the old picture of eggs-and-bacon on the menu had an unappetizing anemic pallor. My head was logy, and my hand shook so that finally my cup of coffee just slipped through my fingers and crashed onto the tabletop, sloshing me and the table with scalding liquid. I jumped out of the booth, shaking my pants, and she jerked a wad of paper napkins from the container and started to sop up the dark stain.

"I'm sorry," I said.

"Look, I do things like this all, I mean all, the time. Don't be stupid. There. You better go home and go to bed."

I took the sticky napkins from her, both of us holding on to them until finally she let go. And smiling I said, "All right. I will. I wonder if you'd like to come too?"

Her face crinkled, the eyes stayed grave. "No." And she sat back down. Then she smiled. "You better go home and go to *sleep*. I'm going to 'European History: World War I to the Present.'"

"That'll depress you."

"No, it won't. It'll make me mad. It always does."

"Yes, you're a warrior, Alice 'Red' MacLeod."

She nodded, pulled over my plate and ate everything on it. While doing so, she told me she had two pieces of news for me: Last night, Graham and Dickey Pope had stormed into the plant when the shift ended, looking for Charlene. They told Alice they didn't know Ron Willis—the white-haired man with the black moustache. And no one else she'd spoken to had heard of any connection between Willis and Charlene; except that one woman had told her she'd heard Charlene had taken up with a man called Luster Hudson, and Ron Willis had once palled around with Hudson when the latter had worked at C & W as a forklift operator. I thanked her, and she said she'd love to help me put Willis away; he was a stoolie paid to keep watch on union activists like herself. She said Willis had once told her floor manager the lie that she had a long affair back in Boone with a black Communist social worker.

"What was the lie?" I asked.

"That he was a Communist."

"Oh."

She looked across at me, her chin up. "It's over. He had to choose between me and somebody else, and he didn't think he ought to have to. But I thought it would be better for everybody if he did."

"You're . . ."

She cocked her head. "Archaic. High-minded. Unliberated. And a hillbilly."

"What I'm trying to say is you're very pretty in the morning. Christ, I sound like a teen-ager. I think I'm falling in love."

This time she didn't blush; she just looked, and then she said, "Go home. I'm late. Here." And hauling a coin purse out of her book bag, she took out three folded dollars.

I said, "No."

"I asked *you*, remember? Plus, I ate your breakfast."

"If you're so unliberated, why won't you let me pay?"

She said, "God, I hope that's not a serious question," and hurried into her parka and slid fast out of the booth. "Look, are you going to bed?"

"The prospect seems to fascinate you. Are you sure you couldn't give World War I the slip?"

"Your eyes aren't even in focus. I think you're already asleep."

I pulled myself out of the booth and touched my toes five slow times. "Wide awake. In fact, I'm about to embark on a new career. Breaking and entering."

"For a good cause?"

"Yes, ma'am, Governor."

"Okay." She slung the bag over her small straight shoulder. "Bye."

"See you tomorrow, seven thirty, Alice."

When I reached the North Hillston colonial I planned to break into, there was a car already parked out in front. A white Oldsmobile, like a big ice floe in the white snow. The house was Rowell Dollard's, and the car was Cuddy Mangum's. In the front seat sat Mrs. Mitchell. I tapped the glass against her skittering paws. Cuddy was already inside, and he started yelling as soon as I opened the door. "Where'd you go, you damn jackass!" He stood at the top of the curved stairs, hand inside his coat, probably looking for his gun.

"What are you doing in this house, Mangum?"

"Guess. Now, Justin, why in holy shit did you run off that way? I come out and you're gone wandering off in the snow like old Doctor Zhivago. And so I ask your pal Sister Resurrection out there wearing I do believe your scarf like she ate the rest of you, I ask her, 'Sister, did you see a good-looking crazy man go by?' But we don't speak the same lingo the way you and her do, and all I got for an answer was that God's in a *real* bad mood and lost His patience with trash, which I hope was not in reference to me."

By now I had crossed the Dollard foyer and had climbed the stairs to the landing.

Cuddy shook his head. "You know, maybe you do need a sick leave. You look bad. You haven't even changed your clothes, and that scares me. And excuse me being lewd, but did you maybe come or pee in your pants?"

I said, "What are you doing here? It's coffee."

A sleepless night had reddened the blue-jay eyes and shadowed the old acne scars. He still wore the three-piece herringbone suit he'd put on (or bought—I'd never seen it before) to take Briggs out last night to dinner. I'd been telling Cuddy for years that if he really wanted to take over the department, he had to stop wearing things like Elvis sweat shirts. Maybe love would be his tailor. I said, "Nice suit."

He tilted his head at me. "I know you, General. I may not know you, but I know you. I suspicioned there might be an attempted break-in at this residence coming up, and I figured the police ought to be on the scene. And since you ain't the police—being as V.D. the old spit-licking toadeater has fired, excuse me, *suspended,* your ass, I figured I would save you from the temptation of committing an illegality. Call me Tonto, for you are sure enough the lonesome Ranger now."

"You're the one waltzing around his house without a warrant," I said.

He rippled his bony hand in his jacket pocket, tugged out a loud tie, and then the paper. "Oh, I gots de warrant."

"How?"

"Mister Ken Moize. And I got something else for you, you just going to love." He crooked his long skinny arm and darted it at the open door of Cloris Dollard's bedroom.

Inside, boxes were piled on the bare mattress of the queen-size bed. Cuddy loped around the bed and patted them. "I was just tidying up the lady's closet a bit waiting on you, because it didn't look to me like anybody'd paid it much mind, and this box here"—he tapped a cardboard crate labeled KORBEL CHAMPAGNE—"well, sir, it was full of little children's clothes still with the price tags on them. I guess she was planning on sending them off to her little grandchildren. So I wonder, maybe this was where she kept stuff she hadn't gotten around to mailing off to folks, like Mrs. Cadmean said she was going to. And so, what you're gonna love, Kemo Sabby, is what was down at the bottom." He reached in and his hand came back out holding a red Moroccan leather book, gold-stamped and gold-leafed. The blank pages of the diary fell open to a small clear envelope. Inside the waxy paper glittered the golden coin. Cuddy held it up so I could see the classic smooth brow of the profile of Liberty, and the date, 1839.

19

Still dressed, I fell asleep and didn't dream and didn't wake until a thudding jarred one eye open to see by the carriage clock beside my bed that it was five thirty. I staggered to the back window and looked down in the gray light at my yard where Cuddy Mangum stood pitching up snowballs at the side of my house. When I jimmied open the window, he yelled, "We got to go to the hospital. Luster Hudson's beat up Charlene Pope. Open your damn door, I've been kicking at it for ten minutes, haven't you got any ears?"

"Bad?" I called.

"Nothing permanent, but it doesn't sound pretty. Contusions, abrasions, hematoma, and as per usual. Mankind! My car's out front."

I couldn't tell if the sky was five thirty dusk or dawn; the snowdrifts looked higher now, and the tree branches sagged with white weight. I yelled at his back, "Is it tonight or tomorrow?"

Cuddy swiveled back around; wearing his neon-shiny parka in all that white, he looked like an astronaut on the moon. He said, "General, don't talk crazy when I'm working so hard to persuade people you're sane."

"Is it five thirty P.M.?"

"More or less. Come on! I've got four more cases besides this one, you know. This crime-doesn't-pay notion has never really gotten across to the populace. I'll wait in the car. Martha wouldn't come. She can't take the weather. Probably home biting the Professor. She's jealous."

As his heavy Oldsmobile crunched out through the snow, he said, "Don't you ever change your clothes? Want a Big Mac?" His hand rummaged in the bag beside him and brought out the dripping hamburger.

I said, "What happened to Charlene?"

"Okay, okay. Desk clerk, real pisspot at the Interstate Budget Motel, heard her screaming. 'Course, he hated to intrude, he hears so many folks screaming out there, so he turns up his TV. Then this pickup zooms off, cutting right through his boxwood shrubs, so now he goes to check, because screams is one thing and shrubs is another. So, when he notices the room door's open and the heat's escaping, he strolls on in and sees Charlene on the floor between the beds, and so he calls us in case she's dead and we ask him why he didn't bother to let us know. He's mostly torn up about who's going to pay for all this breakage and who's going to clean up all this blood. And I say, 'You are,' and then I sort of accidentally drive over some more of his boxwoods backing out in a hurry."

"How do you know it was Hudson?"

"Description matches: big, blond, ox-headed, and pig-eyed. Plus the plates match. He checked in there last night as 'L. Smith.' Catchy. Sounds like he was flashing a wallet as fat as Woodrow Clenny's on Saturday night." Woodrow Clenny was a legendary Hillston pimp, whose throat had been cut years back by one of his employees. Cuddy said, "So he shows at the Budget and then Charlene shows later in her van. Ask me why she went. I'll say this, when our pal Paula told us Charlene wasn't as dumb as Preston, she gave her too much credit."

"Hudson. Did you get him?"

"Nope. Three cars out looking. We leaned on the guy that's been feeding his dogs, but he swears all he knows is Luster says he's going to Asheville, and he pays him to feed them. We got a man on this guy anyhow. Well, too bad Little Preston didn't torch Luster's bike when Luster was sitting on it. Isn't that B.M. good, referring to the Big Mac, naturally?"

It was at least making me feel better than I had in a while.

Cuddy said, "I passed our coin to Ken Moize. It fits the description in Mrs. Cadmean's letter."

"And the one on Bainton Ames's list?"

"Yep. Worth more, lot more, now than Ames paid for it. Mr. Ratcher Phelps would weep to know the appreciation." Cheeks sucked in, he slurped at the semisolid milkshake through the straw. "And I wired a photo of the coin down to that Mr. Bogue in Atlanta to confirm. And let's see, what else. Mrs. Cadmean had no liquor, no drugs in her system. She made no toll call to North Hillston inviting your uncle over. Don't throw up your racquet yet, but I do believe Solicitor Moize is coming your way on the Senator. Dick Cohen wouldn't go for suicide; filed his report 'open pending investigation.' So, really all we need now is for Dollard to make a full confession and we've got him."

"How is Rowell?"

"Resting. No visitors. Fulcher tried hard to keep the newsboys out of the cookie bowl about Dollard's even being out there at the Cadmean lodge, but somebody (it wasn't you, was it?) leaked it to Bubba Percy at *The Star*." Steering with one skinny hand down the blank unrutted road, he dumped a fistful of french fries into his mouth.

"How's Briggs doing, Cuddy?"

"Oh, okay. Like I say, still at my place. After she got back to the lodge, she didn't feel up to staying out there alone. And I don't want to crowd her right now, so mind if I pass the night on that rickety couch with the catpaw feet of yours? If Lunchbreak's coming over for a snack, I'll step out in the yard."

"Fine."

"Junior Briggs's daddy called out there to the lodge after you left, huffing and puffing and tried to make her come stay with him at his house." Cuddy shook his head and sighed.

I said, "He wants her back."

"Well, hey, he ain't gonna get her."

"Who is, you?"

Frowning, he looked over at me. "That bother you? Let's get straight, General." His eyes stayed on me, asking me.

"No," I said. "Damn it, will you watch the road! At first I thought it would, but it doesn't bother me a bit."

He grinned. "Why the hell not? You got a nerve not being dismal. I'll tell you this, when God got around to making that woman, He'd finally figured out how to do it. He was *inspired* that morning. Then He fell into a slump and came up with Lunchbreak."

"Talk about sounding like a Loretta Lynn song! Do you *want* me to fight you for her?"

"Hell, no. You're too good-looking, and rich. Well, I thought you were rich. 'Course, now you're out of a job and gone crazy and let your clothes get all messy, I guess maybe I could take you on. Holy shit!" Suddenly he twisted the steering wheel. "Look at that Buick! That joker's lost it! Jackknifing, look at that, with the brake pedal to the floor!" Cuddy slowed, pumping gingerly, until the wide car ahead of us managed to spin out of its circle without leaving the road. "No chains, no brains," Cuddy snapped. "So hey, Mister Preppie, we gonna duel or what?"

"If Briggs is gettable, go get her, Cyrano."

"Say who?"

"Don't kid me, Cudberth, you already slipped up and told me you had an M.A."

"Well, that's true, but I didn't get it in French drammer of the *fan de sickle*. And anyhow, you want to know what a big nose really means?"

"It means jocular. Take the turn, take the turn, you're passing the hospital!"

Charlene's room was crowded. There were two other patients in it, both elderly, one watching The Merv Griffin Show, and the other telling her to turn it off. Around Charlene's bed were Paula Burgwin, Graham Pope, and Dickey Pope. No doubt, Preston Pope would have been there too if Cuddy had been able to talk Fulcher into releasing the suspect into his custody for the visit. But the law had Preston now. The grand jury had gone ahead with their indictment of the youngest

Pope for the murder of Cloris Dollard; bail was set at $250,000—which was a lot more CB's and cigarettes than Graham and Dickey had in stock to offer a bondsman as collateral. Joe Lieberman hadn't even tried to negotiate.

By the bed, Graham, hairy and bear-big, was shouting. "Now, God damn it, Charlene, you tell me who did this to you and I'm gonna kill the son of a bitch!"

"I'm gonna kill him too," said Dickey from the other side of the tilted bed. He had a comb and a pair of pliers sticking out of the pocket of a black satin cowboy shirt with roses sewn across the yoke. Any inconsistency between their vaunts to avenge Charlene now, and the fact that only days ago both these Popes had described her to us as the whoring bitch whose head they planned to bash in—for breaking Preston's heart, and then squealing on him to the cops for pure spite—was obviously not troublesome to either.

In the chair beside the bed, Paula Burgwin, plump and teary, sat holding Charlene's hand. Charlene's face on the snowy pillow was red with cuts and bruises except for where a white bandage swaddled her nose. Hard red lines were painfully distinct across her throat. The worst was her eyes—they were gorged with blood so red that no white showed, and black circles puffed around their sockets. Her right hand was in a cast. Paula kept patting her left one.

I had to swallow a few times before I said, "Christ, Cuddy," and they all looked at us coming into the room.

Graham puffed up in his huge down vest. "Y'all get out of here!"

"Get out of here!" echoed Dickey.

Tears ran over the sides of Paula's round cheeks. She said, "They want to help, is all."

"Shit!" Graham was wheezing like a bellows. "Help send my little brother to the chair. Mangum, they get my brother, I'm gonna kill you, I'm telling you now."

"Kill 'em both," Dickey said. "Let's bash 'em, come on!"

"Call the police!" shrieked the old woman in the next bed, her stick-thin arm waving her IV tube so jerkily I had to grab at the swaying stand. I stepped over and told her, "It's all right, ma'am. We *are* the police. Excuse us, please." And I pulled closed the white ring-curtain that partitioned the room.

Cuddy said, "Graham, cut this shit. The sad fact is Preston has signed a statement that he picked up that silverware on Wade."

"It ain't true. He never saw it. He knows better'n lie to me."

Cuddy nodded fast. "I wish he'd known better'n tell so many different stories to Captain Fulcher downtown, 'cause it does have a way of giving the impression of a lie."

Graham weaved toward Charlene. "He did it for this goddamn bitch here. Trying to save her ungrateful whoring ass. Excuse me, Paula."

Cuddy whistled. "For Charlene? That's noble. That's not brainy, but that's noble. You hear that, Charlene?" He moved to the bedhead now and spoke softly. "Lord, lord, Charlene. I'm real sorry. Now, I want to hear you tell me who did this to you."

Graham yelled, "She won't tell us. I swear she's in on the goddamn fix."

Charlene's lips moved stiffly until she could whisper, "Get fucked, Graham."

Cuddy smiled. "That's my girl! You haven't lost your sweet-talking ways. Now, how did this bad mess happen?"

She stared at the ceiling. Finally she managed to mumble, "I went to bed and I woke up this way."

Cuddy said, "Come on, tell me, because the fact is, I already know."

Her head moved slowly, painfully, away from us, and the hand in the plaster cast hid her face.

Cuddy said again, "Come on, sweetheart; after Luster finished showing you what a real man he was, where did he go?"

Now Graham swelled almost to the ceiling. "Luster! God damn it, I knew it!"

"Let's go get him," hollered Dickey.

I blocked the door while Cuddy called, "Whoaa, boys. Back up."

"Are you sure you're the police?" came the reedy voice from behind the curtain. "I think I ought to call the nurse."

"Go ahead," Paula snapped. "I sure can't get her to come for me."

I asked Graham, "Do you know where Luster Hudson is? Because we don't."

"He's no place where I can't find him!"

"Graham!" Paula stood up, tugging down on her sweater, then raising her small pretty hands so the charms jingled high as her voice. "Graham! You listen to me for once. What good's getting killed gonna do?"

Dickey said, "Paula, cram it, who asked you?"

Graham knocked him on the back of the head. "Shut your mouth, Dickey!" Then he tried to hug Paula, rumbling, "Little lady, don't you worry about me."

She said, "I'm not, you damn goon."

"She's just all upset," Graham explained to us. "Paula has a heart just as soft as a little baby bird."

Paula replied, "It's not as soft as your head."

Finally we succeeded in pushing the Pope men out into the hall, and I said to Graham, "All right, if you find Hudson, you'll call Mangum, deal?"

Dickey sneered. "Y'all bring a bag to put the pieces in, and bring one that don't leak."

Graham said, "Dickey, will you shut your mouth? Now, listen here to me, Mangum. Charlene planted that crap on Preston. I know it. I talked to him serious today, and he never saw it. The way I see it now is Luster made her do it."

I said, "I'm getting the same feeling."

Graham swayed back and forth above our heads, his hair and beard brown shiny tangles. "So, here it is. I'm gonna find Luster Hudson for you and I'm gonna leave that son of a bitch just about enough teeth to talk through to tell you he made her do it. And then you send me Preston home! Come on, Dickey!" Down the green hall they stomped, twice the size of the old women in robes who clutched the arms of bored nurses and shuffled inch by inch along, trying by constant motion to keep away from death. I watched them, lit a cigarette, and slumped against the wall. Finally, I said, "Hell. It fits. The beating, the money. I think Graham's telling the truth about Preston; Preston's covering for Charlene."

"Yep, Preston's the Duke of Windsor, okay. Well, getting your Harley incinerated and even the *tips* of your fingers shaved off could make a fellow less churlish than Prince Luster want to get even. Okay, if Luster and Charlene planted it, did they know who it belonged to?"

I told Cuddy about the encounter with Sister Resurrection and her intimation that she'd found the earring at the Tucson Lounge. "According to Preston, remember, that's where Luster and Charlene hung out every night."

Cuddy said, "Them and every other honky-tonk freak in Hillston.

You better put that cigarette out before a nurse asks me to arrest you."

"Well, I don't think Charlene knew about the murder until she heard it on TV, just like Paula said. Question is, what about Luster? Where'd he get all that cash the motel clerk saw?"

"Selling dogs?"

I felt sick. "It was just robbery all along."

"Hold on." He yanked at his hair for a minute. "Dollard might still have unloaded the stuff. Or, Luster could have been working for Dollard. Or for somebody."

"Or Luster could have killed Cloris all on his own. You just saw his hands dented into Charlene's throat in there!"

Cuddy nodded. "He's mean enough. And dumb enough."

I thumped back hard against the wall.

"Calm down," Cuddy muttered. "Now, another thing is, this could all be separate from what happened to Joanna Cadmean, or what happened to Bainton Ames, too, okay? And maybe it's not separate. We don't know." He went back into the room, and crushing out my cigarette on the sole of my shoe, I followed him.

The two elderly patients had reconciled their differences and were both quietly watching a game show in which couples clawed their way to the stage for the chance to guess behind which curtain waited the price-tagged paraphernalia of a better life.

Paula was leaning over Charlene, still stroking her hand. Bending down beside them, Cuddy said, "Charlene, listen. Wanting to protect that pig Hudson would be real stupid. Wanting to protect yourself from that pig by freezing us out would be real stupid too. And you're not stupid. We're the only ones can help you."

The red, horrific eyes moved from his face to mine. "Sure," she hissed, flinching, her lips held still. "Like Shirley."

Paula explained. "She means a friend of ours seven or eight years ago, and the thing is, Shirley asked the police to help her because her ex wouldn't leave her alone and said he had a knife and all, and the police told her they couldn't get into it until Jack *did* something. He had to do it first, is what they said."

Charlene turned her eyes, acerbic and dry, back to us as Paula added, "Well, what happened was, Jack killed her. She bled to death right there on her floor."

Cuddy nodded, "Okay, I remember when that happened, Charlene, and if Shirley'd come to me instead of whoever she went to, it *wouldn't* have happened. But this is different. Understand that. Okay? Now, we can go two ways. One is, you tell us where Luster went, and we lock him up on felonious assault. Two is, you don't, and we lock you up as a material witness. Both ways, Luster's not going to be able to get to you."

She just looked away.

I stepped in front of Cuddy. "Charlene, would you like a cigarette?" She didn't say no, so I lit one and held it to her lips and moved it away and then back again while she smoked. Then I said quietly, "You know, we're not the only ones who want to protect you. It sounds like Preston does too. He's risking a murder charge for you. I don't know how much you have to forgive him for—quite a bit, probably—but it does look as if he's forgiven you beyond what maybe most men would go. Is that fair? I don't mean just that you left him. I mean he must know Luster forced you—I think he did force you—to plant that silverware in the Pope house, and then call the station so we'd come out and pick him up. But I don't think you knew what that silverware would mean to us. Because Luster lied to you. You didn't know the silver was connected with a murder. If he's told you you're an accessory, he's lying. I don't think you are."

She kept staring at me as I put the cigarette back to her swollen lips.

I went on, quietly, "And so, maybe it's not Luster Hudson that's the better man. You think?".

As I smiled down at her, tears welled over the bruised eyes.

"Charlene." My voice dropped quieter. "Luster just wasn't what you thought he'd be. That's all. Listen. I've made the same mistake. God, we all have. But I'm very sorry it had to cost you so much." I held the cigarette down to her again. "Now, everything's going to be all right. That's a promise. And so would you mind if I just ask you this? Will you tell me, do you know where Luster is now?"

I waited, and finally her head shook no, almost too slightly to see.

"Or where he *might* have gone?"

Another no.

I leaned closer. "He called you to come to the motel. And you went because you were afraid not to?"

After a longer wait, her head moved slowly up and down.

"Yes. And you were right to be afraid. . . . Here. Look, would you like a sip of your juice here?" I put out the cigarette and placed my hand behind her head and carefully raised it and held the paper cup to her lips. Her eyes, still filled with the unfallen tears, stayed on mine. "You brought him some clothes to the motel? And what else? The rest of the stolen property?"

Her head moved no in my hand, her eyes frightened.

"You didn't know what you were bringing?"

Then, after a moment, she struggled to whisper, "A gym bag kind of. Locked. Had to pick it up from somebody."

"All right," I told her, nodding. "Thank you. Good. Will you say who? . . . No? All right. That's all right." I let her head back down on the pillow, but kept my hand on her hair. "We'll put that aside. Charlene, why did Luster beat you? Did you tell him that you'd been talking to us, and that we were looking for him?"

She nodded yes, and I kept on smoothing her hair back from her forehead.

"And did you tell him you were scared maybe he had killed Mrs. Dollard, and that's why he had the silverware?"

She stared at me, her mouth quivering.

I said, "Were you really with him the night Mrs. Dollard died? It's all right that you said you were before. Just tell me the truth now, just go on."

Charlene's unhurt hand was kneading the starched white sheet. She looked at Paula and Paula murmured, "Tell him," and then Charlene's head turned back to me and she shook it softly no.

I nodded. "You weren't with him. All right. Charlene, did Luster Hudson kill Cloris Dollard?"

The tears now spilled over her eyelids and slid down into the bandage. She winced as the salt of the tears touched her broken skin. Finally, her chest moved and she whispered, "He said he didn't, but I swear he did. . . . The guy gave me the gym bag. Ron Willis."

Paula squeezed Charlene's hand. I stepped back and said, "You did the right thing, Charlene. I want to thank you. All right? You rest now, and Paula'll be here with you." Paula nodded vigorously. I bent back down to the bed. "And we'll have an officer right outside this door. Hudson's never going to hurt you again. I'm giving you my word. Now you go back to sleep. Good night. We'll leave you alone now."

Back out in the hall, Cuddy caught up with me near the nurses' station and said as we went down in the elevator, "My my my. That was fine, Justin." He gave his low, windy whistle. "Now, why can't I get a bedside manner like that? You get that from your dad? I almost fell into a trance myself just looking on. A brain of steel is just not doing the trick for me; what you need in this world is a silver tongue."

When he returned from calling headquarters, I was slumped down in a sofa in the main-lobby lounge. I said, "If I hadn't been so damn sure, so *blind*, maybe Charlene wouldn't be up there like that."

"Well, hey, what about me? Don't hog all the guilt. You told me to pull her in, remember? And what about *Charlene*? She could have told us about Luster any time she wanted to. Okay, so we find Hudson and see what's in that bag. And we find Willis. And we don't know Dollard is out. He sure isn't out of the running on the Mrs. Cadmean case."

I said, "I think I can give you the plate numbers for Ron Willis." I found the piece of paper in my wallet. "WY-2252."

"You sure you're not psychic?"

"He tailed me out to C & W, and was very interested in my talk with Charlene out there. He knows Hudson. But he may not have any more to do with it than the gym-bag transfer."

"My, you keep busy. Okay, I'll put in a call."

"Let's go over to C & W. He works there."

"You work too many hours for a man's already been fired."

"I haven't been fired."

"Well, General, let's just say, you're in the cannon and the match's mighty close to your balls. You took me a little too literally when I advised you to get lonesome. Actually, what you need is some friends in high places. You need to . . ."

Then I saw the plaid parka spinning in through the main doors. I introduced Cuddy to Alice MacLeod at the information desk. She said the hospital had called the plant to check on Charlene's insurance. We waited for her while she went up to visit, and then followed her back to the mills. Ron Willis had not shown up for work. Nor did he ever return to his apartment, across the street from which Cuddy and I sat waiting for him in the cold Oldsmobile.

Late that night, while I threw blankets and sheets on my couch, Cuddy started winking his eyes and making *V*'s with his long skinny fingers, and he said, "Well, you are smooth. You want some advice?"

"No."

"Here it is. Marry her."

"Who?"

"Red MacLeod."

"I told you. I just met her. Good Christ, you're always trying to get everybody married. You and my mother. You go ahead without me, all right? What do you want, a double wedding out in my backyard?"

"Well, hey, wouldn't that be a sweet thing?" He snapped off his galoshes and slid his feet out of his Hush Puppies loafers. Both his big toes stuck out of holes in his socks. "But let's hold off till the snow's not so deep. Because I want Briggs to wear some high-heeled sandals. I just love that kind."

"What in the world makes you think she's going to marry you?"

Shaking blankets out on the couch, he said, with no smile, "Faith, hope, and that poor lady, Mrs. Cadmean. I asked her. While Briggs was getting on her coat. And she said, yes, as a matter of fact, she had that feeling. Oh, well, okay, I believe her, why not?"

"No reason."

That night I dreamt again of Joanna; she was going to marry Rowell, in the white dress she had died in.

At noon the next day I hurried past Sergeant Hiram Davies at the switchboard while he was looking down at his bologna sandwich; he never went out for lunch, fearful he'd be forced to retire if he left his desk. At the end of the hall I waved in at Cuddy Mangum (eating a loaf-long grinder while talking on the phone), then stepped inside my office and shut the door. Everything was the same there; somehow I'd imagined the room would be redecorated, or mossy with cobwebs.

Everything was the same with the case, too. Neither Luster Hudson nor Ron Willis had yet been found. Preston Pope still was in custody. Rowell Dollard still was not. But when the grand jury met again on Monday, they seemed likely now to decide Rowell should be charged. There was simply too much evidence. Foremost was the long letter. It was indisputably in Joanna Cadmean's handwriting. The Liberty coin found in Cloris Dollard's diary was indisputably the same model that Bogue had been shown by Bainton Ames that long-ago summer night. Ken Moize, who had asked me this morning to come to his office, also told me the coroner had ruled out accidental death for Mrs. Cadmean— on the assumption that the balcony rail was too high for her to have fallen over unintentionally, especially on crutches, moving slowly. Between the other two possibilities—homicide or suicide—the coroner had elected not to choose. I said that one thing troubled me: Why had she, so indifferent to her beauty, been so beautifully dressed that night if she weren't expecting anyone? "So what? Maybe she gussied up for Mangum."

This morning Ken Moize, an eagerly earnest native Midwesterner, had his helmet on, and an exalted look; he was prancing to joust, just as soon as someone handed him a long enough lance and a wide enough shield. Moize had wanted me in his office by ten to give him a full briefing on my investigation of Bainton Ames's death, as well as any theories I had about Cloris Dollard's, and Joanna Cadmean's. With his tape recorder spinning, it felt a little less lonesome off the deep end.

I'd had a number of other phone calls this morning after I'd come back from the diner, and my third breakfast with Alice. Ratcher Phelps had called. Rowell Dollard had called. Both wanted to see me. The third call was from Lawry Whetstone, whose secretary I'd asked to tell him to get in touch. He said, small world, that I wanted to see him, because he wanted to see me. Lawry didn't say what he wanted to see me about, but I assumed I knew—he wanted to accuse me of having an affair with his wife, Susan. And so we agreed to meet at my office at one thirty; my office was more convenient for him since he was eating downtown, and more comfortable for me since I didn't want this talk to happen in my house. I didn't want it to happen at all. I'd been expecting his call for months, and worrying about it, and feeling guilty about it, and imagining how I was going to respond to it. But the call had never come.

And now, just when it was clear to me that Susan and I were no more real together than mannequins embracing in a store window, just when I had begun worrying and feeling guilty and imagining how I was going to get *Susan* to admit we didn't care enough about each other to risk the waste and hurt—now here came Lawry's call. Now the secret was out, shame wriggling me up on the scaffold even as the scars of the A were fading from my breast. As Lawry hung up, I found myself in a twitch of resentment—like the thief arrested on his way to return the stolen goods. For more than a year Susan had refused to leave her husband for me; now what was I going to do if, instead of demanding that I leave her alone, he announced that he was getting a divorce, and Susan was mine?

So, not much liking myself, I defiantly walked into my office, and waited. I had no idea what style of confrontation to expect. Lawry and I had, of course, met; we'd even played tennis. But I avoided him: if I saw him in the club locker room, I'd go home without changing my clothes; if I saw him at a cocktail party, I'd keep to the other side of the crowd. This was to be our first and probably our last private conversation.

Lawry Whetstone surprised me. Sleek and Florida-blond and cruise-tan as his wife, he breezed in and sat down on my black wood chair and comfortably rubbed the pastel checks of his wool jacket against the LUX ET VERITAS insignia on its back. He had a great deal of rich hair close-trimmed in back, and a deep dimple in the middle of his chin. His weak feature was a bobbed nose too short for his face, and he had a habit of pulling on it as if he could make it longer. He crossed his legs, looked briefly at his suede boot, and then briefly at me, and said, "How about this snow? Wouldn't you love to go cross-country skiing? Ever tried that? Sorry you couldn't make lunch. This new Italian place in the Monmouth Building, I've got to say, it was great. Some smart people are starting to do some smart things downtown. About time, right?"

I nodded. I was trying not to smoke. I was just waiting.

Lawry glanced appreciatively at his cashmere coat, which hung from my coatrack. "So maybe they'll turn old Hillston around," he said. "Look at what's happened in Richmond and Baltimore. Why not Hillston, right? Tear out all this old junk."

"I like the old stuff."

"Who doesn't?"

I could hear the pulse in my ears as I kept waiting.

"Okay," he grinned. "You're busy, I'm busy." Lawry stroked his close-trimmed sideburn with affection. "Anyhow, Susan says she told you Cloris Dollard mentioned me at that play, the night she died, about how she was feeling 'bad' or something about me?"

"Pardon?"

"Dollard's wife, right? Should have gotten in touch earlier, I guess, but who thinks these little things are going to matter. To be honest, I didn't connect the times right off. Because the damn thing is, I think I was trying to call her from Atlanta just about the time she died."

"What?" My pulse and the muscles of my face hurried to adjust to the news that Whetstone was apparently here not to talk to me about Susan, but to talk to me about Cloris Dollard. "You called Cloris Dollard Sunday, January ninth?"

"Right. Called her twice. The first time she said she was just leaving to go to the Hillston Playhouse—weren't you in that Shakespeare thing they did?—and so would I mind calling her back. So I did, around eleven, eleven fifteen, that night. No later. I crashed pretty early." He finished stroking his sideburn and went back to pulling on his nose. "Thing is, she didn't answer. Phone all of a sudden clicked off. Around eleven. You can check the time with the hotel; don't they keep tele phone records? I was returning her call. How this all got started was, she asked me to do her a favor. I guess that's what she was telling Susan she felt guilty about. I mean, I hardly knew her. Still, it's sort of a bummer hearing she got killed."

The Dollard phone transcripts for that Sunday had, I thought I recalled, included among Cloris's many long-distance calls, one to Atlanta, but given the department's premise that robbery was the motive for the crime, morning calls had not been followed up. I asked, "What favor?"

"Right. Well, I was down in Atlanta on business, and C & W, I guess, told Mrs. Dollard I'm staying at the Hyatt Regency, so she catches me in on Sunday morning. I was half-asleep, to be honest. It was damn funny. Out of the blue." Then Whetstone sat back with a silky rimple of his pastel suit, and waited expectantly for me to invite him to continue. He had an effective rhetorical trick of luring you on by pausing. When I said, "And?" he recrossed his legs and told me that Cloris Dollard had called him for advice: An Atlanta textiles firm had approached her recently about purchasing any drawings there might still be in her possession executed by her first husband, Bainton Ames, shortly before his death; designs for an innovative type of loom that was supposed to cut costs and labor.

"Why should they want a design at least fifteen years old?" I asked.

"Oh, back then they couldn't be bothered with energy efficiency, you know; they all thought Ames was some kind of half-baked genius-type nut." Whetstone opened his eyes wide to symbolize madness. "But now it's the thing; everybody's into saving power, et cetera. So, okay, Mrs. Dollard digs out these old Ames folders, but naturally she doesn't have the foggiest what she's looking for, so she zips over to old Cadmean here in town, and he tells her anything Bainton Ames designed belongs to *him*. And he grabs the papers away from her. So, that was that. Mind if I smoke? Ever try these Ultra Lights? Pretty damn good."

I pushed over an ashtray (one I'd made up in the mountains), and Lawry slid from his pocket a leather-and-gold cigarette case that was exactly like the one Susan had given me and I could feel now in my breast pocket being beaten on by my heart. Why had old Briggs Cadmean lied to me by saying Cloris had never brought him any designs? Why lie? I asked Lawry, "What does this have to do with her calling you?"

"Oh, I'm C & W, too." He gave me a collegial shrug. "She liked to ask men's advice; you know the type. So, okay, she says she's started getting p.o.'d at old Briggs; he's such a senile old bullshitter, I'm not surprised. So, he tore her head off about the designs, and she's p.o.'d, et cetera, you know: 'Who is he to tell *me*?' She's the inventor's widow, right? And what she wants to know is, does Cadmean really have the right to stop her from selling them."

"Well, she had the copies she'd made," I said. "Did he grab the copies?"

"Copies? Oh, I guess, well, I didn't know about that."

Staring down at my note pad, I kept doodling the word *Cadmean*, making stairs of it. "My mother was with Cloris when she had some copies made. She mentioned it."

"Nice tie," Whetstone said suddenly. I looked up and saw him studying my chest. "Dior?"

I flipped the cloth over and read the label. "Valentino. What exactly did Cloris want your advice about?"

"Nice tie. She wanted me to get in touch with the textiles guy who'd approached her. I said I would, and I'd call her back. Just to be a nice guy, right?"

"Was this a Cary Bogue at Bette Gray Corporation?"

He grinned as if I'd just told a clever joke. "How'd you know Bogue?"

"He was with Bainton Ames the night of his death; back in 1968. I've been looking back at the reports."

"Right." Whetstone nodded. "I actually gave Bogue a call on this Mrs. Dollard thing, and he mentioned that drowning episode. Did you know this? Pretty interesting. Ames was so pissed then at old Briggs Cadmean, he was planning on walking out. That's why Bogue was up there, negotiating about getting him to come down to Atlanta. Ames had come up with some new rapier-type loom, I guess."

I had to get out of my chair and start walking. Why hadn't Bogue mentioned this to Stanhope at the time? Had Cadmean known Ames was leaving him? Walter Stanhope's rasping whisper came back. *I were you, I'd be leery of the man with the strings.*

Whetstone gave me the ingratiating smile that he followed with the pause.

"Leaving why?" I asked. "Did Cadmean know?"

"Couldn't say who knew. Way before my time. The story I heard was that Ames had a burr in his butt about old Briggs's roughing up the union types that were agitating back then. Ames—now, this is all according to Bogue—Ames was trying to pressure the old man into going union by holding the designs out on him, and when Mr. C. called his bluff, Ames said he was taking his ball and was going to go play elsewhere. You know how it was in the old days. A little sandbox and everybody kicking sand. A more personal-type life-style, know what I mean?" Whetstone leaned smoothly forward and twisted his cigarette out half smoked. His eyes were as blue and as empty as the sky, and they were the precise color of his pocket handkerchief. I had been dreading the possibility that I would *like* Lawry Whetstone. But I didn't like him.

Now he smiled broadly, his teeth slightly bucked and intensely white in his tan face. "The thing is," he said, "it's all so rinky-dink. I mean, about the dumb designs. You know? Bogue told me it was no big deal; sure, he was curious to see the drawings, but what he really wanted was an intro to talk about buying some kind of coin collection. He's a coin-type nut. But old Briggs, that's just the sort of small beer he has a hernia over, the loom thing. How the designs belonged to him. That man is so out of it. And too full of himself to step down."

I sat back. "What do you mean, out of it?"

Whetstone pulled on his nose and then glanced at his nicely buffed nails. "Ever met our Mr. Cadmean?"

"Yes."

"Well, then you know what I mean. How he *loves* every square inch of C & W. How FDR shook his hand for beating the 'Krauts and Japs' with his parachutes. Et cetera. Right? Whereas, news flash. We *are* Germany and Japan. Old Briggs hasn't got even a rudimentary grasp of what's going on at C & W these days. But you'd have to kill the old shit to get him out."

I leaned back on the rear legs of my chair. "That's not what I hear from him. He says he's down there all day every day."

Whetstone laughed, his tan fingers laced around one knee; on his right hand, a gold college ring. "Right! And the peacock spreads its tail on NBC every day too. But it doesn't negotiate the deals, now does it? I like to say, 'Corporations aren't made out of whole cloth.' Obviously, if we'd counted on the cotton mills for capital, Chink imports would have closed C & W down years ago, the way they have most of the old man's buddies. Nobody wants to tell him, but his beloved mill is just a dinosaur we have to work around until we can cart off the bones." His grin invited me to share in this corporate fun, but instead I tore the scribbled note off the pad, and asked him to repeat the times and contents of his calls to Cloris Dollard on the day of her death. He did so affably.

Then he surprised me by leaning over my desk and picking up the silver letter opener Susan had given me. It was the most recent of her gifts and the one that had prompted my asking her again to stop buying me things, and her telling me again that one of the advantages of having an affair was it gave her someone else to shop for. Shopping was her occupation. Now Lawry tapped his forefinger on the silver blade's tip. "Are you in a real hurry?" he asked. "Susan give you this?"

I kept my eyes on his, their blue blankness impossible to interpret. "Yes," I answered. "She did."

"Nice." He placed it back at a pleasant angle to the rock crystal desk-garniture. "I've got one too," he added. "Listen, have you got a minute, Justin? To be honest, this Dollard thing was a kind of excuse to come in."

Here, then, it came. And what I couldn't understand was why he was smiling the energetic salesman's grin that was too kinetic to be so close to the eyes' blue blandness.

"Justin," he said, and I felt his body as well as his voice hone toward me. "Justin, Susan really enjoys herself with you. She really does. The thing with you's been a good deal for her. You and I have never laid it out, but let's take it as programmed in—and filed. And go from there. Right?"

My throat felt dry as sand, dry as mornings in the mountains when I would awaken to the faint jiggle of the nurse's tray and wonder why she, a stranger, should come with such efficient comfort into my es-tranged delirious room. It took me a minute to wet my throat enough to reply. "I don't know what to say, Lawry. I hadn't realized you knew about my relationship with Susan. I can only—"

He broke in cheerfully. "Come on! Let's be real! This is today. You knew Susan and I have always been open about all our affairs."

I reached into my jacket for my cigarettes. "No, I assure you. I didn't know you *had* 'affairs.'"

He grinned. "Well, you knew of at least one affair that one of us was having." And he pointed at the gold-trimmed case in my hand. "Come on, Justin, everything's fine, not to worry, okay? Long as no-body's got herpes." He guffawed, then looked at me. "You know, Susan told me you weren't going to make this too easy."

"Make what easy?" The sweat was starting across my upper lip, and heat pulsing into my hands. "Make *what* easy?"

Looking at his coat, he said, "Well, to be honest, what would you say to the possibility of a foursome? How does that strike you?"

"A foursome?"

"You know." He gave his nose a few short pulls, and turned to me and smiled.

"No, I don't." But I was beginning to suspect that I did, and the skin of my scalp warmed.

Whetstone's voice became confidential. "Look. I'd really enjoy getting something together, and so maybe you would too. I've got this gal I've been seeing, works in Personnel. She's pretty damn great, believe me. And we've tried it with another couple." He nodded at me encouragingly, as if he were selling me insurance. "It worked out fantastically, just great. So, okay, what I'm proposing is, how about getting her together with Susan and you and me, and see what happens? Susan says fine with her—you know her, she's adventuresome, right?— but she didn't think you'd go for it. But me, I like to say, nothing ventured, nothing et cetera. I promise," he laughed, "we won't do any coke around you. She tells me you really don't like getting into that. Okay?"

I stood up fast. "The answer's no."

Undismayed by my face, Whetstone rose from my father's old chair and advised me, "Remember the old cliché, don't knock it till. Think it over. Maybe you've already got somebody else you're into things with now. I don't know what your life-style is, but somebody new'd be okay with me, if it's okay with Susan. Does she know her? I mean, no real reason it has to be this gal I was mentioning before. Slash is slash, right?"

I hit him. I didn't know I was hitting him, I didn't know I'd come around the side of my desk to do it, until I was watching my fist fly into his jaw and seeing his tan complaisant face shoot backward, the mouth opening surprised. His head clattered loudly down the front of my file cabinet to the floor. From down there he rubbed his blue handkerchief over his jaw and then stared at it eagerly. There was no blood. After that, he looked up at me; his unclouded eyes giving no signal at all of what he might say. Then he bounced agilely to his feet, wiggled his jaw, and said, "What's with you? You some kind of S and M macho cop type or something? I'm beginning to wonder about Susan's taste."

"Me too," I said.

The doorknob turned, and Cuddy Mangum's head poked through. "Excuse me," he drawled. "I thought I heard the sound of violence. Y'all playing squash, or what?"

I said, "This is Mr. Whetstone. He just brought us some information."

"Sounds like it wasn't very good news," Cuddy said.

Whetstone pulled his cashmere coat off the rack, and wiggled his finger at Cuddy. "You ought to do something about this guy." He shook the finger at me. "He's a nut."

"Well, we'll give him some more shock treatments," Cuddy replied. "Let me walk you out, Mr. Whetstone. Our chief's in the hall, and he's not very stable either." He turned to me sternly. "Savile, go to my office."

I said to Lawry, "If you want to continue, I'm at your service."

"God Almighty," Cuddy muttered. "He wants to fight a duel."

21

Cuddy Mangum's cubicle was stacked with crates of paperback books, for which he had the same ravenous appetite that was set loose upon the candy bars and crackers whose boxes and cellophane wrappers littered the area near the wastebasket, giving his floor the look of a movie theater after a Saturday matinee. On one of his walls was a poster of Elvis Presley, and on the other a blackboard, and on the blackboard were scribbled notations of the sort always there, for Cuddy thought aloud with chalk, in what he called an academic way—although I'd often suggested that it was actually from detective films that he'd acquired his diagraming habit. This he admitted: "Well, hey, of course. How do you think the Indians learned how to sneak up on the buffaloes except from watching the dance? The whole twentieth century comes out of the movies—luvvv, everything, don't you know that? You're the smoking detective and I'm the chalking detective. I've got six channels, movies is all they show. Some of them are real *old* black and white ones; you'd like those."

Among the white hieroglyphs now on his board was this triangle:

Cuddy apparently had eliminated Rowell as a suspect in Cloris's killing on principles of schematic parallel structure. Despite his continual reminders to me that it is only in books that the same character commits all the murders, he was in his investigations strongly drawn to any congruity in modus operandi. Here not only the obvious significance of Rowell's presence at the scene on the nights of both Bainton Aimes's and Joanna Cadmean's deaths, and the significance of their both falling (or getting pushed) were figured in; he also had inscribed in his geometric angles the fact that there had been discussion on both nights (Ames at the restaurant to Cary Bogue, Mrs. Cadmean to me by letter) of the 1839 Liberty quarter-eagle coin that was subsequently found in Cloris Dollard's closet. He also seemed to think relevant the coincidence that both falls to death—separated by fifteen years —had taken place on the nineteenth of the month; the only fact in the cases that seemed to me to *be* just a coincidence.

I was studying his triangle when he loped back into his office and poked me pedagogically on the collarbone. "General Lee," he said, "you are on the hill at Gettysburg, and if you will look around you, most of the coats you see are blue."

I said, "Yours is gray." He had on again his new three-piece herringbone suit.

"You are not supposed to be here. You are particularly not supposed to be here whopping your girl friend's husband in the jaw, who by the way has just probably established Mrs. Dollard's time of death for us as about 11:07, which is the time he said her phone clicked off, and which is jest a leetle too quick for the Senator to have zipped in from Raleigh to kill her. However, I must say, I didn't like old Lawry either. He had too many teeth, and every one of them was perfect. On the other hand, why wasn't *he* hitting *you*? You're the adulterer. 'Course, I'm not too up on the customs of the porticos-and-polo set."

"Let's drop it," I said. "I've got to go. Rowell asked to see me this evening. I don't know what for. And Ratcher Phelps wants to see me too, so I'm going there first. Want to come? I'll explain in the car."

Pulling straight up on one of his many cowlicks, he looked like a lanky puppet dangling from his own hand. "Sorry," he sighed. "I've got an armed robbery, and an exhibitionist. And I have just returned from another little drive that was your idea, and that may be enough for me. But I had to testify in Raleigh anyhow, so . . ."

"You saw Burch Iredell? You got out to the vets' hospital?"

"Yep, I slid on over through the slurp and saw your old coroner for you about the Ames drowning. Hiram Davies neglected to give you an update on Mr. Iredell, because Time has bullied him around in the meanwhile, bad. I asked him if he could remember back fifteen years, he said he could remember back to the Flood. I said this was more like a lake. I asked him, Mr. Iredell, you have any thoughts about whether back fifteen years ago Mr. Bainton Ames (since you were coroner back then and you signed the official papers) might have been, unofficially, murdered, and if so, sir, by whom? Well, Mr. Iredell said he certainly did have a notion Ames was murdered. Said the man sitting across from us had done it. Said this man shot Ames with the same rifle he'd used on JFK."

"Come on," I said. "Are you making this up?"

Cuddy flopped down in his chair and threw his long legs over the edge of the metal desk. He sighed, "I wouldn't have the heart. You eat lunch? You tore out of the house so early to eat breakfast with the future governor, I bet you're hungry. You want that extra grinder? It's meatball. I'm losing my appetite from falling in love."

I ate the gooey sandwich, leaning my head over the wastebasket, while I told him why he'd better get back in touch with Cary Bogue, and while he told me more about the former Hillston coroner.

"Now, where the nurse wheeled Mr. Iredell out for us to have our little talk was the so-called recreation room of this veterans' hospital, which speaking as a vet, all I can tell you is, it's a funny way for a country to say, 'We appreciate it, boys,' because this particular snot-green-painted place was truly ugly and gotten all tumbledown and was el-cheapo for openers, and I sure wouldn't want to get re-created there —the reason being almost everybody I saw was about as scrawny and lost-looking as a plucked fowl escaped from Colonel Sanders. All this recreation room had was a little old black and white TV with furry channels, and some wornout jigsaw puzzle boxes of the Grand Canyon, and these plastic checkers that the fellow that had allegedly murdered Mr. Ames was playing a game of solitaire with. Now, this alleged murdering fellow didn't have any legs, had his pajamas folded over with safety pins, and he looked to me more the meditating type than your Mr. Iredell seemed to think he was, what with accusing him of killing Ames, JFK, the little children in Atlanta, plus being a North Korean spy who's been slipping into Iredell's room every night and stealing his desserts and planting electrodes in his head. Which the latter may be true, because your Mr. Burch Iredell, by the way, had a sort of sit-down disco movement to him, including his eyeballs, that didn't seem to wear him out at all." Still seated, Cuddy suddenly flailed himself about in palsied gyrations, his eyes spinning like Ping-Pong balls in a bingo hopper.

I said, "Will you quit kidding?" I had spent in the mountains many unending mornings in such a recreation room, among the checkers and the spasms, where each minute stretched like an orange pulling loose from the bough, too slowly to see it let go. I said, "Look, it's nothing to kid about."

Cuddy shook his head. "It ain't my joke, General. It's the Lord's. If you think that's kidding, you should have seen some of the fellows out there couldn't make it down the hall to get to this recreation room. Let's just leave it that your Mr. Iredell's opinion is not going to be much use to Ken Moize in a court of law. Because law's got no imagination." Cuddy blew out another long sad sigh. "Humankind," he said, "is breaking my heart." Then he shuddered off the subject, and scooted his chair over to a paper package lying on one of his book crates. "Now, tell me, which one of these do you think? Which goes better with my suit?" He pulled out two ties. "I'm trying to improve my image so I can get Briggs Junior to marry me. Women are always after you, and all I can figure is, it must be your clothes."

"They don't marry me."

"Oh, they will when you mean it. Come on, which one?"

The first of the ties looked like a summer lightning storm, and the other one had orange squares on it. I said, "Are you seriously asking me?" He nodded morosely. I took off my own tie and handed it to him. "This one," I said. "Trust me."

"That's what my ex—"

"I know, I know."

So I went by myself and tieless through snow now crunchy as brown sugar to see Ratcher Phelps in East Hillston at the Melody Store. Up front a young woman was clerking, and back among his pianos Mr. Phelps sat in his black suit and black patent leather shoes and sheer black nylon socks. He was playing a banjo and talking a song to himself, as solemn as a family lawyer at the reading of a will. He kept on with it as I walked toward him: "If you need a good man, Why not try me? . . ." His long spoon-curved nails plinked a last sharp chord as I finished the verse for him in a soft whistle, my ears going pink as I heard myself doing it. He said, "Hmmmm," his moist doleful eyes quickly blearing over a look of wry interest. "You know that tune, Lieutenant?" he asked.

"Yes, sir. 'Big Feeling Blues,' isn't it? I have it on a Ma Rainey record, with Papa Charlie Jackson playing banjo."

"Hmmmm." He placed the glittering instrument carefully on top of the spinet behind him, and gave a slide of his hand to his hair. The hair was a flat black color that looked dyed and straightened; he combed it with a deep side-part. "You like the blues?" he asked me. I nodded. He nodded back. He said, "I have it in my remembrance that a piano"—he skipped his hand, a diamond ring twinkling, over the spinet's keyboard—"that a piano is your particular favorite. Who do you like on blues piano?"

I told him, "I like Fletcher Henderson. Lovie Austin. Professor Longhair. I like this lady Billie Pierce a lot. I like mostly old blues."

He nodded in a stately way and repeated his oleaginous "Hmmmm," and then we rested with that.

"Well, Mr. Phelps," I began, "on the phone this morning you mentioned wishing to discuss this matter of reciprocity with me. Here I am." I sat down on a piano bench across from his.

Wetting his lips and pursing them a few times for practice, he said,

"Young man, I have deliberated in my mind, and I have gone to my heart and asked it. And I believe that your"—he paused, searching among the spinets for a word—"your misimpression about my business, which is the business you see here before you, and not the jewelry business, *was* a misimpression."

I smiled, nodding. "Mr. Phelps, I am here as a music lover. And I am here alone. And anything you may kindly choose to say will be held in the uttermost confidentiality. I give you my word."

He accepted it with five slow nods. "Let us then," he said, the voice warming, "let us then take a supposing. Suppose on that constitutional walk I believe I told you I have the habit of taking?"

"Yes?"

"Suppose those particular articles I believe you told me you were looking for, suppose they came to my notice, and the individual which they did not belong to, also came to my notice? Now, in such a supposing as that, what would be interesting to know is if you people have any renumeration in mind for the recovery of those lost articles . . . throwing in that unnamed individual for no charge?"

I gave him a very serious frown. "Mr. Phelps, Mr. Phelps. I thought we had already settled on your remuneration—when we came to our agreement on the matter of your nephew Billy, and his upcoming trial. Here you are raising the rent."

Like a minister of an old Ming dynasty, he stood up, small, portly, and sedate. "Billy," he said, "is my sister's baby. That poor widow grieves over her boy, and I in my heart.at night in bed I grieve over her, and a little extra re . . . muneration would go far to help ease her trials, and rent. That lost property is valuable property. According to you white people that lost it, now. I wouldn't know. Worth more than all you see before you."

I stood up too, and we studied each other. Meanwhile, at the front of the store, a fattish child with idolatrous eyes spluttered notes out of the brassy bright trumpet the clerk had taken down for him; his mother watched, pleasure and distress both in her face.

Finally, I asked Ratcher Phelps if he had the stolen jewelry and coins with him. He said this was a music store. I asked him if he knew where the goods were, and who had them. He asked me to find out what the reward would be if he answered that question, and then ask it again. He offered me another of his suppositions: It would be astute of me to hypothesize that the more quickly I returned with an agreeable figure, the more likely I was to be present at an upcoming rendezvous between Mr. Phelps and the unnamed seller of the Dollard property. I was to suppose that Unnamed had contacted Phelps out of an urgent need for immediate cash.

I asked, "Are we talking about a Mr. Luster Hudson?"

Phelps rubbed his topaz cuff link, big as a cat's eye, on the black sleeve of his other arm.

"Ron Willis?" I asked.

"Young man," said Ratcher Phelps, "we are talking about Ma Rainey and Billie Pierce." He picked up his banjo, cradling it across his dapper pouch. "And," he added, leading me to the front of the store, "up here let me call to your attention a book of Fats Waller's melodies that I am partial to, and I believe you would find them interesting to undertake."

With a hand on his shoulder, I stopped him. "Mr. Phelps, now, let's spell this out, all right? I get this money for you, and you've got to promise me I'm going to be there looking on when those coins are turned over to you."

His perfectly specious smile rippled over the deep black jowls. "Oh, young friend," he said. "Let's just play the tune. Let's not sing out all the words."

22

I don't like hospitals. My father liked the clarity of urgency there. I don't like the sterile smell, the sealed windows, the sharp quality of light and life insisted on. When I was a child, University Hospital meant to me the big square building that wanted my father to be in it most of his time, and that would call him away loudly out of his sleep, insisting that he return. As this building was also the ogre-haunted, inexplicable maze into which from time to time elderly relatives of mine would walk, never to come out again, simply to vanish from my life, I was always terrified that my father too would be snapped up by whatever monster crouched hungry behind some turn of the endless halls. He, a surgeon, always joked that no doctor and no nurse of his acquaintance would be caught dead staying in University Hospital as a patient; they knew too much to risk it. "Good Christ, Peggy," he'd say, "whatever happens, just keep me at home in bed and let me sniff chicken soup." But, of course, when my mother found him that first time, fallen over his desk in a coma, she brought him as fast as she could to the big building where they are supposed to know how to make the bad things stop happening. And years later, the ambulance that sludged through snow to the foot of Catawba Drive where I sat in the smashed car, holding my father, blood from my mouth sliding onto his unconscious face, that ambulance rushed him straight to University Hospital. And after six months more, he was caught dead there; while west in the mountains, in a hospital of recreation rooms, I was caught alive.

Rowell Dollard had once come to visit me in the mountains to tell me I was killing my father and was killing myself. Today I was coming to University Hospital to visit him, and hear him try to convince me he was not a murderer too.

Outside Rowell's door, Officer Wes Pendergraph sat reading *Sports Illustrated*. Inside on the angled pillows, the silver hair gleamed as if it really were indestructible metal not subject to the dissolution of color and flesh that had in two days withered my uncle's face. The face, gazing out the flat window, did not turn until I said, "Rowell."

"Justin. Well." His eyes moved toward me; in them, anger too weak for his customary passion. "Your mother telephoned me from Alexandria."

"Yes, I spoke with her too."

"What did she say to you?" Rowell asked.

I didn't say she'd called crying and bewildered; how could Joanna be dead, Rowell be her murderer, me be his accuser? And crying, asked, had my suspension from work been brought on by a relapse into an alcoholic madness? I told her only that it had not, and that other than so saying, I would not discuss with her the investigation of Rowell Dollard. "He's *family*, Jay," Mother had kept repeating. I said to Rowell now, "She is naturally distressed. She wants to come back to Hillston, but she has to stay with the children until Vaughan and Jennifer return from Antigua. She asked me to send flowers to Joanna's services." Actually, by Joanna Cadmean's will, there were to be no services, merely private cremation. Old Briggs was apparently making the arrangements.

"Will you sit down, please? I can't see you." Rowell's voice, once so heartily senatorial, was now faltering.

"All right." I pulled over the vinyl chair. "How are you feeling?"

"They've brought my blood pressure down. But there's an embolism lodged in my lung."

"Yes, I was told. I'm sorry."

"I'm not supposed to laugh too hard and send it to my brain. That is, under the circumstances, hardly likely . . . You've been taken off the investigation."

"Yes."

"I would still like to talk with you about it."

"As you say, the matter is out of my hands. If your lawyers think you should talk to anyone, talk to Ken Moize."

Dollard inched up farther on the pillows. "I said I want to talk to *you*."

"All right."

"I did not kill Cloris! I cannot believe that you could have thought I did."

I looked at him a long time, then I said, "I owe you an apology for having believed otherwise."

Dollard let his breath out abruptly, as if startled to realize his lungs were filled.

I added, "But it is Mrs. Cadmean's murder the prosecutors are taking before the grand jury Monday."

"I am not guilty of that, either. She died exactly as I told you."

"Would you believe it if *you* were still solicitor! Does it look like suicide to you?"

"No." His protuberant eyes fixed on mine. "No. It looks like murder. It *was* murder. Her own."

"Her own?"

His head raised from the pillow, his neck veinous. "Yes! Listen to me. Joanna murdered herself . . . so that I would be convicted."

"Jesus, Rowell! That's preposterous."

"Is it? I've lain here thinking about everything, and I know it's so." His voice quickened, and he stopped himself, then began again slowly. "She must have been planning it for years. She planned it perfectly."

His eyes closed shut but moved restlessly beneath the lids as he went on in the strange thin voice. "You, Justin, were the perfect one to use. The perfect one to go to first."

"What do you mean by that?"

His head lay motionless on the pillow, the eyes shut. "You are a sympathetic person. And an imaginative one. You are too young to know many of the circumstances of the past, but close enough to care. You are a relative of mine. And you don't like me."

Neither of us spoke. Outside, the clouds filled with a rusted rose color, and day's light slipped lower in the room. From the hall filtered to us the rumbling screak of tray carts.

Then Dollard spoke again, his voice still as the time. "Joanna hated me. She never forgave me for breaking off with her. It was . . . unacceptable to her. After I ended it, while she was still at the university, she called me . . . continually, at all hours, pleading, threatening. She was *obsessed*. One time, she demanded I come to her dormitory room or she would cut her wrists. I refused, I didn't believe her. I was wrong. I found out she had nearly died—*would* have died if her roommate had not returned unexpectedly from home. She has done this before, Justin. Don't you see?" He stopped, pacing his breaths with concentrated effort, while outside the red darkened.

I stood by the sealed window to watch night come on. I said, "You are telling me Mrs. Cadmean plotted her suicide to make it look as if you had murdered her?"

"Yes."

"*She* took the phone from the hook, *she* broke the door chain in the study, *she* tore off her own watch?"

"Yes."

"And your scarf, in her hand?"

"She must have picked it up in the hall. I didn't notice. I was terribly upset, Justin! God! She led me up to the study. Do you think if she had been trying to get away from me—on crutches!—I couldn't have caught her?"

"She could have been already upstairs. You could have forced her upstairs."

His eyes stared at me, but were seeing back to that night. "She stood there, and *smiled*. And said, 'This time I am leaving *you*. And this time *you* will suffer.' And then . . . she jumped."

"Again, Rowell, we're back to, why were you there? She did not call your house on the nineteenth. That's a fact."

His forefinger knuckle rubbed against his lips. "No, she didn't. I had phoned her earlier myself; I admit that. I was furious that she had been in my home. That she'd manipulated you into bringing her there. It was then she told me if I didn't come over that night . . . She threatened me . . ."

I looked around at him. "With what? That's the point, isn't it?"

He pushed the knuckle hard into his upper lip.

I said, "Rowell, you read the letter Mrs. Cadmean wrote me."

"*Lies!* Incredible lies. That's when I knew how long she had planned this . . . monstrous . . ." His voice faded.

"You know we have checked, and she did come to Hillston last summer, and there is a record of a call from your number to hers on St. Simons Island at the time she said Cloris called?"

"For God's sake, can't you understand! *I* called her, to demand that she stop her vile accusations to Cloris. *She would never let me go.*" Rowell's voice itself sounded penned by a furious frustration. "When she married Charles Cadmean, I thought that would be the end of it, but, no, the letters . . . *demented* letters, Justin . . . kept coming. Years later, after Cloris and I married, they still kept coming. This has gone on half my life! I don't mean all the time. But she besieged us. It was maddening. We never knew when. Years even could go by. We would forget. Then late at night, the phone would ring and it would be her again. That voice! You have no idea. . . . Upsetting Cloris dreadfully. Telling Cloris how she'd been made to suffer. Telling her I had . . ." He pressed his hand against his forehead.

I said quietly, "Had killed Bainton Ames?" He said nothing. "We know you were at the Inn the night Bainton died. Why did you take his coin? Good Christ, Rowell, why did you *keep* it!"

Straining, Dollard pulled himself upright on the bed. "Justin, Joanna *put* that coin there in Cloris's closet two days ago. She must have. That's why she made you bring her to my house. She was upstairs alone, wasn't she?"

I sat back down. "And where is she supposed to have gotten it?"

"It's a duplicate."

"No, it's genuine."

"For God's sake, Bainton's was not the only one of that series, was it!

There must be dozens of them. You have to find out where she bought it. Can't you see how *long* this woman has been plotting to ruin me? She wants to kill me!"

I said, "She's the one who's dead, Rowell. That's a rather extreme form of revenge."

"I tell you, she was psychotic!"

I shook my head. "Everything you tell me, especially if true, especially if she did hate you this bitterly, all the more reason for you to get rid of her."

"*She killed herself.* Justin, Justin, please. She actually believed that I would come back to her! When she spoke to me at Cloris's grave, she actually believed that now I would come back to her. She had *waited.* I told her she was out of her mind. *She killed herself.*"

Behind us the door whooshed silently open and a young doctor, an East Indian with deep, placid eyes, entered the room. "Sir," he said in a purr, "I must say to go. Senator Dollard must be staying undisturbed." With long, attenuated fingers he lifted Rowell's wrist to take his pulse. I told the doctor I was just leaving. "Good, then," he murmured.

Passive and quiet in the hands of the hospital, Rowell looked up at me. He said, "Will you help me, Jay? She plotted against you, too."

I said, "Do you have any of these demented letters she's supposed to have written you?"

He shook his head angrily. "Of course not. I tore them up. Why should I keep them!" He saw that I did not believe him, and closed his eyes.

At the door, I asked, "One thing, Rowell. Excuse me, Doctor. Would you be willing to give any monetary reward for the recovery of Cloris's jewelry, and the coin collection?"

"Do you know where they are?"

"I'm in contact with someone who thinks he can buy them."

"Is this coming from you on your own? Or from the department?" Rowell's voice was rising again, and the doctor held up an admonishing hand at me.

I said the department had no knowledge at this point of my informant.

"Send him here to me."

"I can't do that," I said.

He brushed his hand irritably at the doctor, who was trying to wrap a blood-pressure band around his arm. Then he muttered, "Five thousand dollars. If he'll bring those things directly back here to *me*. They're mine."

"Just one thing more. Did Cloris ever mention being approached in the last year by a man named Cary Bogue, who wanted to see some technical designs Bainton left behind?"

Rowell shook his head. "What do you mean?"

"Had she kept any of Bainton's Cadmean Textiles files?"

"There might have been some in the basement. I don't know; what if there were? Justin, what are you talking about? For God's sake!"

But the doctor took me firmly by the arm. "No more. Good evening." He pushed the door shut behind me.

In the hall, Wes Pendergraph dutifully stood up and dropped his magazine on the chair seat behind him. Obviously he hadn't been told of my suspension. "How's it going, Lieutenant?"

"Fine," I said. "Anybody else been in there?"

"You better believe it." He showed me his pad with the names on it. In addition to his private physician, Dollard had been visited by several lawyers, by his senatorial aide, by his secretary, by the lieutenant governor, by the A.G., by Judge Tiggs, and by Briggs Cadmean. Pendergraph shrugged. "The doctors are going nuts, but, gosh, I can't keep men like Briggs Cadmean and them out, can I? And the news guys! This Mr. Percy from *The Star* won't quit!"

"You're doing fine. Take it easy, Wes."

Down in the lobby, I telephoned Etham Foster and asked him to check the coin Cuddy had found in Mrs. Dollard's diary again against Ames's records: was it the *same* coin? I telephoned Miss Briggs Cadmean at River Rise, where she was still staying, and asked her if she had heard what Joanna was saying on the phone to Rowell that time he had called when they were both up in the tower study. She said no, she had left the room so as not to overhear their conversation. I telephoned the Melody Store and said to its proprietor, "That song we're singing without words, Mr. Phelps? I have an offer of five thousand dollars."

Ratcher Phelps hummed. "Well, well now, indeed I believe you and I are going to get along, Mr. Savile. I appreciate this, I want you to know. I'll be in touch."

Hanging up, I noticed through the glass booth Paula Burgwin hurrying toward the elevators; she glided by so smoothly wearing her fake-fur hooded jacket, I thought of a lady bear on skates in an ice show. Paula was carrying a vinyl flowery suitcase. In it, she told me, were clothes for Charlene Pope, who was being released from the hospital and was going to move in with her. She explained, "Cuddy Mangum's promised us some whatdoyoucallit, surveillance, but I'm taking a week off from the Rib House to stay home with Charlene anyhow. I just hope they don't fire me, you know?" Paula asked me to excuse her breathlessness. "I've been racing. I just got off work and I wanted to get here quick as I could. Who wants to stay in a hospital longer'n they have to, do you know what I mean?"

"Yes. Tell Charlene to do what Mangum tells her. You're a good friend." I held the doors as she tugged the bag into the elevator.

"She's family, is all," Paula replied. "Bye bye, thank you."

So I left the hospital, where they can't always stop the bad things, and never the worst. I went out through those wide doors that I had watched so intently as a child from the backseat of Mother's car. Watching for my father to appear again, absently patting the pockets of his long white coat, searching for his cigarettes. I would count every person released by those doors, saying to myself, he will come before I count twenty of them, before I count forty of them leaving. I would sit waiting, watching for him to escape again from the terrible vast building that I imagined as the lair of some invisible dragon who snatched away family, the dragon from whose imperishable thirst I had fled, on coming of age, to warm meadhalls where, of course, I found out the dragon comes too, leering jealous through the windows, watching, waiting.

23

The wall of iron spears around the Cadmean mansion was gated and locked across the driveway. Snow shiny in the starlight was frozen on the turreted bays and conical roofs, and frozen on the winter vines of the latticed arbor, and frozen on the branch tips of all the high, thicketed trees through which, flickering, I could see lights here and there in the dark red house. It was close to ten. No one answered the buzzer I pushed at the gatepost, or even came inquisitive to a window at the sound of my horn. I gave up finally and drove on through Hillston to C & W Textiles Industries.

Back in the 1840s, John Cadmean, the first of the Hillston industrialists, had not only built, on the property where the mills still stood, new homes and a school and a church for his workers, he had erected his own mansion, a huge, awkward attempt at Greek Revival, right next door to the factory. All he had to do was walk across the plank path thrown over the mud street, and there he was among his clattering looms. He wanted to be close. He did everything personally. He had even persuaded the people of Hillston to help him personally lay tracks, in the middle of the night, for his own railroad, tracks to run right up the street to the warehouse doors, tracks to run precisely through the right-of-way of the Virginia line that held the monopoly for freight service through the Piedmont—that Virginia monopoly being the reason why he had to start his own railroad in the middle of the night. And when the workmen from the Virginia line came in wagons and tore up a hundred feet of the illegal tracks, this first of the Cadmeans had talked a state judge of his personal acquaintance into issuing warrants for the outsiders' arrest. The Cadmean line remained.

Hillston then was a roughshod, graceless town where rowdies, some of them named Pope, spilled out from cheap-fronted frame saloons and fought down among the lame vagrants, the whores, and the scrawny farmers crowding with mules in the dirt-swirled streets. Hillston stayed through the century's turn as graceless as it had begun. And although by 1900 the shrewdest brigands to survive the Confederacy had bullied enough bulk of wealth to buy colleges and build conservatories and pave streets and ride upon them in open carriages with their wives, Hillston stayed still what my father, the Virginian, once said it had never stopped being: a mill town founded by a coarse breed with the trite, threadbare vision that the grabbing and holding of money was in itself a pursuit worthy of the word *civilization;* a town of a heart's-core rapacious greed plastered over with a thin smear of bromidic morality and a vulgar aesthetic. He said this at a dinner party to which—as I recall—my mother had invited both Mr. Briggs Cadmean and Rowell Dollard, neither of whom agreed with him. It was probably the only time I saw my father anywhere near as drunk as he all too often came to see me.

Old Briggs hidden tonight behind his iron wall was a direct descendant of that man who had allowed no right-of-way to impede his trespass. Thinking so led me to consider another congruity unmentioned in Cuddy's triangle of deaths: Bainton Ames and Luster Hudson and Ron Willis had all worked for Cadmean. Of course, half the people in Hillston did. Hillston was his; he had inherited it. If there were secrets about these murders the old man protected behind the iron gate, how was I to force a lock more than a roughshod century strong, even if I found the secret out?

The new C & W business offices (whose procedures, according to Lawry Whetstone, old Briggs failed to grasp) sat precisely where that first Cadmean had built his house. The new C & W gate was open, steel mesh rather than wood planks, and I drove through it to wait for Alice MacLeod to come rushing out from among the moil of bundled workers.

I'd seen her once today already. This morning, like the morning before, I had arrived early at the diner, and was waiting for her with breakfast and with flowers—silk ones I'd taken out of a vase in my living room. This morning we had talked more about her and more about me; and listening and talking made me more and more want to listen and talk to Alice MacLeod. In fact, the thought—not the thought, the sensation—came, that I wanted to be near Alice MacLeod as profoundly as I had wanted, seven years ago, to be near whiskey.

"Hi," she said under the C & W lights, and I said, "Hi," and we stood there jostled by the ravel of men and women headed shivering toward their cars and homes.

We moved through our talk slowly in the general direction of the old Volkswagen she'd parked at the far end of the first lot. Then over her shoulder I saw someone I thought I knew. Edging the area of new C & W construction at the border of the lot were three work-trailers up on blocks. Behind them were rust-brown girders, the low skeleton of what, according to signs, would be eventually C & W ELECTRONICS DIVISION. The person I thought I saw peering out one of the trailer doors was Ron Willis, and when the moon slid over the spider tank atop the main factory, so that I could see his oddly white hair before he pulled on the orange John Deere cap, I knew that it was Willis.

"Go home, I'll come there!" I abruptly told Alice. And I started running hard toward the trailer, cutting across aisles of moving cars. I was not close enough to catch him when Willis saw me, and saw that I was coming for him. He sprinted off around the side of the trailer. I heard a car rev, and then the tan Camaro came out fast. I was right in his path. A gun came out the driver's window and shot wildly. Screeching, cars all around us bucked to a stop as I flung myself off the Camaro fender, got to my gun, fired, missed, and started running again back through the lot, cursing out loud because my Austin was parked all the way at the other end of the plant, and Willis, horn blaring, was in a fast weave through the astonished traffic.

Then I heard the VW's horn, and Alice was backing at high speed toward me. I tumbled by hops into the seat as she reversed gears.

"Go!" I yelled. "He's at the gates!"

"Was that Ron Willis!"

"Yes." I reached over her hand and jerked the wheel. "Left! Through there. Okay, just get me close enough to try to shoot out the tire! Watch out! *Jesus Christ!*"

She had sheered in a thudding tilt up on the curb and was passing around the right side of the line of cars exiting at the factory gates. I could hear the metal on my door shriek against the steel post.

"Take a right!" I leaned out the window. "See him?"

"Yes. Damn this damn car!"

By now we'd fallen half a block behind. We were going to lose him. The Camaro bounced over the top of the rise ahead on Wade Boulevard.

"*Now watch it,*" I said, choked with the old fear. "Watch the snow! You're skidding!"

As we came over the crest of the hill, I saw that halfway down the other side, the rear of Willis's car was starting to slip sideways. He brought it back in line, sped up, slid again, and then his brake lights came on and stayed on, and he began to pinwheel in the icy crust, spiraling down the street. A station wagon coming from the opposite direction cut away from him, went off the road, and hit a mailbox on the corner. The Camaro slid sideways up onto the sidewalk in front of us.

"God, I'm going to hit him, I can't stop!" Alice yelled. But she did stop. With two feet to spare.

Gun in hand, shaking, I was out of the VW and at the Camaro door when Willis suddenly accelerated, blinding me with splattering slush. His car lurched forward, and jerked me loose from the door handle I'd grabbed. I fell away, rolled out into the street, fired two shots into the rear tire, and one into the back window. This time the Camaro smacked into a parked van on the other side of the street, and stopped. The woman driving the station wagon screamed. A teen-age couple hopped out of the parked van. As I pulled Willis from his front seat, he kicked at me. I hit him in the stomach and he dropped to his knees in the brown, oily snow.

"What do you think you're doing?" he gasped, his white hair flopped over the dazed eyes.

I said, "I want to ask you a couple of questions." I told him his rights, which assured me he already knew. Then I cuffed his hands behind him to the streetlight.

No one was hurt. The teen-agers were confusedly shaking glass slivers out of their hair. The woman in the station wagon had bitten her lip and was deeply upset because she'd only driven out to buy some coffee. She kept repeating this fact as a great injustice: "All I went out for was a can of coffee." Beneath a scarf, her hair was in plastic rollers.

When I reached Cuddy Mangum on the phone, I told him to send along a squad car, and to radio for a wrecker.

"Justin," he groaned. "Will you please just stay home, so I can?"

I said, "I am at home, on sick leave. This is a big collar for you, Mangum. If you want to score with V.D., better get over here quick."

My weak leg buckled as I walked back from the Dot 'n' Dash to the intersection. The teen-agers were staring at Ron Willis. The woman with hair rollers was staring at the gash now bent into her car's front end. Alice MacLeod was staring at me. "Are you limping?" she asked, her hands tucked under her arms, her eyes filled with a caring so wonderful to me that smiling wasn't enough and I laughed aloud. "I'm fine. How are *you*?"

She was laughing too. "You mentioned us going out somewhere tonight. Was this it?"

"Well, wasn't it pretty exciting for a first date?"

She looked past me at Willis, who scowled and yanked around to turn his back on her. She said, "I was happy to help, believe me. Did he kill Mrs. Dollard?"

"I think he knows who did, if he didn't. Good Christ, Alice Mac-Leod, where in the world did you learn to drive like that?"

"In the mountains. We drive like that all the time."

"*Thunder Road!*"

"That's right. All that bootleg whiskey weighing down the trunk keeps us from fishtailing in the snow. You ever driven in the North Carolina mountains?"

"I've been driven in the North Carolina mountains. I'm going to tell you all about it as soon as we get out of our clothes." We were slopped with mud and slush from head to foot.

Far off I could hear the siren coming as she took my hand and looked at my watch. "It's only ten twenty-five," she said. "Where next?"

24

It was nearly midnight before I opened the door to my house, stepped inside behind Alice, and saw that there was going to be a scene.

Before that, Cuddy Mangum had booked Ron Willis, a surly man in his late twenties whose demeanor vacillated between whining indignation and a drug-sustained loud bravado. Willis denied he had given a gym bag to Charlene Pope to give to Luster Hudson, claimed he had no idea where Hudson was, and snarled that he refused to say anything else. He also said did I know my girl friend had been "a nigger's whore?" Cuddy pulled me out of the room, and locked Willis up for the night.

Down in the foyer, Cuddy told me that my tie had gone over so well with Briggs Junior, as he called her, that he would never forgive me for having telephoned his house when I did. Then he winked down at Alice, standing there with us, and said, "Governor, I'm trying to get this lady I love to marry me. That's her daddy up there on the wall giving me a nasty look." He pointed at the portrait of old Mr. Cadmean above the courtroom doors.

"Good luck," Alice said.

I told her, "Mangum's a little nuts on the subject of marriage."

"Well hey, why not?" Cuddy grinned. "Now if y'all two would come get married with us, and stop this tearing around the streets shooting off guns like *The French Connection*, we could all play bridge together and then go home. Be a foursome. Y'all play bridge? I love it."

"Good night, Cuddy," I said.

He took Alice's hand in his huge gloves. "Now listen, Red, I know old Sherlock here looks pretty pitiful now, but take my word for it, he used to be a pretty snappy dresser."

I said again, "Good night, Cuddy," and he waved his key chain of talismans at us and rubbed the rabbit's foot lavishly against the side of his nose. Then Alice drove me back to pick up the Austin, and then she followed me home.

The scene I saw coming, I saw as soon as I realized that my furnace was clanking heat up through the radiators and that Susan's mink coat was draped over the banister. She had never before come over to my house when Lawry was back in Hillston, so I was shocked. But then I had never before hit Lawry in the face, either.

"Well, sugar, it's about time. Where the crap have you been!" Susan spoke just as Alice walked through the open door into the living room, and it was too late for me to do anything but walk in after her.

Susan was draped full-length on the white canvas couch. There was a bottle of Campari on the floor beside her, and a wineglass. She was wearing black velvet slacks and a black cashmere sweater and she was reading a hard-cover book she'd brought with her, entitled *Mommie Dearest*. She did not move when she saw Alice except to toss her head so that the mane of blond hair shook.

I stepped toward her so annoyed it amazed me that she blandly smiled when I asked, "What are you doing here, Susan?" Then I turned sideways and gestured an introduction. "Alice MacLeod, this is Susan Whetstone. Mrs. Whetstone is an old friend. What did you want to see me about, Susan?" I had told her again on the phone yesterday I wanted time to think; again she hadn't listened.

Now Susan sat up. "God, what happened to you! Have you been rolling around in the slop out there?"

I said, "Yes."

Susan was still ignoring Alice, who stood next to me, still buttoned up in the plaid parka, her jeans and boots as soiled and soggy as mine. I kept talking without much hope for the conversation. "Alice has just helped me capture a suspect over on Wade Boulevard."

"What fun," said Susan, with a grin, and now she looked at Alice as if the latter were modeling a bizarre outfit she didn't plan to buy. She asked, "Are you a police . . . person too?"

"No," Alice said.

"No? Just another old friend?" And now Susan looked at me. "Or a new friend? Mighty sweet of you to play cops and robbers with Justin when it's so cold out, and at midnight, too. I thought you'd been fired, Justin. Are you a private eye now?"

Alice said to me, "Thank you for the offer of a drink, but I think I'll go home now." I could feel from the heat on my ears that they had blushed as red as Alice's hair.

"No, wait." I caught at her arm but it tensed, and I let my hand fall away. "Let me walk you to your car," I said.

"It's not necessary," Alice said.

"Oh, don't leave on my account," called Susan, stroking her hair up from the nape of her tan neck.

"I'm not," Alice said.

"You just got here. And you both look like you could use a drink. Meanwhile, have we met before, Alice? Did you say her name was Alice, sugar?"

I said, "Susan, please."

Her eyes grave and a darkening blue, Alice looked back at Susan. "Yes, my name is Alice. No, we haven't met. But I have met your husband. I work at C & W."

"You do?" Susan smiled. "What do you do there? Let me guess. You work on the line, just like in that movie *Norma Rae* with that short girl friend of Burt Reynolds's playing a redneck with all those children by different fathers. Isn't it boring how little bitty the world is?"

Alice said, "No, I don't find the world little, or boring."

"Lucky you."

"Yes. Good night." Alice walked out of the room, and I followed her.

Outside by the Volkswagen I said, "I'm sorry. I had no idea she would be here. I should have told you. I'd hoped to end—"

"Please." Alice's hand waved away my words. "There's nothing to apologize about. And I'd rather you didn't try." Her voice was as brisk as the air clouding her words. She was in her car now, but I was holding the door open. She tugged at it. "Would you please let me shut this?"

"Alice, let me talk to her, and then come over to your apartment? Will you? Please? I'm so sorry for putting you in an awkward—"

She said, "I didn't feel awkward." And she pulled the door closed, and drove away.

Back inside, Susan stood at the unlit fireplace, watching herself brush her hair in the mirror above the mantel.

I said, "You were a bitch. What are you doing over here?"

She looked around and widened her eyes and then turned back to the mirror.

"Susan, let's . . ."

"Let's what, sugar?" She kept brushing.

"Talk."

"Talk away. Don't you want to change first? And bathe? Look at yourself."

"Lawry told you what happened?"

"He thinks you're crazy." She kept her eyes on her image.

"Because I didn't care to join his four-way fuck!"

"I told him you weren't into group things. He never listens to me. He said you knocked him down." Now she curved sideways, and looked at me, her head tilted into her hair. "That kind of turns me on."

I walked away and sat down in the rocker next to the couch. I asked her, "Will you answer a question? Have you been having other affairs? Since we've been involved?"

"Affairs?"

"Sex." I watched the big diamond move with her hand, dead in the muted light.

She glanced at her brush, pulled the loose hairs from it and balled them between her fingertips. "Do you want to know?"

"That means you have. Why didn't you tell me?"

"You're so old-fashioned, honey, I didn't think you'd want to know. It wasn't serious."

I glared at her until she shrugged and turned back to the mirror. Then she asked, "Who's that girl?"

I was quiet, listening to the rattle of the water in the radiator. Then I said, "I'm in love with her."

Susan spun around. "What? You're reading me the riot act, and you're balling that dirty little redneck hippie?"

"That's enough! And I'm not sleeping with her, Susan. I just met her."

Susan came across the room and stood over my chair. "You *are* nuts, you know that?"

I stood up, knocking over the wineglass as I squeezed past her to move away. "Listen, Susan. I've been trying to say this a long time, and now I'll just say it right out. I don't think we should see each other anymore. You never had any intention of divorcing Lawry. I don't know why I wanted you to. Let's just stop it right here and now."

"No," she said, as if I'd asked her if she wanted another drink. "I don't want to stop it."

"*I do*. I'm sorry. I don't want to see you anymore. I'm very sorry if this is hurting you."

"Oh, crap, Justin. Not again. We've played this scene before. Don't pull this on me tonight about leaving Lawry." She picked up her purse from the floor, put her brush in it, and started looking through its depths for something else.

"I don't want you to leave Lawry," I snapped. "I think you two suit each other just fine."

"Now, don't be sarcastic." She found a gold tube of lipstick.

"I mean it." I raised my voice. "Will you look at me!"

Her head swung up. "What in hell is the matter with you?"

"I said I mean it! I want us to say good-bye. I'll walk you to your car. Is it out back?"

"Are you pissed because I told you I screwed somebody else? Grow up."

"I'll get your coat."

After examining the lipstick tube carefully, she closed it and dropped it back in her purse. "Is this a joke? It's not funny."

"I'm serious."

"Oh, fuck. This is ridiculous." She laughed with a short, harsh sound. "A month from now, when you want back . . ."

I stunned myself by yelling, "I'm going to marry Alice MacLeod!"

Now she stared at me, her mouth in a grimace. Then she hissed, "You shit!" and bounded off the couch and slapped me across the face. I let her do it. The edge of the platinum setting of the big square diamond cut into my lip. I let her slap me twice more, and then I grabbed her wrist and pulled it down.

I said, "I'm sorry, Susan. I haven't behaved well. I wish this didn't have to be painful. You act as if it sounds like its coming out of nowhere, but . . ."

She yanked her arm away. "You are so full of it. I don't know why they ever let you out of that nuthouse." Swooping up her purse, she stalked into the hall and stabbed her arms into the mink coat.

I went after her. "Be honest, God damn it. You don't love *me*. You never have. I was somebody to slip off and eat lunch with. That's it."

She shook the perfect blond hair free of the fur collar. She said, "Sugar, all you ever were to me was a dick. And that doesn't mean cop."

The door slammed behind her, and the hall shuddered.

The next morning I opened one eye to squint at my brass clock, and instead I saw an old loud-ticking tin alarm clock with two bells on top. Beyond it on a papered wall I saw a photograph of Martin Luther King, and beside that a poster of an Appalachian bluegrass festival. I turned over and I saw the red tangle of Alice MacLeod's hair. I was only an instant surprised; after that, I felt that I was looking at my life, familiar and sure as when, after long traveling home from New England schools, mile by mile beside the highway, granite turned to red clay and each bend of the road was felt before seen.

I was awake, and had been visited by no ghosts in white dresses, or in white hospital coats; I was freshly awake and had scarcely slept.

Last night at one when I'd rapped on the door of her basement apartment and, squatting down, had tapped on a window, Alice had pulled back the blue cotton curtains and told me through the glass to "Go away." Had not her upstairs neighbor, a brawny man I immediately detested, come down in his T-shirt to the landing of the old, partitioned house, and asked her if she wanted me "gotten rid of," she probably would never have let me in. Mud-clotted as I was, I didn't look very reputable, and I think that helped her decide in my favor.

Embarrassed, she opened the door, and embarrassed, I followed her in. I stepped down into what must have once been the kitchen of the house, down into a room that was like seeing Alice MacLeod herself, fully, for the first time. The pine furniture looked mountain-made. On the unvarnished floor was a dark-blue oval rag rug, and thrown over the couch a wedding-ring-patterned quilt of pale bleached blue. Filling a corner was a wooden handloom, its shuttle resting among green hues of thread. A typewriter was crowded by textbooks on a card table, and plants in rubber pots leaned toward the light.

"What are you doing here?" she asked.

"This is a wonderful room."

"Thank you."

"I came to ask if you would marry me," I added, shivering in my sodden clothes.

"No, I won't. Good night." In the green wool robe that fell over her bare feet, she stood stiffly upright, like a small red marigold.

"I wonder if you would give it some thought," I said.

"I don't even know you."

"Oh, yes, you do. Don't you believe: 'Whoever loved that loved not at first sight?'"

"No."

"I do," I assured her. "I want to be around you every minute you'll let me." I sneezed.

"You ought to get out of those clothes."

"All right." I pulled off my coat and jacket together, and grabbed at my sweater.

She almost smiled. "You ought to go *home* and get out of those clothes."

"Listen, *please*," I said. "I'm sorry about tonight. . . . Susan is someone I was involved with because I didn't care what I was doing, and neither did she. I just told her I had fallen in love with you. Could I *please* stay and talk to you awhile? I know it's late, but tomorrow's Saturday. No 'World War I to the Present.'" I grinned, holding my breath for her answer.

Alice frowned at me, and then she frowned at a faded photograph on the mantel of the wide, low cooking fireplace. In the photograph a young, thin serious-faced couple looked uncertainly at the camera; he in an army uniform, with Alice's eyes; she in a cotton dress, with Alice's hair. After studying their picture, Alice walked out of the room. She came back with a large pair of folded denim overalls, their soft blue as pale as the quilt on her couch. "Okay. You can wear these," she said. "Bathtub's back there."

I took them from her, saying, "I hope they belonged to your father or your brother or your grandfather and not to that fellow who wanted me 'gotten rid of.'"

"They belong to me," she said, but she called as I walked off. "And the guy upstairs is gay."

And so afterward I went out in her backyard and scrounged for fallen branches to crack over my knee, and together we built a fire with them, and we talked about the mountains. We talked about our pasts, as though we could see them in the bright leaping fire. And hour by hour, our eyes spellbound interwove all difference. So that, when long into the night our voices sank lower, like the fire gleaming quiet and warm, and I took her hand, our palms, wordless, spoke on together in conference too tenuous and sensible for speech.

When we went near morning to her bed, I had learned that her grandfather had beveled the corners and plaited the ropes beneath the yielding feathery mattress on which, in the dark blue dawn, we slept.

Early Saturday as I left Alice's home, I was singing. I was thirty-four and had long ago stopped listening to love songs as though they had anything to say to me. Indeed, I was faintly surprised to realize that people kept on writing the songs, and that new lovers would be forever stepping into the dance I thought I had left for good. And now, walking along the cold crystalline sidewalk in those overalls, I had a feeling of such glad buoyancy, such bighearted, lighthearted amplitude, that I expected my feet not only to dance but, like Paul Bunyan's, to bound over the houses, and my eyes to wink at breakfasting families of birds in the top branches of trees.

26

In my living room, I sat thinking about Alice, thinking that Alice was the source of Joanna Cadmean's vision of my falling into something new, whether good or bad, she couldn't say. I was also waiting for someone to pick up Cadmean's phone. Then, after I was told, for the fourth time, that old Briggs was unavailable, I decided to use a family connection. I called Cuddy's River Rise condominium and spoke with Cadmean's daughter, and with some difficulty persuaded her to find out for me her father's whereabouts. When my phone rang shortly afterward, I assumed she was calling back, but instead I heard a voice whose rusty cough I recognized before he finished asking, "Could I talk to Mr. Justin Savile? This is Walter Stanhope. From the Banks."

"Hello, Mr. Stanhope. This is Justin. How are you?"

"Don't mean to intrude. Wondered how it was going."

This morning, in my own expansive state, his calling felt to me a gesture of enormous outreaching. I told him, "Sir, I'm following in your footsteps. I've been suspended." Then I told him of Joanna Cadmean's death and of the evidence that linked Rowell Dollard to it, and linked Rowell, by the coin, to Bainton Ames's death as well. I told him of Luster Hudson and Ron Willis and Charlene Pope, and of Lawry Whetstone's information. I told him that far from being further harassed by old Briggs Cadmean, I couldn't even get past the old man's iron gates to speak to him about why he had lied to me when he claimed he'd never seen the Ames designs that Cloris had wanted to sell to Bogue.

"Ah," replied Stanhope. "Cadmean lied? Find out why. And why Bogue lied."

I told him everything Rowell had said to me in the hospital: that Joanna had plotted to kill herself in order to take revenge on him.

"Know she tried suicide before?" asked Stanhope. "Back in college."

"Yes, sir, I was told, but . . ."

He cleared his throat slowly. "Something didn't go into the report on that attempt. I guess, her dead, no harm saying it now. Doctor told me at the time he released her back then. She'd just had an abortion."

"Abortion?" I think this fact shocked me as much as her death.

"Not a very good one."

"My God. Dollard's?" And neither she nor Rowell had ever had another child. *Think of me as your father*, I could hear Rowell saying.

"I'd expect so." Stanhope stopped to cough. "I were you, I wouldn't shut out any possibility till you're sure."

"Pardon?"

"Sure that Dollard's not telling the truth about her. People can hate a long time, even ordinary ones, and she wasn't ordinary." In the background I could hear the recording of the baroque violin music stop, then in a moment another record begin.

"But to plan out her own murder like that? It'd be diabolical."

"People can be diabolical, you want to use that word."

"But she *was* psychic, Mr. Stanhope. She told me she felt like there was a phone ringing while Cloris was being assaulted, and now we've found out Whetstone actually was trying to call, right then!"

"Not saying she wasn't clairvoyant. Know for a fact she was. Saw her prove it." I could hear him try to swallow. "But both can be true. The way she used to look at Dollard; it was past what most people would call love."

"Mr. Stanhope, I'm convinced she's right about Rowell killing Bainton Ames. And I thought you agreed."

"Maybe he did. Could be she thought she could get him back by blackmailing him. Could still be true he didn't kill her. You said out here how she told you she was going to die soon. Could be she'd already planned it."

"No, what she said was somebody was going to *kill* her."

"So why didn't she protect herself? Why wouldn't she leave the lodge? Another thing; you just said it struck you funny how she was all dressed up that night—not like her regular style. That sticks out to me too. Excuse me." I could hear his muffled coughing and the wheeze for breath.

I said, "Are you all right, Mr. Stanhope?"

He said, "Okay."

"Do you mind if I ask, have you seen a doctor?"

"Yep, I've seen a lot," he replied, and changed the subject. "Well, think about that white dress. I'll tell you what I thought when you told me: dressed up for a wedding."

I had thought of that too, while Rowell was talking, there in the hospital. And I had dreamt it. But I didn't want to think it; I didn't want to believe she'd made me a part of her plot.

Stanhope was asking, "Could she have planted the coin in that closet?"

And I could remember how she'd suggested she go see Cloris's bedroom, remember her going back into her own room before we left the lodge, remember the shoulder bag pressed tightly to her side as we climbed the Dollard steps together. "Yes," I said. "And I guess she could have had the letter to me already written. And I guess if Mangum hadn't come to take Briggs out to dinner that night, she could have already figured some other way to get rid of her, once she knew Rowell was coming." I was fighting hard against what I now knew I had already started to believe yesterday as I looked into Rowell's eyes in that white room. "But the broken chain and . . ."

"Just saying," Stanhope whispered in his graveled voice, "keep it in mind. Up to you, but I'd try tracing that coin, and same if you can for the leather diary. Where were they bought, who by? And what's the C & W connection? That's what police can do. It's just no fun."

Before hanging up, Stanhope made a dry noise that could have been a laugh. "Never knew why people figured justice *ought* to be stone-blind, but I always knew she *was*. Looks like, here you've got plenty of evidence to get Dollard for killing Mrs. Cadmean, which maybe, maybe now, he didn't do. And no way at all to convict him of killing Bainton Ames, which maybe he did do."

"I've got the coin."

"Well. You know juries. And after fifteen years, well."

"Maybe, Mr. Stanhope, if Joanna Cadmean did commit suicide, she realized exactly what you're saying now; she knew we couldn't get Rowell for Ames, but could get him for her."

"Could be. Kinda doubt that was her motive." His cough started again.

As we said our good-byes, I told him I had hopes of getting married by summer. He wished me well. "Hope is all I have to go on now," I said, and thought that I was beginning to sound like Cuddy Mangum. I added that the woman I wanted to marry me was from the mountains and had never seen the Banks, and that I'd like to bring her out there. "And I'd like to have her meet you then, if that's all right. Maybe in June?"

There was such a long pause, I wondered if he had put down the phone, but then he said, "Okay. I'll try to be around."

I didn't ask him what he meant, because I knew. And I stood still by the phone, with the sense that I was suddenly pinioned by this unspoken sentence of death, as if my happiness with Alice were some great bird shut into a cage so small that its wings crushed bent against the bars. But soon enough I would forget to think there was a cage; everyone does, even the dying.

I hadn't moved when the phone rang again, scaring me. This time it was Briggs Junior, who told me that her father could be found for the next hour at the Hillston Hunt Club, and could be found later this afternoon at Joanna Cadmean's cremation, which she herself did not plan to attend. "Such rites seem beside the point," she explained.

I asked her to have Cuddy meet me at my house at five, and added, "Let me just say, Briggs, I think Cuddy Mangum is one of the finest men I ever knew."

"Are you saying that because you don't expect me to realize it?"

"No, not at all." Somehow, whenever she and I spoke, we were quick to assume the other's hostility. I mentioned this observation to her now, and said, "You know, you and I so instantly got off on the wrong foot, I thought we were destined to end up in love."

She said, "That's only true in books."

"I thought most of the true things were in books. I just wanted to say I shared your view of Cuddy, that's all." She didn't answer, and I went on, "Sorry, I'll keep quiet. But if we're going to play bridge together for the rest of our lives, we're going to have to learn how to talk to each other."

"Bridge? I don't play bridge."

Poor Cuddy's suburban dream of a table for four. Alice had told me she didn't play any games at all. And I had already played too many hands in a pacified recreation room, feeling beneath my fingertips the ruffled corners of the worn cards; looking out at winter mountains leaf into spring, swell into thick summer, then fall. Cuddy believed if he waited until he could get everything ready at once, make all arrangements, forget no detail, then life would begin for him like a birthday party at last, and keep on noisy and warm always. But in Briggs's voice I kept hearing a disengagement cool as her stars, and it worried me for him.

At the Hillston Hunt Club I found old Mr. Cadmean. In a mammoth black hunt coat and a fur cap, he stood smoking his cigar in the middle of the club's indoor riding ring. At his feet in the loose sawdust earth lay a fat elderly cocker spaniel. Cadmean held in his arthritic hand a lunge line; at the other end on an enormous black horse trotted his little granddaughter Rebecca Kay, plump and glossy as an apple in her red snowsuit. She was so tiny, the stirrup leathers had been tightened right up into the saddle skirts, but she was posting with a determined scowl and in good rhythm and thudding with her boots on the huge horse's withers whenever he forgot her slight weight was up there and slowed to a walk around the circle Cadmean was turning. A woman stood by, watching, her teeth tight on her lower lip; I assumed she was the child's mother.

"One two! One two! One two!" called Cadmean from the hub of the moving wheel. "Manassas, move your fanny! Kick him, honey! Good girl!" It surprised me to hear that this dutifully trotting horse was Manassas, the stallion who had thrown Joanna Cadmean weeks back.

"Can I jump, Grandpa?" yelled Rebecca, pointing at a low set of crossed bars behind Cadmean. She raised herself up and forward into a half seat.

"No!" cried the mother, and Cadmean growled, "No, ma'am," at the same time.

The little girl said, "I'm not a baby, I'm almost six!"

"Manassas is a baby," Cadmean was saying as he turned and saw me walking toward him, my shoes digging deep into the soft dirt.

"Hello, Mr. Cadmean." I stood outside the circumference of the stallion's trot and watched his white eye roll at me each time he snorted past. In a few minutes I said, "I've been trying to reach you for days, Mr. Cadmean."

"Have you?" He didn't look at me. "Well, looks like you found me too. I thought I heard tell you were excused from work due to illness. Might be dangerous traipsing around sick like this." He switched hands on the line, and his bent fingers came up to shift the cigar along the small fleshy lips.

"No, sir. That's not why I was suspended. It was for tracking dirt onto the parlor rug."

The lidded yellow eyes stayed with the horse and rider. "I believe I warned you about that very thing," he said.

"You did."

"That's right. I thought I did."

"Let me offer my condolences about Joanna." My offer was met with a nod. I added, "I'd like to attend the services this afternoon, if you have no objection."

"She put down she didn't want services, but I'm certainly not going to let her go without Reverend Campbell saying a few words over her. She was a Cadmean by name, and no nuttier than some of the others, God knows." Then abruptly he flung out his arm and introduced me to Rebecca's mother, wife of another of his sons, a gentle-faced, timorous woman whom he obviously terrified. As we exchanged hellos, the old man pulled in on the lunge line, halted Manassas, took Rebecca off over her protests, hugged her over her protests, handed her to her mother, and told them to go across the street to the Fox and Hound Restaurant and order their lunch. Rebecca parted unhappily while issuing her own command. "You better come soon, Grandpa."

"Isn't she something?" he beamed as they left the ring. "Reminds me of Baby. Did you come here to ride, Justin?"

I stroked Manassas down the white blaze of his head, while his mouth nibbled wetly at my hand. "No, I came here to see you," I said. "But I used to ride."

"I know you did. Now, who told you where I was?"

I smiled. "Why did you refuse to talk to me?"

"Where's my daughter?" He moved his cigar over to the other side of his mouth.

"Why did you call Walter Stanhope and tell him I was crazy?"

Cadmean laughed out loud. "Well, son, we got the kitty full. Somebody's got to call."

"Go ahead."

He laughed again, and we stood there until Manassas shook himself and backed away tugging at the lunge line.

Cadmean handed me the line. "Here. Ride him."

"No, thanks."

"Oh, come on, let him get the kinks out. I'll tell you this. I wish I could still get up on an animal that pretty without every joint and bone in my body screaming its goddamn head off. These are the good times, son. Don't throw them away saying, 'No, thanks.' Things just get worse and worse. They truly do. You'll wake up one morning and it'll hurt just to move. Go on. I've got to go take a leak. I just took one, half an hour ago. That all goes to hell too. Come on, Duchess."

His old cocker spaniel lurched to her feet and paddled after him as he left me standing there with the horse and walked with his stiff carefulness to the stable office door.

I thought about it, and finally unhooked the lunge line, climbed up, and rode Manassas. At first I was tense enough to let the horse fight me with a skittish backward dance; I was nervous that I would not be able to stop thinking about Joanna Cadmean and that Manassas would feel this and would try to throw me as he had her. But finally his rhythm took me over and I met him there and we had worked up to a canter when Mr. Cadmean came back, scraping his fingers up against the shave of his fat cheek as he watched us. When a young boy in chaps entered the ring, Cadmean called me over, and the boy took Manassas to walk him, and Cadmean, the spaniel, and I went outside, and crossed the snow-curbed street. I said, "Maybe Hillston ought to invest in snowplows."

"Look over your head." Cadmean pointed at the glassy sun in a cloudless sky. "Let God plow. He's the only one doesn't come begging me for donations to buy His equipment." He paused. "I take it back. Every time I turn around, His preachers are sliding their buttered hands in my pockets."

We entered the paneled bar of the Fox and Hound Restaurant. It was busy with boasting businessmen and Hillston women rich enough to ride. Between us we knew most of them. The bar was ostentatiously sporting: hunting horns, crops, ribbons, and etchings of redcoated riders hung on all available wall space. The bar had been modeled on the proprietor's notion of a British country pub; all the wood was varnished almost black and gouged with scratches, all the fabric was faded cabbage roses, and even the Cokes were served in pewter tankards. Above the rows of liquor was a stuffed fox who appeared to be running fast without caring where he was going, for one of his eyes glanced at the mirror behind him and the other one stared out at us. In the middle of the floor was a large Franklin stove; beneath it, Cadmean's spaniel, which he'd brought right inside with him, flopped over exhausted from her walk across the street. Cadmean took us to a far corner away from everyone else. He sat down in a chintz armchair under an engraving of two fox hunters taking a fence while a third fell from his horse on the way.

Sitting down across from the old man, I said, "All right. I rode your horse. Now, will you answer my questions?"

"Good horse. Am I right?"

"Very."

"Fine, fine horse, Mr. Manassas. Whiskey?" The bartender had come over with a deferential stoop.

I said, "Bloody Mary, very weak."

"No whiskey?" asked Cadmean. "Well, I'll have my whiskey, Mr. Gilbert. A double, how about?" Then he settled into the upholstered chair and gave one long slow stroke to his bald scalp. He said, "I called home. It was Baby found out for you where I was. Selma was glad to hear her voice after all this while."

I said, "You don't waste much time."

He nodded. "I don't have much time to waste. Where is she? She hasn't been at the lodge since the accident. Is she coming to the services today?"

"No, she said she was not."

His mouth twitched. "I don't understand her, I just don't. Where is she, son?"

I shook my head. "I'm sorry. I don't think it's for me to say. If Briggs wanted you to know, she'd tell you."

"Justin, you just told me you're not going to play the only card you've got in your hand." His puffy lips pushed in and out like those of an old sea bass. "That sort of stymies our game, doesn't it, hunh?"

"Maybe it's not the only card I have," I said. "But before I turn over any others, I'd like to know why you called Walter Stanhope." We sat waiting while the bartender placed down our drinks tentatively, readjusted them, lifted them, rubbed his cloth over the wood beneath, put them back, and finally left.

Cadmean said, "I told Stanhope—good man, Walter—the same thing I told you: No sense in muddying old stagnant water, making a mess." As if in demonstration, he swirled his drink until the amber liquid slopped over the sides.

I said, "That water was already stirred, Mr. Cadmean. And now, not only are Bainton Ames and Cloris dead, so is your daughter-in-law."

His big head swayed sadly. "I know. I know. It's just pitiful. I couldn't even believe it at first. But I told you," he sighed, "Joanna was a crazy woman. She's proved me right. I certainly hate to think of something that bad having happened out at my lodge. I built it, and I had some happy times in it."

I took the plastic stick with its fox on top out of my glass and sipped at the Bloody Mary. "You understand," I told him, "Monday, Rowell will be charged with her murder."

"Why don't we wait till Monday to see what happens on Monday, how's that?" Sucking in a piece of ice, he bared his teeth and crunched it in two. "Tell you what I know today. Know Rowell's in a hospital bed and it's a goddamn shame. Shame about his health, and his primary, and shame about the shit that geese are going to gabble."

"Yes," I nodded, "I expect whatever happens Monday, you'll have to find another friend to run in your primary this spring, Mr. Cadmean."

Swallowing the ice chips, he smiled agreeably. "Oh, well, I have lots of friends."

"Perhaps you should have made Lawry Whetstone one of them."

"Why's that?" Cadmean's lidded eyes squinted at me. "Fact is, I don't like Lawry. I don't believe there's a natural fiber in him. I believe he'd as soon put his pecker in a plastic balloon as a living moaning woman and I got no use for a man not more particular."

I said, "I don't like him either. But I appreciated his coming in to say Cloris told him herself—the day she died—that she'd brought you those designs of Bainton Ames's. And that you had confiscated them from her. It made me wonder why you bothered lying to me about that." He watched me sip at my drink. I went on, "It made me wonder so much, I started wondering if maybe you decided you better get hold of *copies* she told you she'd made on those papers. Copies she probably kept in her safe. Maybe in her purse. Like the purse we found thrown into the grass beside her driveway."

Turning the whiskey glass in circles on the dark table, Cadmean shook his big bald head as if I'd given the wrong answer to an easy question. "Shit, son, that's pretty farfetched, isn't it? You know I was watching a Shakespeare play while poor Cloris was getting robbed. A play where a fellow has himself turned into an ass, am I right?"

"Oh, I didn't wonder if you did it personally. I don't believe you'd personally crack open the head of even a loose woman."

His eyebrow went up at this and stayed there, sardonic. "I appreciate your good opinion," he said.

I took out a cigarette; I kept them now just in the pack—the case I'd put in a box with the other gifts I was returning to Susan. I said, "No, sir, I didn't think you were over there personally rummaging around in the Dollard house. What I've been wondering was if maybe you arranged to have someone else do that errand for you. Or arranged to have someone else arrange it. Someone from C & W. You know, the same way C & W men come over and unfreeze your pipes when you ask them to. Maybe two somebodies. Maybe Luster Hudson and Ron Willis."

He took a cigar out of the hunt coat, rolled it between the stiff, twisted fingers. "Luster Hudson. And Ron Willis. I don't recall those particular names." Now he began to lick at the cigar with a tongue pink as a cat's.

"No? They're C & W. I was wondering if you'd asked Ron Willis to follow me around town the last few days. Which he did."

Cadmean looked at me, his lips puffing in and out.

I smiled back. "I know you've taken a real interest in my whereabouts, from your long-distance calls. Problem is, Mr. Willis got a little nervous from being wanted for questioning in a murder case, and he got a little more nervous, it turns out, from being pretty full of cocaine, and the result was he took several shots at me."

"Mighty happy to see he must have missed," said Cadmean, pulling out a box of wood matches and waving the flame of one beneath his cigar. "Where is he now, this drug-addict fellow?"

"He's in jail now."

"That so? You think he killed Cloris?"

"No. He has a very good alibi for that night. Not a Shakespeare-play alibi, but just as good for his purposes. I'm interested in whether he got those papers from this friend of his, Hudson, who maybe did kill Cloris."

"I read it was gold and jewelry that robber took, not papers. What would some old robber want with those?"

I finished my drink and patted my mouth with a paper napkin that also had the fleeing fox on it. "Mr. Cadmean," I said, "the bad thing about using violence is, by its nature you can't keep it on a lunge line. You can harness a waterfall to your mill, but what if there's a flood, and the dam breaks? You can hire a thug to take some papers from a lady's house while you and she sit watching a play, but what if the lady gets a stomachache and leaves early and catches that thug helping himself to her silverware and anything else he sees, and what if that thug got scared, or just thuggish, and killed her? You see what I mean? Once you let violence loose, it's out of control."

He nodded. "A lot like alcohol-drinking. Am I right? All depends on the drinker." With a noisy gulp he finished off his whiskey. "A lot like car-driving in the snow. All depends on the car. And the driver." The ice snapped between his teeth. "No, I don't believe I know these two fellows of yours. 'Course, if they did kill poor Cloris, I'm going to have to let them go from C & W." He watched his ash as he slowly rolled it loose on the edge of the ashtray. "Now, let's go back to Rowell a minute. Hunh?" His eyes seemed impervious to the smoke coiling past them as they peered at me. "Now. What you got against your uncle, son, except he helped your mama put you in a loony bin to dry out."

I leaned forward into the smoke behind which Cadmean's moon-wide face bobbed. "What I have against him," I said, working to keep my voice as tranquil as his, "is I believe that he's a murderer."

"Who of? Joanna?"

"That's certainly what the prosecutors think. And can prove. But the person I *know* he killed is Bainton Ames. One reason I know it is that Rowell has never said to me that he didn't."

"No hope in hell you'll get proof, son."

"That may be true."

"And why want to?"

"You say you wouldn't want to have murderers in your factory. I don't care to have any more of them than I can help in my state's senate."

"Oh shit, Justin." With a cracking snap of his fingers he called over the bartender from the other side of the room. "You can't clean the dung off the world. It just keeps flying. You can't dig out the road back to Eden, don't you know that yet? Another drink?"

"No, thank you."

"Sure?"

"Yes."

"Allrighty."

"I do know you can't," I said. "So let's just say I want to find out for sure, for my own satisfaction. How's that?"

Cadmean gave his skull another stroke. "That's different. Check, Mr. Gilbert, if you will, sir." He slid an ancient curved wallet from his back pocket, and paid with cash. There was nothing in the wallet but a great deal of cash; credit cards were not to his taste, he said. Pawing up a handful of jelly beans from the bowl on the table, he pushed himself with a grumble out of the chair. With a snort, the old cocker spaniel shook herself instantly awake and followed her master on his progress through the room, stopping when he stopped to squeeze a shoulder, rub a head, or kiss a hand. At the door he suggested that we go for a walk.

I buttoned my coat. "Aren't you supposed to be joining Mrs. Cadmean and Rebecca in there for lunch?"

"The girls'll be fine. That woman's so scared of me—now, isn't that amazing?—she can't even eat when I'm around. Just diddles with her fork."

So I crossed back over the street with him, slowing my steps to his as we trudged into the snow-splotched wet field of the jumping arena bordering the stables. There we wandered about among the scattered red and white gates, and the hogback rails, and the plasterboard walls painted to look like either bricks or stone. We could hear the snow melting, and the earth sucking it in.

"Sun's working," Cadmean grumbled. "I told you it would. Now. Let's play some poker." He put his gnarled hand through my arm as we stepped around a gully of icy mud. "You see my Baby, am I right?" I nodded. "You interested in her?"

"She's interesting, yes."

"She's damn pretty."

"Indeed she is."

"Smart."

"Yes."

He bobbed his head, and then slid his hands into the deep pockets of the old hunt coat. After a few more yards, he growled, "Well, I want her to come over and see me." I nodded again. "I want her to do something else." He looked at me. "I want her settled down before they dig my hole. I want her with a man can make her happy. Right sort of man."

"What kind is that, Mr. Cadmean? Surely not the sort with a history of mental trouble. I believe I'm quoting correctly your remark to Mr. Stanhope about me." Leaning against the fake brick wall, I thought with some pleasure about the inevitable clash between the old man and Cuddy Mangum, whose name the industrialist had doubtless never heard, unless he'd heard it from Cuddy's father, who'd worked on the line at C & W all his adult life.

Cadmean navigated the puddles, came up to me wheezing, and stood to scrape the bottom of his old black-laced boot against the wall edge. "Oh, shit," he grinned. "Forget what I said to Walter. I'm the one all for burying the past. You're the gravedigger won't let it be." His small eyes smiled with a sleepy malevolence. "All right, son. Let me hear your answer. Can you bring my Baby over to her own home, to sit down and talk with her own daddy for one evening's time—and doesn't it crush your soul to hear me have to ask it? Can you bring her?" The only sign of his feelings was a rapid twitch that began at the side of his mouth.

I looked at the bearish eyes; in the sun they were yellow as sulfur. I asked, "And if I do?"

"Well, then," he started to walk again, Duchess tilting toward his heel, dottering along beside him, as fat and old as he. "Well, then, I guess in trade I'd lend you a shovel to help close up that grave of yours. I guess I'd tell you a story. Now, understand me, this would be *just* a story, and it's not one I'll ever tell again, and it's not one if you wanted to tell it to somebody else and give me the credit for it, I'd ever say that I'd told you. Hunh? If you were to go blabbering, I'd be obliged . . ." (And he grinned, his discolored teeth oddly old behind the baby-pink lips.) ". . . I'd certainly be obliged to tell whoever you'd talk to, that, well, you had a history of mental trouble. This here is a private story for your own satisfaction. Not for Ken Moize. I'd like your word on that."

I looked across the road to the stubbled farm fields where a chicken hawk swooped tirelessly on the watch for a snake or a careless mouse. I said, "All right. You have my word. Tell me the story."

He grinned. "Why don't I tell it after you bring over my little girl?"

But I shook my head and kept walking, too quickly for him to keep up.

He called, "Hell, hold up, son." So I waited for him to slush stiffly through the sinking snow. "Hell, I hate being old," he was muttering, "Truly, truly hate it. But I like your gumption. You're stubborn as me." He took my arm again and we ambled on around the maze of jumps. His other hand scraped its monotonous song against his cheek as he began to tell me his story: "A while back, one summer, let's say 1968 or so, a man who designed my machinery—and this is a man I treated so well, giving him so much stock, he came to hold the chits for a god-damn ten percent of my business—this particular man decided on the sly to peddle his fanny to the highest bidder. And, same time, to peddle those designs he'd been doodling behind my back, besides."

I interrupted, "As I understand it, Ames opposed you for trying to keep the union out of C & W."

Cadmean stopped short. "Now, wait. Wait. Don't 'understand,' just listen. This is a made-up story, wasn't that clear? And I'm the one making it up. There's no names to this story. Hunh? You just listen, all right?"

I said all right, and he clumped forward again through the mud. "Well, now, I happen to hear that some business acquaintances who'd come up to see *me*, were sneaking around on this visit and setting up a private-type meeting with this particular two-timer. I happen to hear because I make it my business to hear. Everything." He gave me a sideways glance. "Now, pretend the place they were meeting was mighty close to where I have a summer home, and say I also keep a nice boat. Still have it. I enjoyed a spin in that boat. Pretend that night I spun it over to the marina next to Pine Hills Inn, just to keep a personal eye out, see if my sad information of this two-timing was accurate."

I whispered, "Go on."

He nodded, "Good story, am I right?"

At the end of the field, out of the stable trotted two young matrons, one on a gray, the other on a dun mare. They'd been in the Fox and Hound earlier, and I knew them both from those social and civic affairs that like medieval feast days ordered the calendar of Hillston's inner circle. In their black and red riding outfits, the two waved merrily, and Cadmean swept off his fur cap with a bow as they whisked by us. "Ah, woman, lovely woman!" he groaned. "I truly could have married another half a dozen if the Lord hadn't shut off my tap." He guffawed loudly, and the women turned their heads and waved gaily again. Watching them trot away off among the trees, Cadmean squeezed my arm. "Why in hell don't you get married? You and Baby, now. You two are certainly good-looking, both of you. Good blood. Good families. I believe I could get a fine litter of grandchildren out of the two of you. 'Course, they'd be goddamn stubborn."

I stepped away, folding my arms, but I said nothing to disabuse him of his suddenly evident plans to breed me to his daughter. Instead, I told him that yes, his story was fascinating.

"I figured you'd think so," he chuckled. "Well, I'll finish it. Say I took a glance into that inn window that night and I see all my old pals are indeed having a little gab with the two-timer. I also see, looking miserable over by himself at the bar, a certain good-looking fellow, maybe about what your age is now, who I happen to know is cross-eyed in love with a foolish woman that's already married to this betraying man I've been talking about. You follow me?"

I said I did, and he smiled.

"So, I go back to my boat, diddle around there—pretty damn put out and trying to ease my soul." Cadmean stopped again and hoisted himself up on a hay bale we'd come upon; he gazed complacently around him, as if that too were a way to ease his soul. He looked on one side at the dark feathery trees fronting the blank sky, then turned around and looked across the street to where small white swamps of snow seeped into the brown and yellow grass of the meadow. The hawk still circled.

Cadmean beamed. "Isn't that the prettiest thing in the world? Winter fields. I got no use for people putting down the Piedmont like it was some scruffy patch between the mountains and the beach."

"The mountains and the coast are beautiful," I said.

"It's all beautiful. God on the land never went wrong. People now, I think He gave up and turned people over to Lucifer." Cadmean pulled out another cigar, while I found a last cigarette, and we each lit our own, and I waited.

Finally he mumbled, "So," his lips a circle of smoke. "Here's the part of my story for your special satisfaction. Say, when I'm sitting down there in my boat, I see my false friends out on the Inn porch arguing with that design man, and he looks a mite weavy on his feet from not being the kind to hold his liquor. After the others walk on back inside, he stands there looking down at something he's pulled out of his pocket."

The coin. So far, each thing Cadmean had said fit precisely with what Cary Bogue had long ago reported: the arguing would have been their trying to convince Ames not to take his boat across the lake after having so much to drink. It was what happened next that I wanted to know. I asked, "And?"

"And? Well, *and* this in-love fellow pops out of the Inn and catches the other one up, right about where his boat's moored. And they talk a bit. And they yell a bit. And maybe it's talk about this also two-timing woman they both want to hold on to. The way I said before, men are rutting hogs, and, son, that's a fact of nature no sense denying. And, another *and*, this in-love fellow gets carried away with his feelings, and slugs my design man right in the face a good one, and down he goes, clunk, on that hard concrete walkway by the dock. And off the other one goes not even looking back."

My heart had quickened fast enough to sweat my hands inside their gloves. Had Rowell simply left Ames lying there on the marina walk?

"He went off to his car in the lot?" I asked.

Cadmean shrugged, puffing up smoke at the cloudless sky, watching it rise. "So, there I sit and there the other one lies flat out. I'll tell you this. I didn't feel like going helping that man up after he'd stabbed me in the back. But he didn't move and didn't move, and I'm starting to think, maybe he's accidentally dead from that fall under the influence.

But pretend, here comes the in-love fellow back, and he about jumps out of his skin when he sees the other one still laying where he'd socked him. So he picks him up. Now, son, let me rest my old voice. You use your imagination." Cadmean's sleepy yellow eyes moved back toward me.

I stared at him. "He put the body in the boat and took off."

"All right. That sounds like a good ending to this story."

I said, "And he motors out into the middle of Pine Hills Lake, throws the body overboard, jumps off himself, and swims ashore."

Cadmean's cigar slid around in his pink puffy lips. He shook his head. "My story ends at the dock. My eyes are good, they truly are, but not good enough to see across a big old lake in the middle of a summer night."

"You heard the explosion when the boat hit the pump?"

"My ears are good as my eyes."

I tried to keep my voice even. "And you never said *anything*? Why didn't you tell Stanhope?"

Cadmean's little eyes widened innocently. "Tell him what?"

"Christ! That Rowell murdered Bainton Ames!"

"Now, son, now." He leaned over and squeezed at my shoulder. "I don't know what you're talking about."

I walked off, wheeled and stared back at him. At the stable end of the muddy arena I could see the teen-age boy leading out Manassas, now unsaddled and looking like some Tartar chieftain's steed, the winter hair of his pasterns like high shaggy black fur boots. I said to Cadmean, "Fifteen years! And you know what! You *told* Rowell what you saw, didn't you? Christ, you've had him by the balls for fifteen years!"

Pulling off his fur cap, Cadmean scratched his bald skull. "Well, that's a mighty uncomfortable figure of speech. . . . I'll tell you two things about Rowell. He was a good husband to Cloris. He's been a good state senator to this area. He's a Piedmont man. He does what he can for us."

"He's *your* man."

Cadmean squished the cap back on. "I'm a Piedmont man. So are you. I love where I live. Don't you, son?"

I told him, "Ken Moize can subpoena you. You've withheld evidence in a felony."

"Have I?" He pulled out the cigar and studied it curiously. "Have I?

I thought I was just telling you a story. In exchange for you arranging a visit. And seems like you gave me your word you'd get Baby to come see me. So why don't you go do it, son?"

"You're amazing! You stand there and tell me you'd commit *perjury*, and then you expect me to 'keep my word'!"

He looked at me with an astonishing benign affection. "Justin. I don't believe you think a gentleman's word has anything to do with what other people do or don't do, or say or don't say. Keeping his word just has to do with his having given his word. Am I right? That's the kind of gentleman I want to see my girl bed down with."

By now I was pacing back and forth about twenty feet off from him. I yelled, "Just what are you going to do if Hudson and Willis won't keep their mouths shut! If you sent them over to Cloris's, and we can tie you to it, you better believe that's a subpoena you'll *have* to answer. Christ!"

Cadmean spit out his cigar and ground it into the mud. "Oh, now we're back to *your* story. Well, I don't believe I'll worry about that. I'm an old man, and worrying's bad for the little bit left of my health. Like I said, son, this philosophizing of yours about brute violence and all getting on the loose, and how it can't be controlled . . . It all depends." And then with a jerky quickness I wouldn't have thought possible, he jumped down from the hay bale, threw up both arms, clapped his hands sharply, and in a booming shout called, "Manassas! *Huh! Huh! Huh!*"

Off at the field's end, the black stallion broke loose from the startled stableboy, reared with a shivering whinny, then bolted toward us. Duchess bounded to her feet and started barking.

Mud flew up with a smacking pop as Manassas' hooves slapped at the ground, flying closer. He was galloping straight toward me, his neck stretched, mane shaking, nostrils huffing out white smoky air. His eyes wild on mine, he kept coming almost as if old Cadmean, like a wizard, had communicated to him some silent command that he come trample me to death. At the last instant, when I could feel his breath in the air, I leapt sideways to the barrier of the hay bale.

Cadmean stood right where he was, as serenely as if he watched a child skip toward him bringing flowers. Only inches away from crashing into the fat old man, the horse sheered off at an angle, legs prancing mud up on Cadmean's pants legs, then whirled around and stopped himself in front of his master, who reached calmly in the deep pocket, pulled out the jelly beans and held them up. Manassas mouthed them out of the big twisted fingers while Cadmean, cooing, rubbed the sweated neck. "Good boy," said the old man with a chuckle, and peered over at me. "Controlling brutes, now, son. It all depends," he said quietly, "on who's in control. Hunh?" He thrust his fingers through the bridle strap, and tugged the nuzzling animal into a walk beside him back across the thawing field.

Two hours later, when I came quietly into the crematorium of Pauley and Keene Funeral Home, Mr. Cadmean in a dark suit, his bald head bowed, stood alone among the empty chairs, as the Reverend Thomas Campbell, who had baptized generations of the inner circle, including mine, prayed that in heaven Joanna Cadmean's soul would find the peace that life should not promise and cannot give; while Mr. Pauley with a discreet forefinger pushed the button that slid her rich black coffin smoothly and slowly into the fiery furnace.

Afterward, I walked Mr. Cadmean out to his limousine and said I'd like to ask him one question. "Did you ever tell Joanna the story you told me?"

"What story was that, son?"

"The one about the designing man and the in-love fellow."

His driver opened the back door to the C & W company limousine. Cadmean carefully lowered himself into the plush seat, then shook his head. "I don't recall that particular story," he said. "But I never told Joanna any love stories. I truly never had the feeling she was the kind of woman would want to hear them. Would you excuse me now? I need to get back to my mills. I've got a young snot been giving me a hard time. He's in for a surprise. I'm an old man. But I'm not as old as they think. Hunh? I appreciate your paying Joanna your respects. I like a man with good manners. Principles, I've got no use for. Ever notice how most of the slime of the world gets flung there by men with principles? Take care, now." The big car turned slowly toward home. Home was Hillston. All of it.

27

"General, I had made plans to fling my skinny body over what you might call the chasm between Junior Briggs and her old man Fatso the Bald because I hate to see a family frost each other when it's a family I want to put my name to, and I'm the one liable to end up catching the icy breeze. But I don't know about talking Briggs into going over there. All this terrible stuff you tell me that old rascal's said, not to mention *done*, lordy! I don't know. Why did you say we can't go to Moize? My future pa-in-law ought to be in jail!"

I said, "Cadmean does love her, Cuddy. It's been five years since Briggs's even gone to his house."

"Well, now, love. Nero loved Rome. To hear him tell it, he only burnt it down so he could redo it prettier. I saw that on TV."

"Don't worry. I didn't think you'd been sneaking around reading Suetonius."

"Who?"

Cuddy Mangum roamed my kitchen drinking my beer and complaining to Mrs. Mitchell about the contents of my refrigerator and shelves. "Honey, just eat it. I know it looks all crumbly and rotted, but he doesn't have any *American* cheese. What kind of soups are these tall skinny cans supposed to be? Bisque? Vissysuave? Don't you have any meatball vegetable?"

We were there waiting for a visitor. Mr. Ratcher Phelps had telephoned shortly after my return from the funeral services to say he was ready to pay his call. I confessed I wasn't going to be able to hand him a check for $5,000 today. In his sonorous dirge of a voice, he replied, "Patience is a woman I've kept company with all my life, and I've got the trusting heart that gives a man tranquillity of mind."

We were waiting, and Mr. Phelps was an hour late.

"Maybe," said Cuddy, gnawing at an old stale loaf of French bread, "maybe Parson Phelps and his girl friend Patience took time off to go at it back behind the pianos." And he gave his crotch-pumping gesture.

I shook my head. "Mangum, I thought love was going to refine you."

"You never know what love's gonna do. Look what it's done for you:

losing your job, punching husbands out, you and Red running wild and slobby in the streets. Is this bread bread, or is it bricks?" Teeth clenched on one end of the loaf, he was yanking wildly at the other with both hands.

"It's old."

"Of course it's old. It's yours, isn't it? I think it's got two of my teeth in it too." He gave up and let the loaf clatter to the table. "Anyhow, what you don't know is, one reason Professor Briggs Junior is so crazy about me is because I'm so, let's call it, loose. How's that? *Loose*." He jiggled all his lanky limbs in an attempt to convey a languid easygoingness. "And she's uptight. I mean, not really uptight from the inside out, but a little bit from the outside in. Due to her losing her ma and hating her pa—wonder why?—and due to that phony-leftist ghoul she slipped up and married back in the sixties when everybody was nuts. That creep actually *beat* her, on his way to a Hooray Hanoi march, and if I ever come across him I'm gonna be tempted to do to him what a guy from Hanoi did to a friend of mine. Oh, lord, you know: We all plum lost our twenties to the sixties. I oughta be ten years younger. Know what I mean? 1965 to '75, Uncle Sam was an old acidhead. Good politics, though."

I sat down across from him with my yogurt and said, without planning to, what I never had said in five years of almost daily conversation. "Cuddy. I want to tell you something, all right?"

"Shoot."

"You say you lost your twenties. Well, so did I. I was in a sanitorium. Twice. For several years. A hospital up in the Blue Ridge." His jay eyes looked into mine, warm in the sun coming across my shoulder onto the table's clutter of food. "They called it 'acute alcoholism.' But it wasn't just drink. I was, well, okay, I was crazy." Blushing, I rubbed hard at my ear. "It's not the sort of thing I want people to know. But I've told Alice, and I've always felt bad not being open with you about it. So . . . well, that's it."

The sun moved in among the bony shadows of his face. "Aww, General," he said quietly. "I'm glad you said so." Then he smiled. "But I've known it for years."

"Known what?"

He rolled his blue eyes extravagantly. "That you'd gone to the bin, as my grandma used to say when they took her spinster sister there for being too much of a friend of Jesus'—even though the hymn says you're supposed to be. But she fell into the habit of too long nightly phone talks to Him, and they were on a party line."

I was rattled. "Don't kid me. You knew?"

"'Course I knew. So what? I told you, everybody went crazy back then. You should have seen me out in those rice paddies." He grimaced. "No. I take it back. You shouldn't have seen me."

"That's different."

"Not much."

"You didn't bring it on yourself."

"I brought my first wife on myself trying to get out of going."

I found him another beer in the back of the refrigerator. "Who told you?"

"Guess." He snapped off the can top. "Right. Old V.D. Wanted me to keep an eye out, let him know if you slipped up."

"Why didn't you tell me!"

His Adam's apple bobbled as he drank. "Never saw you slip up."

I pushed the yogurt away. "Rowell must have told Fulcher."

"Probably." Cuddy squatted down by the cabinets. "So, I wasn't open with you either. And another thing I never told, I'll tell you now it's true confessions. Your old love Lunchbreak made a play for me about a year ago. That time I came to that cast party y'all had when you did, what was it? *The Philadelphia Story*. She was high, and wanted to know if I wanted to step into a back room and get that way too." He had his head in the cabinet, looking among the cans there.

"Did you?" I asked.

"Nope." His head poked around the corner of the cabinet door. "Don't you have *any* junk food in this house? Nothing in here but a million jars of vitamins. I crave junk food. Some of us never had the willpower to kick our bad lunch habits the way you did."

Then the doorbell rang, and Ratcher Phelps came in, sanctimonious in his black suit, as if he'd arrived to show us a catalogue of caskets. Instead, what he carried was a cardboard box. Holding it on his knees, he sat on the edge of the couch cushion and accepted a snifter of brandy to war against his lumbago. "Young gentlemen," he said, "my party was not punctual, and consequently I apologize for keeping you waiting, but I needed to ascertain for certain that my party was not hiding and watching where I went."

"Let me see the coins," I said.

Phelps smiled sadly and snuffed at the brandy. "Suppose." And now he began another of his hypothetical propositions. "Suppose when I leave, you were to find a box on your stoop, and maybe it has coins in it, and maybe it doesn't."

On his feet quickly, Cuddy snapped, "Look here, Parson, why don't you—"

But I waved him down and asked him to show Phelps the mug shot of Luster Hudson he'd brought with him. "Mr. Phelps," I said, "I have a photograph here I wonder if you'd glance at, and give me a nod if it reminds you of your unpunctual party."

After the briefest look, he gave me the nod, adding, "Ummm. I guess that's what you white people would have to admit was a ugly face."

Cuddy said, "Yep. Luster's the bad kind of ugly. I'm the good kind. Now, let's move on. You told Lieutenant Savile on the phone that you'd explained to Mr. Ugly you had to check out this merchandise, and locate your capital. You have such a fine reputation in the business—"

"The music business," interrupted Phelps.

"That Ugly actually trusted you to cart off this stuff! And you're going to meet him with the money. Right?"

"Well, this isn't all the merchandise, and there was a down payment." Phelps moistened his lips, and then he chugged the entire brandy as if it were water.

Cuddy asked, "Meet him where for the rest? And when?"

Phelps's moist bereaved eyes were peering into the empty snifter.

"Would you care for another?" I asked him.

"Why, just a morsel," he replied, and stared politely at the ceiling while I poured the snifter half full. "Thank you. As to the 'when,'" he said, "one o'clock this morning." Phelps peeked up through the bottom of his glass. "As to the 'where,' where might you say my remuneration may be at?" Now he spun the snifter and scrutinized me through it, his eye like an owl's, shrewd and inquisitive.

I assured him arrangements were being made, but repeated that I'd already explained I didn't have the money with me.

He nodded. "The thing is, I'm accustomed in my business, the music business, to deal on the down-payment plan, and being as I've just put down a thousand dollars on this particular transaction, I am short and I am troubled by that fact."

I said, "I could give you a check of my own for eight hundred, but anything more would bounce."

Cuddy whispered, "Are you crazy?" but I wrote out the check anyhow, while Phelps tossed down his second brandy with long liquid swallows.

Neatly folding my entire bank account and tucking it into his vest pocket, he said, "The 'where' is a little alleyway next door to a white people's dance place named the Tucson Lounge, if that name's familiar to you."

"Yes, all right," I said. "We'll be there at one A.M. You stay away."

He shook his head mournfully. "It would be agreeable to me, Mr. Savile, to stay to home, being that I am not partial to the music they play at the Tucson Lounge, but this party is going to be waiting and watching for my car to drive up. And then I get out and walk and then I put down the money and then he picks it up and then he puts down something for me. The fact is, you need me there."

He was right, and we worked out a plan together. When we finished, Phelps stood up and handed me his empty glass. "You people be just as careful as I'm going to be," he told us. "This particular man is a running man and a scared man and this man already showed me a gun and rubbed it a little too hard into my neck." Phelps pointed out the small bruise just under the drooping lobe of his ear. "That gun was by way of impressing on me *not* to do just exactly what I'm doing." He studied each of us in turn. "And I ask myself, why *am* I doing it?"

"Well, sir, you're a good citizen," suggested Cuddy.

The short portly body bowed its Mandarin bow. "Exactly what I decided must be so," said Ratcher Phelps.

Cuddy added, "Plus, you love your nephew Billy. Plus, five thousand dollars' reward is better'n messing with stolen goods nobody smart would try to fence for the next ten years. Plus, I've heard Luster Hudson's views on the race to which you have the honor of belonging, and I imagine he hasn't been too shy about sharing those views with you."

Phelps bowed again.

Cuddy asked, "Just how much more does Mr. Ugly think you're going to pay him for this stuff? And where does he think he's going with the money?"

The box under his arm, Phelps sauntered over to my old upright piano, where he played a run of scales with his left hand. "He didn't specify his travel plans, but he knows he needs to go somewhere new, fast. And the sum he mentioned was twenty-five thousand, and the sum I mentioned back was fifteen thousand. Of course, you gentlemen tell me those articles are worth twenty times that."

Cuddy whistled. "Whooee. He thinks you've got fifteen thousand in cash! That's a lot of pianos, Parson."

Phelps changed keys, modulated through a series of chords, while his whole face sagged into a mask of despair. "Mr. Savile," he sighed. "Talking of pianos, you need a new one."

I told him, "Well, it needs to be tuned."

"It needs to be . . ." He rolled his tongue thoughtfully, and then smiled. "Ostracized. That's what it needs to be. Ostracized." He set the box down beside him, and standing there back in his overcoat and fedora, romped through "Maple Street Rag," wincing at the sticking keys and flat notes.

"Well, hey!" Cuddy clapped. "That was fine!"

Phelps told me sadly, "I hate to see a man that says he likes Fletcher Henderson, having to play his tunes on a piano this bad." He flashed his aggrieved specious smile, and wished us a good evening. We were to meet again at midnight.

When Cuddy came back inside with the cardboard box, he rolled his eyes. "My, my! Look what I out of the blue found on your front door-stoop."

"You know," I said, holding up the Photostat, "this picture of Hudson? Remember that mug shot of the punk we showed Joanna Cadmean? The big blond guy you said had gotten killed in Vietnam. That guy and Hudson look a lot alike. Remember how she kept staring at that photo out at the lodge?"

Cuddy had opened the box. "Stare at this," he whistled. Out of the satin jewelry bag, he poured bracelets, a necklace, and a single emerald earring. Unsnapping a leather case, he held it up for me to see the ten clear-plastic labeled envelopes, within each of which was a single coin.

"Damn it," Cuddy yelled. "Don't put your fingers on them."

But I had already seen an envelope that I was astounded, and sickened, to find among the others in that case. It wasn't supposed to be there. It made no sense there. On the other hand, it was the only way that everything did make sense. This envelope was labeled, like all the others, in Bainton Ames's methodical spidery handwriting; the words identified the coin inside this envelope as his "1839 Liberty-head quarter eagle, Charlotte mint." With my handkerchief, I held up the packet by its corner. The profile of Liberty gazed with the same exquisite disinterest I'd seen on the coin now at headquarters that Cuddy had found in the diary that was supposed to have belonged to Cloris Dollard. The same coin, and Ames had only owned one.

Twenty minutes later, we were in Etham Foster's lab, and his saturnine face, brown and dry as toast, was glowering at us. "I ought to report you two."

Cuddy winked. "Why, Doctor D. We're the ones got the goods for you."

"Yeah. And jumbled them all up, too. If you Dick Tracys have smeared my prints!" Away he stalked on the stilts of his legs.

And so in another hour we knew that the two coins were exactly the same model; that according to Ames's records he had at no time ever had two of the same model; and that the envelope in the stolen case was definitely in Ames's handwriting. There had not been anything at all written on the envelope found in the diary.

I slumped against the wall. "Well, that's why Joanna Cadmean told us the envelope was blank when she supposedly saw the coin in the case last summer. She couldn't risk trying to forge Ames's handwriting."

Foster had dusted the leather case and was working with his microscope on the prints. Now he looked up. "Come here." Elation inched into his voice. "It's Hudson, okay. A big fat juicy thumbprint, right *there*. On the corner of the case. Look." He pressed his own huge thumb over the Photostat of Hudson's print. "The size of mine. Look." Glee, pushed out of Foster's voice, escaped by making him rub his hand rapidly up and down his long thigh. "I *got* him," he said. "He stopped being careful. They always do. And that's all I need. Now it fits. Didn't fit before. No prints at all on that diary. Except y'all's, of course. Why not Mrs. Dollard's, see? That lady flimflammed us, Justin, that psychic of yours. She was good. I'll say that. Flimflammed us, see?"

Yes. I saw. Finally. Joanna had done just what Rowell had claimed. And Rowell had done just what Joanna had dreamt.

And neither of them had been careful enough.

Foster stood, one gigantic foot on his metal stool, his hand outspread as if he were dribbling an invisible basketball. "Another thing," he said. "We got in touch with that auction gallery of yours in D.C., Savile. One of these quarter eagles did come on the market there a few years back, like that guy Bogue said. Agent that bought it wouldn't reveal over the phone who he was bidding for. But we can subpoena him if we need to."

Cuddy sighed loudly. "I think we know who he was bidding for. Joanna Cadmean. Fuck the ducks." He tilted his head at me sadly. "We've been had, General. You know, that night at the lodge she was hustling me and Junior out the door so fast and saying how we should make a night of it, and I thought the whole time she was just match-making."

"Theories," snorted Etham Foster, stooping over his microscope. "Real evidence is where it is at, my men." His mood broke through again, giving his voice almost an effusive sound. "I knew there had to be more for me than a dumb Marlboro butt. And here it is!" His hand rubbed happily along his lean flank. "Don't slam the door."

"I think Doctor Dunk-it is bidding us adieu," said Cuddy. "Come on, General, let's sneak out of here before somebody gets the idea you're trying to do your job."

On the way back to my house, Cuddy said, "So we grab old Luster, good old all-American solo, and bring him to V.D., and get us some medals, and unlock poor little Preston Pope so he can try to win back Charlene's affection."

"Fine. Will you please be sure you have your gun?"

"Listen, Sherlock, I've got to go to Moize with all this crap. The coroner's got to be filled in too. Remember that thin ice you used to spout about? We're dancing on it."

"I don't know whether I wish we could suppress the two coins, and let Moize go ahead and prosecute Rowell for Joanna. Or let Rowell just fade in peace."

"Whoaa." He turned to stare at me. "Don't go closing family ranks on Lady Justice, General. I'll bust right through your ivy vines and come after you. I mean it."

"Watch the road. I know, I know, hell. Well, he didn't kill *her*."

Cuddy leaned back, pushing his thin arms straight out on the steering wheel. "Yep. That Mrs. Cadmean took us in, rolled us good and left us in the street in our shorts. Lord, imagine that kind of hate dripping drop by drop down on your brains for thirty years. Humankind! Maybe I oughta go into a monastery and just pray. It's gotten so sitting on the benches in the damn River Rise shopping mall is enough to break my heart just watching the sadness and meanness go by."

"He didn't kill her. But he did kill her baby. She'd had an abortion just before she slashed her wrists."

"Don't tell me any more."

"And he did kill Bainton Ames. Let me out at my car. I'm going back to the hospital."

Now Cuddy grinned, his sharp features splintering into new angles. "What hospital? No need to check into your old room at the booby hatch. How about a Trappist retreat for us both? We'll find one with cable TV, where they'll let us bring Junior and Red, and we'll live happy ever after, planting zucchini."

"I suppose you haven't read *Candide* either."

"*Candy*? Sure, I read it. I read everything with a blowjob in it."

I said, "Cuddy, I hope just because I told you about being in that sanitorium, I'm not going to have to listen to you joke about it from now on."

He pulled to a stop behind my Austin, and waved out the window at two Frances Bush students, one of whom casually gave him the finger and went on talking with her friend as they walked through the gate. "My my, such rudeness," he sighed. "Aww, listen, if people can't joke about the ones they love, next thing you know they want to burn queers and bomb Iran. Love's a joke, General. Why, it's just the best joke on life there is in the world, if you wanta know the capital T Truth. How about a 5th Avenue Bar?" He tugged a candy bar out of his pocket. "You know, now, our generation *worked* on being rude, on a principle of anti-Agnewfication. But these youngsters don't give the appearance of knowing the difference. Imagine that." He tossed the candy bar into my lap.

I asked, "What's in this thing?"

"You never had a 5th Avenue Bar? No wonder you went totally psycho and had to be locked up. These are sorry times. I can't believe that young woman flipped me the bird! It must be enough to drive a gentleman like you crazy again. Here everybody is, lonesome shitbags in satellite orbit around a big black hole, meaning so-called civilization, and not only does this generation not even bother pretending to *ape* any ethics at *all,* they're rude! Speaking of apes, you just gonna love Luster Hudson. *Adiós.*"

28

"How are you, Rowell? Rowell?"

"Yes. I suppose you came for your informant's money, Justin. It's there by the bed."

Rowell Dollard had made out the check to me, his signature less thick and sure than it had always been when scrawled across the bottom of the homiletic letters I used to angrily crumple in the waste can at law school.

Seated in the wheelchair beside the flat hospital window, he looked shrunken within the gray wool robe, black monogrammed with his initials but now too large for him. The unlighted room was nearly dark, and empty anyhow of belongings that he would want to see as part of his life. On a tray, food lay untouched in glutinous positions. On a table, ribbons drooped from flowers in cardboard vases.

I stood across the room from him to say that the man to whom I would be giving the check was risking his safety, if not his life, to lead us to Cloris's killer.

Dollard might have been blind, his eyes looked with such fixed opaque blankness at the window glass. "Who killed her?" he asked quietly.

I sat down in the vinyl chair. "A man named Luster Hudson. He worked at C & W."

"Robbery?"

"Yes. But it may be more complicated than that; he may have been working for someone."

Nothing in his face changed. He wasn't interested.

I said, "I have the jewelry. And the coins."

"You didn't bring them."

"No."

The perfectly combed silver hair was motionless; the outline of his head as still as a medallion, and lined by moonlight slatted through the half-raised venetian blinds. "I didn't think you would," he said finally.

I was watching his reflection in the dark window. "I expect you know what I found in the case," I said. "And what finding that second coin in the case means."

"What is that, Jay?" He asked the question politely, but as if he were not involved in the answer.

"It means that Joanna put a coin in the diary. To convict you of murder."

"Yes."

I leaned sideways in my chair so that I could see his face now. "And the same coin in the case means that the night you killed Bainton Ames, you did pick up his coin from the marina walkway, and you did keep it. Odd how the same coin both absolves and convicts you."

He didn't speak, but his body seemed to become even slighter inside the handsome robe, as if the aging of years had been collapsed into minutes and his flesh wasted as I looked on.

I asked him, "Why did you strike Bainton Ames that night?"

Dollard's head turned carefully toward me. His face, all ruddiness clarified, was frail now and nearly delicate, the eyes and mouth expressing nothing. "I assume you've talked with Briggs Cadmean. He surprises me, telling you. But he always did surprise me."

I asked again, "Why did you knock Ames down?"

Rowell was looking past me out the window. After time went by long enough for me to hear the calm noises and the blurring hummed voices that are the sound of hospital evenings, he answered, "Bainton said something about Cloris I couldn't allow him to say."

"All right, but *then*, when you came back, Rowell! And found him still lying there!"

He said nothing.

"Was it," I asked, "because your car wouldn't start that you came back?"

Preoccupied, he slowly nodded.

"When you saw Bainton was still unconscious . . ." And I bent farther forward, into his line of vision. "Why in *hell* didn't you go for help! So you knocked him out, so what? Why come back and kill him!"

Rowell's eyes blinked, and he pressed his hand over them. "I thought he was already dead."

"But he *wasn't*, Rowell. There was water in his lungs. He drowned. If you hadn't panicked about protecting your precious political career. If you hadn't taken him out in that boat, and thrown him over, and *killed* him, Rowell, he wouldn't have died."

Earlier today, imagining confronting Rowell, I had assumed he would deny that he'd taken Ames into the boat; I thought he would claim he had picked up the coin where Bainton had dropped it and then left, and that the dazed man had eventually gotten up, motored off alone, and toppled overboard. But instead my uncle gazed at me, curiously. He asked, "Political career?"

"Come on! Christ! That's why you covered it up. And you got your reward, too. Old Cadmean's blackmail took the curious form of financing your ambition. Your goddamn ambition."

He turned his head calmly away from me. "My ambition? . . . Considering my name, I don't think I had much of that. Certainly not enough." The robe slipped and he pulled it back over his legs. "I had a little. But I had to flog it. My brother Kip had to flog it in me." Rowell's voice was so hushed, I kept myself perfectly still in order to hear him. "Even then," he went on, as though in private meditation, "even then, I knew Dollards were supposed to play in a different league."

"You're a state senator."

"State senate isn't much, Jay. Not much to end with; maybe to start." His hand, bruised bluish from the IV needle, moved gently down the gray wool over his legs, which rested on the props of the wheelchair. "I think I was a good solicitor. Probably I should have stopped there."

"Yes!" I burst out. "My God, how could you bear being under Cadmean's thumb all these years! Him, and Joanna Cadmean! Both! Jesus. I pity you."

His face flinched and some of the color came back and some of the old anger deepened his voice. "Your pity is not something I· want or need." He pulled himself straighter in the wheelchair, tightening the gray robe around him.

And so we sat together in silence in the dark, impersonal room, until he asked mildly, "What have you said to Fulcher and Moize?"

"Nothing yet. Cadmean won't say anything. Ever. Doubtless you know that."

"Moize, I expect, will try to indict me only on Joanna, whatever you say." His tone was bizarrely detached, as if he were discussing some court case in which his interest was merely professional. "The other . . . is so long ago."

I said, "There's no statute of limitations on murder."

Moving his forefinger softly along the rubber wheel of the chair, Rowell said, "Jay, this will disappoint you, no doubt. But if you'll think back to your criminal law classes . . . Perhaps you never attended many . . . Though I had hoped when you enrolled at Virginia . . . Well. If you'll think back, you'll recall casebook examples I expect Mr. Moize also recalls."

"What are you talking about?"

Dollard waited for the energy to speak. "If I struck a man in anger, that was assault. If I then returned and discovered that man—as I thought, dead—and I removed his body, that was disposing of evidence. Neither striking him in anger nor removing him is murder. Nor, by precedent, is the combination premeditated murder." Rowell said all this seriously but dispassionately, as though he actually were in a law school classroom.

"There is no statute of limitations on manslaughter either, Rowell."

"True." His hand began to move again on the wheel, barely touching the rubber tread with his fingertips. "But I rather think . . . I have been through . . . a lot. And I have already paid this state—as the play says, doesn't it?—some service. And I rather think a jury will be inclined to mercy." His head kept staring straight out the window when he added, "I'm just sorry you can't feel the same inclination."

Upset, I stood and started walking. "Why, Rowell? Why didn't you call an ambulance!"

"I told you, I thought he was dead. I couldn't hear his heart at all. And . . . And . . ." Now the voice faltered for the first time, and the silver hair began to tremble slightly. "And then, I didn't think. You don't know what you'll do until you do it. Yes, I must have picked up the coin. I must have carried him into the boat." He spoke softly, pausing often, seeing what he said. "I didn't think, until I was swimming and I heard it blow up and the light was in the water and then I had already chosen . . . what I couldn't even regret." He fought through a slow, struggling breath. "Do you want the truth? I was too weak to bear the shame of having killed him. . . . I was afraid it would cost me Cloris. I would lose Cloris. I . . . She . . ." Rowell's head fell suddenly to his chest, then came quickly back up, and his throat tightened with a strange constricted noise. "Ambition? . . . She was my ambition. She was my ambition." His bruised hand squeezed hard around the wheel. "And her, I won."

High in the window, moonlight shuttered through the blinds and shadowed his face. And when the moon moved on, I saw that he was crying, tears following one another down into the tremulous mouth. He made no gesture to brush them away, and they hurried from his eyes and nose onto his neck and soaked into the collar of the gray robe. Grief shook through him, breaking up his words as he said, "She's gone, Jay. I didn't believe it until these last few days here. I put off believing it. I put it off and off and it wouldn't stop being true. I've lost her. She's gone." And he bent over in the chair as if an unbearable pain had twisted through his body.

"Rowell." I came around the back of the wheelchair so that I stood close beside him. "Please don't. . . . You're not supposed to get—"

He grabbed up at my hand and crushed it in his. "I don't care. You see? I *have* lost her. When you've lost, you're not scared you'll lose." Letting go, he breathed in a last long shudder until his body was still again. I waited there beside him. Finally he pulled a handkerchief from his pocket and blew his nose. He said, "I'm all right. Go sit down."

"I'm sorry," I told him quietly. "I'm sorry for your pain. To have kept this inside too; for so long. I can't say I wish I had left it all alone. But I hope you will forgive me for the poor way I handled it. I . . . I judged you unfairly. I ask your pardon. I wanted to think you guilty. Even of killing Cloris to protect yourself."

He twisted his head to see me. "Why? Why? Was it because I pushed at you so hard?"

My eyes closed, weighted shut. "Why flog in me an ambition it seems neither of us really had?"

"I just wanted you to be better than me."

"It always felt like you wanted to prove me worse."

Rowell shook his head, the silvery hair whitened by the moon. "I'm sorry. No . . . I loved you."

"It didn't feel like it," I said.

"All I hated was your weakness." He looked away, back to the window.

"I hate it too, but I'm forgiving myself. So should you, Rowell." Reaching across the bed, I picked up the coat I'd left there.

His arms stretched out along the rests of the chair, his hands hanging motionless above the wheels. He said, "I think I'll leave that to a higher judge than I'm going to get in Hillston. . . . Are you leaving now?"

"Yes, I have to." I buttoned my coat. "You should rest. I'll go talk to Moize, now. I'll come again tomorrow. I'll do what I can."

At the door, I looked back at him, still and gray by the black empty window. "Good night, Rowell. I'm sorry."

He whispered without moving, "Jay? This isn't the life I meant to have."

29

The Tucson Lounge on Saturday night was a place for Hillstonians to go in fumbling sentimental quest of a feeling they had heard in the sound of songs and seen in the size of films, and thought would be theirs, and would be better than their insensible weeks, if only they clotted together in a place like the Tucson Lounge. This feeling was some amorphous heightening of impulses nationally inherited and both fed and sedated by a week of television, which was too small and flat for the size of the impulses. This feeling was some mixture of anarchy and of nostalgia for undefined hurts, and of lust enhanced by the romance of love, and of xenophobia boiled over by sports and news into a fine and otherwise failed (not even attempted) sense of all American spirits joined, and so each enlarged to the size of film and the sound of song.

And all this was made possible for these Hillstonians by the alchemic solution at the Tucson Lounge of beer and music and bodies and flaring lights. All this found expression in bloodied knuckles, in throats sweetly choked-up close to the band's booming speakers, in couples rubbing hot-eyed against one another on the dance floor. All this found its correlative with the national heritage in the Tucson Lounge's western decor. Outside blinked the red neon cactus. Inside over the long bar ran a mural of a cattle stampede in a dust storm: steers plunging off the wall away from the endless open background; a train rushing westward into space; a solitary cowboy sitting his horse in bittersweet patriotic lonesome sufficiency and self-regard.

Across from the painted cowboy, I leaned on the bar, gun heavy beneath my arm, and watched the hand of the big round Budweiser clock fall from the twelve. Behind me up on a roughwood platform, the Boot Hill Boys, a country-and-western group (mountain-country taught on fiddle and piano and guitars; western-dressed in fringe and boots) wailed of invisible tears and trembling lips and the solace of barroom buddies.

Cuddy Mangum and I had arranged with Ratcher Phelps that I should be the one to wait inside the bar, since, of us three, I was the only one Luster Hudson had never seen. "Not that I think even Luster's dumb enough to show up in public," Cuddy had said, "but if he does, you'll spot him."

I'd stared again at the photograph of the cropped-haired, ox-sullen head whose thickness narrowed nothing at all as the neck bulged into the shoulders. "I think so."

"Yep, you'll spot Prince Luster right away. He'll be the one snapping folks' backs in his biceps, and chomping the tops off the beer bottles and spitting the glass chunks at the band."

An hour ago Cuddy and I had left our hurried meeting with the stunned and fretful Ken Moize, who had until Monday to decide what to tell the grand jury he wanted them to do with Rowell Dollard. I told him why Joanna should want us to think Rowell had killed her. I didn't tell him Cadmean's story about that summer night at the Pine Hills Inn.

As Cuddy dropped me off in front of the Tucson Lounge, he said, "The cavalry *is* coming. Wait for it, you hear me? If Parson Phelps chickens out on us, I'll just take his car and stick Sister Resurrection up front wearing his fedora. The black people all look alike to Luster anyhow."

It was now twelve thirty. I'd drunk one whiskey and four Coca-Colas. I'd seen a Dodge mechanic bloody the nose of a collegiate fellow who kept insisting (from the rules of a different protocol) that a tap on the shoulder gave him the inalienable right to slow-dance with the mechanic's date, who giggled each time her escort was tapped, and giggled higher when the collegian was knocked backward into the passion-glazed couple behind him. I had heard from the Boot Hill Boys a dozen variations on the sad imperfectibility of human love. I had gone three times to the bathroom (posted COWBOYS), and the third time had side-stepped somebody's vomit on the floor.

The rest rooms were off a rear hall across from a fire exit, and it was from the small glass pane in that door that I was to watch the alley for Hudson. The Tucson Lounge fronted Crowell Avenue, where Sister Resurrection had brought me in the snow to see the trash. Beside the bar was an open-ended pedestrian alley, and there, blocking the entrance, Ratcher Phelps was to drive his black Buick, with Cuddy Mangum hiding in the backseat. Exactly at 1:00 A.M., Phelps was to walk to the middle of the alley, set down the brown bag containing the money (actually, wrapped packages of Cuddy's memo pads), then instead of waiting in his car for Hudson to replace this bag with the rest of the jewelry, Phelps was to leave. As soon as Hudson touched the bag —which Phelps was to position just across from the fire door—I would move to arrest him, Cuddy being by then out of the Buick and covering me.

This short alley backed onto Jupiter Street, which ran one-way and was not much used: most of the buildings in the block were empty victims of the suburban River Rise shopping mall. I had been worried about not having anyone in position to block off the Jupiter Street end, from which we expected Hudson to approach, but Cuddy was certain that if Hudson (who was slow) ran, we could outrun him.

On the Jupiter Street corner leaned a decayed hotel, its shaded side-rooms hiding from the alley's view. This hotel, the Piedmont, had decades ago lost, with the closing of the nearby train station and the extinction of that migratory species of salesmen called drummers, what-ever respectability it may have once claimed. For years the same drunks grew old in the lobby, watching the same parade of hookers, runaways, illicit lovers, and the drifters whom Fulcher delighted in sending patrol-men to hound out of Hillston. I had taken the photograph of Luster Hudson to the desk clerk, and had passed it among the limbo of dere-licts in the musty foyer, and no one had seen Luster Hudson tonight inside the Piedmont. The clerk was hostile and averted his eyes; the drunks asked me for money.

Queasy with the thick sour stink of urine and beer, I kept waiting by the Tucson's fire door. At twelve thirty-five I called Alice on the wall pay phone. I said I wanted to tell her what I could only say by saying that last night with her I had felt, finally, what I had in the past asked, unanswered, of drink: that there was nothing else to ask for, because there was nothing missing. She said only, "I know." And I said that I already knew that she knew. "I know," she said.

From then on, I just stood waiting; pretending—when men lurched past me headed for the cowboys door, and women lurched past me, some with wide smiles, headed for cowgirls—that I was using the phone again, or waiting to use it, or waiting to be sick, or looking for love.

Then, at twenty till one, I saw Dickey Pope, bright-faced with sweat and high blood and drink, staggering up to me on his heeled boots. He had a deep cut over his cheek, and his black satin shirt with its yoke of roses was ripped open to his navel. Dickey was unzipping his jeans, his other arm thrust out to shove open the men's room door, when I registered on him.

"Fucking Lieutenant," he belched. "What's happening?"

I said, "What happened to you?"

"Nothing. I'm just having me a *good* old time!" He took his hand from his open fly and waved it back at the blare of noise down the hall. "Hey. Joe Lieberman says you're gonna turn Preston loose."

"Maybe."

He swayed toward me with unfocused belligerence. "You better. You savvy? I'd love to kill you." Dickey threw in this last remark casually, not even looking at me.

"Really? Is Graham here with you?" I was thinking that if Graham were around, I should either get rid of him before Luster arrived, or tell him what we were doing and ask for his help.

Dickey chortled, throwing his arm around me. "Graham's on a goddamn hunting trip. He don't even sleep. He's *tracking* something." Dickey was so delighted with this conceit that he hugged my shoulder.

I said, "If you mean what I think you mean, Luster Hudson's still in Hillston."

Dickey pulled away, crafty-eyed. "My brother Graham raised Preston from a baby," he said, and backed through the door to the men's room, with a slurred, "Fucking Lieutenant!"

When Dickey came back out, I followed him into the bar to see if he'd lied about not being with his brother. But I didn't see Graham—the size of a buffalo and hard to overlook—anywhere in the crush. Dickey fell into a booth beside an underage, overripe girl wearing a sequined jersey, inside which he immediately plunged his hand. She poured a stream of beer over his head and he rubbed his hands in his black curls and then stuck his fingers in his mouth.

I walked back to the hall and waited some more. At ten till one a drunk couple went behind a recessed partition at the end of the passageway, and made love. I could hear their grunts between the band's twanging chords, and could feel the thumps along the wallboard.

At twelve fifty-nine, craning my neck to peer down the dark alley, I saw the nose of Ratcher Phelps's black Buick. I checked the push bar on the door again, my palm so moist it slid along the steel cylinder. Slipping my gun from its holster, I held it inside my coat. There was no one anywhere in the alley.

I felt Phelps coming an instant before I saw him, small and straight in a checked overcoat, his feathered fedora at a conservative angle. He carried a brown paper bag rolled at the top.

Phelps had come only a few yards toward me when, from Jupiter Street, two of the old scavenger drunks I'd seen in the Piedmont lobby wobbled into sight.

Mr. Phelps hesitated, reluctant to put the bag down until they were gone. But one of them, scratching at the stubble on his chalky face, came wheedling over. "Hey you. Got any change?"

His companion slapped at him feebly. "You asking a nigger for money?"

I was straining to see around them as they crowded against Phelps, and then suddenly Hudson was coming up fast behind the two old drunks. He was not as tall but he was as big as Graham Pope. He had about a two weeks' growth of dirty-blond beard and wore a muddy fleece-lined jean jacket.

Hudson knocked through the tiny derelicts, grabbed Phelps, half his size, with one beefy fist, snatched the bag away with the other, and then, almost lifting him, slammed the small black man without a word into the brick wall. "God's sake," moaned Phelps, his hat tumbling away. Hudson grunted, "Shaddup, coon, and lissen." I was terrified to wait, fearing that if he opened the bag, he'd kill Mr. Phelps. I was terrified not to wait. Phelps said, "Just a—" and Hudson shoved his hand over Phelps's face and banged his head harder against the bricks. I jumped out around the door yelling, *"Hudson! Police!"* He reeled about, Phelps slumping to the pavement behind him, and fired the big automatic suddenly in his hand. The bullet burned past my ear, wood chips splintering back from the door into my neck. From the left I heard another shot, Cuddy's, that missed, and I was shooting too, as Hudson spun already running and Cuddy was already flying past me after him as I stumbled over the crouching drunks in my way.

Swinging off-balance around the corner onto Jupiter Street, I saw everything with the most intense swelling of sensation. The Piedmont. By the snow-heaped curb, Hudson's pickup with three basset hounds howling in back, lunging on their chains. Cuddy in a crouch, gun out, shouting "Halt!" Hudson turning. The Mustang behind Hudson across the street. The huge shaggy shape jumping to the Mustang's hood, lifting something shiny to its shoulder.

Hudson was firing and Cuddy's revolver flew spinning away over the sidewalk.

And then I had stepped in front of Cuddy, pushing him down behind me, my arm shoving him back, and in my other hand I felt my gun keep shooting and I heard Hudson keep shooting and I heard a cracking echo.

And the whitest light exploded inside me, blowing up too fast and too big, distending the light through me so there was no room for me inside my body. And still so expanded were my sensations that I even had time to think how strange I had time to think I was dying, time to think how strange it should be Rowell's words I was hearing—*Jay, this isn't the life I meant to have.* And time to think of Alice. And time to feel beneath my head the sliding sheen of Cuddy's parka before the black sky whitened.

III

THE SEASONS
ALTER

30

Of the first long timeless night, I have no memories at all. How long it was, I was not to learn until much—until months—later. Of how far I had traveled into that darkness, how nearly I had touched the faint sinking banks I floated toward, I had no sense at all, until slowly and from a dim, clouded immensity of height, pain reached down for me and in a blast hooked through me to snatch me up. The dark water felt so restful, felt languorous warm, and the huge squalling shape that grappled to lift me was so cold and screeched at me so loudly, that I kicked out at it to let me fall back, drop deeper and deeper into the muffled lake, to let me slip listless down deep into the quiet quaggy muculent dark.

And so falling I would escape again into the timeless night. But more and more persistent, this intolerable creature would come back for me with its grapple to gouge me up into the sharp cold. More and more precipitant, more and more intrusive, until, unable to fight free, I was snatched through the eclipse.

I was jolting with convulsions I couldn't stop, and thinking, "I have to get back. This is too far to ask me to go, and too fast. If I'm not held back, I'll die, sucked up into that mire of light."

Then there was an *I* there, hearing voices that were not me.

I heard voices, calm and medical. "Dad?" I was saying, but there was no voice to take the word outside me, and no one answered.

Time came back voluminous.

My mouth moved. With the strangest labor it brought out the sound, "What's wrong?"

A cry I knew came saying, "Oh, my God." Then I heard my mother's weeping and felt her hand. "Jay? Jay? Jay?"

"Can you . . ." I sank away and, flailing, swam back. ". . . make them stop this pain?"

But she couldn't stop it. Nights and days labored on and were the same to me. The same black, as profound as the slime at the lake's unfathomed deep. My eyes were pressed shut, closed with tight weight.

Time wove on, and finally my hand came up and felt, and my head and eyes were wrapped with thick tape and gauze. I heard someone moving gently around me. I asked, stuttering and frantic, "Am I blind?"

"No. No. We don't think so. Just sleep. You're all right."

"Alice?"

"Yes."

"Alice?"

"Yes, it's me."

"Where . . ."

"Yes, you're in the hospital. Don't try to talk."

"Where . . ."

"You were shot. But you're all right, you're all right now."

Memory blasted everywhere through my body. My fingers grabbed up at the mask of bandages over my head and at the tubes tangled in my nose and the tube needled into my hand.

"Justin! Stop it, stop moving!"

"*Cuddy?* Where's Cuddy!"

"He's fine. He wasn't hurt. Lie back!"

But by now I was heaving in spasms, and then there were doctors back, hands and voices looming around me.

Day by night, like the old delirium, my self drowned and surfaced, plunged and swam back to air. Ghosts already drowned clutched at me, or groped sightless past me. Joanna. Cloris. Bainton. My father. Day by night the pain funneled toward the places where two bullets from Luster Hudson's gun had entered my body. The first had passed through my bent leg into my stomach. The second had taken away a tiny back corner of my skull.

Voices came and went. Cool medical voices that advised in whispers, they couldn't promise anything. "I'm afraid he isn't out of the woods yet, Lieutenant Mangum, but don't say that to Mrs. Savile at this stage in the game."

Voices of my relations. Alice's voice, reading to me from her textbooks, hurrying history by me, and with it, time.

Day by night, rambling quietly in a stream of words, Cuddy's voice: "Hello, General. *O Bottom, thou art changed!* I saw that in a play. Onc't again, you took them too literally when they told you to go on sick leave. You came close to showing us Stonewall Jackson had nothing on you, jumping in front of me like that, you're so dramatic. Being in reference to the fact that General Stonewall got himself shot and went west to the Great Chancellorsville Above, and being in reference to the fact he was what you might want to call a hero, which don't ever do again, you hear me? Welcome back."

"You still here, Sherlock? What? 'Come again?' as my grandma was always saying to her pappy after he got the palsy and lost the free use of his lips. Can't you talk any plainer than that? 'What happened?' You mean nobody bothered to mention that Luster shot you? Well, Luster shot you. Next time you save my life, would you try to do it so you can keep a little closer grip on your own? I can't keep taking all this time off to troop over here to University Hospital to see if you've checked out. I'm a busy man. I'm trying to get engaged to Junior, plus V.D.'s flying all over the place to the Southwest Moneybelt, licking toadies, trying to get a big-city job out there and leaving behind a mess on his desk that's a revelation of his so-called mind.

"Come again? I think Justin's asking us about Luster. I know it's hard to believe, Alice, but this man used to be a real smooth talker. Well, now, Luster. Luster is a corpus delicti. Nawsir, you didn't kill him. You did just what it says do in the manual, Wild Bill. You shot him bull's-eye as anything, right in the leg.

"Nope, it was Graham Pope gave Luster the *coup de grass*. I don't know if you had a chance, you were so busy knocking me down and trying to squish me, chance to notice somebody great big standing on the hood of a Mustang with a Western Field 550 pump gun, twenty gauge, firing three-inch magnum shells? Well, that was my deputy, Graham.

"No, you're right. It's a shame. I was looking forward to asking Luster a couple of hundred questions about him and C & W myself, but Graham hadn't read the manual."

"Good evening, General Lee. Now, you scared us bad last night, slipping away again. Pull yourself together. Bubba Percy down at *The Star* got halfway through your obituary, had you joining all your fancy ancestors up in Preppie Heaven. But I told him, 'Bubba, you rot-eating hyena, that man's not about to die. He's got a closet full of clothes he's never even worn. Plus he owes me $69.50 for jumping on top of me and bleeding all over my J. C. Penney parka.'

"Speaking of owing money, we got a *bill* here from Mr. Ratcher Phelps. He wants the city to reimburse him for the $233 in cash he claims he was carrying in the wallet he claims was removed from his person by those two old drunks in the alley. Says I, 'My my, you mean right there in the middle of the guns of Navarone, which you might have thought would scare off such jittery tiny little rummies as those two, you mean those two eensy-weensy winos whipped around from where I saw them scrabbling away, and coolly relieved you of that much untraceable money?' Says Phelps back, 'Young sir, Greed knows not Fear, and an inebrious man has no ears, and it is devastatabalistical to me that when the white people get robbed, you people come running; but when the black people get robbed—yea, in the very midst of laying down their lives for the white people—that's when you people turn your backs, and perambulate the other way.'

"Well, he had me there. Says I, 'Parson Phelps, think of nephew Billy, out of jail and back on the streets up to his childish pastimes. And doesn't a citation of gratitude from the mayor of Hillston himself mean more to you than filthy lucre?' Know what he said? He said, 'No. No.' Now, who'd suspect he could talk so short? So, I get him the money, don't ask where from, but Hiram Davies would go rabid and chew up his desk. So now Phelps says, 'Here's the rest of it.' The 'rest' meaning a bill for, one, dry-cleaning his coat; two, replacing his fedora; and three, outpatient services to paint Mercurochrome on his noggin. Meanwhile, Savile, *you* owe Phelps seventy-five dollars a month for the rest of your life, which needs to be a *real* long one.

"What for? Why, the new piano installed in your living room you gave him that eight-hundred-dollar down payment on. He threw in the stool 'cause he took a fancy to you."

"Well, my my! They took those coils out of your nostrils. Tell you the truth, they didn't do a thing for your looks. 'Course, you still look a little too much like the creature from the black lagoon, what with all your hair gone under that wrapping, and I'm really not all that crazy about your scruffy beard. But on the other hand—now don't rile up, Peggy Savile—ma'am, you do have yourself a handsome son somewhere underneath it all. Now if he'll just go back to sleep and stop pestering us with all this begging for sips of water, maybe we can play us some more bridge before they throw us out. Is that Ms. Woods, R.N., on again? Umm ummm, she was *so* short-tempered to Mrs. Mitchell last night. Where'd Junior and Alice go? I swear, sometimes I get the feeling those girls aren't really trying all that hard to learn how to play this game, Peggy. Do you get that feeling? Lordy, they already owe us four hundred and fifty thousand dollars, and they're still trumping their own aces. Can I offer you a glazed doughnut, ma'am? I see you're watching the basketball game. A blue-through Tarheel, you *sweet* lady!"

And days of nights passed by. And not until then was I told how long the timeless while had lasted. Not until then was I told that outside the sealed window of my hospital room, everywhere on the trees along the branches swollen buds had burst to petals, unleafing snow and rose.

31

They said it was the third week of March. It might as easily have been in my dreaming one night or one year since I'd felt myself fall back into the sheen of that blue parka, but by the moon's time, a few days more than two months had circled round, passing by. Two months that would have no past. I thought how less than a twinkling of an eye must time be to the dead.

They told me I had been unconscious for three weeks, and only semiconscious for three more. They told me that two doctors had given me up, and a third had flown into Hillston from Baltimore, and contradicted them, and snapping off his surgical gloves had flown back away. They told me that I was lucky, and that I would be living from now on with a shorter intestine, a stiffer right leg, and a head made harder by a sizable plate of steel. They waited no longer to tell me that Earth had turned tumbling on without my knowing, slanting the Piedmont to spring, because doctors were going to cut away my bandages to see if I could see, and everyone was concerned that for me to see the world so changed since last I saw it, would bring about a relapse.

But what I saw after the chilling blade snipped, and weight lifted gauze by gauze, was light brightening until it hurt, and then the white and rose Highlander face of Alice MacLeod. And that hadn't changed at all.

"Hi," she whispered. "I was saying when you hung up: I love you."

After a few minutes, another face leaned down and winked a blue-jay eye. "Let's move on out of the mush, you two," said Cuddy. "I've got an official ceremony to perform. This is business." He waited until the warm limpid eyes of the doctor from India finished searching in mine, finished touching my face with the same long thin careful fingers I had seen months ago feel for Rowell Dollard's pulse. Then Cuddy said, "Here goes. Now watch me mess up. *Dulce et decorum est pro fratè* just about *mori*."

In his hands was yellow shine that unfolded into a long, fringed yellow sash. With studious pats he draped it across my hospital shirt. "I memorized that," he said. "You want me to tell you what it means? 'How sweet it is to throw your body down for your soul brother.' More or less. Doctor Dunk-it was my consultant. Don't you just love it? It's old. That sash is old too. That sash is genuine Confederate sash I bought in Washington, D.C. This auction agent that found the coin for poor old Joanna Cadmean helped me locate this sash. I told him you were dying, and I wanted you to be buried in it."

"I don't know why in the world," said my mother to Alice MacLeod, "men think *women* are so sentimental."

"But, General, even though you fooled me, you can keep it anyhow if you want to."

"Why, my God, Alice, I remember how Justin and his father both cried all the way through *Bambi*."

"Oh, didn't that movie just break your heart?" sniffed Cuddy. "But now, *Dumbo* was even sadder than that. Did y'all see *Dumbo*? Remember when they chained up his momma? Oh, my!" Cuddy blew his nose, yanking a Kleenex out of the box beside Mother's Shut-in Surprise.

The next week I was put in a wheelchair by the window so that I could watch the Lenten sky blossoming, and the cardinals swaying on the thin branches of the dogwood trees. Seated there, by the window, my thoughts were often with Rowell.

The state had made its decision. At a new inquest, Hillston's coroner had ruled Joanna Cadmean's death an apparent suicide. Probably no one would ever know if she had really spotted the original Liberty-head coin in the case. Perhaps she had seen it, but I preferred to believe that Joanna had never seen the coin Rowell confessed he had picked up from the marina pavement and, years later, returned to the case. And returned there as a token of what? Possession? Guilt? Cancellation of the killing itself, itself tangible evidence that Bainton Ames had never removed the coin from the case that night, and so had never left his house that night, and so had never drowned?

If Joanna Cadmean had *not* seen the Liberty-head coin, but had only dreamt it, then her final case for the Hillston police department transcended all the other mysteries the department had brought, in earlier years, before the oracle of her extraordinary gift. If she had only dreamt it, she was (as Rowell told me) preternatural; and I think she was.

And, ironically, if Joanna had only trusted her gift, had she not assumed she would need "real" threads to weave her spell, had she not found—as we now knew—a duplicate coin in Washington, and bought a diary in a St. Simons shop, and used the brass letter opener to break off the door chain inside Briggs's tower study (leaving on the brass blade some fragments of the chain's metallic paint for Etham Foster's microscope to find), had she not erred in the other infinitesimal inevitable ways people in the tangle of the real world must err, no doubt we would have all gone on believers. No doubt Ken Moize would have persuaded a jury to condemn Rowell Dollard for killing her, killing her, though, in only thirty seconds and not for the thirty years she believed he had actually taken to murder her heart.

But as it was, Ken Moize accepted the coroner's new verdict that a mentally unbalanced woman had killed herself. Moize still did go to the grand jury about Rowell Dollard. And he did obtain an indictment. Because Rowell voluntarily confessed. After long discourse with our attorney general and with the other men who live at the capital of the state, Moize agreed to accept the plea of nolo contendere then entered by Dollard's lawyers. The charge agreed upon was involuntary manslaughter, resulting in the death of one Bainton William Ames. The judge, who was not Judge Henry Tiggs, found Rowell guilty, sentenced him to ten years in prison, reduced the sentence to five years, then made him eligible for parole in one year, and then allowed whatever time the Senator needed to recover from what proved to be a paralysis of his right arm caused by his embolism—that time would be counted toward his serving out his sentence.

It was entirely possible that Rowell would be paroled before he ever entered a cell. And if this did not seem just (as it did not to some local journalists), the judge announced in his summation that, in view of Rowell Dollard's personal suffering and his public service ("And," said Cuddy, "let's face it, his family name"), the court was inclined to be merciful. Naturally, Dollard had resigned his state senate seat and his candidacy in the upcoming primary, and our state, said the judge, could be assured that this man was thus punished well enough to satisfy Justice.

They told me that before his transfer to the new state medical facilities in Raleigh, Rowell Dollard and I had lived for two weeks on the same hospital floor along the same corridor, and that often in the long nights after visitors from the world outside were required to leave my room, he had come in his wheelchair to wait beside me, never speaking, just waiting there, beside the sealed window, watching out.

One bright day when haze motes spun up in my room like seafoam, Cuddy Mangum stuck his head in the door. "You decent?" Then he ushered in a thick cluster of Popes, all noisily hushed and stiffly dancing so as not to take up too much space.

Dickey had his comb and his pliers in a new aquamarine cowboy shirt yoked with lariats. Graham had taken off his down vest and put on ten pounds. Somewhere lost behind Graham, Preston moved furtively. And on either side of Cuddy stood Paula Burgwin, in a muu-muu, and Charlene, whom I'd last seen as a platinum blonde and who was now staggeringly black-haired and appeared to be wearing a Puerto Rican costume from *West Side Story*. Of Charlene's own recent stay in this hospital, there was only a thin white scar over the bridge of her nose.

The Popes jostled for position until Cuddy, like the nervous director of a school play, prodded Paula forward, and she—obviously elected speaker for the group—said, "Mr. Savile, how're you doing?"

"Call me Justin. And much better, thank you, Paula, and how about you?"

"Well, I am trying to lose weight, is all, if you can believe that, and I'm on this Scarsdale Diet thing, you know the one where that lady shot him, and," she giggled, "it's a real good diet for me because I can't even afford half the things he expects you to—"

Graham bellowed, "God damn it, Paula, will you get on with it?"

"Yeah, Paula," said Dickey from the mirror over the sink where he was combing his hair. "Will you stop running your mouth?"

"Shut up, Dickey." Graham cuffed his brother in the side of the head.

"Listen, y'all goons," Paula said, "Justin *asked* me how I was doing. I'm doing *fine*." She turned to me with the Snow White smile that showed her small perfect teeth. "Well, I lost my position at the Rib House, but I'm seeking other employment at this time."

"I don't know why," growled Graham.

"Anyhow," Paula told me, "if they'd let me get a chance to say so, we all just wanted to come see how you were doing and tell you we're sorry about your getting hurt and we appreciate what you did to help Preston out. And Charlene got a suspended sentence, for giving evidence against that goon Luster. We appreciate that. And, well, that's all."

Preston sidled out from behind Graham and nodded and ducked back.

I said, "Listen, I appreciate what *you* did, Graham. I probably wouldn't be here if it weren't for you."

"Hell with it," Graham grumbled. "I'm just sorry Hudson's dead. I wanted to mess that son of a bitch up in person, and I wanted him to remember who was doing it."

Charlene had stuck a cigarette between her magenta lips, but Cuddy pulled it out before she could light it. She stepped forward now, orange skirt flouncing, and frowned at the ceiling. "This is all my fault, I guess. I hope you ain't going to hold it against me." She stepped back as if she'd finished a recitation.

I told her, "Don't be silly, Charlene."

Cuddy sighed. "Let's say there's nobody here without some M&M's melted on their hands; by which I mean Messing Up and Mixed Motives."

"Not Paula." Graham tried to hug her, but the muumuu slid away from him. "This little angel here never bad-mouthed a soul in her life."

Paula giggled. "I guess you never heard some of the things I've said about you, Graham."

"She was teasing," he explained. "Okay, Lieutenant, you ever want to go hunting something with *four* legs, you look me up. We got to hit the road, I guess."

"We got to split," echoed Dickey, and they all left but Preston, who passed quickly by my bed, his hand inside his leather jacket, and dropped out of it a car's AM/FM tuner onto my sheet, then hurried away after his family.

"I didn't see that," said Cuddy.

I asked him, grinning again, "Did you round them up and make them come here?"

"Well, it is April Fools' today. But I believe this was Paula's program."

"Good Christ, did she give in and go back to Graham?"

"Let's put it this way. She went back to the Maple Street house. Because Charlene came to our conclusion that Little Preston did a noble deed trying to keep her out of the state pen where her sweet-talking ways might have gotten her face torn off and her hair (umm! you notice that?) ripped out by some of the inmates there—whom I have seen at the lady convicts' wrestling finals, and I don't believe even Graham would take them on without a sledgehammer. So Charlene the Hot Tamale has kissed and made up with Preston and love's gonna live there again. Paula went on back because she didn't want Charlene to have to live in that house again with the Pope boys unchaperoned, which she believes no woman should have to do, and I can see her point. But Paula is *not* living there, as she put it, as man and wife. She is holding herself in reserve, like those Greek ladies in *La Strada*."

"*Lysistrata*."

"That's right. One of those foreign films. And speaking of man and wife, look here." He loped around to the bedside, tugging out a small jeweler's box; in it was a diamond ring in a circle of tiny sapphires the color of his eyes. "You think Junior'll like it? I put it on my Visa card. I just have the feeling she's going to say yes. Don't you?" Head tilted, he grimaced.

"I hope so, Cuddy. She ought to."

He flopped down into the wheelchair and spun it in a circle. "Oh, lordy, if she doesn't, I'm gonna, I'm gonna . . ." He stopped and sighed loudly, for the first time in our acquaintance robbed of his rich mint of words.

I said, "Did you buy those clothes to propose in?" For he was wear
ng a Harris tweed jacket with a gray wool knit tie.

"First, I tried on a bunch in your closet, but the pants were knicker-
ockers on me. Tell you the truth, I came into a little extra money.
This is going to spook you, Justin. I almost didn't want to tell you. You
remember those basketball scores Mrs. Cadmean gave me the night she
died, off the top of her head? I won the pool. I won the damn
N.C.A.A. basketball pool! First time in my life! Can you believe that?"

I could see Joanna's face, see the perfect smooth profile, feel the calm
gray eyes on mine, hear her voice soft and absolute as a dream saying to
me, *Let go*—saying to me what she could not tell herself. I said, "Oh,
yes, I believe it." The face moved close to mine, translucent now.

Cuddy was saying, "No, I already wore these clothes when I took Junior over to see her old man."

The gray eyes closed and the face faded away.

I said, "Sorry? You got Briggs to go see Cadmean?"

"Ummm."

"How'd it go?"

He spun the chair in a slow circle. "I'll say this. If you stood between her and her dad in your shorts, your pecker wouldn't be too
much use to you afterward, due to falling off from frostbite." Cuddy
yanked up his hair. "I hate to confess this because I am a strictly moral
man, but I *liked* the fat old bastard."

I laughed, and winced. "I also hate to confess it, as he is *not* a
strictly moral man. . . . Any chance Ron Willis will tie Cadmean in
for us about those Ames papers?"

"I deeply doubt it."

"It's not over, Cuddy. Luster was working for somebody. I just know
it."

"Doctor D's happy. He found some of that yellow carpet's fibers on
Luster's sneakers. Plus a speck of Mrs. Dollard's type blood, plus a
sliver of some kind of expensive grass the Dollards had planted out
there, plus a few white Persian cat hairs, plus Lord knows; so he's
happy, and Ken Moize is happy. Luster did it. And the state rests.
We've got nothing on Willis except his whinging a few shots at you,
which appears to be a popular Hillston pastime. He can prove where he
was the night of the robbery. Just because he knew Hudson and just
because he handed Charlene a bag, doesn't make him a murderer. Or

even an accessory. Meanwhile, hophead Ron has come up with some *real* fancy lawyers that wouldn't use Joe Lieberman to lick their stamps, and they are arguing he wasn't even shooting at you. Just disturbing the peace, under the influence, and driving so as to endanger."

"I think old Briggs hired Willis to find somebody to steal those copies of the Ames papers. Cloris *had* them. Somebody took them."

"Oh, lordy. You are stubborn. Well, it wasn't Cary Bogue; he said he never saw them, and for us to stop pestering him. Anyhow, Fatso the Bald and I didn't get into that aspect of our relationship when I was over there. It was personal."

"What did you say to him?"

"Not much. I've been told that I'm a talker, but between your mama and my future pa-in-law, I believe I've been overrated."

"So, what did he say?"

Now Cuddy jumped out of the chair and blew up his cheeks and poked his finger at his pursed lips. "Says, 'Who the shit are you, son? Hunh? Hunh? Hunh?' Says, 'I truly truly believe I know you from somewhere, your particular ugly face strikes a chord of memory in my old ossified vicious self-adulating mind. Didn't your daddy used to work on my line? Hunh? Hunh? Now, shit, you're not diddling with my Baby, are you? Even if that child did sew a stone up in my heart. Because if I hear—and my ears are big as the sky—if I hear you are not doing right by my Princess, I'm going to have to send some boys from C & W over to pull off your arms and club you to death with them. Son.'"

I said, "Let me quote a friend: 'You are messing with the big boys now, Mangum.'"

He winked, "Oh, I expect that man is going to just love me if he lives long enough. I'm not going to let him see his grandchildren unless he improves his character."

"Forget it, Cuddy. He's too old for improvement. And I'm not sure what's coming along behind him is any better."

"Are you in reference to Lawry Whetstone?"

"For one."

"The Whetstones are on a cruise to the Caribbean. What with your whopping him, and throwing her over, they needed to rest up. Fatso gave me the news when I was over at his castle that he personally sent old Lawry off on this vacation and told him don't rush back. They don't appear to be too friendly." Cuddy ate two chocolate turtles out of the box on my bedside table, then leaned over and shook my foot. "All right, now, when are you going to unhook your catheter and come on back to work? Not that it's as much fun around there now that old fathead V.D.'s left us to go tame the West."

"Have I still got a job?"

"Yep. Fact is, the new captain's a friend of your family's, you know how family connections always help. He even got you a raise so you could make your piano payments." Cuddy draped his (apparently new) London Fog raincoat over his lanky shoulder.

I pulled myself carefully up on the pillows. "New captain? Have we got a new captain? Who?"

At the door, sun twinkled the blue-jay eyes. "Oh, a real brainy guy."

"*Who?*"

"Me." He waved a salute and closed the door.

32

I was home by Easter, sleeping on the couch downstairs across from my new ebony spinet. Above the piano, beside my father's water-color, now hung the pencil sketch Joanna Cadmean had drawn the first day we met; Alice said it didn't look like me.

Propped on my cane, I watched Alice day by day move through the house, and leave it rich with her presence, with a vase pulled forward on a table, with apple juice shining in the refrigerator, with her small earth-dark gardening gloves placed one upon another in the window-sill.

While she was gone, I followed her days, walking with her along the aisles of looms at C & W. Lying on my couch, I was taking tests with her across the street, worrying if this morning's exam had indeed, as we had predicted, begun with this question or that. I was going back, sober, to college.

Seated at my new piano, I was always listening for the click at the door and the quick steps coming closer. At every car's brake squeaking outside the house, my heart expected her, hours before I knew she could possibly return.

My own first public outing was to take place shortly before I resumed work at the department, under my new chief, Captain Mangum. I was asked to Easter services at the Presbyterian church I had attended as a child, as a restless captive peering at the back of old Briggs Cadmean's glossy skull, but that I had not entered since my father's funeral. It was Alice who (to my mother's delight) asked me to go to church with her.

Across from her at the kitchen table, I said, "Red MacLeod, Lenin is writhing."

"Why?" she asked, and poured more syrup on her pancakes.

"I thought you were a Communist."

"Wasn't Christ? I'm a communist with a little *c*." She smoothed the syrup in swirls with her knife. "Most Communists with a big *C* are just Fascists without the nice clothes."

"Are you speaking as a weaver, or as a politician, or as a churchgoer?"

"All three," she said, and began eating.

I watched her. "Alice, why don't you marry me now, and then run in this district primary? It might be nice to have a Christian communist state senator named Savile."

She laughed, leaned over and kissed me, tilting the small, stubborn chin. "First of all, Mister Savile the Fifth, even if you do con me into marrying you next month, which is not practical, and not reasonable . . ."

"How about if I say, all right, *take* the damn sideboard out of the dining room, will that do it?"

"This sideboard is hideous. And second, if somebody out of this house goes to the senate, the name's going to be MacLeod the First. Unless, of course, you want to run against me."

"Ah *tempora*. You and Briggs." I poured her a third cup of coffee. "You ought to get old Cadmean to finance your campaign. You're one of his. He'd love to buy you. . . . Can you be bought?"

"Bought to do what? And for how much? I'm practical. So's Cadmean. Just last week the union and he bought each other off. What he wanted to buy was 'cooperation,' and we sold it to him."

"Meaning what?"

"Are you really interested?"

I was very interested.

"Well, Mr. Cadmean invited all the shop stewards to this special board meeting, where he got us to testify so the board would vote through his plans to put this new loom system in the cottons division. That's my section. To update, instead of cut back. Now, that means, shutting down for the time it takes to install the system, and then, after it goes in, laying off some workers."

I put down my fork. "New loom system?"

"Okay, so why does the union agree to 'cooperate'? Because, Mr. Cadmean makes a big tearjerker speech about how it's better to lay off a few people now, than to let the division get shut down completely because we keep running at a loss. Because if we have to shut down, everybody loses." Alice cut some more squares of pancakes with quick sharp slices.

I asked, "Why should the union believe him?"

"Because there *is* a faction on the board fighting Cadmean to phase out a lot of the textiles; they want C & W to move into developing computers; they want the plant space. And frankly, if they're willing to give me assurances they'd pay to train the people now assembling their clothes, so they could assemble their computers instead, that would be fine with me. But Mr. Cadmean comes out sounding like the great American philanthropist and making the board sound like heartless capitalist capital *P* pigs, and everybody gets choked up about loyalty to 'the old mill,' and fighting the Oriental import peril, and they vote him everything he wants. Why aren't you eating your pancakes? Are you in pain again?" She looked at me seriously over her coffee cup.

I said, "Are you talking about a direct projection inertial-loom system?"

Alice stared at me, her cup dark blue as her eyes. "Well, you're always a surprise." So was her boss.

Sunday night, rain thudded at the bedroom's bay windows, and the big oak scratched at the glass, but to me wind and rain sounded peaceful as mist.

Unfastening her green robe, Alice said, "So, you think old Cadmean's really going to show up tomorrow to see you? What do you think he wants?"

"He's the one who made the appointment and what I think is, he's too conceited to miss a chance to grandstand. But who knows what he wants, except he wants his daughter. And who knows what *she* wants, except to spite him. Good Christ, I can't believe she turned Cuddy down."

Alice slipped beneath the covers. "Justin, how many times do I have to tell you, Briggs didn't say *no*. She told Cuddy, 'Ask me again in a year.'"

I pulled myself up, careful of my leg. "Why? You don't have to wait a year to *decide* if you love somebody. If you do, you do. Like us."

She hugged against me, her cold nose on my chest, and wove her fingers through mine. "You're not fair to Briggs. She wouldn't say, 'Ask me later,' unless she was pretty sure she was going to say yes. Briggs has a lot of bad junk to sort through about her dad. I mean, to be sure that she's not marrying somebody either because Cadmean *doesn't* approve, or because he *does*. And, Jesus Christ." Her hair, scratchy silk, made goose bumps along my shoulder. "Who in our generation wouldn't be at least a little ambivalent about marrying the local chief of police?"

"How about a local detective lieutenant?"

"That's bad enough."

But her mouth and her hands as she now slipped up over me was evidence beyond doubt that she and I were stubbornly perfectly right.

She whispered, "Now, don't hurt yourself again."

"About that sideboard. We'll haul it to the backyard. We'll sprinkle it with the leftover cigarettes, and the leftover Jack Daniel's, and set it on fire. Say yes."

"Yes."

She moved above me like a flower swayed, like white peonies and red poppies and rose mountain laurel swayed; and I was the new shafts of spring earth, and so joined with her that there was no way to tell what was earth growing up, and what was flower.

33

Easter Monday two letters came in the mail. Both were endings; one was also an inheritance. The first was a postcard from Susan Whetstone of a hotel swimming pool in St. Thomas. It bore neither salutation nor signature and was brief: "Why did you send those things back? You are so full of it." Unless she'd already found someone else to give the gifts to, Lawry now had two of a number of expensive things, including a gold chain I had never worn, with the initials JBS.

At the heading of the other letter was the name of a legal firm in Cape Hatteras. It advised me formally of instructions received last month from a client, Walter Charles Stanhope, regarding a bequest. Mr. Stanhope's desire was that in the event he should predecease me, I should come into possession of property of his, consisting of a three-room house and a lot fifty by a hundred feet at 5 Shore Walk on Ocracoke Island, North Carolina. This letter ended: "I regret to have to inform you that Mr. Stanhope passed away at his home during the night of April 10. The house has been closed. Please advise us at your earliest convenience as to your wishes in this matter."

In my living room, holding the lawyer's letter, I saw myself creak open the bleached-gray door of the small house, shadowy under moss-bearded oaks. I saw the fishing rods inside the door, saw the phonograph records still on the turntable, saw the conch shells dusty pink in their cabinet. Standing by my car in Hillston, I walked into Mr. Stanhope's bedroom, which I had never entered, and took down the black frayed dusty case of his violin from atop a mahogany wardrobe, and sat down on the bed where he had died, and held it. Standing in the noise of downtown Hillston, I traveled back along the coast of the silent Outer Banks, back along the thin, flurried wild oats rustling together as they bent away from the sea, back where spume of the gray waves rolling in from an old world was salt in my eyes.

At the Municipal Building, Cuddy Mangum stood in the corridor outside my office, pinning to the bulletin board more of the notices with which, Etham Foster told me, our new captain was rapidly reorganizing his unnerved department.

"You're early," Cuddy said, spitting thumbtacks out of his mouth into his hand. "B.M., referring, of course, to old Briggs Monmouth, isn't showing up till four, if then. Plus, he says we're going to meet downstairs in the courtroom. Says he's too old to climb all these stairs and too fat to ride in the elevator. Fact is, the old bastard just wants to refresh our memories about who paid for that courtroom and who thinks he still owns it." Cuddy rubbed his eyes; there were dark circles under them now.

Leaning on my cane, I followed him into the big corner office where the Elvis Presley poster had replaced Fulcher's bowling trophies, and where there was finally room enough for all Cuddy's books. He tapped his pencil on the large metal desk. "Now, listen here, Justin. The hard-headed truth is we just haven't shown Mister Moize enough to tie Willis in on the Dollard case. He's not going to take it to the grand jury. So I don't want you to limp off brokenhearted." His head at its old waggish tilt, he added, "You must have come in here six hours early to traipse around showing off your cane, which does have that Ashley-gimping-home-to-Tara look to it, I'll give you that." He stood, looking out his window over the little skyline of Hillston, now flat-edged in the bright spring sky. "Maybe I should get a cane," he said. "Maybe that would help."

I told him, "Alice says Briggs is going to say yes one of these days."

"Well, I hope Alice is going on inside information." His head shook away thoughts, and he turned back. "Seeing as you have shown up a week before the doctor said to . . ."

Then there was a knock at his door, and Hiram Davies, frozen-faced as a palace guard, stepped in. "Captain, Mr. Moize needs to see you right away. I'm sorry if I interrupted. Excuse me." With a starched nod, he backed out.

"What now?" Cuddy said. "Okay. How about start going through these reports, General." He tapped a stack of papers on his desk. "Crime marches on, you know." He sighed and yanked up on his cowlick and left.

So for an hour I read laconic tales told by patrolmen of my fellow Hillstonians; most of them mysteries only in God's plot, which has always escaped detection. A car dealer on the bypass borrowed a friend's shotgun and blew off his own head because his business was failing; his body was discovered by his eight-year-old daughter. A fight took place outside the College BierHaus between two high school students and two Pakistani university undergraduates whom the locals mistook for Iranians; one, an epileptic, was hospitalized. A battered wife blinded her husband by throwing liquid Drano in his face. An East Hillston senior citizen's lung was punctured by a knife wound inflicted by a fourteen-year-old mugger. A North Hillston boy on speed killed his mother's miniature chow. Last, there was a report with the heading, "Refer to Savile—homicide." The body of a coed had been found Friday night; someone had raped and strangled her as she walked back to her dormitory from the library through University Arboretum. I was supposed to find out who.

I heard Walter Stanhope's hoarse whisper. *Forty years, it's enough. I stick to fish now.* Forty years, before he'd retreated to the outermost edge of the land, retired to the place where prophetic Indians had stopped the first Lost Colony, and then with all their people had fled west and west and west away from the endless waves of pale dreamers from an old world, themselves fleeing west. Forty years; that left me thirty-five more to go.

I went to the morgue to see the body of the young murdered woman, and then I drove across town with Etham Foster to walk the path through University Arboretum to the place, strewn with rain-blown pink and white petals, hidden in a canopy of leaves, where she had died, and where no one had found her until Saturday morning, in the rain. "Just my luck," grumbled Foster. "Rain."

At four fifteen I was sitting at the table where, when court was in session, the prosecuting attorneys sat. I sat and blinked at the afternoon sun angling through the tall sets of dusty windows, and thought about my new case. On the dais in front of me rose the high empty judge's bench, flanked by the furled flag of the state of North Carolina, with its motto, *Esse Quam Videri*, "To Be Rather Than Seem." Beside me, the empty pews of the jury box sloped up to meet the oak wainscoting.

The murdered girl's name, said the report I held, was Virginia. Virginia. That name of the first girl born to the first colonists, the name of the first Protestant born in the new world, born on the Outer Banks to a governor grandfather named White and a father named Dare, christened in honor of a Virgin Queen for whose favor Sir Walter Raleigh had dared the dream of gold. The Lost Colony had vanished, including this firstborn of my people, this Virginia White Dare, had vanished and left only a mystery carved in a tree, a single world of warning or prophecy, the word *Croatoan*. But no one had been able to interpret the mystery, and no one had been warned away, and whites dared to keep digging the gold beneath the forests of tall pines. Raleigh had died on the block, and his dream was now a land of Hillstons.

Briggs Cadmean, wearing a rumpled poplin suit and holding an unlit cigar, came into the courtroom. He squinted at the hard light for a moment before he moved. Then down the tiered aisle he shambled with leisured interest, running his stiff fingers along the backs of the empty oak chairs, stooping with a groan to pick up a littered newspaper off a brown-cushioned seat.

"Good afternoon." He smiled, reached for and shook my hand. "Justin. Mighty happy to see you in church yesterday and on the road to recovery. You had my prayers, son. I know a parent's heart. I've lost five of my flesh and bone. None left to me but my Baby and two foolish sons so scared of me they moved out of the goddamn state." He waved his cigar at the windows. "Isn't this the prettiest day you ever saw? All that rain just washed the world young. Between the apple trees and the cherry trees and the azaleas, I just want to fill up my lungs with Hillston! You know what they say, 'If God is not a Tarheel, then why is the sky Carolina blue?' Am I right? What can I do for you today?" By now Cadmean had settled himself carefully into the large spoke-backed chair where during sessions the court recorder sat.

I said, "You're the one who made the appointment."

He nodded. "Where's Captain Mangum?"

"He had a meeting. He sends his regrets."

"Hunh. You like Mangum? Smart man, am I right? New breed."

"Yes."

"His people were tenant farmers, you know that? Country people. His daddy came into town applying for a job at the mills, came in his bare feet."

"What did you do, have his genealogy traced?"

"Captain Mangum like his new job?"

"Yes."

Cadmean grinned. "I talked to a lot of friends of mine. I heard they were getting ready to appoint a new chief. I'm all for progress, always have been."

I said, "No reason why if you're asked your honest opinion, you shouldn't be happy to give it."

Old Cadmean rolled the cigar between his palms while he told me, yes, he was always happy to be of service to the city he loved. His huge bald head swiveled slowly as he spoke; doubtless to indicate that the perimeters of this courtroom were a ready example of his affection for Hillston. He said, "Shame you never got to see the old courthouse, Justin. Man with your fine taste would have liked it. I was a teen-ager when it burnt down. I remember getting shown the ruts in the steps where the colored people had rolled up the whiskey barrels back when they were running the town for the Yankees in the days of Reconstruction. Couldn't even read, and they were running the town drunk as baboons. Well now, progress."

I said, "While you're throwing your unprejudiced voice behind the new breed, Mr. Cadmean, I've got a name for you. Somebody who believes in progress and wants to get into state politics one of these days."

"Who is he?"

"It's a she. Alice MacLeod. Your great-grandfather sent her to college."

He grunted. "Oh, her. Bush Scholarship. Yep, Alice is something. She's not a scared woman. Scared women give me the fidgets. Wants to get into politics, hunh?" The fingers scraped up the fat cheek. "Hunh. Well, maybe I ought to sit down one of these days and have a talk with her."

I said, "You'll run into the same problem you're going to run into with Captain Mangum. She's not for sale."

"That so? Wouldn't it depend on what I wanted to buy?"

"What can I do for you, Mr. Cadmean? I'm afraid I need to get back to work pretty soon."

"That thing over in the Arboretum Friday night?" He shook his head. "Didn't that make you sick? What kind of girl was she?"

"Not the kind that wanted to get raped and strangled."

Turning his chair so his back was to the shaft of sun, he squinted at me. "I saw Rowell last week."

"Yes, he said you'd come. I went to Raleigh yesterday afternoon to visit him."

"Must weigh down your soul."

"Mine, yes. But I think his own actually feels a little lighter. Confession has a way of doing that. Is that why you're here?"

"Joanna was a crazy woman. I believe I told you that. Pitiful. It just makes me want to cry."

"Does it?"

"Doesn't it you, son? Killing herself for spite."

"Yes, it makes me want to cry. I'm sorry she died. I'm sorry she couldn't let go."

"What of?"

"Believing she could force someone to love her. As you know, Mr. Cadmean, it can't be done."

The eyelids lifted to show more yellow.

I pulled my leg off the cane I was resting it on, stood up, and, sun in my eyes, walked toward Cadmean's brooding face. I said, "I hear the board at C & W met this past week and decided to install a new inertial-loom system in the textiles division."

He pursed the sea-bass lips. "Well now, Justin. Who told you that? Yes, I won that vote. I had some opposition."

"I heard you had to scramble pretty hard."

He nodded. "I truly hate it when I have to. It reminds me I'm getting old and that's something I hate even more."

"Mr. Cadmean, tell me something about this new system of yours. Are your engineers making use of Bainton Ames's designs?"

"Could be."

"Where'd you get them?"

He surprised me. He said, "Cloris gave them to me day before she died. Brought over a whole box of Bainton's other old stuff besides."

"Why'd you tell me she didn't?"

The old man patted his hand at the air near me. "Something the Preacher Solomon says, I believe, is a prudent man concealeth knowledge. But a fool's mouth is his destruction. I make it a practice not to answer folks, till I know *why* they're asking a particular question. Hunh? You told me those particular designs were tied up with poor Cloris's getting herself killed. Well, I didn't believe they were. I thought you'd gone haywire, tell you the truth. But, naturally, every now and then I'm mistaken."

I asked him, "Did she give them to you of her own free will?"

Cadmean bared his small even yellow teeth. "It's not my way to use force against a member of the fair sex. I love women."

I said, "Not 'loose' ones. Not Cloris Dollard."

"That's true, son. And I told her so to her face. Told her something else. She had no business holding those designs back from me all these years, a whole carton of stuff mildewing down in her basement, not letting me know Bainton had advanced his ideas as far as he had way back then. 'Course, she didn't anymore know what was in those files than a cat can read."

"So why'd she bring them to you when she did?"

"Well now," he rumbled. "That's a long story."

"Is that why you came here? You enjoy telling these long stories, don't you? I'm not sure I have time for another one. But I'll listen to a short version."

I walked back to my chair and sat down. Cadmean pointed at my cane. "How long you going to have to be on that cane, son? Is that leg busted for good?"

"Probably not. *Do* you know Ron Willis?"

"Mighty happy to hear it. Well now, Mr. Willis used to drive a forklift on the night shift; in cottons."

I smiled. "That's another thing you were too prudent to reveal last time we talked?"

"No. I didn't know it then. You obliged me to find it out after that pleasant walk we took. I like to know as much as I can about anybody working for me."

"Did you arrange for Ron Willis to rob Cloris Dollard of the Xerox copies she'd made of those designs?"

"Oh, I already answered that question for Mr. Moize and the answer was no."

"You would so testify?"

Cadmean pushed the fat pads of his fingertips together. "I recall Solomon also saying there were six things the Lord hates, and one was a false witness who breathes out lies." The big gnarled fingers interwove, flew apart, interwove. "And another one was a heart that devises wicked plans. You want to hear this short story?"

My shadow, looking strange to me with its wavery cane, nodded.

He pulled out a thick brass lighter and held it up into the sun. "Why don't we wait for Captain Mangum?"

"No, sir. I'm afraid you're going to have to put up with a small audience."

"All right, then." The fat old man scratched his song against the shave of his cheek with the lighter, his little lidded eyes on me. "Say there was a man from Atlanta named Cary Bogue, a sort of rival of mine, a ferret and a hog. Maybe you already heard how he came up into our state and tried to work a shady deal that fell through when Bainton died. Say this ferret had gone right then and there to Cloris; says, 'Let's *you* and me dicker, and while we're at it I would truly love to get my hands on all those old coins of your departed one.' Well now, maybe Cloris was not the sort of woman I'm particular to. But she was a feeling woman, and this Bogue showing up the day after her husband died, came across to her a little too much like a carrion crow, so she told him she was making a vow: 'Not you, not now, not ever.'"

I said, "Skip on ahead some, Mr. Cadmean."

Slanted light made a play of our shadows against the wall while Mr. Cadmean gazed around the sunsmoky courtroom. "Fine," he said. "Let's skip to a few months back when Mr. Bogue fell into conversation with somebody from Hillston who knew Cloris. And Bogue mentioned how he'd all those years ago wanted those pretty coins *and* those designs and how maybe he still did, because maybe Ames was so smart he could see the goddamn future far enough ahead nobody could be sure they'd still quite caught up to him. You follow me?"

"Yes."

"That's good, Justin. I appreciate a good listener."

"Who is this somebody from Hillston?"

Cadmean flicked open the lighter; flame shot up and he blew it out with his pink puffed lips. "You know him, son. I believe I heard you did to him what he tried to do to me."

I knew he meant Lawry Whetstone, and saw in the sleepily watchful eyes that he was aware I knew.

I said, "I don't appreciate the comparison. Another thing, Lawry knew what I was 'doing to him.' And he didn't care. And that, I'll confess, makes me feel even shabbier about it."

He nodded. "You're old-fashioned. Like me."

"Not exactly."

"Well, I *didn't* know I was getting two-timed. But I found out." The lighter flicked again. "And I did care."

"And?"

"And I'm afraid my vice-president's liable to be disappointed when he gets back from, what do you call it again? cruising? I'm afraid Lawry was hoping my board wouldn't want to tie up so much capital in any new looms just now, when he's so pressed for cash to finish that electronics plant of his." Cadmean shifted his huge bulk in the chair. "My vice-president spends a lot of time conglomerating and socializing in big-money places, like Atlanta. I'm truly a simple old man. I've found out it's easier to keep your house in order, if you stay home and live in it. Sort of like keeping your wife to yourself, am I right? Another thing I'm old-fashioned about is credit. It appears my vice-president had arranged to lease on credit a bunch of machinery for his new plant from a place in New England that pitifully enough had to go out of business. But this credit was on a mighty short leash. That's why not getting my capital is going to be a disappointment to him."

"But I bet you're going to enjoy telling him."

"Oh, I am." Cadmean probed at the bones padded beneath the bald scalp. "I don't believe he's going to be all that surprised. Lawry and I already had a little talk about his last trip to Atlanta, when he ran into Mr. Bogue and Mr. Bogue was in a position to offer him a little capital in a hurry to hold off those creditors."

"And in exchange, what was Lawry offering Bogue?"

"Using my imagination, I'd say he promised he'd talk a foolish woman into selling Mr. Bogue some coins, plus some designs she had no right to sell." Cadmean's puffy lips pushed in and out as he got up from his chair now and came across the room. "Problem is, Lawry forgot to remember one thing about women. They change their minds. Like *that!*" The fingers snapped in a loud crack, and then he continued his walk, going all the way over to the other side of the large room from me, to the jury box, where he eased himself down into the front pew. He put his cigar back into his breast pocket and set the lighter down on the rail in front of him, turning it to the sharp slant of sun.

"She decided to give those papers to you," I said. "But then you were so obnoxious to her, she decided she'd sell Bogue the copies she'd made."

Cadmean leaned his crossed arms over the jury rail. "I truly wouldn't be surprised. I didn't know about those copies. Didn't know till you told me. Cloris was too sly for me. Women have fooled me all my life."

I ran my pencil through my fingers, tapping it on the report in front of me, point to top, top to point, while Cadmean stuffed his hand into the pocket of his jacket, took out and slowly unfolded a piece of paper. "This thing here is another copy. The original came to my attention a few weeks ago, and I had this made up because I thought you'd be interested." He pulled out some bifocals and slowly put them on. "This was in an envelope addressed to my vice-president Mr. Whetstone at his Atlanta hotel, but Cloris didn't get a chance to locate a stamp to put on it before she passed away." The old man rubbed at his mouth and then began to read slowly. " 'Dear Lawry. You were so upset on the phone this morning. . . .' " Cadmean looked up, over the glasses. "By the way, this letter's dated. Dated January 9. Day she died. You all right over there, son? You look puke green."

I pushed my cane out to rest my leg on again; it had been a long time since I'd been up this many hours. "I'm fine. Go ahead."

"Well, Cloris goes on a little about being sorry to let Lawry down; then she says, 'When you first asked me if Bainton had left any papers, I thought, well, my stars, why hold a grudge against Bogue after all these years. And the girls could have the money. Still, it just didn't seem fair to C & W. That's why I took them to Briggs. But after that old S.O.B.' "—he paused and waved the sheet at me. "Can you believe that woman called me an 'S.O.B.?' "—" 'said what he did to me, I thanked my stars I'd gotten those Xerox copies made, and I called you back. But, like I told you this morning, now I can't bring myself to sell them' "—Cadmean's thin copperish eyebrow lifted—" 'without talking to Rowell about it first. I know we agreed I wouldn't mention anything about this to him, because of his loyalty to Briggs. But he and I have never kept any secrets and I don't want to start. So, like I said, I'll put the copies in the safe, and we'll wait until you get back to Hillston and Rowell's home, and if he says okay to give you the copies, and not tell Briggs about them, fine. And there's no reason why Mr. Bogue ought to get mad at *you*, but I just want to say I'm sorry if I put you in an awkward spot. Apologies, Cloris.' Interesting letter, am I right?"

Sun reflected back from Cadmean's glasses as he refolded the sheet. Then with that surprising suppleness I'd seen once before out in the muddy field by the stables, he picked up the lighter off the rail in front of him and set fire to the paper, holding it by its edge in the big stiff fingers until I would have thought they'd be burnt. I jumped, then sat back. With my cane, I couldn't have reached him in time to stop him, even if I'd been willing to give him the satisfaction of trying.

I said, "These are handsome oak floors. Seems a shame to burn holes in them. It's also against the law to deface public property."

"Justin, you're a wry man."

"Not as wry as you, sir."

He grinned. "That's true too."

"What was the point of that little bit of drama?"

"Son, you suspected me of hiring some bumblers to rob a woman that ended up getting killed." He groaned, bending over to pick up the ashes and to dust the floor with his hand. "Well, that's insulting."

I said, "I assume Luster Hudson got this letter out of Cloris's purse when he went over there to get those papers for Whetstone. Willis got it from Hudson. And kept it, as insurance. And what do you want to bet, you got it from Willis. Now, how did that happen?"

"I've learned a lot of sad things in a lot of sad years on this pitiful earth, Justin. One of them is, if a man can be bought once, he can be bought twice. Hunh? You just have to offer him a little bit more than he was getting the first time. A sad tale of betrayal came with that letter."

I looked up. "What'd you give Willis? The mills?"

Cadmean swayed his big head. "Now, you know that's something I'd *never* sell." The teeth flashed. "And not about to let anybody else sell it. Or shut it. Not till they dig my hole."

I clipped my pencil to the report. "Willis has somehow acquired some very expensive lawyers. I can use my imagination too. As far as imagination goes, you're a lot of things, Mr. Cadmean, but I'm not sure being a psychic is one of them. How do you know Whetstone was negotiating with Bogue for fast capital?"

Cadmean smiled. "You're right. I don't have visions, like poor Joanna. What I have is friends. All over the South. When you've been in a business for, let's see, almost seventy years, because I was ten when I started on my daddy's line, when you've been at it that long, and you're not a *complete* son of a bitch, and I'm truly not, son, you're liable to end up with a few friends. And my vice-president was not a discreet man."

If Cadmean was right—and the fact that Lawry Whetstone was cruising the Caribbean while the board canceled his plans to cut back the textiles division suggested that Cadmean was right—then Lawry had taken a considerable risk when he came to me with a story so close to the real one in order to find out what I knew; when he even insinuated that Cadmean was behind the theft. As, indeed, I had concluded. I saw Whetstone, blandly tan, turning the gold college ring, waiting for me to ask him another question. *This Dollard thing was really just an excuse to come in.* Had he planned deliberately to end our conversation with his proposed foursome to outrage me and obscure his motive in making the only personal contact with me we'd ever had? *Sugar, I told Lawry you wouldn't be interested, but he never listens.*

Yes, there was little reason to doubt Cadmean was right, and that Ron Willis, for who knows what price, had sold him the letter that told him he was right. Whetstone must have decided Sunday after Cloris called him that he'd rather not wait to hear what Rowell would say, because he knew what Rowell would say, because Rowell was Cadmean's man. Cloris must have not only told him in that Sunday-morning call (*She was a totally open person, Jay; she never kept anything back*) where she was putting those copies of the designs, but told him she was going to be out at the play all evening. Easy enough to call that evening to be sure she was leaving. Easy enough to call Ron Willis from Atlanta and tell him to go take the papers and make the theft look like an ordinary robbery. Whetstone knew what Willis would do for money, because he was already paying Willis to spy on people like Alice. He already knew Susan would be at *A Midsummer Night's Dream* that night, and so he phoned her and left her a message to call him back as soon as she got home. Easy enough too to call the Dollard house to warn Willis to get out because Cloris was also on her way home.

Easy enough to think nothing could be easier than getting those copies for Bogue (for whatever reasons of rivalry with Cadmean or revenge against him or curiosity about the designs themselves, Bogue had wanted them), in exchange for whatever financial help Bogue was going to give Lawry to help him rival or revenge himself against Cadmean's power at C & W.

It must have been a shock to find out Willis had subcontracted the job to a man as stupid and vicious as Luster Hudson, and that Cloris had come home too soon from the play. To find out Hudson had tried to take revenge on Preston Pope, and had returned to Hillston from wherever he'd been sent. To find out Susan had been talking to me about what Cloris had said. That Willis wouldn't stay put, and was terrified of Hudson and paranoid about me and in the habit of taking more cocaine than was fashionable, and then shooting off guns. The last shock must have been when old Cadmean showed him Cloris's letter.

I stood up in the sunlit oval and pushed in my chair. "Of course, Mr. Cadmean, I don't believe you want Lawry's felonies to come to light. You like things the way they are. As I recall from your other little story, this is just the way you like to have people in your employ. I'm not sure Lawry's going to be as much use to you as Rowell was; I very much doubt you're going to run Lawry for office."

He rubbed his hand roughly over his face. "Thank God his daddy's dead and gone."

"I don't know why you even bother mouthing the words." I picked up my report. "The thing is, I'm not interested in playing cat and mouse with you. I'm on a cane, and don't enjoy the scampering. So I won't. What I am going to do is tell Ken Moize everything you've said. It's his job to decide whether he wants to spend the taxpayers' money to listen to Willis perjure himself, or whether he's just going to put him away for assault against me."

"There certainly doesn't seem to be any *proof* that Mr. Willis sent Hudson to poor Cloris's house. Or that Lawry hired Willis."

"Like I said, it's not my job to make that decision. And chasing you for my own satisfaction has gotten to be a waste of my time. What accommodations Lawry and you and Moize make don't interest me as much as finding out who just killed a girl named Virginia Caponigri."

There was a noise and the doors behind us opened. Cuddy Mangum, shielding his eyes, stepped inside, a clipboard under his arms. "You two still here? Hello there, Mr. Cadmean. Sorry I got held up, but Justin here can fill me in."

I said, "One thing we were talking about was how Mr. Cadmean had given you his vote of confidence over at the city council."

"Was I saying that?" Cadmean threw up his old hands in innocent openness.

"I appreciate everybody's vote," Cuddy said.

Cadmean grinned. "Some votes count more than others, that's a sad fact of democracy."

"Umm," said Cuddy.

Mr. Cadmean puffed up his lips. "Well now, you think you deserve this job?"

Cuddy said, "I know I do."

"I'm as smart as you are, son." Cuddy had started back up the sloped aisle toward the double doors when Cadmean added, "I want you to bring my Baby over to see me again."

Cuddy turned. "I don't know if I would even if I could; but I can't. Briggs's not going to be around for a while, soon as her term's over. Seems like she said she was going off west somewhere to look at a telescope."

"Well, shit, son!" Cadmean roared. "Shit! Don't let her get away! Women are truly the wonder of the world, they're Eldorado and the mouth of the Nile. But you got to remember. Not a one of them has got a lick of sense. I married four of them, and two of those got a pack of coyote lawyers to gouge through my pockets. And there were some others I woke up in time *not* to marry. Women are going wrong. I swear, they're getting to be just about as hoggish as men, plus all of them being as crazy as loons on top of it."

Cuddy blinked and sun flashed through the blue. "You old bastard, if you hadn't believed all that bullshit, maybe you wouldn't have had so much trouble with your women." He waved the clipboard at me. "Meet you back upstairs, General Lee. We got a lady thinks she saw somebody suspicious hanging around the Arboretum." The oak doors closed behind him.

As Mr. Cadmean shambled over to my chair, he held out his gnarled hand. "Good man, Mangum. Come on. Between my arthritis and your leg, we ought to be able to keep up with each other."

"I think I can manage," I said.

And so we walked back through the courtroom and out onto the black and white marble floor of the rotunda. Cadmean turned at the doors to look up at his varnished portrait. "Shit," he whispered. "I was old *then*. If there's one thing I can't stand the thought of, it's the world going on its merry way without me in it."

"You want it to come to a halt when you do?"

He grinned. "That's exactly right."

"Well, that's something else you can't do anything about."

"What was the first something?"

"Acquiring your daughter's affection."

From the middle of the patterned floor, he circled back to me. "Justin, you don't want to waste your time? Don't waste it trying to hurt my feelings. Don't get yourself believing I care whether you want to listen to my stories or not. There's always somebody who does. Always will be."

"Till they dig your hole. Or are you planning to keep talking from the grave?"

He chuckled. "Could be. Keep your ears peeled. Hunh! You sure were something in that donkey head, son."

I pushed against the brass filigree of the door bar. I said, "What if Rowell hadn't made that nolo contendere plea? What if there'd been a trial and we'd subpoenaed you? Would you have perjured yourself?"

The pink lips pursed against his forefinger. "There wasn't a trial," he said.

"But if there had been?"

The old stiff fingers squeezed my shoulder. "Son . . . son. 'Sufficient unto the day is the evil thereof.' Hunh?"

Outside, the afternoon sun glowed red on all the buildings. I stood with the old industrialist at the top of the broad stone steps that were guarded by empty antique cannon, fired last in 1865 for a lost dream and a cause undefendable. Beside me a long sigh rumbled from Cadmean before he spoke. "I'll tell you this, Justin. Sometimes I think when I think about my Baby looking up at those tired old stars of hers, what if it was my privilege to be up there, looking down? What do you think I'd see? Hunh?" His sulfurous, low-lidded eyes gazed down over Hillston. "Well, I'd see a little tiny ball of slime, wouldn't I? And nations of bugs crawling crazy all over it. And I bet up there I'd be able to hear something I've always suspected. God laughing His damn head off like a scorching wind. Am I right? Take care of yourself, son."

I stood there, watching him carefully descend the gray stone steps one by one, watching him stiffly pull himself into the backseat of the waiting limousine and with a wince of pain tug shut the door.

All he couldn't do was make his child want to spend a night under his roof. All he couldn't will, with the powers of influence, was love. Just as Joanna couldn't will it, not even with sorcery, or revenge its loss with death.

I stood there until from behind the stone balustrade, I heard the voice of Sister Resurrection, as always, faithful at her station by the house of law. She began to speak suddenly, as if she'd been listening to the old man whose bones, like hers, were brittle, and whose eyes were as ancient and as hard. I heard her before I saw her, so her sharp impatient chant came up to me in the warm sun like the keen of a ghost too haunted to wait for the dark.

"The time is come. How long, O Lord? God fixing to melt the mountains. Make a path. God fixing to overthrow Pharaoh. Joseph's neck in a collar of iron. Cut it loose. The blind shall see the mountains tremble. Make a path for the anger of the Lord. Praise Him!"

Around the corner of the cannon the small figure of rags came marching, her hair snow wool and matted with bits of earth. The filthy sweaters hung fluttering to her knees, and she had again her wood handmade cross in both small black hands. Leaning on my cane, I made my way down the steps to where she stood, still speaking. "God Almighty's sick and tired. He gonna loose the Devil's chains."

I touched her arm, and she spun to face me. I said, "Mrs. Webster, God knows I don't have any right to ask you this, but don't you believe there's any chance for love at all?"

The clouded black eyes blazed out at me like a sudden flame. "I carrying it!" She spit the three words up at my face, and then thrust forward her crossed sticks of wood. "You want it? Take it!"

Startled, I stepped back and said, "No, ma'am."

Clouds passed over the eyes like smoke and she turned away and began again to prophesy.

LEWIS SHINER
DESERTED CITIES OF THE HEART

Finally, being a rock star just wasn't enough for Eddie. He used booze, sex, smack, 'ludes, anything to help forget his need to know it all meant something. Then he went crazy and disappeared.

The sacred mushrooms at Na Chan kept calling Eddie, and while he dreamt among circles in time, lots of crazy things started: His brother Thomas and his wife Lindsey caught up with him; Carmichael, a journalist for Rolling Stone tracked down Carla, the charismatic leader of a guerrilla outfit struggling for survival; and the fighting 666th, a US private army – funded by Irangate profits and CIA-backed, fighting under a fanatic quasi-religious banner to save the world from communism – is about to overtake them all. All of them at Na Chan – just in time to see the beginning of the end of the world.

Lewis Shiner brings us face to face with the paranoia and confusion of a nuclear age; dragging hidden longings, guilt, fear and passion protesting into the open in one violent thriller of politics, ancient civilization and twentieth-century corruption. DESERTED CITIES OF THE HEART is an extraordinary achievement, exciting, erotic and totally fascinating.

0 349 10001 2   FICTION   £3.99

ROBERT RANKIN

The Brentford Trilogy

Can that be Jim Pooley himself? Layabout, bookies' best customer and dedicated pint-of-Large-fancier? Yes, unquestionably, it is he.

And by his side, isn't that the professionally unemployed ladies man. Flying Swan worshipper and bike rider, John Omally? Indeed. It is that lad.

Once more the dauntless double-act must outwit the fiendish Unknown Powers of Darkness, and defeat alien superpowers, crushing the legendary ancient Evil which, from time to time, crawls out with a new game plan, intent on nobbling life On Earth As We Know It! But the plucky Brentonians are never alone – even when facing the Big One. There's back-up from Professor Slocombe, Norman, Neville and Soap Distant – throw in a camel, some magic beans, Penge, the Great Pyramid, Norman's Morris Minor, a fleet of robots and a uncanny feeling for atmosphere – with expert consultation and guest appearances from Edgar Allan Poe and Sherlock Holmes . . . it all makes you wonder why Evil ever bothered to have a go!

'A born writer with a taste for the occult . . . Robert Rankin is to Brentford what William Faulkner was to Yoknapatwpha county'
TIME OUT

0 349 10028 4   FICTION   £3.99

Donn Pearce

COOL HAND LUKE

Lloyd Jackson was caught red-handed, abusing the system. So he was brought before the wrath of the Law. And he left an anguished chorus of forlorn voices praying behind him, and danced his way heel and toe right into his cell and on to the chain gang.

Donn Pearce's own experience on a chain gang in central Florida created COOL HAND LUKE and later the screen play to the classic film, starring Paul Newman. This story of one man's refusal to let the prison system grind him down has a poignancy and vitality which immediately caught the imagination of everyone who read the novel when it was first published in 1965. It remains just as powerful today.

'Rhythmic prose, tragic drama, and realism made larger than life'
PUBLISHERS WEEKLY

0 349 10004 7   FICTION   £3.99

S·U·M·M·I·T

D. M. Thomas

Age and soggy brain cells are not a safe combination for a US president and 'Tiger' O'Reilly's got a big helping of both. Let's just say he makes big blunder and impeachment looms. In the circumstances, a summit meeting with the new Soviet leader, Grobichov, seems a good thing to go for.

Quickly, the two world leaders take protocol into their own hands, dismissing the ranks of fawning advisors and second-rate interpreters, deciding to hold discussions on a private man-to-man basis, to cut the cackle and really get to know one another. And it has to be admitted – Alexei and Larissa, 'Tiger' and Wanda make a great double-date. A coup of Class A misunderstandings *do* slip through the fine mesh of presidenti intelligence . . . something to do with twenty million contraceptive coil and California being presented to the Soviets . . . but world leaders are only flesh and blood, after all . . . anyone can make mistakes!

'With its canny political satire, its hilarious insights into the sex of politics and the politics of sex will delight and amuse even Thomas' most devoted readers.'
Erica Jong

0 349 10024 1   FICTION   £3.99

A DARKNESS
IN THE EYE
M.S. POWER

Seamus O'Reilly, 'Godfather' of the Provisional IRA, was a
ruthless, vicious man. But he found the times demanded such an
attitude. He was also thoughtful, humble, and tired. Tired of
always losing in the struggle for peaceful, political solutions. Now
the British Army is determined to infiltrate and exploit an angry
new splinter group rising up within the Provos. O'Reilly's
superiors make their decision, and the pale image of a settlement
fades out of his grasp again.

This final novel in M. S. Power's haunting trilogy about Northern
Ireland takes O'Reilly closer to defeat than he had believed
possible. It carries us directly to the heart of an eerie world of
shadows, ghosts and muddled beliefs, where another war is
fought: against the stupid, misunderstanding the very nature of
power, and against the ignorant, unable to value a future beyond
the thrill of their own violence and revenge.

Also by M. S. Power in Abacus:

THE KILLING OF YESTERDAY'S CHILDREN
LONELY THE MAN WITHOUT HEROES

0 349 10024 1   FICTION   £4.50

Also available in ABACUS paperback: